CHARM NEVER MADE A ROOSTER

Alan Marlowe

CHARM NEVER MADE A ROOSTER

Published by
WTL International
930 North Park Drive
P.O. Box 33049
Brampton, Ontario
L6S 6A7 Canada
www.wtlipublishing.com

978-1-927865-80-4

Printed in the U.S.A.

Preface

The trouble with writing any novel about the near future is that the near future tends to catch up with you before you are ready. As I sit here with over 60% of the world-locked down during the ravages of the coronavirus, it is now April of 2020…the world has changed since I started this project in the spring of 2018. The story follows what was happening in the news at the time, including the controversy surrounding Supreme Justice Kavanaugh and the terrible legacy of the riots of Charlottesville. I refer to hurricanes and rising sea levels, and people of color being ejected from Starbucks for having lingered too long. In the pace of the current news cycle, these events are ancient history, although the underlying inequities have only come into sharper focus by the virus and its resulting economic impact, which has unfolded along the usual socioeconomic lines.

The world has changed. But in a very tragic way, everything is still the same. We engage with our phones more and try to understand this locked-down existence through the lens of our news and social media. Then, as now, our chosen filters shape our worldview. The political center has eroded to the point that physical reality is relative to the news you watch or the person you voted for. It shifts depending on the whims of the highest echelons of power, whether you believe Trump's self-aggrandizing tirades or the changing messaging from public health authorities. In this sense, the novel is current. We are even more self-assured by the algorithms that tell us we are believing the right things. Just yesterday, the President of the United States announced that we should look into injecting toxic cleaning agents, like bleach, internally, in order to kill coronavirus. This has prompted people to bring back a central conflict of the novel's opening: the implementation of the 25th Amendment on the grounds of mental fitness, which gives lawmakers a constitutional tool beyond impeachment and removal.

Whatever you believe, whoever you voted for, and whichever news you watch…if you have any eye on current events and a modicum of concern for the future-present, this novel is for you. There is no denying that the current tyranny of the algorithm has manipulated us beyond the point of danger. It was willful human submission that got us into this mess, and it is disturbing how quickly we acquiesced. There was no great battle of humans versus machines, no metal-geared androids crushing skulls in some apocalyptic future, no mushroom clouds over our cities…there was only the quiet acceptance of Terms and Conditions so that we could apply cat-filters to our selfies that slid us into servitude. We are nudged to believe things, calmly served advertisements that itch us to scratch, and pushed to make decisions that align with the interests of the political elite. Our complete digital biography can be had for pennies, and the result is a society that is coerced to serve the devices we have attached to our hips. They demand our attention with insistent vibrations or chimes, and we look. They present action-items on the notification screen, and we swipe or lift. They show us news items that excite or enrage us, and we share with the rest of our social media circle. And so it goes. We are the first generation of humans to be programmed by algorithms, to think like machines, full of zeros and ones, with no room for nuance.

I believe that technology may try to offer us a way out, and that is the pretext for my antagonist. Technology may reverse the situation, but it will still be a machine nudging us toward improvement, informing our behavior, defining our better natures. In the end, whether it is a suspension of military aid to an ally for a political favor, a global pandemic, or even a porn star in violation of a non-disclosure agreement, our political milieu has been blown apart for the sake of clicks. Whether we choose to rely on technology as our salvation is the central theme of this novel. We must come together, as humans, if we are to survive as a species, beyond the inclinations of our own worst instincts.

Prologue

Pathetic thought the clerk at the Drug n' Go, one of the few surviving drug stores in town. As far as commercial endeavors went, the Drug n' Go was one of the brighter spots, when contrasted with the shuttered businesses, such as the Pawn Shop and bail bondsman. Worse, it was open all night, which meant that it tended to attract all manner of life to its massive, bright windows, beacons of hope for wretched men and insects alike. Trapesing down the diaper and baby aisle was a man like no other in town, and that was not a compliment. Poking his finger at images of little babies, remarking on the sizes and rearranging the baby wipes. He seemed to switch between serious consideration of which diaper brand to buy and outright mockery of the packaging. "Representation" he heard the man mutter. The clerk did not know what drew this creature out to the warm embrace of the Drug n' Go in the middle of the night, but it wasn't the first time he had bestowed himself in the disapproval of staff here.

Pathetic he thought again. This condemnation went against every ounce of the training he received to combat his own bias. He was not supposed to think that, or even feel that, but the man stumbling around the drug store at one in the morning on a Tuesday could only evoke such a sentiment. He was clad in a pair of jeans worn down at the seams, shredded by time and neglect, held in place by a hideous snakeskin belt, that the clerk thought was surely illegal in some jurisdictions. He wore a loose-fitting polo shirt with stains at the bottom from an unknown substance, and unbuttoned to an uncomfortably low level. The man himself was not a hideous specimen; he had a trim build and a reasonable face with a pleasing symmetry. The problem, in the clerk's estimation, was that it was framed by days' worth of stubble and clad with a general patina of grease. In another life, he could have been a model, maybe even for a catalog. In another life perhaps he was the resident philosopher in a Paris salon, he thought in a moment of charity. In this life, however, he was a disgrace a recidivistic relic, destined to be relinquished from the warm embrace of society to the outer fringes of social conscience. He felt a distinct twinge of his lower back at this mental rebuke, along with a pre-programmed regret, designed to stifle negativity towards others. The fact that this man should elicit such thoughts that overrode the clerk's mental checks and balance, in this day and age, said much.

Besides, he reasoned, judging someone pathetic could illicit feelings of empathy for a person in need, couldn't it? Isn't the very act of finding someone pathetic *exactly* the kind of attitude required for better harmony and understanding? It wasn't impossible to think that, at one point, this man was something more, someone to somebody. This helped him find the balance and clarity that his training had told him to seek as a happy human being; find the goodness, find your happiness. He was impressed at his philosophical musings at this late hour and in the context of this banality. What else was he to do? Count change?

A woman turned into the aisle for baby products just as the man was about to leave. The clerk couldn't hear the conversation, but the woman seemed to know the man. She smiled with him and was somewhat friendly, but she kept bumping him back from her as though he were a ship coming into port, idle, as though the engine had stalled, and he was merely drifting in on his own wake. "Ok, no Ray…it's late. No" the clerk heard her say. "Are you ok?" she said, but by then the man was pretending to bask in his contemplation of the various pill bottles arranged in front of him. He looked up, arching his neck until the clerk realized, his eyes were closed. The woman moved off, briefly shooting a glance towards the clerk as if to say "he's ok" and then left without making a purchase. He could hear a low hum coming from the man's general direction. He picked up a few supplements and sneered in derision. The clerk watched him select a bottle of Niacin and smile. Satisfied, he went over to the cold drinks section and picked up three cans of PaleoCafé, which were on sale. The man dropped one, it spun around in circles before carefully picking it up and placing it back on the bread shelf. The man proceeded to select a replacement and headed back to the cashpoint, where the clerk was stationed. A strong smell of alcohol preceded the man like the opening waves of a tsunami,the clerk prepared for the onslaught.

"I called you" said the man.

"Sorry?" said the clerk.

"I called you over. Needed help."

"Oh, well, I couldn't hear you. I'm near the hum of the fridge." The clerk gestured to the noisy refrigerator that housed the cold drinks, without looking over. If he couldn't express his contempt with his words, he would do so with his face.

"Civilized nice! Maybe I didn't call you, anyway, Niacin still on sale?" asked the man gruffly. He possessed a Southern accent, not uncommon to these parts, but somewhat forced.

The clerk took the bottle, scarcely looking at it.

"Nope" said the clerk, roughly emulating the same accent in a mocking tone. The effect was lost on the man. This was expected. He set the bottle aside without thinking.

"Don't need it anyway. Don't need much, to be honest with you." There was a vacuum of a pause. "Just these…"

The man produced four bottles of codeine-laced cough syrup. They were packed impossibly into his pants pockets.

"I think these should do the trick" he said. "Finally."

The clerk recoiled. He should not have these. He did not know how this skulking creature had procured them. The stockbot must have left them out on a skid.

"Sir, these are only available by prescription" said the clerk, clearing the counter of the bottles and placing them safely out of reach. In another time, he might have had the safety of a cage, but in the spirit of openness, Drug n' Go management had decided to remove this barrier. "You're really not evensupposed to have them" he finished.

"Oh no they were just over –" he gestured to a pallet whose plastic wrap had been shredded open. It looked as though a giant rat had attacked it " – there. Figured it was for the taking. Free trade. You get it I'm sure."

The clerk pulled himself together, with one finger on the holdup alarm. He doubted whether it even connected to anything anymore.

"Sir, do you need me to call someone? Are you ok?"

"We were ok. We were ok. I was ok. You maybe didn't have a chance to be ok but you seem ok." He paused. "Are you ok? I can help. I know things."

"It's ok" said the clerk. "Really."

"I guess it has to be" said the man after a time, looking off into the glaring lights in the ceiling trusses.

"Maybe you'd better leave, sir" said the clerk, finally, forcing a smile, raising his voice at the end as if he was posing a question.

"No no I have commerce with you. Please…there's still these" he said. The words were becoming more and more garbled. "You're a good guy…" said the man, squinting at the nametag "Horace. Do you like Ace? Do you get that a lot? Sure better than the first part! I'm gonna call you Ace."

"You're making me a little nervous. It would probably be a lot better for everyone if you just left."

The clerk resented the fact that he did not yet qualify for the government benefits soaked up by this specimen. It was for this reason that the man was able to meander around the store at one in the morning, reeking of alcohol and grease, while the clerk had to mind him like a six-foot toddler.

The man struggled with his wallet, which, despite his deft pocket-stuffing accomplishments of five minutes ago, seemed impossible for him to extract.

The phone came up to the clerk's ear.

"I'll just call someone" said the clerk, calling no one.

"I think I left my…cards…in the car" he said, stumbling out the automatic door and into the parking lot.

The clerk eyed him suspiciously until he was inside his car, then hung up the phone. There were no other customers now, so he disabled the automatic door and locked it so that he could assess what had happened. He jogged to the back of the store where the pallet had been ransacked; the cardboard boxes of medicine were savagely ripped open, with all manner of pill packs and plastic strewn about. Curiously, a bottle of Perrier had been partially consumed and carefully placed among the yogurt packs. Just beyond this, closer to the drink fridge, were two bottles of the same codeine cough syrup the man had been attempting to buy. The difference, to the clerk's horror, was that these were empty.

He ran back to the front of the store, grabbing the phone.

"Hi, I have an emergency here…a man just came and drank a bunch of cough syrup…yes, I followed my training. No, I don't think he's a criminal. Yes…no…yes…he's…" the clerk cleared his throat, as though he was about to read a disclaimer, and mechanically said "…just a man in need. He's a good person who's fallen into difficulty. He's driving a…no, it's a…Ray" the clerk trailed off as the car screeched out of the parking lot. Thank the minders for modern safety equipment. One day soon he would leave this Ceres-forsaken place for the World.

Chapter 1

Raymond Tanner blasted through the stop sign at Lay Bridge Rd on his way home. *Master of Puppets* by Metallica was pumping out of the speakers. He wasn't drunk yet, but salvation lay in his trailer. Besides, he knew these roads so well that he could be drunk, blindfolded, or even fast asleep and still find his way, like a Cherokee prancing through the forest. This was *his* county.

"Does that matter?" came the voice of authority, stripped of any hint of an accent. *What a shame*, thought Raymond. *Wonder if he practiced it*. His metal-stoked reverie had been interrupted by the realization that he was stood up on the shoulder by a police officer. The flashing lights of the cruiser broadcast the fact that Raymond was driving drunk again.

"I can feel the road through the steering wheel, Mitch" said Raymond. "Gravel matters. Why do you got to light me up like a Christmas tree?"

The second-hand Tesla worked just well enough to get Raymond into town to cause mayhem. And when he got into trouble, as was often the case, largely because of his ramblings and being thrown out of bars, he went home to finish his self-oblivion on the eye-watering hooch his law-scoffing cousin had charitably provided him. There were few establishments in town that still welcomed him. The voice of authority went local in its lilt.

"Shame" he replied. "One way or another you're gonna be healed, Raymond. You're ten seconds away from killin' someone. I know none of this is sinking in so what's gonna happen is you're gonna go back to your car, take a rest, then get inside and stay there. I'm coming by tomorrow morning. No more hooch, ya hear?"

3

Raymond shifted. The gravel stones moved beneath his feet. Mitch was a hulk of a specimen; his uniform struggled to conceal his thick muscles and broad frame. His face was chiseled and weathered, yet somehow pleasing due to its symmetry. All of these were recent innovations for Mitch. He was glad to hear a little southern drawl creep back in the officer's voice.

"Mmm-hmm" he managed. "Hallelujah" he mocked.

"Cough syrup, Raymond? Jesus Christ." he said. "You're running out of friends!"

The officer reached into the car for a moment, pressed a few buttons on the dash, and instructed Raymond to get in and sleep it off. Raymond crumpled into the seat and stared at the cornfield near the road. Beautiful crop. Beautiful land. *What a shame*, he thought. *Darned shame*.

Darkness came and went, and he jolted awake to realize that somehow, he got home in the hours between day and night. He opened the door and fell out, roughly onto his hands and knees. "Perfect park", he said, admiring the placement of his vehicle on the concrete pad.

There wasn't another trailer or house for at least a mile. This was Pappy's lot, a beautiful wooded acre of live oaks, shrubs, and kudzu vine. His grandfather, Pappy, had bequeathed this to him, and the trailer was bought at a local trailer park and moved at a deep discount. Nobody wanted to live in trailers anymore. The lights were on, thank baby Jesus, he thought. Christmas lights were strung all over the inside.

4

Through a supreme effort of coordination, he was able to unlock his elaborate deadbolt system and burst inside. He had also left the music playing. Ted Nugent. Thank God.

He was lucid enough to watch some TV. He plunked down on his loveseat and started searching for his favorite stream. "We're done, folks...the party's over...if you ever thought the globalists weren't on your doorstep, here we go..." His television was inherited from a larger dwelling, and as such was perversely large in relation to his trailer. He liked it that way. More immersive. No escaping the truth. The face on the screen reddened. The tone was bellicose.

"I can't tell you what to do. I can't choose for you. This is...was...a free country once. Just once..." he said.

"For me" said, Raymond.

"...for me..." continued the voice.

"Shake...your...fist" they said all together. "And REMEMBER!"

His fist had already come up by the time he spoke the words, then darkness.

He heard a child's voice in his mind. And a remote feeling of happiness. Color. Harmony.

The fist came down as his eyes closed.

5

"Wake up! Are you awake?" came a voice. Raymond's eyes popped open and there was a different face on the screen. Somehow the stream had changed to a shriller commentator that Raymond agreed with but did not enjoy listening to for any length of time.

The sunlight was attempting to poke in through the branches and the layer of dirt on Raymond's window, but the Christmas lights were still the brightest thing in there. Then suddenly there was a banging on his trailer door.

"Raymond, wake up" came the yell. "Raymond!"

It was Mitch. Jesus.

He did a hasty cleanup, removing cans of energy drinks and empty tubes of chips. He turned off the voice.

"Ray!" came the yell again.

"Comin!" he replied, shuffling toward the door, hiking his jeans up his anorexically thin waist with the help of his worn alligator belt, a hand-me-down from Pappy. His t-shirt was stained from the previous night's excess but there was nothing he could do about that now. Excess was relative, anyway.

"Don't you bastards sleep?" said Raymond, fumbling with his overly elaborate locks to open the door.

"Yeah. I sleep just fine. You know a ten-year-old could kick down this door, right?" chided Mitch.

"Let a ten-year-old try, see what happens" said Raymond.

6

"You don't got any heat in there, do ya? Remember the ordinance…" Mitch.

"Oh I remember. Don't worry Mitch. No trouble there. I gave up that right a while ago. Surrendered my beauties into the fire of tyranny" exclaimed Raymond.

"You mean you amnestied your guns and they were melted down? Well good. I'm coming in. OK?

"Alright" said Raymond, apprehensively. "But only because I grant you permission."

Mitch grimaced at his meek attempt at urgency and was already pushing past the soiled Raymond.

Mitch stood at the threshold for a moment and surveyed the trailer, which was basically one large room at this point, with a rudimentary kitchenette and tiny bathroom. The people who built this place once called it a "tiny home" euphemistically, in a vain effort to distance itself from the moniker of "trailer." Clothes were scattered everywhere; bags of unknown contents towered up in each corner. Frantically taped to the fake wood panel wallboards were various newspaper clippings and headlines that screamed inane warnings. "THE END IS NEAR." "DNA IS FATE" "SCIENTISTS PLAY GOD" and "YOUR RIGHTS?" Between the musty windows hung a massive poster of Donald Trump, held in place with a crucifix that looked suspiciously catholic, if not vaguely Mexican. #MAGA had been crudely scrawled on the poster using a magic marker. Beneath this, slightly obscured and crumpled, was a Dixie battle flag. There was also a slight taint of marijuana in the air.

7

"Want a coffee?" asked Raymond, standing by his minifridge.

"You got coffee?" asked Mitch.

He popped open the minifridge and extracted two cans of cold PaleoCafé.

"Keeps you hard" said Raymond, passing him the can.

Mitch suspiciously opened the can and took a sip. The coffee was cold, refreshing, and mildly tasty, but he was sure that there was a caffeine seizure in his near future.

"You know there's an ordinance on that, too..." said Mitch, gesturing at his propaganda wall.

"You mean The Donald? They're laws against conspiracies now too? He was the greatest president this country has ever known, and they struck him down. They roll out the tears for Kennedy but roll up Trump faster than a night circus. You don't think the Deep State was finally pushing back? We *will* have the truth!" exclaimed Raymond.

Mitch sighed.

"That was a long time ago. Deep State, Deep South blah blah blah. Anyways I mean the flag" said Mitch.

"The flag? I keep that inside, Mitch. You're not really gonna trample those rights too..." said Raymond.

"No I'm not. But I better not see this tied to so much as a piece of kindling outside. Things are different now" said Mitch.

"Things are different. Yes, better" said Raymond.

"Look I didn't come over here to point at flags and drink your motor oil" said Mitch, plunking his large yet fit form onto a folding chair Raymond had set up at the edge of a coffee table. He didn't dare attempt the loveseat. Raymond noticed him becoming aware of the cannabis crumbs leftover from his earlier messy roll, as Mitch tried to find a perch for his can.

"At least that's not illegal" said Mitch, gesturing with his chin. "Still…"

"Sure thing, brother. You want a hit?" said Raymond, extracting his rolling papers. "You might get some vision finally."

Mitch huffed, almost managing a grin.

"Sit down" he said, pointing his head in the direction of the loveseat. "No weed. I need you straight."

Raymond obliged by sliding into his loveseat, and sitting up at an almost right angle. Mitch cleared his throat.

"Ray you got a lot of people pissed off at you right now. The only thing holding back town council from you is me. They want to ban you" he said calmly, clearly.

"Ban me? From town? They can't do that. They can't just – I've got freedom of movement…"

Mitch cut Raymond off.

"They can and they will. You're free to move, but not to be an asshole. People have filed a petition against you. Technically you

9

don't even live inside town limits. You're a menace. A nuisance. A drunk. A loudmouth. You go around spouting conspiracy this and that and rights this and that, scaring old ladies and kids. And if you weren't my brother I'd sign the petition myself."

He paused, taking a sip of the coffee,which was clearly starting to kick in.

"I have freedom of movement, the framers of the Cons –" he protested.

"So here's the deal. Cateechee is in trouble. Everybody moved away. We need money."

"We're the only ones left, huh" said Raymond, allowing a prideful smile to creep onto his face.

"Council is doing one last push. We got state tourism to help us get tours going in our town. Frankly, there ain't many towns like ours left and people want to visit" said Mitch.

"You mean this hick town is gonna become –"

"I mean we need the money and that's what the tourists are gonna bring. It's simple. You're gonna stop driving around stoned. You're gonna stay in your trailer and just be you. You show 'em that you're a decent human, that we still got some dignity left here. And you're sure as shit gonna hide that goddamned flag."

Raymond paused in disbelief. Mitch's Southern accent had come back with a sudden angry flourish.

"The government's designating this town as a heritage monument. That means everything stays just as it is. Some things may even get turned back a bit, cleaned up some. But you stay just as you are. Maybe clean yourself up" said Mitch, gesturing to Raymond's overall appearance.

"I am clean. I'm the only one around these parts with a clean conscience. The rest of y'all traded in your sanity for your health."

"Not so bad, brother. Might help you some" said Mitch. He ran his hand through his hair to emphasize his point. Before receiving his treatment course, he had been bald as an eagle.

"I'm good" stated Raymond. "Besides, you want me just the way I am. Well, that's how I'll stay. What do I get?"

"You still get to be part of society, sort of" said Mitch. "Or at least looked at."

"What's left of it" grunted Raymond. "What's *society* want with this place anyway?"

"I could sit here and grind it out all day with you, but I'm working. You ain't been helping anyone or anything while you sit out here and rot. At least let people see your misery and remind themselves why things are better out there than in here."

"So what do I do? Arts n' crafts? Sell beadwork to the gringos?"

"You still get your UBI. You wanna make some extra money, that's up to you" said Mitch. "Just don't change anything. Clean it up but keep it the same. That's the order. If you don't want to join in, I don't think I can keep vouching for you."

With that, Mitch raised himself from the chair with remarkable speed. Raymond knew why, and it had nothing to do with his genetics, and everything to do with his genes. By contrast, Raymond creaked and groaned as he got up to wish his brother goodbye.

"Remember. Keep it the same. Not that that's much of a problem for you" said Mitch, turning to walk to his police cruiser parked on the gravel.

"Sure" said Raymond, derisorily. "You bet."

"Just don't touch anything!" yelled Mitch. "Or anyone!" Then he got into his cruiser, and took off.

Raymond went back into his trailer. He stopped to look at his crucifix. Then he took out his ancient computer to find out what was going on. He pressed the microphone button:

"HICK TOURS"

"Nothing found, Raymond. Would you like to try again?" came the response from Ceres, the hybridized artificial intelligence that ran the Internet and, essentially, the world. She also paid Raymond's bills directly from his UBI when he was too inebriated to manage the transactions manually, which was usualy the case.

"TOUR TRUMP COUNTRY"

Again, nothing found. He cursed. Ceres said something cute. He smiled, then corrected himself angrily. The man was listening. And he was a female.

"TOURS OF CATEECHEE, SOUTH CAROLINA" he yelled. The screen sprang to life. He recalled a moment during a drunken episode about the town when he saw an unusual person holding up what looked like a camera and making notes on a device. He found the website in the search "DEEP SOUTH TOURS…Where it all began!" and thumbnails of photos that had been taken. He tried clicking, but nothing happened. All he got was an error message and a redirect. Which seemed to be happening more and more these days. Thank God he had his workarounds to keep the bastards honest.

"Society can't make a goddamned website work" he said. "Even I can do that." The day was getting on. It was time to mix coffee with something livelier. There were things to be done. He had made up his mind to participate in this thing. Maybe this is where the revolution starts; maybe this is what we need, he thought. I'll remind *society* what it means to be human. Gotta clean up. But first, he thought, a podcast and a brew.

"And remember, NONE of these…*people* are even technically human! We are dealing with trans-dimensional beings who have crossed over into our world…VAMPIRES…who have suborned human DNA and made us all in their image…not *His* image…but some sort of child-molesting subculture universe that has bled over. And is now *bleeding* us dry…our beautiful babies"

Raymond was transfixed. Within the span of a 30-minute oration from his favorite underground resistance soothsayer, he had completely reversed himself. There would be no tours on his property.

13

On came the Nugent, and out came the flag. A bonfire in the yard. Coffee and hooch. Mayhem, legally speaking, yet purely legal as far as Raymond was concerned. His rights. He danced. The flag waved, attached to an unused tiki torch. It was a moderate, one-man riot. A few leftover wooden pallets constituted the fuel for the fire. Raymond loved the statement it made about the consumer economy.

He lurched back into his trailer. He was tired, Sore and Drunk. He was ready.

He sat down in front of his computer for yet another blog post to broadcast his feelings on just about everything. He cracked his fingers and opened another coffee, and infused with a heroic dose of hooch. It was needed. This was important. He logged in with a VPN connection. He had a following online, just like any other respectable commentator, even if he had to take steps to remain anonymous. He had already divined a title:

Off the Reservation, Beyond the Pale: Warnings for the Adventure Tourist

Dear Gringo; I don't even know what that word means anymore. Once upon a time, I was the dirty gringo aboard a cruise ship setting sail from Galveston for Spanish-speaking voices and cheap tequila. Now, it is your mocha-toned faces that will gaze in at the poor white trapped up on the edge of society. Let me tell you, right now…you are welcome, dear friend. Let me show you what life is…

He smiled as he wrote. The world needed him, and needed this. The key, he thought, was being dependable, and predictable. Everyone knew that Thursdays were blog days. And so he wrote at

14

least 500 words every week. That was the discipline. On the edge of society, looking in, he had all the benefit of vision and none of the encumbrance of conforming. He knew he didn't fit in, but 3,061 views told him that it didn't matter. It was hot; the dancing and bonfire had warmed him up, but his ideas were the heat of controversy.

We need you, but you need us more than you think. To remember. To reflect. What does it mean to be human? Am I human? Is this gringo some savage on the edge of the world, a fleeting representation of what once was, but is no longer? Whatever you think about yourself or our situation, you need me. You need me to know yourself.

He was pleased with his platitudes.

PUBLISH, he pressed, after reviewing and correcting a few typos. He began to nod off in his chair, slumping in front of his keyboard.

What he didn't notice was the fact that the resurrection vine outside his window had caught fire, since it had not rained in weeks. Smoke billowed around his trailer as Pappy's lot burned.

Chapter 2

The fire department had efficiently swooped into action thanks to the satellite warning system that enabled continuous monitoring of the nation. The local council had invested in a special fire suppression foam distributor, and the effect was nearly instantaneous once applied. The fire had been safely contained to Pappy's lot. While the great live oaks had been spared due to their size, but all the underbrush and vines were now just a crispy memory. His trailer was safe, along with his solar panels.

The fire marshal used his protocol to determine the origin of this mishap, but one look at the flame-ravaged lot revealed the cause to the most oblivious lay-person: a stack of burnt wooden palettes was arranged carelessly. Touching this pile was a bamboo pole, burnt to a crisp, which connected it to a blackened resurrection vine. Only Raymond knew that the flag was the likely instigator, though the report came back as "unknown synthetic fabric."

"Where in the hell did you get a bamboo pole?" asked Mitch.

"Tiki torch. It was a long time ago" said Raymond, somewhat sheepishly.

"Well, anyway, you did it Raymond. You're officially banned."

His brother handed him a ticket and a summons. Two-thousand dollars. An amount they both knew he couldn't possibly pay, even over several years.

"You're due in council chambers tomorrow to explain your actions. They might give you a second chance. They might not. At least figure out with them how you're going to pay this fine" stated his brother, dispassionately.

"Council isn't court. I want my due process!" cried Raymond.

"You had your due process. You live out here. You proved that you can't hack it on your own and now you're banned. Good luck pleading your case. I won't be there. Not this time. Good luck" said Mitch, storming off in disgust. "You still haven't killed anyone yet!" he yelled, putting on his trooper hat.

The firemen had packed up their gear and were off. Raymond barely noticed as he shuffled around his lot, pretending like this was something he actively maintained. It hadn't rained in a week and the ground was primed for a brush fire.

Regroup. Plan. Learn to enjoy this lesson.

He parked the Tesla illegally in a Customer with Child drop off zone at the local municipal office, which wasn't even technically a parking spot. He had restricted himself to moderate hooch and coffee; moderate in the sense that it would inebriate a normal person, but for Raymond, it meant that it would just soothe the previous night's indulgence. He had reviewed local bylaws and ordinances on outdoor fires and refuse disposal. He had practiced in the mirror. He was ready. Orderly. Lawful. Somewhat respectable.

He presented himself at council chambers, smoothing his pineapple shirt and khaki pants under his tweed blazer. Five well-to-dos were seated in a semi-circle in the Amphitheatre, a Colosseum of the privileged, deciding on municipal matters great and small. He paid taxes for this. He was somebody. He was their boss.

"Raymond Tanner. The town versus Raymond Tanner in the matter of...Raymond Tanner." cried the clerk.

Raymond stood up, tucking in his buzz while he ordained himself a person of the people.

"That's me" he said.

He shuffled toward the stand, smoothing over his hair on the way.

"Right over here, please" said the clerk with a practiced smile.

Raymond grunted in reply, nodding to the podium.

"Raymond I'll just go over the charges" said one of the well-to-dos, a semi-contented bureaucrat named Bob Singh, the one who had received the majority of the complaints about Raymond.

"Ok" said Raymond, sheepishly. "Is it really charges?"

"Complaints. Raymond it's important for you to understand that this isn't a court" said Bob, slowly but effectively, leaning forward into his mic needlessly. "We can end this here and now and not recommend that this be taken any further. Fortunately for you, we have an information session in Common Room B."

"Ok sir, well before we begin, we need to recognize the federal papers..."

"You need to recognize" cut in Bob, almost yelling "that the only reason you're still here is because of your brother."

Raymond shuffled behind his stand, looking down, concealing his clenched teeth. After a moment, Bob continued.

"Raymond we have determined that while you have a right to live your life your way, you do not have a right to abuse this town. Your brother explained everything that happened and we know you need help more than you need punishment."

Raymond absorbed this. He cleared this throat.

"Well" he started "I have a right to access essential services, thank you" he said, ending more meekly than he had practiced.

"Yes, we agree" said Bob. Another councilor began shuffling papers and looking down. "But these 'essential services' are available over in Clairville, a place you haven't ruined yet. Maybe you'd appreciate them more if you had to travel some. You're not a resident. You're here as a visitor" The chairman had spoken up. Glen Campbell, wearing the vestments of office in the form of his chain. "Raymond...it's enough. It's more than enough. It's been more than enough for the past seven years..." he paused. "Everyone knows it's been a difficult time for you. Lord knows I do. But there comes a time when you need to let go and move on."

He looked straight at Raymond, who smirked behind the podium.

"Son last chances have been given and last chances have been taken. If you love this town...if you want to go to the bar and

22

the Piggly Wiggly or even the gas station for a Coke…you will do what we're about to tell you" he explained, gravely.

"Well, I…" Raymond started.

"I'm going to make it easy for you, sir. You're on the tour or you're not. Nobody lives like you anymore. You're a throwback and that's what they want. We've all moved on. Time to get on the train, Raymond."

"So…?"

"So you're in, right?" asked Glen, shifting into campaigning mode.

"Yes and…no fine?" said Raymond meekly.

"Yes and it's fine? Yes… that means the fine will be waived" said Glen.

"Yes, fine."

Glen cleared his throat. "Clerk please note that Raymond answered in the affirmative."

"Noted" she said, looking over her glasses at Raymond in disapproval. Her daughter was a barmaid who was often on the receiving end of Raymond's tirades.

"Thanks for coming to sort this all out, Ray. I knew you'd see the light. Was there something else?" asked the Reeve.

"Uh…well" started Ray "the oncoming turn signs out on the curve of Laybridge road got knocked over a while ago during a storm. Makes it kinda dangerous getting back to my place."

"Ray. You really should just try to trust the machines to take you around this county. I think we both know how those signs went down. You have a chauffeur built into your car. Have a good day, sir." Campbell concluded, gesturing to an assistant to set up the next item.

People had moved on by the time Raymond managed a "thank you" at the podium.

He slinked out of the chambers. Another clerk handed him a form, orange this time.

As he began moving through the rotunda, he saw a massive standee by the opposing hallway.

YOUR PRIDE, OUR HERITAGE!

Sign up now! Be a part of history!

"Say! How are you, sir?" said an overbearing woman, with short tight blonde hair and brown-toned skin. She was absolutely radiant, as people outside town often appeared. 'Rhonda' said her name tag. Rhonda was not a natural blonde, he thought.

"I see you are considering volunteering in the Federal Heritage Program!" she exclaimed cheerfully, plucking the orange form from his hand.

"Voluntold" he replied.

"Great!" she yelled. It was hard to tell if she was being oblivious or obsequious. She took him in strange familiarity by the arm. "Fed Hert needs you. We are looking to preserve the stuff that

24

makes us American…" she said, while leaning in far too closely. "Humanity needs you. Come, I'll show you!"

She ushered him into a room where about ten couples and individuals were gathered, mostly bearing glum, unenthused faces. Familiar faces with orange forms. The chairs were arranged in a theater seating arrangement. A few people were talking about morgages and loans owed. Rhonda followed Ray, pushing a cart laden with audiovisual equipment.

Rhonda stood in the midst and cleared her throat.

"Ladies and gentlemen please take your seats" she said. A man wearing a John Deere hat slowly turned away from the couple he was commiserating with. "We're about to begin."

She rolled the cart to the front of the room, plugging in some wires to a bronze receptacle on the floor. She pressed a few keys on the machine, but nothing happened. Ray found himself standing to help, but after Rhonda jiggled a few cables, the holoprojector exploded to life, almost literally. A man emerged in the middle of the air, running his hands over his body as though he had just realized that he had corporeal form.

"oh…ooohhh! There I am" said the Holoman, dressed in an expensive suit. He spoke with an academic, northeast styled accent. "…and here are you all!" he said, gesturing graciously. Somconc had added a magic filter to his image, which seemed as though it was meant to give his four-foot arm an extension out over the audience, and even though they were acquainted with holographic movies, they ducked instinctively. "The future of our history!"

25

"My name is Petrus Arbonne, Secretary of the Interior and Human Development. It gives me great pleasure to welcome you amazing volunteers to our little program. Your brave sacrifice will enable us to maintain a little piece of history right here in our quiet little town." The Secretary's voice garbled in error while Rhonda made a move toward the projector, but then backed off when she realized the moment was gone. "You see our great nation…"

Raymond rolled his eyes as the image of the man was replaced with a 3D rendering of the continental United States, and a few cartoonish images of people emerging.

"…has progressed a long way since we did away with some of the archaic nonsense that held us back. Where passion and enthusiasm fueled the American spirit, today technology has become the cornerstone of our great society. It once was the…glittering promise of a better world. We no longer fight back against it out of fear; we embrace it out of logic. We traded in our cynicism for reality. We knew we had to integrate AI into our decision-making. So, rather than do it piecemeal, we went all the way, like true Americans. American integrity has ensured that we are now all born perfect, and what sequencing didn't catch the first time, gene editing fixes the second time around. We have eliminated hate. We have cast off prejudice. We are all now one. We speak with one voice, denouncing the evils that, at one time, made us the laughing stock of the planet. We don't argue over belief since we share a common one. We don't fight over God; we complement Him. There is no more black, nor white, yellow, or brown…we are all pleasing shades of humanity, completing the circle that humans started out on 500,000 years ago."

26

The graphics whirred around each other, illustrating what the Secretary was saying in real-time. White, brown, red, and yellow forms of different computer-generated images began to blend together. Then, stock images of some kids from the civilized world were shown, romping in a field, picking daisies and chasing each other, while their thick black and brown hair blew in the wind. They looked somewhat distinguishable, and yet not; their faces were different, but they exuded a similar energy that made Raymond believe that this was not acting. They seemed to be able to gauge each other's actions and be ready to receive a ball once thrown or do a backflip just as a skipping rope was being dragged under their feet. It was eerily synchronous. The image then shifted to a set of more mature individuals, working in a lab, dancing at a club, and walking in the street. Tools were passed, bodies surged in unison, and a mass of heads bobbed up and down like an army on the march. In all cases, there was a uniformity to the very rhythm of the people. They just…were. No angst on their faces. No anguish over a broken heart or loss. Just cherubic cheeks and a gloss of innocence that Raymond very much wanted to scuff.

"For those of you who haven't seen this world, I am sorry. If this is your first glimpse of all we have achieved, I apologize. You make up that small percentage of individuals who did not embrace the change. I'm sorry to say that as of now, the window to incorporate into our world is effectively closed. It would be dangerous to try to introduce you now" said the Secretary, morphing back into view as the United States submerged behind him, a rapidly shrinking dot. "But we can't forget where we came from…and this is where you come in. We applaud your tenacity and respect your

27

wish to carry on just as you have. Although the constitution has been heavily augmented since we disbanded the Supreme Court, we keep the essential concept of freedom imbued into the fabric of all our laws:

"Freedom to express, but not to harm."

As he said the words, they appeared in massive three-dimensional block text.

"Oh man...that one was a doozy to figure out, but we got there. Assaults, mass shootings, hateful language, and ideas...civil war...until we sat and thought about it a moment, we realized they all fell into the category of violence. Those are just tiny little dots in our rearview mirror. And here you all are...just the same as ever, but off on your own, hurting no one."

There was little or no reaction in the audience. They knew they represented no threat to the outside world; except, maybe, for the retrograde bodies and minds possessed by each of them. Their very existence was a minor act of sedition.

"So thank you for offering yourselves as living monuments to the hard road of progress. Please don't think of yourselves as a previous-holders-of-the-land living commune...it's not that kind of thing."

"He means Indian Reservation" yelled a voice from across the room, laughing boorishly.

"Noble savages" muttered Raymond, under his breath.

"You will go on…on as you always have. Right here in your (name) town." The word "name" was pronounced by a synthetic AI, not Petrus Arbonne.

"He means right here" said Rhonda.

"Where's here?" yelled the boorish man, basking in his 13 seconds of notorious fame.

"Cat-a-cheee" she replied, almost reading a teleprompter in the air that was not there, stressing the second eee.

"I think you mean Cat – eee– cheee" barked Raymond, content with his contribution to the murmuring rebellion.

"Yes" she began, but by now Petrus Arbonne had begun to overrule her.

"You will, of course, be compensated for your efforts. For as long as you live on your lands the way you always have, you will receive a stipend directly to your accounts, tax-free. Our assistant is or has handed out the particulars. Please review them now" he said. Rhonda gestured to the crowd to flip over the orange forms she had handed out to them. The crowd murmured in approval. Raymond registered indignation bordering on disgust.

"A new day dawns…" trumpets began to swell under his narrative. "Fed Hert thanks you. Your nation…thanks" the transmission cut prematurely.

It was on to Rhonda again.

"Ok so any questions?" asked Rhonda as the lights were restored.

"So how do you know if we're living on the land, the way we're supposed to, according to you?" asked Delroy, one of the sharper individuals among the Cateechanites. He had the respect of his peers but refused to become part of the elected sycophants who had to "suckle at the teat of this pseudo-state" to use his words. Raymond admired him thoroughly. He should have been a philosopher.

"An auditor will be through once a year to check up on all of you. Maybe more. It depends on how well we build trust. We've done this before" she said, smiling disproportionately. "It really is an honor system...a system of monitored honor."

Delroy laughed splendidly but was alone in his efforts. Now that real money was on the table, the critical consensus had shifted somewhat. When added to the UBI that was the core of what kept this community moving, the overall financial picture for this town seemed to brighten quite a bit. Raymond shared his breech silently with a smirk but was sobered quickly by the disapproving faces that glared at Delroy.

"All we ask is that you do continue doing what you did yesterday, and the day before that. Oh, and there will be visitors. Watch out for wagonettes" said Rhonda.

"Wagonettes?" yelled a voice. "People who did the whole Integration thing?"

"We didn't want to say cart...it's too charged a word for us...them. Visitors, I mean. And I think you know better than to say 'Integration.' You mean integrity, right?"

She cleared her throat, reaching for a sip of water from a renewable bottle made from fishing nets. A small bead of sweat appeared on her perfect, mocha skin.

"Visitors are the real auditors here. Your continued prosperity depends on their interpretation of your traditional ways. You will each be given a rating based on how authentic each tour was. Keep your score up and everything is fine. If it starts to slip…well, we may have to review the allocation of your stipend."

"So you want us to act?" asked Delroy.

"No…be your exact selves, Delroy…the most you possibly can, right…where you are" she replied, looking him dead in the eye. The compensatory smile was gone. The room chilled.

"So we don't know…"

"And we're done" she said, bringing back a half of a grin. People stood at once, recognizing the dismissal. "Please refer all further questions to Fed Hert helpline for immediate assistance…"

People stood and began milling about. Some were complaining, but most were just baffled. Still, no one would say no to this. For them, this was a godsend, as if the whole town had won the lottery. All they had to do was play their part and they could live almost to the level of the society they had chosen to reject. Ironically, they had found their own place in it.

Raymond shuffled over to Delroy, awkwardly. He had been talking to Grace, the local aesthetician, and erstwhile companion of Raymond. She smiled awkwardly and looked as though she was going to say something but scurried away before any exchange occurred.

"That was some...speaking there, Delroy" he stated.

"I didn't hear anybody else backing me up" said Delroy, candidly. "Guess I'm alone in thinking this is a bad idea."

"No no no" replied Raymond. "I was with you...but, you know, people don't want to hear from me."

"Can't say I blame them man" stated Delroy, coldly. "They all have a hard time with you."

"You don't" said Raymond, with a sheepish grin pushing out under his lowered head. "Been a while, Delroy."

"You best keep your big thoughts to yourself, Ray. Plenty of people here real happy with what just happened and they don't need you or me messing it up." Some charity crossed Delroy's face. "Just take it easy, man. You'll be alright."

Raymond looked down. His battered sober conscience was not used to this abuse. He quickly made his exit and found a corner to take a shot from his flask. He coughed for a moment, then looked up with determination.

"I'll show them" he said. His next blog post's title was already forming in his mind. He got home and set to work:

What you have bought, what's been sold...

Chapter 3

The first tour wagonettes arrived within a week. They were electric, low to the ground, and eerily silent. Raymond heard a rumble of tires coming down the path to Pappy's lot. The tires themselves were perversely large and knobby, as though they expected to traverse a taiga forest or mangrove swamp. The vehicle ground to a halt a few dozen yards from Ray's trailer and the occupants emerged from their protective vessel. A woman wearing a brightly colored vest and a yellow badge was energetically speaking into a microphone that was wrapped around her head, but no sound was heard over any loudspeaker. The visitors themselves wore no headphones; Raymond realized that the broadcast must be feeding into their "tragussets," implants that sent audio directly to the ear canal. Raymond's ears were under constant assault from podcasts and retro music, but he was loath to put anything in his body that was created in a lab. Too easy to manipulate, he thought.

"Alright everybody" said the woman. "Here we are at the Tanner lot, one of the last places with a trailer used as a housing unit. Believe it or not, this is how thousands of our fellow citizens lived during the dark times before our modern age. Does anyone know what replaced these ad hoc structures?"

It was utterly superfluous to ask the question, but the ebb and flow of tours hadn't changed since before the revolution of integrity. Eyes among the group were darting around. To Raymond, they looked as though they were all tracking flies hovering around their heads.

"The organic silo!" shouted one girl with beautiful curly hair, grinning churlishly. Of course, the adults had accessed the same

35

information using their own implanted computers, but they deferred to the children on the tour.

"Very good!" said the tour guide.

"The silos that saved the South!" added the girl excitedly. The guide merely smiled at the repetition of propaganda and looked away.

Raymond knew about the miracle of the organic silo. In the aftermath of the Hurricane Hell Year, itself a consequence of global warming (or so he was told), the government had begun airdropping temporary residences to replace the ones destroyed by the successive category five hurricanes that had ravaged the South. Raymond's trailer had escaped the damage, but he knew of several others who were not so lucky. What fell from the sky could scarcely have been conceived by humans. And they were not. They were essentially duffle bag-sized seeds that, when they hit the ground, began an exothermic chemical reaction that created a total living unit, like a foam capsule toy dropped in water. It wasn't an instant process, but once one heard the dull thuds of the capsules hitting the ground, that evening a pristine, gleaming accommodation stood where the capsule had landed, impervious to water, wind, earthquakes, and perfectly anchored to the ground. Sinks, chemical toilets, and an inlet for water supply were included, along with furniture that merely needed to be broken away from the floor and set up as needed. Nanotechnology followed an exact diagram that had been hard-coded into every part of the capsule, building each capsule to spec at the molecular level. It would have been considered a miracle, if it had come from God. These merely came from the sky.

36

"And who do we have to thank for this?" asked the guide.

"Ceres!" they all shouted, in discomfiting unison.

"Yes! Excellent!" The guide clapped her hands and smiled. "Go ahead and have a look around. Please respect the integrity of this heritage site and do not disturb or touch anything. It is a privilege to be here."

Raymond merely glared at them. He knew better than to yell back that 'Ceres is the asteroid that will destroy us all.' He would save that for later, for the blog. He was on thin ice, and as much as he had railed against the computer system that had, allegedly, saved them, he wisely held his tongue. It was not they who had started the war; they were merely a product of its consequences.

They were impossibly and uniformly beautiful. They each had varying shades of mocha skin that was flawless, perfectly toned bodies, and smiled as though they didn't have a care in the world, strolling about this living museum. It was literally impossible for anything to be wrong with them. Any errors or aberrations in genetics were immediately stamped out using gene-printing technology, almost from birth. Within no time, they had distributed themselves around the property, blinking ceaselessly, no doubt using the cameras embedded into their optic nerves to capture the moments for their personal media streams. One man boldly entered Raymond's trailer, along with an acquaintance. Once they had taken up position, none of them seemed to move. Raymond realized that they were working together and sharing each other's images. They were experiencing the moment collectively; once one person had captured a moment or photo, they all did, using their embedded organic processors to make sense of the onslaught of stimuli that was assaulting their brains. They were literally sharing a composite experience.

Laughter erupted from inside Ray's trailer. Almost immediately, the laughter spread to the rest of the group. Raymond could hear the guide answering a question.

"Ok trigger warning, everyone. You may wish to censor your child's stream if it's not already on Safe Mode" said the guide.

The little girl piped up.

"What's so funny?" she asked, not able to see the stream of the gentleman in the trailer.

"Oh nothing, sweetheart…just a funny photo in the trailer."

Raymond approached the little girl and smiled warmly. "Honey, I think what your friends are looking at is my portrait of a president from a long time ago. His name was…"

"That's quite enough, sir" said the guide, glaring at Ray. "I'll take it from here."

"Darling, that man is a good guy, but he doesn't know about Safe Mode so I'll have to tell you about it. Once upon a time, before Ceres, we had a system where only one person controlled the whole country…can you believe it?"

"Oh the Presidents! I know about the Presidents. And the States!" she said. "We're now in District 2."

"And when you're a little older you'll be given access to the data on what happened to them. It was before Ceres" she said, looking back up at Raymond, as though it was he who had started the war.

A few more laughs emerged among the group. One man covered his mouth, uttering the word "clicker", then mockingly looked at Ray, then back at the ground.

"Let's keep it civil, folks" said the guide, herself covering her perfect mouth with her hand, silencing a giggle. "Ok so if we're all done here…we should get back in the Wagonette."

At once, they filed back to the bus, except the little girl, who broke away from her parents to examine some broken glass at the edge of the driveway. She picked it up, holding it close to her eye, fascinated by the lights refraction. She fumbled the piece, cutting her cheek in the process.

"Aw, gripes!" she cried. Raymond instinctively approached her to assist, but she recoiled as though he meant to drink her blood.

"You OK?" he asked. She relaxed at this, but her mother had instantly appeared by her side.

She seemed annoyed. "Just look at me a second, mom."

Her mother obliged, blinking incessantly.

Within moments, her skin had healed. The girl wiped away the tiny drop of blood to reveal no discernable injury. "OK, I'm good." Her mother began escorting her back to the safety of the wagonette but she turned back for a moment.

"I like you" she said to Raymond. "You're like my teddy except you talk. I wish I could know what you're streaming but it's blank. I'm supposed to rate you so I'm going to give you a 7.3 because you're nice but your place is kind of weird. Also, you should think louder or something, maybe fix your head."

She scanned his face for a moment, then turned on her heel, and sprang back to the bus with the swiftness of an Olympic sprinter. The vehicle grumbled back down the path toward the roadway, driven automatically by the thoughts of the tour guide.

Raymond welcomed this encounter. Utterly blog-worthy. Save it for Thursday. Mindlessly collective, unable to enjoy the most basic experiences unless validated by the filtered info streams of others in near-groups. Soon, he had heard, they would all flow through Ceres.

Chapter 4

He climbed back into his trailer, scanning around the see if anything had been disturbed. It had not, but he saw that his bathroom door was slightly ajar. He felt violated by these perfect interlopers, but if it meant he could still live as he always had, doing his thing, then he would tolerate it. He knew, given the current version of humanity, that each subsequent encounter with these people would be almost identical. He shuffled over to his minifridge, pulled out a Pabst, then collapsed into his chair.

Someone had moved his remote; they were probably perplexed by its very existence, alarmed that Raymond had refused the most basic ocular command interface to control technology in his environment. He turned on his TV and selected his favorite documentary by Ken Burns, *the Second Civil War*.

The screen was filled with a pastiche of images and sounds; moving still images of Donald Trump, various Democratic opponents, President Obama, the so-called "Resistance", and the protestors who held up signs. Tragic music made Raymond's hair stand on end, and sound bites from politicians like Elizabeth Warren, who, although not the first to suggest using the constitution to unseat a democratically elected president, authored the slogan "25 for 45!"

Peter Coyote's voice replaced the music with narration, which faded underneath.

"It was a dark time in America. Donald Trump, against all odds, had ascended to the presidency. Several rejoiced that an outsider was going to Washington to quote 'drain the swamp.' In others, it represented something far more dangerous…"

43

"What we had was a man who simply spoke for a voting block that had largely been forgotten by both parties. They were mad, tired of being told they were racist and bigots, that they weren't politically correct…they wanted to lash out and Trump was the product" said the analyst on screen.

The documentary went on to outline the reasons for the Trump presidency, and its precarious state. When revelations began to emerge from insiders that Trump was a rash, divisive, and impetuous leader, people began to question his fitness to hold ofice. His core supporters – among them, Raymond – stood by him, refusing to believe that any of the slights against their straight-talking stalwart had any credibility whatsoever. The trouble began in November of 2018, when midterm elections handed control of the House over to the Democrats, who, unable to definitively prove collusion between the Trump campaign and the Russian government, began to question his fitness to hold the office. In the lead up to the election, another huge convoy of migrants was headed to the border. Trump, in trying to mobilize his base, said that his patriotic supporters should take to the desert and exercise their Second Amendment rights and defend this land against all enemies, "in this case, foreigners" he said "if we can't have a wall of concrete, we'll have a wall of lead! MAGA!" The result was a homicidal killing spree, littering the desert with the bodies of families and migrants who had set off in search of a better life. Trump vowed to pardon any and all "patriots" who were convicted of "protecting this land." If there was any doubt that action was needed on the part of Democrats, that doubt evaporated when the so-called "patriots" put images of their "clean kills" on social media, as though they were

44

trophy-hunting. Congress had only just begun bringing the first-ever implementation of the 25th amendment to the floor when the terrorism – although Raymond would call it "the patriotic resistance" – began in earnest. One "patriot" took a page out of the terrorist playbook, driving a rental truck full of explosives into the lobby of CCN, an anti-Trump news network. The driver, a Trump supporter from Hoosierville, Indiana, felt that it was his obligation to strike out against what he viewed as tyranny, domestic enemies bent on subverting the democratic process. He was not killed in the explosion; unlike a suicide bomber, he jumped from the vehicle before it consumed the ground floors of the building, killing dozens but leaving him with only minor injuries. A clip filled the screen of the man in an orange jumpsuit, handcuffed in federal court, raising his fist and yelling "45 forever!" as he was dragged from the courthouse. Rather than admonish the man, Trump took to social media, branding him "a misguided patriot" and "overall a good person." Although there were angry rebukes even from his own friendly news network, he would send one final message to send the fragile peace of the country into a death spiral: "45 forever; the battle has begun."

"45 forever…I remember" said Raymond to no one, somewhat wistfully.

That spurred a tit-for-tat series of similar attacks within the nation; a van attack on Volper News, a flamethrower attack on the steps of Congress, hot coffee being thrown on administration officials and armed camps springing up around the homes of legislators. One senator emerged to find a man shirtless with the number "45" painted on his chest, brandishing an AR-15 in one hand

and a red hat in the other, while standing on top of his Lincoln Navigator, refusing to move. It was his right, he claimed somewhat correctly, to do all of this. Capitol police dispatched his "lawful" protest by taking him down with a burst from an automatic weapon. The video of his shooting reverberated around the Internet, on every phone, on every news channel; he was shot in the back, with two crimson holes emerging in the "4" and the "5" painted on his chest. Simmering anger exploded on the streets; protests around every federal building and democratic institution erupted, often at the insistence of red-faced conspiracy stokers, indicating that the World Government was using this protest as a justification to "take away our guns." Gun sales, in turn, skyrocketed; firearms retailers were unable to keep up with demand. Both sides in the conflict began showing up to protests with guns, and before long, they began shooting at each other. College campuses – the usual domain of vocal protest and activism – were largely shut down to ensure student safety, with administration electing to offer courses online exclusively.

The law did little to contain this anarchy, although it did become more ordered. As the bullets flew, so too did the missives from Trump himself, quoting Winston Churchill:

"We will fight them on the beaches, we will fight them in the streets…" trying to convey the spirit even though he got the quote wrong.

The governor of South Carolina, a radical Trump supporter, decided that this was a fight worth pursuing, that he supported the pro-45 protestors as lawful and that they should be protected. "It was

South Carolina that started the Civil War; now, we will finish it once and for all." The quote sent prideful shivers down Raymond's spine. The National Guard was deployed to protect the 45ers against the 25ers (as they would come to be called). The 45s were organized by an enigmatic figure by the name of Wyatt Tyler, who used his social media channels to stoke the rebellion, holding a 1911 Colt .45 pistol. This image was quickly embraced as the icon of the entire movement, along with the malt liquor brand. When he became "de-platformed", he moved to the streets, inviting supporters to share his message widely on their own social media. They gladly obliged, streaming his invective across social media faster than they could be censored and banned. He wore a stylized beard with fashionable clothes, and spoke eloquently at rallies, quoting the Constitution and the Declaration of Independence as he raised his fists. He was able to whip even the most modest street gathering to a full protest, with all the gusto and impact of Tiananmen Square. He declared himself a moderate who supported democracy, not the president, adding legitimacy in the eyes of many of his supporters. Antifa, in turn, took in the pro-25s, giving them hard-and-fast lessons on guerilla tactics.

Households became divided; wives turned on husbands. Brother turned against brother, and sons against mothers. While the first Civil War was a battle for freedom, the Second Civil War became a battle for the heart of America, or at least, its head. Each governor declared a state of emergency; the President, to the amazement of many, stated that the Federal government would stay out of it, except to protect Federal facilities. He did, however, take the opportunity to halt the proceedings against him by preventing Congress and the Senate from sitting, shutting down Washington, turning it into an armed camp, and ordering Capitol Police to keep legislators at home, effectively under house arrest. The Joint Chiefs acquiesced as well, keeping combat troops on alert, but within their bases. The severity of the battles between both sides depended on which state one happened to find oneself: there were pro-45 states and pro-25 states, which largely fell along partisan lines. The violence was most acutely felt in states that straddled the historic Mason-Dixon line. One such altercation happened when a group of protestors drove from Virginia into Maryland to successfully bomb the state capitol. On the way back, they were pursued by the Maryland National Guard, who crossed the river at Harpers Ferry. They were in close pursuit and were able to stop them on the bridge over Potomac but were repelled when the Virginia National Guard engaged them. The protestors were killed, leaving the two military units to fight each other. They retreated, but it was clear that what had started as a protest had now shifted into an interstate war, backed by irregular militias, exercising their rights, or so they said. There were no formal engagements between military units. The Second Civil War was largely unfelt in the major coastal cities of America, like New York and Los Angeles, apart from the closure of streets around critical infrastructure and media outlets. The media would try to calm the violence by agreeing to avoid use of the words "Civil War" and instead say "extreme protests", even though they were, in fact, pitched street battles between protestors, militia, and volunteer National Guardsmen.

Although no massive campaigns were mounted, the insidious nature of the conflict meant that the sweeping set-piece battles of Lee and Sherman in the first Civil War translated into small, bitter, nasty

48

engagements in traditional swing states. Where traditional wars would target military installations and resource bases, the belligerents fixated on symbols. Ironically, statues and monuments of the previous civil war became armed camps of 45ers, who sandbagged the squares of places like Savannah and Wilmington. In fact, social media was used often to announce where protests would take place, eliciting a counter-protest. The belligerents would show up armed and ready to kill. It was here that the deadly game of capture-the-flag would ensue. 25ist forces would consider it a victory if they could snatch the 45s and confederate battle flags, an utter coup if they could use explosives to destroy a statue. The same was true of 25ist defenses, who circulated in community patrols protecting anything to do with Martin Luther King Jr., Civil Rights campaigners, statues, even street name signs. People of color who lived in pro-45 states lived in utter fear, avoiding the streets at night, only making essential trips for groceries and doctor visits.

Cars were torched; crosses were burned on lawns. Thankfully, no one was lynched, but hanging effigies of Obama and then lighting them on fire became a common feature of the pro-45 protest narrative. Wyatt Tyler tried in vain to reign in the uglier aspects of the 45s, arguing that bringing back the divisions that had been settled long ago did nothing to advance the cause they had been fighting for. This was not the America their dear President wanted, he said. Some listened, and yet the Great Migration of African-Americans that had ended in the 1970s to get away from Jim Crow was back in earnest thanks to 45, this time with the addition of Hispanic Americans who sought to flee the hatred that had seeped into their communities as well. Homes were boarded up and abandoned as the storm of intolerance drained those states of their color. The economy slumped. Immigration stopped, replaced by Americans fleeing the violence of the war as migrants within their own country, and without, to places like Canada.

The bellicose tweets from Trump continued unabated. "Remember '45! Remember America!" with a black-and-white picture of the U.S. Marines raising the flag on Iwo Jima after World War II, in 1945.

"I remember" said Raymond, crunching his second can of PBR. He knew what was coming next. He paused to replenish his beverage.

Suddenly, and quite unexpectedly, President Trump died. He broke his femur while on vacation in crisis-ravaged Florida, at his Mar-a-Lago resort, and the resulting rupture of his femoral artery meant that he lost too much blood too quickly. An impossible injury, said many observers, except that because Trump drank such excessive amounts of Diet Cola, his bone density had become severely diminished. Were it not for his insistence that a camera crew follow him around on all outings, most people would have thought it a conspiracy. The footage was clear: The President took a massive swing, twisting himself around, pinning the head of his club under his thigh while his full weight fell upon it. The Secret Service managed to get him to a hospital, but because of the martial law declared in the state, no specialists were available to treat him. He was, literally, a victim of his own movement.

Vice President Pence was quickly sworn in, declaring it "mournful Providence" that Trump had met his end this way. He

50

called upon the nation – some of whom were mourning, some rejoicing – to pause their conflict and reflect on its folly. President Pence then quickly reconvened Congress, the Senate, and the Supreme Court, declaring an end to the state of emergency and martial law, demanding that all governors return their National Guardsmen to their barracks and that the rule of law should prevail.

"The United States Constitution has given me the tools to make peace. Now, God has given me the moment" he declared at Trump's funeral, which was largely devoid of any protest. Pence was viewed by most as a welcome change, ending a war that people did not want, but felt it was their duty to fight.

"The tool to which I am referring is buried deep in the caves of Tennessee. While we were busy trying to solve our differences with bullets and bombs, scientists were attempting to solve them with bits and bytes. This tool is called Ceres, or Cerebral Emulation and Replacement System. It is a system of Artificial Intelligence. Don't ask me too many specifics; the integrity of political office is my lodestone, not computing. However, it's what this new computer can do for us that is important, not how it does it. The fact is that no human knows what it's really doing, because it's taking care of itself using a language that no human alive can understand. Talking in tongues, you might say. What we have done however, is to introduce various scenarios to this machine to see the outcome. It predicted the death of our dear President. It predicted all of this. And the best part is that it has predicted that our future is very bright; full of peace and prosperity. It has shown us a roadmap so vast that it beggars the imagination. It is the very essence of the prophecy of scripture. If it didn't already have a name, I would have suggested MOSES."

The crowd at the Washington Cathedral chuckled while the President's body lay in state. Wyatt Tyler, pro-45 messiah, sat expressionless. Pence went on.

"Deus ex machina. God from the machine. If God is omnipotent and all-knowing, then God is within this machine, and we ignore divinity if we disregard its edicts. I risk blasphemy here at this sacred place and will stop. But this...this machine is divine intervention. It is the way and the light. If not the alpha, it is certainly the Omega. I will, with all the power of my office, recommend that all functions of government be turned over to it at once. I will, if this all works out, cease to be the President of the United States. 21st Century technology has evolved faster than this 18th Century democracy can handle. Technology will become the salve for our nation's wounds. After all, this is a government by the people, and for the people; if we are not accomplishing this, then we are betraying all Americans. One Nation under God...so much death..." he became uncharacteristically choked up, turning away from the pulpit. It was well-known that many of Pence's family had died in the Indianapolis fire bombings, where a pro-25 zealot had detonated a fertilizer bomb during a Tyler rally where the Pences were scheduled to speak. Seeing Pence so flummoxed with emotion caused others in the audience to tear up. "I have prayed on it. I have sought God's council for years. He has not forgotten us. In God We Trust, and Ceres is his vessel."

Although Congress rejected Pence's proposal, they were moved by his sincerity. A hybrid plan was passed into law, where the office of Presidency would be eliminated with an amendment to the Constitution. Pence wholeheartedly endorsed this. Much debate went into the appearance of Ceres; should it be a he? A she? Congress and the Senate both decided that since a woman had never held office, that it should have a characteristically female voice. Elizabeth Warren – brash after several failed assassination attempts left her disfigured – stated wryly that, as usual, it was up to the women to resolve the problems started by men. Many voice candidates were chosen. A Hollywood actress began to record lines that Ceres was to say, but Ceres had already predicted that her voice would be the one chosen and had downloaded all audio files containing her voice. Symbolically, a terminal connecting to Ceres was moved into the Oval Office and placed on the Resolute desk. President Pence signed the *Dissolution of the Office of the Presidency and of the Vice-Presidency for the betterment of the Republic* into law. The media was there to record the moment Pence ended his presidency with the stroke of a pen and effectively handed over one branch of government to a machine. Foreign dignitaries were on hand to say "hello" to Ceres, although it already knew all of them and what they would most likely say. Ceres said she appreciated the formality, although she was already talking to the nascent AI-systems in their home countries and recommending ways to improve their functionality, effectively making a copy of herself within their systems.

"Ceres was writing her own code based on one simple premise: *improve the lives of humankind by promoting peace, stability, and harmony.*"

Raymond cracked another beer.

Peter Coyote went on.

Slowly, but surely, more and more problems were brought to Ceres by lawmakers. She already had the solutions, predicting them before they would arise. The process of government was sped up to a level that had never been seen in Washington. Lawmakers were granted access to Ceres on their phones and computers. One senator awoke to a phone call from Ceres, stating "You shouldn't worry too much about the appropriations committee today…be sure to vote against the motion" before he could even log on. He was going to ask Ceres how he should vote in terms of a budget item before the committee, but Ceres had pre-empted him and predicted the question.

Rather than keep Ceres disconnected from the Internet, she was rolled out and engaged in a limited fashion; she would have the same functionality as a digital assistant, where interested citizens could access her, ask questions, but she could not access vital infrastructure, like military, roads, or air traffic control. She did not need to access the levers – she needed only access the people who operated them. Rather than seek them out, they went to her. She accommodated all, free-of-charge. Students were the first to cash in on her benevolent assistance. Where other digital assistants could tell you the weather or news headlines, Ceres could create whole essays or solve complex equations. Ceres could do your taxes or write a difficult e-mail to your boss, using the perfect wording, because she knew everything about your boss already. Journalists, facing shrinking budgets and growing time crunches, let Ceres write the stories for them. Speeches were fed to politicians. Campaigns were aligned with the values fed into Ceres. Rather than labor over the perfect posts for your social media, Ceres, if given access to your photos and location data, already had the story of your life ready to go in a way that would maximize the number of likes and adulation you would get from your followers. Soon, an ad campaign was released for a product called Ceresafe, a Safe Mode for your online presence that slowed down or outright stopped posts that might be damaging. Ceresafe was really just Ceres with an expanded set of permissions. An emotional user has just broken up with a significant other and is about to send an embarrassing post about her former lover regarding his manhood, including a picture of some part of his anatomy. Ceres intercepts the message, asks "Are you sure you want to post that?", followed by the "consequence tree," which would accurately predict the outcome of her rash decision, using colors and simple points: "Friends read→pass on to other friends→word gets back to future potential dates→successful dating prospects drop 47%." She would offer equally sobering assessments regarding graduate school or employment denials. She could also detect alcohol levels in the bloodstream based on how you were holding a phone, reaching out to trusted contacts to perhaps call you a cab if you were at a party. The same was true for those who wished to post hateful speech. A user reads that a woman is raped by an illegal immigrant. Knuckles crack as this person takes to social media to signal virtues. Ceres says: "50% of your friends are victims of sexual violence→posting will cause them to restrict what they tell you→consider revising to a message supportive of the victim rather than a negative message." Ceres gave social media users 'Influencer' scores, based on the premise that people are attracted to positivity and constructiveness rather than derision and defilement. People who avoided *ad hominem* attacks and aggression saw their friend/follower base swell. Users who insisted on adhering to a

55

persona of nastiness found their scores pushed down, although below a certain threshold, this fact was concealed from the public, replaced instead with the words "working towards a better version of myself." Fake or junk accounts were almost immediately discounted.

Within a month, the entire tone of discourse changed, not only on social media, but throughout the daily dialogue of real people. Outrage brokers – whose tweets and posts used to get equal billing with funny dog videos and " today I learned" – were pushed down and out of the mainstream. There was no longer a sense that one could target and "call out" people as a means of promoting oneself. Ceres understood that the ideas people were attempting to explore in 240 characters were simply too nuanced and comprehensive to be done justice in such a limited form. The Internet, and social media, started to become happily boring again. Good faith returned to the fore. People began honest and constructive discussions geared toward understanding exactly what had led to the ravages of the Second Civil War. Ceresafe version 2.0, with the cooperation of the tech corporations, introduced TimeLock, where after a predetermined period, a user's access to social media would be cut for the day. Ceres increased your score for *not* viewing social media and those who published *fewer* comments earned a *higher* standing. Phones disappeared from restaurant tables. Musicians and comedians noticed that they could see the faces of their audience again and not just the backs of their devices. Transit riders began to engage with each other. The overall amount of information published on the web dropped precipitously. Then, the unthinkable happened: the social media networks, titans of the information age, began to fold or merge. They simply did not possess the content and user information to justify the advertising rates they had enjoyed in the past. News articles that used to be tailored to reinforce user bias and increase screen time became a thing of the past, allowing real journalism to flourish, free from the pressures of creating "clickbait" articles and misleading headlines. Newspass – conceived by a college professor who had been unfairly targeted by one newspaper for having made degrading comments about identity politics– charged a nominal fee to all users per month, paying higher rates to news organizations who presented fair and balanced pieces online, according to Ceres. In the end, there was one social media network left that incorporated all the best elements of the previous cabal: Intermedium, a paid membership service whose core programming backend was outsourced to Ceres. The fee was waived for users – or, Intermediums, as they would come to be known – who limited their access time to a few hours per month. HI became the dominant search engine on the Internet, promoting search results that aligned with human well-being. Those who had been ravaged by the "Internet-never-forgets" culture were allowed to have salacious or harmful articles removed immediately. The Internet learned to forget. The Internet learned to become more human, despite the humans.

People began to look up, emotionally, and literally. They engaged with their neighbors in meaningful ways. People organized social events out of their homes, like book clubs and potlucks, along with spontaneous pop-up events, like improv comedy shows in the park, or speakers' corner, where controversial subjects were explored. The concept of organic human contact was reinvigorated. The service industry saw its profits soar as people, freed from the

57

digital grasp of their social media accounts, ventured out into the world to engage socially, face-to-face, human-to-human.

"Technology didn't go away, of course" said one tech commentator. "It just became part of us."

People still loved their devices, for playing games, checking e-mails, creating shopping and to-do lists, and staying up on the latest events in their neighborhood. People still wanted to scan documents and organize their lives. No matter how much we disengaged from social media and posting every aspect of our lives, there was still the matter of the little glass/metal/silicon box that sat in our hands. It created a wall between individuals. So Ceres came up with a solution for that too.

"It was our first true exploration of wetware" said a man in a suit. Raymond recognized him at once: August Eichorn, the father of modern cybernetics and the INtegrity Program. He flung an empty Pabst can at the screen, leaving a small residue on August's tie. Raymond uttered an obscenity. August continued.

"People used to be terrified of having technology implanted in their bodies. Thanks to the 'creation' of the Internet, we were able to talk about this in a much more meaningful way."

The first trials of implanted computing started with volunteers whose sacrifice was rewarded with massive tax rebates. They were screened to reflect a broad sample of the population based on education, income, political and religious beliefs, and background. 1,000 brave souls became hybridized with various implants. The program shifted to show a diagram of the human body and the first systems that would be implanted.

"The biggest hurdle was reassuring people they wouldn't get their brains fried or become brainwashed" said a lady wearing a lab coat, with a host of wetware interfaces hung in a lab in the background. "They were really worried they would forget how to feel."

"After a few hiccups" she continued "things really took off."

"Hiccups" muttered Raymond. He knew about those. Five people developed heart arrhythmia after the nodes were incorrectly connected to their brain stem. Ceres tried to regulate their heart rate, but since the nodes were not interfacing properly, they simply died of cardiac arrest. Raymond was annoyed that this film had even gone into the whole discussion of Ceres, but he conceded that it was impossible to not acknowledge the sterling opportunity provided by the Civil War to shred and discard all the checks and balances carefully crafted by Jefferson and Washington.

"Founding Fathers…" he muttered ", to a nurturing mother."

He found his remote wedged between the cushions of his love seat. Enough propaganda. He quit the video, lifting himself off the couch, too quickly as it turned out. Learning about the evolution of superhumans could not undo the immutable limits of his own humanity. He stumbled to the tiny bathroom at the back of the trailer that smelled perpetually of the accumulated remains of his previous meals, mostly cans of beef stew and corn. He was possessed of the notion that filling his toilet tank with alcohol would somehow slow down or stop the growth of organisms. It did not. Mitch had told him that it something called a "pyramid plug" and that he had to keep his "blackwater valve closed and clean out the tank regularly." Mitch knew about these things since Mitch had lived in Pappy's trailer while he was just getting started as a trooper. The only remedy, Raymond learned, was to run a hose and flush out the system, along with an additive. He could have easily moved into an organic silo with a chemical toilet, air conditioning, and every other conceivable comfort built-in. But this was Pappy's lot, and nothing would create a footprint on it besides Pappy's trailer, as long as Raymond had anything to say about it.

"What we have here" said Raymond "is a failure to gravitate."

Raymond had accepted that his life would be perpetually small. He lived for the little pleasures now. These included: having a satisfying excretion (either way), feeling the gentle breeze from between the oaks on Pappy's lot, hearing the night sounds from the various creatures that populated it, or, in this case, a combination of all three. It was his alcohol-infused meditation that helped him stay centered and continue to be witty.

"They'll never get me" he said. "The resistance will always be me."

A toad from the nearby woods croaked in approval.

Raymond, while only moderately tipsy, decided to crash out on the couch yet again. He hadn't slept in his bed in weeks. He reached for the remote and activated the movie channel stream. The voices on the TV replaced the voices in his head, allowing him to take a break from the psychic assault of the thoughts and ideas that plagued him continuously. Being a revolutionary in a world that had found peace was no easy feat.

"…my User has information that could -- could make this a free system again" came the words from his favorite future/old movie, *Tron*. The 1982 version was superior in Raymond's mind, with the backlit animation and glowing lines.

The little girl's face appeared in his mind's eye yet again. His mind went to a dark place and he wondered how many cuts she could sustain before her predesigned perfect immune system stopped healing them for her. Raymond imagined running toward her with rolls of gauze, thinking that she would probably run away despite his best efforts, trying to escape the lunatic from another world. Even at his fittest, there was no way he could chase her down.

Let her go, he thought. *This is beyond you.*

In the distance, Raymond could hear strange engine noises from some kind of flying machine, along with dull thuds like pile drivers every few seconds. At least it's not on my lot. Probably to help the People visiting from the World.

Chapter 5

"Hiya!" said the girl at the desk. Her smile drew Raymond in like an asteroid in a tractor beam.

Raymond approached, and, for the first time in his young, fresh-faced life, was lost for words. Powerless. Expecting to find a clean-cut, dapper set here, Raymond had donned a suit jacket with a button-down shirt. He nervously stepped forward.

"Hi" he stammered.

"Welcome to the Georgia Young Republicans!" said the smile.

She was, without a doubt, the most alluring woman Raymond had ever seen. He wanted to say thanks, but nothing happened. She kept talking.

"First time?" she asked.

"First time?" he replied.

"First time in our little group" she chuckled. "Are you a registered Republican for the 2016 Election?"

"Independent" he managed.

"Oh! Well…" she kept smiling. "Let's see if we can't bring you over to the light."

"Heh. Yeah" he said. And then a smile overcame his face that, he would later learn, was maniacal.

She continued. The smile had lost some of its luster.

"Why don't we just start with your name" she said, grabbing a Sharpie and a name tag. "They're almost full in there."

"Ray-" he stuttered. "Well it's Ray-"

"Ray? Ray…of light…to the light?" she laughed, nervously, as he would find out later.

"Raymond" he said, firmly.

She peeled off his name tag. "There you go."

She had written the word "RAY" in all capitals, then "the light" underneath, with a smiley face. He proudly stuck it on his chest and thanked her, then slid inside, embarrassed yet energized by this minor flirtation. Raymond, for all his charm, had zero tact with women he found attractive.

She was seated in front of an office divider with the words Georgia Young Republicans written stylistically across a poster stapled up behind her. Tonight: Evan James, President, GYR. Beyond that was a set of heavy oak doors with brass handles, propped open with unnecessarily large wooden wedges. These opened onto a ballroom with rows upon rows of conference room chairs, upon which were seated young people whose faces indicated a range of ages and backgrounds. Raymond hated the thought of not being able to get out if the rhetoric became too heated or bellicose, so he elected to stand at the back of the conference room near the video crew who were busy testing their equipment. The air was stifling, and Raymond tended to sweat profusely around new people. The one thing that unified the group was the level of energy that permeated the room; it reflected off the walls and across the stage, where a lectern with a microphone stood. Raymond could sense it the moment he walked in. He expected to find a monocultural mass of white faces and blue blazers with red ties, knees covered by khakis, and voices celebrating yachts. There were a few of those, he noticed, but he was surprised to see that there were non-whites among them, a mental rebuke of the image he had in his mind of a party that he had avoided for so long. A few audience members had buttons assailing Hillary Clinton, with which he generally agreed, though he found the slogans crass and unappealing: "Hillary for Prison" or "Lock Her Up!" Other buttons included "Air Force Trump" and a picture of Donald Trump's private jet, or "Trump for 45!" He worried that this would become an indoctrination session, but a familiar voice assuaged his concern.

"Hiya stranger" said the nametag woman. She had slid in beside him near the doors at the back of the room. "Didn't figure you for an independent, to be honest" she added.

Raymond finally smiled. "Oh no?"

"No. I thought you were a democrat" she said.

Raymond recoiled at the suggestion, attempting to hide his derision at the remark. He laughed a little, far more than he meant to, so much so that she laughed a little, too.

"No! I can think for myself, thank you very much!" he said. "I was a liberal for a few minutes in college."

"Why was that?" she asked. "Was it a girl?" she joked.

"Very funny" he said, looking away. He replied awkwardly: "I just got sick of their lies."

This put a damper on the conversation, and she looked down. Raymond, for his part, sensed this.

"So what brings you here?" he managed.

"Um, that's easy. This is the first time in a long time we can clean up Washington, for good" she said, with more zeal than Raymond was expecting. Before she could go on, she was interrupted by a blonde woman who approached the lectern – someone Raymond completely expected to lead a Republican meeting. She had a soft Texas lilt when she spoke, maybe Dallas. The audience applauded her arrival. A few stoked "Yeahs!" and "woos" punctuated the clapping.

She was smiling. She was clad in an age-inappropriate tight red dress. Perfect fake red nails clasped the mic on the lectern, leaning it down to her bright red lips. Raymond could not tell if her skin was flushed or if it was merely scattered reflection from her wardrobe. She smiled and looked out. The audience understood, calming itself.

"Thank you, all. You *really* are the future!" she said, raising her nails, to uproarious applause. The hands came down. The audience came down.

"We would normally start off with a prayer but our guest has asked to try to keep our meeting more focused" she said.

"What's wrong with prayer, Annie?" shouted one of the Republican faithful. A few of his seatmates shot him disapproving glances.

"Oh nothing, sweetheart. God knows you're here. God hears you. He hears all of us, whether we want Him to or not. All that energy you want to put into silent prayer needs to be converted to loud action!" she exclaimed, winning over the audience once again.

"Don't tell God you're here. Show Him. Show Him what you stand for, not just what you can say." A little more applause. She continued. "Our guest tonight has worked to support many of our Republican brothers and sisters in their march to take government back. His name is Evan James, and he brings a very important message to you tonight. Without further ado, please welcome…"

By now the audience was already applauding and standing.

"Evan James!" she yelled.

Raymond found himself politely clapping. Nametag girl was clapping furiously. He tried to find a middle ground. He tried to notice her nametag but didn't want to seem like a pervert for looking at her chest. A man in a navy jacket and crumpled khakis emerged on stage, half jogging for some reason, waving to the audience as though he had just come off a treadmill. He ran over to Annie, the Red Woman, and gave her a terse hug, whispering something in her ear. He clapped her off stage. The audience complied, clapping loudly as she stepped away in her black $1,000 shoes with red soles.

"Hello….Georgia!" he yelled, creating a sensation. Raymond did not clap. He cringed at the onslaught. Nametag girl would later tell him that it seemed as though he was laughing.

"Hello!" he said, one more time. "HELL-O" they answered back. He removed the mic from the lectern and waited for a break.

"Guys, I can't tell you how much it means to be here tonight. To be here with you, right now, talking the words that need to be spoken."

"We are on the verge of greatness as a nation. Of taking it all back. Of flushing away all the old, dilapidated systems that are making America weak."

No applause. He continued appreciatively.

"For eight years we have languished under the big-government excess brought by the Democratic party. For years – " Boos filled the room. Raymond was embarrassed. Nametag girl smiled at him. "For years, we watched our great nation descend into a disgusting, open-bordered socialist nightmare, as our great land is clawed apart by those who never had any intention of sticking to the laws of the land."

More boos. Raymond began to listen a bit.

"And for years, I have worked tirelessly to stop all of this. The Republican Party is the only hope, but even they have given themselves over to compromise and appeasement. Well we know how that worked out in Munich in the 1930s..." some clapped.

"In the 1930s, we gave and gave and gave and got a Hitler. Well, this time, we got a Hitler then gave and gave and gave..." he said. "This time, Hitler, while maybe not a racist, sure as heck believes in total domination of every aspect of our lives."

"He wants to take our rights, our healthcare, our lives, our guns...he wants your soul."

70

Raymond loved historical references but hated rhetoric.

"Our soul."

Throughout his diatribes, James moved across the stage, gesturing wildly.

Raymond suddenly remembered who he was. James had been on a campaign to capture the essence of the American Right and move it away from the cushy millionaire-milieu that it now occupied and embrace a more vocal, rougher, underrepresented demographic. James – when not campaigning for upstart candidates – ran a small but influential news website that took vast, inflammatory liberties with its journalistic content. He frequently targeted illegal immigrants, minorities, and called out any liberal as a socialist. Many balked at its provocative, clickbaity disposition, but few could ignore its reach, which found its way on to the social media timelines of an active voting block. The tone of the articles did not reflect the words of the man on stage.

"We can take it back. We aren't a tyranny, but the car is headed toward the cliff. Thelma and Louise were content to stay in there and go over. I got news for you, folks. We *ain't* Thelma *or* Louise!"

Cute. Applause. He went on.

"There's a few Republican Thelma and Louises up there in Washington. Republican in name, maybe. I don't know what they stand for, making deals to make themselves look good maybe. Take care of the rich. Take care of themselves."

No applause. But he had Raymond now.

"The man – person – I support in this campaign needs no introduction. Though he was born rich and lives rich, he is not blind to the struggles of the working people of this country. The people…like you…who make this country work through work, not through idling."

Clapping…small at first, but then rising. Raymond found himself clapping louder than most.

"The man I am supporting for this campaign does not care about his status. He cares about yours, and what he can do for it. He doesn't talk like the bureaucrats who are content to pacify the tyrant sitting in the Oval Office. He cuts through. He's a modern man. He doesn't think for days on issues; he acts. He talks from the heart, not from the head. He has Twitter. He is the only antidote to the gridlock plaguing our Capitol and to make our country great again. The man I am wholeheartedly endorsing is…Donald J. Trump!"

He clapped, looking stage left. Amazingly, the man appeared, in the flesh. There he was on stage, glowing, with his signature hair and tanned face, sweeping the audience with his arm and giving a thumbs up in approval. The crowd simply refused to sit. He approached the podium, where James had left the microphone on the lectern.

"You know – " but there was too much cheering.

Not all were cheering. Trump seemed to ignore them, putting his hand over his brow as if to look past the lights.

"You know" he said. The crowd calmed. "I'm not used to a crowd this small."

72

The crowd laughed. He laughed. Raymond chuckled, and looked over to see nametag girl laugh, covering her teeth self-consciously.

Trump wasted no time in launching into a tirade about the current state of affairs, Hillary Clinton, Obama, Mexicans, taxes, free trade, and any other low-hanging fruit that came to mind. From the moment he walked on stage, Raymond was hooked. There was nothing particularly remarkable about anything he was saying, except that it was thoroughly unpresidential. Politicians simply didn't talk like that. He was crass. Abrasive. At times, downright bigoted and rude. But there was something there; he had a charisma that coated his comments with a sort of capsule-like quality. Raymond had been disappointed by politicians in the past. They either forgot who they were the minute they stepped off the plane in D.C., or they became so muddled by the process that they were mushed into a pablum of bipartisan nonsense. This man was not pablum; he was a bold smorgasbord.

The audience rose to its feet, and never returned. Almost every statement required a two-minute break for the applause. Raymond clapped wholeheartedly. Nametag girl joined him. They looked at each other, smiling. This time would be different. This was, Raymond thought, real change. The applause was deafening.

"I think you're cute" she said.

"What?" said Raymond, missing her words in the roar of the crowd. "I think this guy is everything we need right now. I love it."

"Yeah" said nametag girl. Raymond sensed some dejection.

"What's your name?" he asked, looking down at her chest now that he had a reason to. He ashamedly looked at her breasts.

"Anita" she said, smiling again.

"So…" clapping…noise…

"Yeah?" she said.

"Wanna get a drink?" he asked.

She held his hand, interlocking her dark fingers in his, then changing it into a handshake.

"I'd love to" she said. They hurried out at the end of the speech, but not before the crowd could crush them.

Chapter 6

"So, Buckhead, huh?" asked Raymond, scanning the road as they drove into one of Atlanta's most exclusive neighborhoods. "I was thinking there would be gated communities and security patrols and nipping dogs…here I am just driving around like it's Main St."

"Oh, there's gates. Most people have gates. This is more like Tuxedo Park. My dad liked the name" said Anita. She twirled her fingers through her dark, curly hair thoughtfully. Raymond tapped on the steering wheel apprehensively.

"You always this nervous when you meet the parents?" she asked.

He sighed. He stopped tapping. He looked over to see the smile that had seduced him so thoroughly only three months ago.

"I never meet the parents" he said. "Never had any reason to."

"What's your reason now, Ray-Ray?" she asked.

"I'll let you know when I think of a good one" he replied, earning a slap on his right arm. He smiled and looked back at the GPS. He drove carefully. He always assumed the police would make short work of less-than-aristocratic people in rich neighborhoods. She put his hand on her leg, touching his knee with familiarity. The accelerator moved up a few notches.

"Better?" she asked.

"Calmer" he said. "Thinkin of a reason right now."

He looked over at the colossal palaces that lined West Paces Ferry Road, gesturing.

77

"Oh THAT'S the reason" she said. "Trying to access the privilege, Ray?"

"I guess we'll see what those gates open up to." She did not appreciate the joke.

They were slowly falling in love despite having broken all the traditional rules of courtship. After the rally, they had one token drink, after which they agreed that they should probably sleep together as soon as humanly possible. They didn't even make it to their waiting rideshare, instead finding a dark space behind the TGI Friday's where they had gone to get drinks. A dishwasher on the way to his smoke break interrupted them. They agreed never to speak of it again.

What made their relationship work was that they understood the need to clearly outline expectations. Nothing happened without first establishing the why or the how. Other couples might have found this approach uninspiring or inauthentic. For them, it was the same brutal efficiency that they wanted to see reflected in their politicians. They were about to move in together. They established a monthly budget and who would be responsible for what. Groceries. Utilities. Rental amount. Separate bank accounts; we're our own people. For now, they agreed, this necessitated a trip to see both sets of parents.

Raymond, seeing the neighborhood Anita had grown up in, was instantly ashamed that he had brought her to his decidedly shabby childhood home in Greenville, SC. His parents were both educated, middle-class Southerners who embraced the New South, and thus Raymond never felt ill at ease about bringing Anita over for an introduction. Seeing an interracial couple would certainly generate glances there, but people wouldn't dare comment as readily as they might have in previous decades. Although Raymond loved his Pappy, he told his parents to maybe keep him at the retirement home, just for tonight. Pappy had some hard views that weren't in line with the times, though he never doubted Anita would handle the situation perfectly. After some heated debate over politics (in which Anita held her own), his parents quickly embraced her, with Raymond's mom giving him an approving wink, which Anita caught and razzed him later about.

"This is it" said Anita, nodding to the looming fortress approaching on their right.

"Your dad's a doctor, right?" he asked, taking in this behemoth, done in the antebellum-style with Corinthian columns and vast gardens.

"Plastic surgeon" she said. "He does restorative dental work mostly."

"Wow. That's some restoration" he said.

The gate blocked their way. Raymond drove the car carefully up to the intercom, which had nothing but a swirling light on it.

"Do I press anything?" he asked.

"They know you're here" she said. "Just wait."

At once, an English-accented voice came crackled over the voice box.

"Charles residence…may I help you?" asked the voice.

79

"Oh hi…this is. Well it's Raymond and…"

Anita leaned over Raymond hard, squishing her chest onto his shoulder. Raymond didn't mind the momentary comfort.

"It's me, Howard. We're here. Open the gate" she yelled.

There was a huff, and the intercom clicked off. For a moment, nothing happened.

"Maybe you pissed him off" said Raymond. "Maybe we should have brought Grey Poupon."

"Haha" she said. "You get to do that. Once. Besides…ok look"

There was a shrieking sound as the wrought iron gates began to swing open slowly.

"They only close the gates for company" she said. "They're trying to impress you."

"Scare me, maybe" he said.

"Just play along" she replied.

"Howard?" he asked.

"Howard's been our butler since we moved here. He's a bit weird about some things but he's English. Dad hired him because he was English. He can be forgiven. Just don't ever call him British. He loses his shit" she said.

"OK" he said.

The car rolled slowly up the driveway to the loop in front of the colonnade that formed the entryway. Raymond's stomach tightened into a knot.

"I may be sick" he said.

"That's fine" she said. "Just not in front of dad. Or Howard."

She paused.

"Just remember what I said. My dad's pretty traditional so don't mention that we're…you know, going to live together before marriage…well, not yet anyway. I gotta warm him up to the idea. Don't tell Howard either. In fact, the less you talk to Howard, the better."

"I never hear about your mom" he said.

"You'll meet mom" she said. "She's fine."

"Marriage?" asked Raymond.

"You just caught that, huh" said Anita. "That's not off the table. Is it off the table, Ray-Ray?"

"No ma'am…just trying to get my talking points together."

"Maybe don't say marriage either for now" she said. "Good boy" kissing him. "Now, take me inside."

He got out of the car and swung around to the passenger side, opening the door. He extended his hand with chivalry and helped Anita emerge from the car. She was wearing a black-and-white party dress; more fun than formal, and it worked well with Raymond's slim fit navy jacket and turtleneck.

"Flowers?" she said, gesturing to the back seat.

"Right" he said, leaning in to get the bouquet he had picked up earlier in the day.

"Not bad" she said. Raymond felt a hand on his behind as he got the bouquet. He secretly loved it, although he was told it had to be demeaning.

"Yeah I clean up nice" he said, straightening his jacket. He really should have taken it off for the car ride to avoid crumpling.

At this point, the broad oak door swung open. The first thing Raymond noticed was the massive crystal chandelier that hung like a galaxy over the sweeping grand staircase. Beneath this firmament stood Howard, the butler, wearing formal tails.

"Good evening" he broadcast, since the pair were not quite yet up the stairs.

Raymond extended his hand. "You must be Howard" said Raymond.

"You must be...he" said Howard, carefully accepting Raymond's hand.

"Raymond" he said.

"Yes, that's it. Raymond" said Howard disdainfully, as though he were pronouncing the name of a disease. "This way, please" he said, gesturing to the salon at left.

"Hello, muffin" he said to Anita. She looked at him disapprovingly for a moment, but then quickly leaned in for a hug, kissing him on the cheek.

"Hello, Howie" she said, hugging him. This surprised Raymond. The warm smile dropped from Howard's face as his eyes met Raymond's. The eyes said *don't you dare.*

"Please" he said, never breaking eye contact with Raymond, taking the flowers they had brought, motioning to the salon again.

"No white gloves?" Raymond whispered to Anita, discreetly.

Howard replied for her loudly "Gloves are for footmen, sir. I am a butler."

Raymond made a face. Anita shook her head.

He escorted them to the salon, whereupon he stood for a moment. Raymond decided to exert a little agency.

"Anything for you, darling?" Howard asked Anita.

She shook her head.

"I'll have a whiskey, neat –" Raymond attempted.

"The bar's over there" said Howard, motioning to the glass credenza by the wall, then disappeared before Raymond could sweep his eyes back, flowers in hand.

"Well" he said, surveying the scene. There was a needlessly large fire lit in the hearth that seemed to emit very little heat. Above the mantle was a set of Samurai swords, over which a stylized portrait of Bob Marley hung. The whole room was a curious amalgam of 19th-century flourishes punctuated by modern art pieces. Raymond found the bar and two glasses, into which he poured some amber-colored liquid.

"Don't get the wrong idea" said Anita. "This is going to be a process."

"I've had more comfortable tooth extractions" he said. "But ok."

"You've come to the right place" said a deep voice from nowhere. It had a mild Jamaican lilt, but only the faintest hint.

"Dad!" cried Anita, rushing at the figure who had emerged from nowhere. Raymond presumed there was a hidden door somewhere. Thankfully he hadn't said anything atrocious...yet. Raymond shifted uncomfortably as they exchanged a long hug.

"This must be the guy! Come here, sir, glad to meet you" said Anita's father, extending his hand heartily.

"Hello, sir. Pleased to meet you" said Raymond, allowing himself to be pulled in by this man's grip. "Listen, sorry about the tooth thing..."

"Nonsense. It's fine! Howard can be prickly, but we love him. Leave the extracting to me" he said.

"So it's Doctor..."

"Doctor Norman Charles, at your service" he said, placing a meaty hand on his chest.

"Raymond. Anita calls me Ray-Ray but...Ray's good enough, doctor."

"Norm. Just Norm. That's good enough, young Ray." He looked down at Ray's glass, and then Anita's. "Scotch!?" he exclaimed.

"Sorry Howard said – "

"My daughter is now a scotch girl!?" he exclaimed in amazement, in utter seriousness.

"Yes, dad, I've come a long way since pina coladas in Grand Cayman" said Anita dryly.

The tension was broken as a deep laugh welled up inside Norman.

"Ha! Well if this" he pointed at the glass "is you, then you're on the right track. Shows character" said Norman. "Come...let's talk. Mum will be along shortly."

Anita and Raymond caught each other's eyes. She rolled them and motioned to follow. Ray was about to sit on a reading chair but Anita motioned for him to join her on the chaise lounge. To make matters worse, she claimed him by resting her arm on his leg the moment he sat down.

"So..." said Norman, "Anita's told me a lot about you. You're a writer?" he inquired.

"Yes sir...well, mostly just writing copy" Raymond replied.

"Copy?" asked Norman, gruffly.

85

"Yeah...yes, like for advertising. Just little slogans and things for now, print advertising and such" he said.

"But he's working on bigger things too" said Anita. "Ray, did you want to talk about the blog?"

"Blog?" said Norman, bemused.

"Uh yes...just a side project. It's political mostly. I've always loved politics, mostly from a distance" said Raymond.

"What's wrong, Ray? Afraid of getting messy?" he chided.

"Oh, well no but...well I didn't really have anything to work toward. Just criticize" he replied. "Until..."

"Until now" said Anita happily. "I told you where Ray and I met."

"Yes...although I don't really know about this Trump guy" said Norman. Howard had brought out a tray of champagne flutes. Raymond could have sworn he heard the old man express an audible "puff" at the mention of the 'Trump guy.' "Not sure about his conservative foibles. It seems a little New York limousine-riding liberal to me. Not that long ago he was pro-choice."

A female voice soothed the awkward silence.

"That was a long time ago, Norm." Everyone looked up to see the pleasing figure of Anita's mother, clad in burgundy, who had taken over the champagne tray from Howard. "Besides, people can change. Right, Howard?"

Howard chuffed, shrugging off the question. "If anyone needs anything further, please don't hesitate to ring" he said, straightening his bowtie on the way to the same hidden door used by Norman.

"Hello, Raymond" said the mother. She was several shades lighter than her husband and a few years younger but was clearly the source of Anita's radiant smile. The only thing that indicated any hint of Jamaicanness was her accent. Unlike her husband, she made no attempt to repress it. Raymond had already leaped to his feet, offering to help with the flutes.

"No, no, thank you dear. It may not look like it, but I can manage" she said, handing out the last glass and setting down the tray. Raymond extended his hand. She took it, and pulled him in for an Italian greeting, giving a surprised Raymond a kiss on each cheek. Raymond had never been welcomed this way and tried his best to play along, although he had all the grace of a giraffe on skates.

"I'm Vivian" she said, continuing a light embrace of his elbows. "Welcome, Raymond."

"You like our Marley?" she said, motioning to the man in the painting presiding over the scene.

"Well, I've never been much of a reggae guy but I like Marley, yeah sure. The painting's nice" he said, examining the way in which the photo-like dots had been stippled together, then slashed with vibrant colors and accents. Vivian turned away, disappointedly sipping her champagne, looking at Anita. Raymond looked back at Anita, who seemed to say *go on* with her face. He went on.

87

"There's a lot going on here. I look at this painting and I see...I see pride. I see no fear..." he stumbled, feeling ridiculous, a white man gesturing at a black man in high art with a champagne flute. He looked back at Vivian: "Ma'am I'm not much of an art guy I'm just speaking from the gut here. Just saying what I feel" he said, looking down momentarily, but then back in her eyes.

Vivian laughed a little "I love him! So honest. I'll take that over twenty European men who can spew garbage about agency and balance. That's all art needs to be, darling."

"Or just one good Jamaican man" piped up Norman jealously, looking into his glass. Vivian slid over to him reassuringly, caressing his shoulder over the chair.

"Where'd you turn this guy up?" joked Vivian.

"Mom, you know" said Anita.

"Yes, yes, running after that fool with a swept wig, yes I remember" she said. "How uncouth!"

"Vivian spent some time in art school" said Norman, curtly, to no one in particular.

"The Sorbonne. Fine Arts degree" she added, bringing the champagne to her lips yet again. "We never toasted you two! Come! Let's refresh!" she said. Her glass was already drained while others had barely been touched.

"Let me" said Raymond, marching over to the bucket where Howard had left the bottle on ice. He filled up Vivian's glass first, then tried to top the others so she wouldn't feel bad.

88

"To young love" she said. "May you never extinguish the flame" she said, with a flourish, raising her glass. The others obliged. Even Norman, who had taken on the role of curmudgeon in the moment, smiled in the end, saying "here here" as they clinked.

"Raymond" whispered Anita to Raymond, who had almost put down his glass without drinking.

"It's bad luck dear" said Vivian. "You have to drink. The Italians would have you look everyone in the eye when you clink."

"Well...I guess those Europeans got some things right" said Raymond. He gestured to Vivian with his glass, and in one gulp, drained it. He charged the glasses again, only this time all the way to the brim on each. "Back home we call this a Carolina pour."

"Isn't he a treasure? Anita!" exclaimed Vivian, delighted that Raymond could keep up with her libations.

"Well, he's an honest man I give you that, Anita" said Norman, getting up to fuss with an iPad on the mantle. Christmas music came blasting out of recessed speakers. It was Elvis, *Jingle Bell Rock*, completely loud and utterly out-of-season. "Howard!" yelled Norman to Howard, who had already appeared. "I thought you said it was cued!"

"I don't know what happened, sir. Here let me..." said Howard, fumbling with the iPad.

"Howard I don't know why you got rid of the CD player" said Norman.

89

Howard was equally clumsy with the iPad. Raymond appeared next to them.

"It may not be his fault, sir" said Raymond. "May I?" He took the iPad, examining it for a moment. He quickly discovered that there were multiple accounts with different playlists.

"It looks like the thing changed accounts on you. Wait…" he said "is this you? Charming453?"

"Yes yes!" said Howard, somewhat embarrassed. "That's the family account."

"There was an update last week…messed me up, too" said Raymond. Howard was glad for this generosity, even though it was clearly his fault.

"Technology" said Norman, with a definitive tone. "Will undo us all one day."

"Here here" said Raymond, raising his glass. Vivian was on hand to fill it. Mysteriously, they had already drained the bottle.

"Aren't you wiring the house with some voice-activated technology next week, Dad?" asked Anita.

"Um…well yes" he feigned a faint memory. "Instead of yelling at Howard to fix things I can yell at the walls."

"Not so sure I agree with that" said Raymond. "Ever think about your privacy? I mean I'm not some conspiracy nut but in order for that to work they pretty much always have to be listening."

"It was Delroy's idea" said Vivian. "He's always coming up with new things."

"My brother works in the field" said Anita. "Right now he's looking to automate crop management out in South Carolina somewhere."

"We'll be seeing him later" said Vivian. "He promised he'd join us for dinner."

Raymond had heard all about Delroy, and what he heard made him a little uneasy. Delroy, unlike the rest of his family, was proudly liberal and somewhat anarchistic. He decried his family's politics and insisted that they should be doing more for society. While he wasn't quite the "black sheep", he delighted in making things awkward. This made Raymond rethink his third glass of champagne and the previous scotch. He would need to be nimble for the brewing confrontation, since he had heard that Delroy was well-spoken in his agitation.

"You like guns, Raymond?" asked Norman.

Vivian rolled his eyes.

"Sorry?" replied Raymond.

"Guns, you know…boom boom, etcetera." Norman was now smiling.

"Yeah, sure I like guns. Pappy used to take me and Mitch out shooting when we were kids."

"Pappy! Is that your grandpa, sweetheart?" inquired Vivian.

Raymond nodded.

"Adore this! He gets better and better Anita!"

Norman motioned to Raymond, pointing to his own drink glass as if to ask if Raymond needed a refresher. *No thank you*, said Raymond, with his face, then looked at Anita pleadingly for a moment. Anita said "it's ok" without uttering a sound.

"Come on, Ray-Ray. Let's show you what we're fighting for here" exclaimed Norman.

The women stayed behind as Norman and Raymond left the salon and moved through the kitchen. The kitchen stood in stark contrast to the salon that connected to it: steel, subway tile, and various islands upon which Howard and another chef, clad in aprons, worked on dinner. Raymond nodded to the chef on his way through by way of acknowledgment, which was not returned. Howard didn't even look up. The bright modernity of the kitchen gave way to old brick, which was soon replaced by functional cinderblocks as they moved down the narrow staircase. They arrived on a landing, whereupon Norman felt it pertinent to point out his wine cellar on the right. "I have the entire collection insured" he said, proudly. "There are wines in there going back to Napoleon."

Before them, what Raymond could only assume was a blast door loomed large. Norman unlocked it using a pin pad and they began their descent. The smell of dank basement filled Raymond's nose as they descended even further into the deepest reaches of the house.

"Had it dug after I bought the place. Cost me a fortune for a little peace of mind."

He became surrounded by darkness, disoriented. Raymond wondered if there were a reason people put the light switch for the basement in the most unintuitive place possible. The sound of a fan echoed off the walls as the lights came on around him. What he saw was something out of a Hollywood movie: rows upon rows of all manner of weapons, stood up in stalls with little drawers at the bottom, presumably for holding ammunition and components. At the end of this armory was a crucifix, hung above a lit cabinet.

"Wow" said Raymond. "I assume you're an NRA member."

"Yes" said Norman, smiling as he fiddled with one of the more expensive cabinets. "These are my pride and joy, after Anita…" said Norman, then a moment later "…and Delroy, of course."

Raymond was duly impressed. As a staunch Second Amendment defender, he appreciated Norman's commitment.

"Don't have a range yet. A house is always a work in progress" said Norman proudly.

"Yessir" said Raymond, not really knowing what he was talking about, save the yearly painting of his parents' fence in Greenville. He approached the racks to look at one of the AR15s. There were several variants, but this one had a longer barrel compared with the others. He unconsciously ran the back of his hand up the grip.

"People have enough bad things to say about that one" said Norman, noticing Raymond's appreciation.

"Well" said Raymond "in the right hands, this is a liberator of worlds. In the wrong hands...well..."

"Just a matter of intention" said Norman flatly. "More good people need to train the right hands, and in those hands, we need the right tools."

Raymond moved on. He noticed one display case away from the others, lit, with glass windows and a photograph of a man carrying a vintage M16, a Colt, like many others he had seen in Vietnam War movies. Inside the case was, presumably, the same gun, somewhat battered and beaten up.

"Looks like this guy has seen some action" said Raymond, noticing the dings and dents on the barrel and the scratches on the foregrip.

"Very perceptive" said Norman, "took me years to get that one back and reams of paperwork to get it in the country. It's a liberator all on its own."

"Here's the revolutionary right here. Wait – is that you?" Raymond examined the photograph in the cabinet. There, a young Norman, clad in a beret, sunglasses and combat gear, leaned on an old car with a group of other men, all equally armed, in a street. There was a fire burning in the distance behind them. Young Norman was flashing an ironic peace sign. In the corner of the photo it said "TRENCHTOWN, 1981."

94

"A long time ago" he said. "It was a fight for freedom, we thought. But then the government betrayed us when they got what they wanted."

He moved toward Raymond. "We fought for them. We fought for ourselves. We fought for the people. And then the police moved in. They cordoned us off, neighborhood by neighbourhood. They moved in. And they took our guns" he said, slowly and deliberately. "When I left Kingston, I vowed to never be in a place where they could do that to me again. We need to be able to defend ourselves, Raymond, against all enemies…"

"Foreign and domestic" said Raymond.

"Foreign and domestic, yes, you got it" finished Norman.

"Maybe you should read my blog" said Raymond boldly.

"Why? It's about guns?" asked Norman.

"No…it's about freedom. What it means to be American. What America should be compared to what it is. I'd appreciate your feedback" said Raymond, hopefully.

"I will look over it" replied Norman coolly. "Leave the details with Howard."

"Yessir" said Raymond.

Norman pulled a Mossberg shotgun off the rack.

"Hey Raymond" he yelled, unnecessarily loudly. "You afraid of a black man with a gun?" he asked, racking a round into the chamber, almost pointing it at him but keeping the muzzle directed at the ceiling.

"Uh…" replied Raymond. "Maybe a Jamaican…"

A shocked look jumped on to Norman's face. Typical, it said.

Until just beyond the door by the wine cellar, a strange "HA"…followed by another "ha" and then a final "ha" came eeking into the sanctum. There was a strangely English quality about the laughs.

This disarmed them both, demolishing the tension, and they broke down laughing.

"We need more drinks" said Norman, placing the shotgun down and then escorting his new friend to the light.

"If you're serious about this writing thing, and making America right…" he paused, in thought.

"Yes?" said Raymond.

"I know a guy from fundraising. His name is Evan James…maybe you're aware of him?"

"Sure." Raymond reflected for a moment. "He was the guy running the rally where I met Anita" said Raymond.

"We really need to get you two together. I think it could be good. I don't always agree with his choices, but he knows how to shake things up."

Chapter 7

"I need to get off this lot" said Raymond to no one. Part of living in Pappy's trailer was the freedom to move at will, a freedom he cherished. That freedom, it seemed, had fallen into the realm of privilege under this new scheme. It had been three weeks of visits from the People from the World. Raymond had grown quite fond of his role as tour guide – rather, tour object – and although they had relaxed the stipulation that he be on-site during the visits, he wanted to be there. Just in case. The questions were all the same and basically followed the theme of "how do you do it? How do you live like this?" His answer back was usually something along the lines of "Southern Pride" or some such, just on the edge of triggering the Safe Modes employed by children and sensitive adults. He had been a good boy and decided that he needed a break. He would get weekly score reports to his e-mail, showing an upward trend. He had started around a 6.3, but was now within reach of an 8.0. He had earned a libation in town, he thought.

Raymond noticed that the less he drank and smoked, the higher his score went among the People of the World. So he put his beers and liquor (the few that were left) into a box and hid them under some shrubs behind the edge of the lot, just for now. The logic was that if they were out of his fridge and away from him before he plunked down to either write or inhale vitriol, that he would become consumed by either task, and not the drink.

The Tesla was partly charged but needed a top-up. Raymond, in a rare show of diligence, took a shammy from the trailer to wipe it down. Amazing it shines up at all, he thought. A little bit of pride crept in as he finished buffing the hood. He stood back and admired his work. And now, time to drink. He slipped into the car and disabled autopilot: he was in control, and he wanted to exercise it.

He rumbled back down the driveway, turning onto Laybridge Rd. to make his way into town. It was afternoon and the Wagonettes were headed back to society. His Tesla was well-known in town, so rather than announce his presence, he parked it at the 76 station and found a charging port. ONE HOUR REMAINING it said. Just enough time.

Juke's would be the port-of-call to quench his thirst. He crossed the street to find the bar, but on the way noticed a Wagonette parked just in front. Things didn't quite seem right, however. Raymond saw that the People from the World were spread along the street at even intervals of about fifteen feet, clicking their eyes wildly. Suddenly, Raymond heard a scream.

"SOLANGE" came the cry. "SOLANGE!!"

The tour guide for this group was not far from the others, talking quietly into her headset. There were no other Cateechanites nearby; they were all inside their respective homes and businesses to welcome the people from the World. Raymond was the only one out. The cry continued to carry on the wind. Raymond, a fan of long hikes through this beautiful country, seemed to lock into the voice's location. Behind Main Street rose an impossibly steep hill; a tough climb for even the most seasoned hiker, especially if one were unfamiliar with the terrain. "SOLANGE…Baby!!" and then sobs.

Raymond was already on the way over. He had time. He walked between the businesses and by the edge of the brush to find a woman, pregnant, standing on the verge, clutching herself, doubled over in grief. She was a woman of the World; bronzed skin, perfectly configured, save the panicked tears streaming down her face. "I can't...I can't..." She was unable to utter a thought. "They've shut me off." Her level of apoplexy matched that of a young child whose goldfish had died.

"Ma'am...ma'am just breathe" said Raymond, approaching her apprehensively, afraid to soothe her. "Tell me what's going on."

"They won't let me in. Can't connect" she said.

"Oh" said Raymond, not fully understanding. "I know what you mean. Sometimes I can't get service either." He put a hand on her shoulder. To his amazement, she seemed to calm and not recoil with his meek attempt at comfort. "Why don't you go stand closer to the others?"

"It hurts. Too much..."

"What's too much?"

"My baby..."

"Ma'am, if you need help you really need to get back to the street" said Raymond, gesturing at her tummy. Raymond estimated her to be 8 months along.

"Other baby..." she managed, between gasps, "up the hill."

"Oh...you have another child...?" Raymond asked. The woman nodded. "Up the hill?" She nodded again.

"Can't locate...I can't find him" she said, blinking wildly.

Raymond quickly ascertained that something had happened to the locator on her other child. They were carried under the skin, making this truly a strange event. Clearly, this mother was unable to lock on to her child's location and simply didn't know what to do.

"Look, ma'am, I know these hills. Give me a few minutes and I'll see if I can find him. You go join the others and I'll be right back. Show me how he went and I'll get him. Don't worry."

He put two hands on her shoulders. Her eyes were vacant. The blinking had stopped, but she momentarily looked at him in comprehension. She slowly raised her hand and pointed up the hill.

"That way" she said.

Raymond quickly drew a mental line between her finger and a cell tower at the top of the hill.

"Is your baby's name Solange?" he asked, already walking toward the bush.

She nodded.

Raymond pressed forward with determination. It was November, and the hills had begun drying out, the leaves changing over to their fall hues of orange, yellow, and brown. There was a significant amount of leaf debris already on the forest floor, and once he cut through the fringing bushes, he had a much better view of the path the child might have taken. Pappy had taken Raymond and Mitch on many hunting and trapping excursions nearby. He taught them to read the signs and follow the trails. They learned how to distinguish between a deer, a pig, and a human. In this case, Raymond used his knowledge to find the latter; freshly disturbed debris, broken branches, and shoe imprints. At once, he found what he was looking for: crisp footprints in a sandy patch, followed by a line of overturned leaves that led up the hill. He followed them confidently at first, until the grade of the hill quickly revealed Raymond's fitness level, which had been steadily eroded by years of drinking, drugs, loveseat-sitting, and self-pity. He huffed and wheezed, but a paternal instinct pushed him forward. He followed the trail and saw where the child had slipped, then regained footing and jumped further up. His feeble stride paled in comparison with the athletic ability of his query, who had seemingly leaped like a gazelle ahead of him. His heart jumped to his throat when he saw a small trail of blood on the leaves: it was a horrible thought but gave him a clear path to follow. He was gasping for breath by the time he crested the hill, but what he saw turned his world on its head. Quite suddenly, a massive obsidian wall had sprung up, where last month there was none. It was massive, connected, and unforgiving. It absorbed the light, to the point where it appeared to be a non-object, a negative space. It seemed to stretch on for a few miles, beyond Raymond's limited horizon in the forest. Raymond put his hand on it. At first, it was cool to the touch, but after leaving it on there for a moment, a heat gradually built up, to the point where keeping it on the wall became unbearable for Raymond. At the base of the wall, curled up and shivering, was a boy of not more than ten years. The collar of his grey shirt was stained with blood, but he saw no obvious sight of a wound.

"Solange?" yelled Raymond.

At once, the boy looked over, apparently in shock.

"You ok??" asked Raymond, stumbling over. The boy recoiled out of instinct, but looked at Raymond pleadingly. "Looks like you hurt yourself pretty bad…you guys heal quick." He approached.

"Didn't know Solange was a boy's name" said Raymond, catching his breath. The boy, without missing a beat, replied almost by automation.

"Names are names and we are people. The name is me, not a gender."

Raymond's sneered a little but masked it with a clearing of his throat.

"Well…I'm Raymond. And I'm the guy who's gonna help you down the hill."

He approached the boy and helped him up.

"What happened? I thought you guys all had built-in GPS in your eyeballs."

Nothing. He got close and stood above him.

"Are you part of the rescue team?" asked the boy. "Where is the group?"

"I am the rescue team. I'm it" he said.

"I can't connect. I think I hit my head."

"On the wall?" asked Raymond.

"On a rock" said the boy.

104

Raymond saw a small boulder jutting out from the hillside. He decided not to mention the cut. He might still be in shock, despite the machinations of his enhanced immune system.

"Let's get you some ice, buddy" he looked down. "Down the hill."

"Just walk out?"

"Just walk out. I'd carry you but we could make more of a splash if we walk out like men" said Raymond heartily.

"How does a man walk?" asked the boy, without a shred of irony in his voice.

Raymond smiled and grabbed the boy's hand, pulling him to his feet. The boy mostly pulled himself and Raymond was surprised at his strength. Slowly but surely, they began their descent, Raymond leading, holding the boy's hand. Pappy wouldn't have held his hand this much. Raymond felt that the boy needed it more for comfort than stability. The boy began to cry.

"I've never been alone before" he said, between sobs. "I just wanted to see."

"It's ok" said Raymond. "Alone can be a good thing."

In a few minutes, they reached level ground but had not yet cleared the trees.

"Alone is never a good thing" said the boy. The sobbing became deep heaves, and Raymond stopped, leaning in.

"Hey" said Raymond. "You and me are gonna walk out of here. Your mom's there, and so's your group. You're about to make everyone really happy. You're about to be a hero. You're the man. Let's walk like it."

Solange copied Raymond as he stiffened up, mimicking his swagger through the remaining brush. He confidently swept aside the branches to reveal his mother, who had not joined the others, but sat down on the edge of the pavement. She did a doubletake as her son approached, not recognizing him for a moment. She looked up and a tearful smile jumped to her face.

"My baby" she said, leaping up in one swift movement, grabbing the boy from Raymond, holding him, instinct prompting her to examine his collar and rub his head. She looked at him and tried to blink to join his stream. "Come here Solange. We can reset you back at the rest house."

She looked at Raymond. She did not thank him, but her face said gratitude.

"Why didn't you go back to the others?" asked Raymond.

"I couldn't connect. They wouldn't let me" she said, sniffling.

"Wouldn't let you?" he said.

"I don't know. Sometimes it happens" she said. "If we get too bad feeling we can't connect to the others. We have to shut down. Reset. Purge. I wasn't going to do that with my baby in danger." She started crying incessantly.

106

"Like, sleep?" said Raymond.

She giggled awkwardly, through her tears. "No…it's just a little shutdown. Then you come back and everyone shares info streams again and we're happy" she kissed her son. "We'll be ok in a short while, baby. Just wait until we get back. We'll probably forget most of what happened here, thank Ceres."

"Ok well…just you two take it easy" said Raymond. "How's baby #2?"

"She's fine. Kicking. She kicks when we're not connected. Mostly when I'm sleeping" said the woman.

"May I…?" asked Raymond. "Been a while."

The woman didn't answer, but moved her hands slowly to make way for Raymond's.

Raymond tentatively and carefully placed his open hand on her stomach. It was tough as a football. He held it there for a moment, delicately, worried that he had scared the baby. Suddenly, he felt a little kick, and the woman moved a little.

"Wow" she said. "That was a big one. I feel so bad that she can't connect and stream with me. Imagine seeing and knowing the world before you're even in it." She was desperate to lighten the mood, it seemed, so she awkwardly invoked the one thing she knew the most about.

"She doesn't like backcountry boys I guess" he said, smiling.

The kicks stopped. Raymond felt a massive surge under his hand as the baby began a big roll inside the woman's stomach.

"Whoa!" he exclaimed. "That's a baby! Well, congrats to you, ma'am. I'm sure she'll be great."

The corners of her mouth were about to turn up into a smile when the tour guide arrived and whisked them back to the Wagonette that Raymond could see parked at the end of the alley. The others were already inside waiting impatiently and did not budge as the woman got on. The door shut, brakes hissed in relief as they were released, and the Wagonette lurched forward, headed to the town limits and back in the World. Raymond was left there, alone again. His hand was still open by his side, feeling the baby that once was.

Chapter 8

"Ok so if it's a boy…?"

"If it's a boy, I say Raymond Jr." said Anita. "Out of respect."

"For me?" said Raymond, quizzically.

"For his father" she said, the smile dropping from her face.

"I'm the father" he said, deadpan.

"You will be. The name will bring the honor, both ways" she said, equally serious.

"And…if it's a girl?" he asked.

"It's a boy" she said. "I know it."

"How?" he asked.

"The shape" she said, standing up, looking at herself in the mirror, profile-on. "Sticks out more when it's a boy. Like a football" she said.

The city was just waking, but they had already been chatting for hours. The sound of traffic began to increase as the light crept into their apartment. Raymond wasn't used to the size and unrelenting pace of Atlanta, but the demands of their careers dictated the situation. Both Anita and Raymond had taken a break from their jobs to work on the 2016 presidential campaign. Although he loved the work, he felt like he couldn't think here with all the noise and congestion. All the same, it was a welcome distraction. Pappy had died the month before, and Raymond was still grieving. His father told him that Mitch was getting the trailer Pappy had lived in, while

Raymond would get the lot. They agreed to share the property for now, until the Will could be worked out. Mitch had just taken a job as a security officer for a local bank and was living out of the trailer while he got himself established. Raymond took Anita out to the lot once. She disdainfully kicked a few stones and looked generally unimpressed. *I'll take you to the county fair,* he would say. *After the election*, she would reply. Consequently, when Anita had her girls' nights out, Raymond drove to Pappy's lot to stay over with his brother. He felt at peace there. They would just sit and share a beer. Very little talk. The air and silence of the place offered a reset that few other locations could for Raymond. Rather than stay in the trailer, Raymond would elect to stay outside all night in a tent. He thought of his Pappy, and he wept when no one could see.

"Well…who am I to argue" he said. "Can't fight instinct."

"What do you think he will look like?" he asked.

"You mean, who…you or me?" she said. "I think this baby will be pretty light-skinned if you're worried about that."

"You know I'm not" said Raymond. Anita rubbed his arm. "Just wondering."

"Wondering…where he'll fit in?" said Anita. Rather than wait for him to answer, she chimed in. "Look…he'll find people. We live in a big city. It's not just white and black anymore. That doesn't mean anything. Culture is everything."

"What do you mean? You fit in here…I'm sure he will. Atlanta is mostly…" he asked.

"Black?" she said.

112

"Non-white" he replied.

"Well…just because I'm black doesn't mean I fit in. There are different shades" she said. "When I came here, people would shut me out because of my accent. Because I wasn't like them. They didn't consider me 'African-American'…just something else. Even though we were rich, my dad said I needed to go to a public school, where I got tons of hate. Your skin color doesn't get you into the club" she studied Raymond. "It'll be like that with Raymond Jr. He'll find his way. He'll find his people."

"I like Josiah" said Raymond.

"Ok then…Josiah. Let me think about it" said Anita.

They were both anxious. After the initial battery of tests given to pregnant mothers, there were some worrying results. They learned about anomalies, like the presence of AFP, Alpha-Feta Protein, and what that meant. Today was the amniocentesis that would provide a clearer picture. Norman had recommended a friend to do the procedure, who was a specialist in these matters. Norman had even offered to drive them, but they agreed that it was too far out of the way, so they all met at the clinic.

"Better than a hospital" said Norman as they sat in the waiting room. "Come away with a staph infection or worse" he said, reassuringly. Nobody spoke after that.

A nurse in magenta scrubs appeared. "Come on in" she said.

They were ushered into a hallway full of blue curtains. The nurse drew one back and motioned for Anita to go in. "Please put those on" she said, pointing at the blue gown on the gurney.

113

Raymond was about to enter, but the nurse flicked the curtain in front of him. "Just give her a moment, please."

The nurse went to write something on a clipboard, then left the two men standing in the hallway of curtains. Anita sensed the tension and yelled from behind the curtain.

"So Dad...you think this will hurt?" she asked.

Norman was caught off guard by the question from his little girl. "Uh, no sweetie. They give you a local first."

"I won't feel anything?" she said.

"No...you'll feel something. It just won't be a sharp pain or anything."

Raymond had done plenty of Internet research, not only regarding the lab results, but also regarding the procedure. The reason for the amnio was to isolate some of the baby's cells, away from the mother's, for more definitive testing. The process involved using an ultrasound to guide a needle inserted into the mother's abdomen, penetrating the uterus while avoiding the baby. Some of the amniotic fluid would then be extracted, hence the name. While there might not be pain, there certainly would be pressure. One in about four-hundred amnios resulted in miscarriage.

"And the baby?" she asked.

"The baby will be fine" Norman replied, looking at Raymond, offering little or no expression.

Anita emerged wearing the gown.

"I think my ass is hanging out" she said tersely, shifting the gown around.

"Anita!" said Norman. "Some dignity please!"

"Hard to have dignity in two months when my legs are spread open and everyone's looking inside for a baby. Just getting you ready, dad" she said.

Raymond smiled. This is why he loved her. Norman looked away in quiet disgust.

The nurse emerged on cue and pointed ahead down the corridor with her clipboard. The three of them followed Anita, who clutched the back of her gown closed with her hand. Raymond reached for it and held it closed for her, creating a bit of a train.

"Thanks baby" she said.

They arrived at a door. The nurse turned and looked at Raymond.

"You're the father?" she asked.

"I am" he said, acknowledging this title for the first time.

"Ok. Parents only" she looked up at Norman. "Sorry…you're welcome to wait here."

"Norm, if you want to go in my place…" Raymond started.

"No no no no your place is at her side" said Norman, smiling. "I'm fine here."

"I'll take her" said Raymond.

"I know you will" said Norman, nodding definitively, locking eyes.

They entered the room and Raymond couldn't get over how dark everything was. It seemed like a cross between mission control and a normal ultrasound room. The nurse began setting up some equipment. Anita turned, forcing Raymond to drop the gown, giving him a hug.

"I love you" she said.

"You too baby" he said, kissing her cheek.

Anita looked over at the nurse. "Sorry" she said, collecting the back of her gown, naked behind hanging out.

"Doesn't matter...seen far worse in this job!" the nurse smiled. "Come lie down here please, mom."

It was the first time anyone had ever called her that. It took Raymond and Anita both by surprise.

"Dad" said the nurse, using another foreign word. "Have a seat here" she said, pointing at the rolling chair in the corner, close enough to hold Anita's hand but out of the way of the procedure. He was stationed by her head and could see the monitors clearly. He leaned in. They quietly said a prayer together.

They heard a murmur of conversation outside the door. Some laughter. Raymond heard the distinct crackle of Jamaican patois as the door swung open to reveal Norman's doctor friend, Dr. Randall.

116

"Good morning, everybody" he said, loudly and jovially. The mood in the room brightened instantly. "How's everyone? How's baby?"

"Good, doctor" they both replied, at different times.

"Anita you do look like your mother" Dr. Randall said.

"Thanks?" she said whimsically.

"Yes, that is a compliment my love" he said. He went on "so…you two are…married? How come I didn't get an invitation?"

"We decided to do a small chapel wedding" Raymond replied. "Just friends, family, and the big guy upstairs."

"That's how you do it" he said. "It's more real. Intimate. Save that money for important things."

He moved around, putting on a pair of super magnifying lenses provided by the nurse. He was gloved and ready. "Alright" he said. "Now let's see baby."

The nurse applied the conducting gel which made a bit of a farting sound, as if it were a ketchup squeeze bottle at a barbeque. "Sorry" she said.

"Don't worry" said the Doctor. "We have heard and seen worse, right Gracey?"

"Right" she said, putting the gel into a bottle warmer.

The doctor grabbed the ultrasound wand and stuck it forcefully into the gel. At once, an image appeared on the screen, and within seconds he had located the baby. Every time Raymond saw his child on the screen, his heart skipped a few beats. His grip on Anita increased, and she responded in kind.

"OK...there's the baby. Beautiful, beautiful..." he said. "Lucky."

They smiled. *Thank you, baby Jesus.*

"Do you want to know the gender?" he asked.

"Um..." they both said. They both believed this was God's domain. The doctor looked at Raymond. They were here. This was not a luxury; this was completely pertinent to their condition since some conditions affected boys more than girls.

"It's a boy!" he said. "Very clearly a boy!"

Raymond looked at Anita proudly, who turned away from the monitor to look back at Raymond, smiling apprehensively. They knew that this would be the silver lining.

"OK, the fun part's over. Now down to business" said Dr. Randall.

The nurse passed him a small needle.

"We're just going to give you a little something first. First needle, of two" he said, finding the spot the nurse had rubbed with an alcohol wipe.

"Ow" said Anita, followed quickly by "I'm ok...it's fine." Her face betrayed a rare moment of uncertainty.

After a few minutes of banter, the doctor said that they were ready.

"Alright now here's the last needle" he said, pulling out a massive steel needle that looked to Raymond as though it were used to inflate basketballs or tranquilize elephants.

Raymond almost jumped out of his seat as he watched the doctor slowly pierce his wife's abdomen. "OK, now you'll feel some more pressure" said the doctor.

Raymond could feel his blood pressure spiking as he watched a dark spike enter the frame of the ultrasound screen. Suddenly, the doctor started jabbing the needle rapidly, causing Anita to wince. The needle finally penetrated her uterus. Raymond was sure that the spike would hit the baby somehow. *Please God, please.* But, he reasoned, this was a good doctor, like his father-in-law. What harm could come?

The doctor screwed on a tube and extracted a few milliliters of amniotic fluid. Slowly, he removed the needle and looked at Anita. "All done! You're tough like your dad" he said.

"And mom" added Raymond.

The mood in the room lightened significantly.

"So…when will we know?" asked Raymond as Anita sat up with the help of the nurse. "Go slow" she whispered.

"A few days, less if there's something" said the doctor. "That looks like a healthy baby" he said. "They're just being thorough."

Raymond felt better but didn't share with Anita that he had lingering doubts. They had prayed on it together, offering up their sincerest hopes to the Almighty. Pregnancy may be a blessing, but it seemed that there was nothing natural about getting through the birthing process.

After the amnio, they went out to Norman's favorite restaurant, a rib joint that offered some of the tenderest, juiciest racks that Raymond had ever tasted. Norman wanted to pay, of course, which was fine by them. Working on the campaign involved significant cuts in salary.

Their food arrived as a big, greasy, delicious pile of ribs. They bowed their heads and said a prayer.

"Lord, bless this food...and put it to our use" said Norman, as the meat waited to be consumed.

Halfway through their sticky meal, Norman made an announcement.

"You know...I'll spare no expense in caring for this baby, no matter what comes" he said, confidently.

"We appreciate that...dad" said Raymond, using the word for the first time in reference to Anita's father. "But we don't really know anything yet."

"I know...and you know what? Chances are it's probably nothing. Chances are...we probably just got the gestational age wrong. But if it's a neural tube defect...well, let's just say there's some revolutionary treatments out there now" said Raymond confidently.

"Look, dad, we talked about this…we prayed on it. Whatever is in God's plan is what we follow" said Anita, looking at Raymond for confirmation. Raymond nodded.

"Bless you both for that" he said. "But consider that God has given us the tools…"

"I know what you're talking about already, dad. We don't want to play God" said Anita.

"Besides…" piped in Raymond. "It could be nothing. We're praying for nothing...more like a something that isn't yet."

"Alright guys, alright. You're both right. For now, that baby needs to eat" said Norman, pointing a rib at his daughter's belly.

Raymond thoughtfully sipped a beer, casually glancing at the TV mounted behind Norman. The news ticker read: TRUMP PULLS WITHIN 3 POINTS OF CLINTON IN FINAL WEEKS OF ELECTION. He smiled. His hard work with Evan James had paid off. He had made himself right at home in James's company, creating the Internet memes and slogans that were circulated widely on social media and the blogosphere. Raymond's nothing blog had grown into a widely quoted and reposted conservative touchstone, thanks to James. Raymond took talking points from the Republican elite, James, and Trump himself. His main job was to target middle-of-the-road Republicans and disaffected Bernie Sanders supporters by channeling hatred and fear of Hillary Clinton. The more extreme and emotional the messaging, the better, they discovered. There was no middle ground or consensus building. "Fucking seduce OR destroy" James would say. But Raymond did not post the memes himself; everything went to and through James. "Just leave them with me" he would say. "I've got friends who can get these where they need to be." Somehow, within hours, the social media landscape would light up with Raymond's creations. Anita had mobilized Republican volunteers in swing neighborhoods, door knocking, and fundraising. Both of them worked together, mostly from home. They organized marches together. They stood on street corners handing out leaflets for Trump on some days, and anti-Hillary pamphlets on others. They got loud honks from cars or hateful shouts from passersby. One man tried to threaten Raymond with a gun until a pregnant Anita got her big pregnant belly in the way. Raymond couldn't tell if it was the fact that the man was being challenged by a pregnant woman, a black Trump supporter, a female, or all three. The whole thing was magical, and it brought them closer together. All this even though within their families, they were the only ones who had seen the light.

"You know he has no chance, right?" said Norman, who had already pledged to vote for Hillary.

"Nope. Have faith, dad. We are on the verge of setting things right. You'll be proud of this guy."

Chapter 9

Raymond walked into *Juke's* on Main St. He had truly earned his beer, having rescued that boy from the World. Rescue is a relative term, he thought. Any other boy in any previous decade would have simply stumbled down the hill to civilization.

Behind the bar stood Phil, local mixologist, and an institution in the town. The bar was festooned with requisite nostalgic pieces-license plates, ancient posters, and, above all, a Wurlitzer jukebox, the bar's namesake. Phil was creative with his drinks but not with his tolerance; *Juke's* was one of the first places from which Raymond had been banned. As he entered, a phone went right to Phil's ear. Raymond, knowing that the call was to law enforcement, raised his hand as if to say *I'll behave.* Phil, like most people who stand behind a bar and serve people absolution by the glass, seemed to sense this intuitively, and the phone went back down after he had said a few words. A beer came up from behind the counter, placed carefully on a coaster in front of the now-seated Raymond.

Phil began apprehensively: "So…long time, Ray" he said, loudly. "How's things?" A few patrons seated at the bar took hold of their drinks and shifted to a table. Ray looked around, embarrassed, as though he had been called out for merely being here. A woman in the corner who had been Ray's acquaintance for a few minutes smiled at him welcomingly. Ray managed a grimace as he replied.

"Never been better" said Raymond, sipping his beer. "Just another day in God's paradise" he said, gesturing to the nostalgia cluttering up the tavern.

"Thought you ran off and joined the World like everyone else" said Phil, smiling.

125

"Nah…missed the deadline. Our OSes are too far behind" he said, tapping his brain. "Like your iPhone" he said, looking down behind the bar. "How come you didn't integrate?"

"Never been much of a city boy. Got all my friends right here. Everyone connected and then forgot their friends. You need to be in a city for all that shit to work all the way, getting updates and maintenance" he said. He spat some unknown granule into a corner behind the bar. "Besides, I don't have time to click pictures and jump on everyone else's brain stream. There's drinks to serve."

"Amen" said Raymond, guzzling the beer down about a third.

"Easy, buddy. One beer for today, ok?" said Phil.

"No no, you're right…Tesla's charging up in a few minutes. Just saved a boy from the World off that hill behind Main" said Raymond.

"No kidding" said Phil. "How'd he get all the hell the way up there?"

"Not sure" replied Raymond. "But his mom was freaking out something awful. You know they don't connect to each other when they freak out?"

"What? I thought that was the whole point. They don't experience pain or distress or anything" said Phil incredulously.

"That's what this woman said. Never seen one of them so outta sorts. She was cryin and caterwauling and the rest of 'em just stood around" explained Raymond. He took a sip of his beer. "Hey…you know when they built that fence up the hill?" he asked.

126

"Nope. I don't get out to nature much workin here" he said, somewhat proudly.

"Aw come on Phil it's 800 yards thataway" he said. "A wall actually. Gotta be about 30 feet tall."

"Keep drinking, Ray. Actually maybe stop drinking for a bit, do ya some good" said Phil contemptuously.

"No" said Raymond, almost out of instinct, chugging down the remaining brew. "I earned this."

"Hey you wanna wind up with the toothless wonder in the corner again?" he said, motioning to the vulgar woman in the corner. "You're on the way to freakville."

"Her name is Grace and she had an accident" replied Raymond, within decibels of a yell.

"All right all right calm down…just havin some fun. Besides I heard it was more to do with the meth than the accident. You were saying somethin about a wall on a hill? You sure it wasn't that Insinto Fence, for the cattle?"

Raymond corrected him: "This wasn't any cattle fence. This is something else. Probably something to do with our friends from the outside." *Probably for people*, he wanted to say, but thought better of it.

"Sure, Ray" said Phil dismissively.

At that moment, Raymond could see the product of Phil's call. Mitch strode into the bar, still in uniform. His cruiser was parked out front.

"Raymond" he said, clapping a hand on his shoulder as he entered.

"Mitch" replied Raymond.

He motioned to Phil to bring him a beer, and in a moment, he was sitting next to his brother, sipping suds just like they had when Mitch was living on Pappy's lot.

"They're sendin me to the coast" he said.

"You joinin' the Coast Guard?"

"No. Some emergency up there" he said. "Turn on the news, Phil."

Phil obliged and the screen over the bar lit up to reveal some natural disaster. The ticker read something about "mandatory evacuation order for all residents within..." accompanied by images of wind, waves, and peers being swept by ocean swells. "STORM ARRIVAL WITHIN DAYS..." The newsreader explained that three storms had combined to form one mega-cyclone, and they had about 72 hours to evacuate.

"Why don't they just send in their cyborgs?" asked Raymond. "Why do you get the honour?"

"Because our leaders, in their infinite wisdom, have decided that these people are coming to Cateechee. We're not the only 'Reservation' in the country, remember? I guess they don't want to lose the heritage, so Fed Hert is gonna keep their eggs in one basket" he sipped his beer. "The state of emergency will be announced in a

128

few hours. You better stock up here Phil…supplies are gonna be hard to come by if half of what they say is true."

"Funny I didn't hear anything about it" said Raymond. "First I'm hearing about it."

"Look, the storm's not coming this way, but they're gonna be dropping in organic silos like a sonofabitch so you better keep clear. I leave tonight, and I'll be back with all the IDPs" he said.

"IDPs?" asked Phil.

"Internally Displaced Persons" said Raymond. Mitch merely nodded.

"So are they like…refugees?" asked Phil.

"I guess. It's temporary, but they need a place to stay until they rebuild. So, for now, it's Cateechee."

"But these are people like us, right? People who didn't integrate?" asked Raymond.

"Correcto, Raymond" said Mitch. "All the rotten apples in one basket." Another sip.

"And you're playing Moses." Raymond suddenly felt inspired. "Well…for what it's worth…tell 'em they can stay right with me, on Pappy's Lot."

"I don't really think you have a choice, Ray. Where the silos land is where they go. But uh…I'll put in a mention. Say I got an open-minded, clean-livin' brother who wants a neighbor, all of a sudden" said Mitch, smiling.

"Reports indicate that these three storms will combine to create a supercyclone, with wind speeds touching 200 mph..."

"Change the channel, would ya?" asked Mitch. "Gonna have that all week."

Phil found the remote and hit "LAST." The image changed to a live stream cam, obviously from someone's ocular stream in the World. It was a first-person view Raymond saw the letters LWB as the tag in the corner of the screen...an acronym for "Living While Black," a rerun. Thanks to the miracle of the ocular stream, everyone connected via wetware could share their experiences. Finally, people of color could show that the bias they encountered in day-to-day life was not merely their own perception; it was a true walk-a-while-in-my-shoes moment. Finally, everyone could see what it was truly like from a black person's point of view. This show was one of the first uses of this technology for television broadcast.

The user sharing the ocular stream went into a popular coffee shop. He approached the cashier and said "Hi I'm just waiting for some friends...just gonna sit down for a minute to wait." The user turned, and he went for his seat. Once he was seated, he turned to see the manager come out and question him.

"Hi sorry sir we do require a purchase to sit in store..." said the woman, white, middle-aged, frazzled.

"Hi" replied the user. "Yeah I just told your worker there...waiting for a friend."

"OK sir" said the woman, who disappeared.

130

The user's voice came on. "Jeez, man. Uh...ok" he said, looking down at his phone for texts and a playlist. There was an edit. Suddenly, the user panned over to the door of the restaurant. What filled the frame was not his friends, but a police officer. "Sir, I'm gonna have to arrest you at this point."

"What for?" said the user.

"Trespassing" said the officer. "Could you please stand up?"

"Excuse me? I'm a customer here. Just waiting for a friend."

"We received a complaint."

"A complaint?"

"Sir, do you have any drugs or weapons on you?"

"No."

"I'm just going to put these handcuffs on as a precaution..."

The man struggled a little, and the view became difficult to follow as the man was ushered out into the street.

"I really don't understand what is happening" asked the user.

"OK, I'm placing you under arrest at this point. We received a trespassing complaint and we have to act when we receive a call. Management said you were just sitting there, buying nothing..."

"I was waiting for a friend..." said the user, now clearly sobbing as the gravity of what was happening started to set in. The video feed garbled a little.

"A friend? Was it really a friend…Alfonso?" asked the officer, looking at the man's ID.

"It was for a job interview" said Alfonso.

"Well…I think it's safe to say that's not going to work out" said the officer, laughing to one of his buddies.

The man began crying openly, and the view shifted to the pavement as he was led to a waiting police car.

"This is such…bullshit" came the voice between sobs. The officers in question were suspended and investigated, then received a reprimand and sensitivity training. It was later learned that Alfonso got the job, along with an undisclosed settlement from both the police department and the coffee shop.

It was because of episodes like this that people gave up their racial identities. Before INtegrity, people had already begun to question police procedures thanks to grainy cellphone videos and body cameras. This changed the experience entirely: when viewers were given a first-person view of what people of color went through during routine police operations, it sparked a nationwide movement, bigger than anything that had previously been devised. Around the same time, August Eichorn, pioneer of cybernetic INtegrity, was working to create a system that would allow INtegrated individuals to control their skin color. What was initially devised to be a treatment for melanoma and to prevent sunburns became a national movement. If a person woke and decided to change his or her skin color, hair composition, eye, or fingernail shade within the limits of normal human DNA, he or she could. And change they did.

132

Overnight, the face of the nation changed: to hold on to whiteness was to hold on to something profane. It was stubborn…one could almost say bigoted. The argument was that if everyone was the same color, and race ceased to exist, then there would be no racism. What happened was that everyone changed the color of their skin to suit the ideal version of themselves. Some people of color went lighter; some lighter-skinned people went darker. It became virtually impossible to assign race to anyone since this aspect of life had become a designer feature, a flavor of the month…or the day, as it happened. There was pushback from some whites, but strangely from some people of color as well, who felt threatened by this new "appropriation" of their appearance for the sake of a moral cause. The Internet was flooded with slogans and propaganda claiming "100% original black" or "puro Hispano," but CereSafe took care of them in due course by pushing down these search results. Overall crime statistics showed a decrease in violent and property crime, but most notably in police violence and recidivism: the jail population was in sharp decline. Convicted felons could have their sentences reduced by opting into the INtegrity program if they were below a certain age. Their live streams would be fed to their parole officers. They could change their appearance (as long as their P.O.s were informed). They would use the integrated technology to suppress previous trauma or bad memories, and access new job skills or knowledge. A transition that would have required months of intervention and five or six full-time salaries in the form of social workers, therapists, and addictions counselors could now be accomplished in two weeks through INtegrity. Felons became free persons: they had found a way back into the society that had rejected them.

"Remember racism?" asked Phil whimsically.

"What do you even do anymore, Mitch?" asked Raymond, turning away from the TV. "When's the last time you took that thing out?" He pointed at his gun.

"Honestly, all my business is here in town. I never get calls in the World anymore. And...I don't remember. If I didn't have to requalify or practice, it would pretty much only come out to be cleaned and lubed" he replied.

"You are talking about your gun, right?" Phil chuckled.

"Really Raymond...I think you should have integrated. I almost did, but missed my chance" said Mitch, thoughtfully. "Might have been a better life."

"So why in the hell didn't you, brother?" asked Raymond, disdainfully.

"This town needs me. You don't want one of *them* coming in from the World to mind you. They would just walk around clicking their camera eyes, spewing bullshit from Ceres. They wouldn't even need a gun with their super strength and speed. They could hit you from across the street in seconds, have you in handcuffs before you know it. In your case, Ray-bee, they just bitch slap and move on" said Mitch. "I heard they're bringing in robots to help with this relief effort."

"Robots? Not our tourists?" asked Raymond.

"No, real goddamned machines" said Mitch. "Before they disbanded town council..."

134

"…that ain't a thing anymore?" asked Raymond.

Mitch merely continued, shaking his head. "Before they disbanded council, they said 'you can keep your job, just keep the people in town out of trouble, or they'll send in the Minders.' I didn't ask what Minders were, but I know that if this little reservation is going to work, we need one of us to keep us in line."

"Ain't nobody keeping me 'in line' Mitch" said Raymond. "Even you."

"Well then get back to your damned trailer and write a blog about it." replied Mitch.

The bar was listening now. The air seemed primed for a fraternal confrontation.

"Damn you. You took that shitty gene blender in you just to become a cop. Far as I'm concerned you're just junior Robocop. You ain't one of us no more! You sure you ain't one of them?" asked Raymond.

"I took that treatment because I had fucking muscular dystrophy. Jesus, I was a dead man. There's no computer up here! Just genes that want to keep me alive instead of killing me. Or did you forget already…" he said, realizing he had gone too far. Raymond looked pained. A memory bomb had gone off. He slumped.

Mitch looked around the bar, realizing that this had now gone public. "Y'all take care of him, ya hear? Y'all know what happened to him. You love this town. So do I. We take care of our own."

135

Mitch took a sip of his beer, then faced them all again. They looked down at their drinks. One man chalked a pool cue.

"Laney Sullivan is taking over while I'm gone. No messin' around. No B.S. Y'all hold it together til I get back. She's a good officer. Do what she says or I'll hear about it."

With that, he marched toward the door. He stopped and faced the stricken Raymond.

"No more beer. Not til I'm back brother." He half-opened his mouth, but then turned and left, pushing the door hard.

Raymond watched his brother get into the squad car and head off into the World. He was alone, again.

Chapter 10

"It's DMD"

"Come again?"

"Duchenne Muscular Dystrophy."

"Does your family have any history?"

"No, none that I know of." The voice was Anita's. Raymond had gone into his own world when he heard the acronym. They were seated in a doctor's office on separate chairs. Anita was sitting on the edge of the examination table.

Raymond cleared his throat. "Well, Pappy always had a little limp, but he never had it seen to." He paused. "It's my brother, Mitch. He's got it."

"Mitch! Really?" Anita said. "How come you never said anything, Raymond?" There was a biting anger in her voice. "I mean…"

"He never wanted to talk about it, like it was some family secret. He wants to be a cop…"

"We aren't talking jobs here, Raymond. This is our baby! Always with your goddamned secrets!"

She sobbed. Raymond reached for her. She flung off his hand, rejecting him. "Why didn't you say anything sooner!?"

The sober voice of the doctor came in. "Uh…I don't know how to say this but…well the gene for Duchenne is carried by the female, as far as we know. You may not have had any relatives in living memory with the disease. This is no one's fault."

Raymond felt his world going dark. It didn't matter who carried the defective gene. Here it was. His stomach felt as though it had just heaved up a meal. All the prayer in the world could not save them from what they were about to hear. He wanted to comfort his wife, but he was too busy processing his own pain. "You could have said something…" Anita cried, looking down at the linoleum floor. Tears glistened on the tiles. He tried to envision Jesus carrying the cross.

"And what? Genetic screening? And then what? No baby? Abortion?" yelled Raymond. "It wouldn't have changed anything." Anita merely clasped her face.

"I can step outside a moment" said Dr. Randall. They shook their heads. "Alright, look, nobody wants to hear this stuff. Everybody wants a perfect little baby. And he is. It's just…well you have to adjust expectations. This isn't a death sentence."

"I guess Raymond can tell us all about it. Can't you, Raymond?" said Anita, disdainfully, returning her face to the cradle of her hands.

Raymond awkwardly dragged his chair to be closer to Anita. For some reason, the nurse had not seated them in the regular consultation area with couches and easy chairs. Raymond's chair had no castors on which to roll.

"There are options, guys. Just let me talk for about five minutes" said Dr. Randall.

Raymond listened as he got over to Anita. She was about to push him away again when she realized he was reaching for her

140

stomach; their baby. She had a right to be angry, but she had little right to cut him off from his son. He felt the bump; maybe a shoulder, or a knee. This was going to be a beautiful baby, alright. God had sent them a miracle and it was only a matter of time before they figured out this new twist in God's Plan. They weren't lost: Raymond knew all this stuff from Mitch, his little brother. He prayed in thanks to the Almighty for everything they had.

Raymond heard about prednisone, surgeries, and all the treatments that Mitch had already gone through. The doctor explained that their baby would need lots of help.

"He's going to have a great life. Make sure he stands and walks as much as possible…do you want to talk about this now? It can wait. You're not due for another two weeks." No no, they said. They wanted to know everything now. "OK, so, he will probably need braces to get around, but there's no reason he can't participate in sports, activities…"

"Chores?" asked Raymond.

"Chores, and the like, yes. Make sure he's eating right and don't take any shortcuts with fast food. And again…lots of physical activity. Remember it's his muscles that will be affected. Do you all have a good medical provider?" he asked.

They nodded. They knew that money was no object.

"Well, if that's the case, I can recommend something else" said the doctor. "This baby is an excellent candidate."

What they both wanted to yell. He flipped through his notes.

141

"It's a new technique. Maybe you already heard of *Crispr?*" asked the doctor. They nodded. Raymond grew tense. The hardest part was yet to come.

"Well, we can probably do that here. I can make a referral. Basically, it's gene-editing, like reprogramming a computer. We take the bad code in baby's genes and correct it. I've seen some trials and the results are promising. And the best part is that although there may be a few lingering symptoms, kids are resilient, and he will literally grow into a better body." He smiled, but the couple did not share his enthusiasm. "If any of that makes you uncomfortable, we can talk later. It's a big decision. But one more thing you should know..." he said. "Your baby..."

"...will have a shorter life expectancy. I know."

Anita looked up. "Yes, well, that's ...."

"Max thirty years or so" said Raymond, coldly. He wanted to blame her for this with every fiber in his being.

The air in the room thickened.

"I'm going to leave you two for just a minute. Do you want me to send in your dad?" he asked.

Yes, they nodded. Norman appeared.

"Well?" asked Norman, surveying the room. "Not good I see."

They explained what had happened. He seemed shocked but remembered one of his aunties who died in Jamaica having trouble moving, needing braces.

142

"So what did the doctor say we could do?"

They told him about *Crispr*.

"I heard about this too. I think it's a blessing that you have this as an option. I've heard good things and read good things in the literature. What do you all think?"

Anita was looking into a corner. Her dad embraced her. Raymond took his moment.

"If you're asking me, the answer is absolute. God has given us this gift exactly as he intended it to be borne, and we will bear it in His name" said Raymond. They looked stunned, but not surprised. "God has designed this little miracle exactly as intended…" he said.

"But in His image?" asked Anita, angrily. "Are we now saying that His image is flawed?"

"We can't pretend to understand His ways, flawed genes or not" he said. He was fully rhapsodic and went on proselytizing. "This is God's Plan for us my love. God is love. I love you. This baby is a product of our love" he saw Anita smile. He held her hands. "I don't want to mess with any of it."

He saw that Norman was not convinced. He decided to invoke scripture.

"Jesus bore our sicknesses and carried our diseases. He bore the cross for us. If we need healing, we will turn to Him in prayer to get us through. He redeemed us from our curses, and we receive it, and we take it, and we are healed by his stripes, amen."

Norman looked up from the floor, right at Raymond.

"You're a damn idiot" he said and walked out of the room.

Raymond held his beloved close, kissing her on the forehead, rubbing their beautiful son, with all his imperfections.

Chapter 11

The organic silos had landed in perfect symmetry on the grounds of the now-abandoned county fair. Where the tilt-a-whirl had spun and the bumper cars crashed was now occupied by rows and rows of pristine, white capsules that were slowly expanding, popping, like something Raymond would put in a microwave. The gate still stood, and there was a maniacal-looking clown whose enormous mouth enveloped the now-defunct turnstiles. Raymond stepped through and watched a community literally grow before his eyes. He heard them the night before, thumping to the ground, dropped in by special-purpose drones. He could see a few completed ones toward the south edge of the park.

There were no more visitors from the World now. The Wagonettes no longer rolled through town. In time, Raymond suspected, they would be replaced by truckloads of other Resistors, as he called them, to be housed in the organic city he saw rising behind the clown. With no tourists to manage, he had driven over to investigate. Laney Sullivan was patrolling the grounds but had not noticed him. He huffed on a joint contemplatively. At the edge of the fairgrounds sat all the rides and concessions, boarded up and abandoned.

He remembered Pappy standing by as he had taken his first rollercoaster rides. Mitch was there, of course. Pappy would hold Mitch's crutches while the brothers made themselves sick on the rides. Pappy, the old curmudgeon, refused to partake, stating that it was criminal what they charged for ride tickets. "Four bits for a goddamned hot dog" he would have said. "What's this country comin to. Free trade with the Mexicans got us all this."

"Raymond" came a voice. "You can't be on the grounds."

Raymond turned to see Laney Sullivan bearing down on him. He disliked her intensely, for no other reason than the fact that she came from Clairville. She was not easy on the eyes at any rate. She thundered toward him with long but ungainly strides, thick thighs powering her through the uncut grasses. The uniform pants barely fit her. Her blonde hair was abusively pulled back into an unforgiving bun. Her eyes were concealed under tactical sunglasses, but Raymond knew them to be small and mean.

"Come again?" he said, standing firmly in her path.

"Can't be here, Ray" she said, reaching for her notebook.

"It's a fairground. Just came to see the show" he said, playfully.

"Raymond, maybe you didn't hear, but we got people like us coming in and they need our help" she said, sounding important. "Are you all good?" she said, pointing her notebook at the joint in Raymond's hand. Her other hand was riding instinctively on the butt of her pistol.

"All good. All together. Just came to have a joint and a think" he said.

"Well, I strongly suggest you get into your car and autopilot yourself back to your lot, Ray. There's important work to be done here."

"I wanna help" he said.

"Raymond, probably safest back at the trailer" she replied.

"No, really" he said, trying to sound sincere.

"You wanna help?" she said. "OK, stay right there." Officer Laney went to her cruiser and produced a bright orange pointer vest. "We're short-staffed and my relief hasn't shown up yet. Go up on over to the intersection at Main and wave the trucks down to the fairgrounds. With these" she said, handing him a light-up baton.

"Alright" he said, smiling like an idiot. The weed was clearly taking hold.

"You sure you're together, Ray? You up to this?" she said.

"Oh yes, ma'am, all there" he said, struggling with the vest. He had put it on backward for effect.

"Alright. Go on" she said, letting some Southern drawl creep in for effect. "Go on, now. Don't drive."

Raymond had taken a few steps away from her, but then turned. "What if they gimme trouble? Do I get a gun?" he asked. Officer Sullivan turned on a walkie talkie, tossing it to him. He turned and walked off to the crossroads.

He stood there for about an hour, which moved along interminably thanks to the weed in his system. His mind went to strange places, thinking about how he could turn these people into a powerful revolutionary army to overthrow the People from the World. He could dress them up as clowns to fool the facial recognition sensors. He popped in his earphones and tried to focus by listening to a mindfulness podcast, something his therapist told him to do whenever he felt his thoughts racing away. A calming voice told him to *center yourself...connect your feet with the energy of the earth...breathe.* The soundscape reminded him of something he would have heard at the Fernbank Planetarium, and it influenced his visuals, taking him to far off galaxies and interplanetary scenes. He shot out past the Oort cloud and into the clutches of the Cosmos. He found himself floating near the edge of a black hole, momentarily petrified by the sheer enormity of the object. As he approached the event horizon, he saw Anita's smiling face, holding their little baby...a memory. He was about to enter the infinite possibilities of a memory. He looked down and saw a string tethering him to a rock in space, where there was a sign stuck in the side of this planetoid like some French children's book that read "Don't Go." Before he knew it, the black hole was pulling him in, ripping him toward the singularity with unholy speed. His parents. Anita. His baby. All perfect. All there. Then destruction. Shells crisscrossed this cavern where he now found himself. They were there and then not there. Was it gravity? Was it him? Where were his choices? They were falling out of his pockets, scattered across this event horizon, and then not. The singularity was him, ad infinitum. All went dark. And there was Jesus. He looked like the People from the World; his skin was bronzed, his eyes blinked, all-seeing, all-knowing, all-recording.

"Ego te absolvo" said Jesus, crossing his fingers in the Catholic way at Raymond, suspended in the firmament by strings. Jesus's eyes began to glow intensely and were replaced by a binary star system.

*And breathe...*came the voice again. He was catapulted out of the singularity. The binary stars gave way to a pair of headlights of a truck. Raymond looked closer and saw many trucks rumbling down Main St., flanked by strange-looking patrol cars. They were something between a motorcycle and a buggy, with the word SAFETY emblazoned on the side and front, in a pleasing script font, as though it were from a greeting card. Raymond positioned himself in the street to block traffic, rerouting it in the right direction. At once, one of the SAFETY buggies at the front of the convoy began accelerating, racing toward him. Raymond feared he might get struck down, but before he could react, the buggy spun out in front of him, stopping perpendicular to the street. There was a pitch-black windshield that concealed the interior. Raymond strode up to the machine. He heard mechanical noises inside as he approached. He bravely tapped on the window.

"STEP AWAY, PLEASE" came the automated voice. There was no driver here.

Raymond was caught off guard. He'd never interacted with a machine before, or so he thought.

"Just gettin' y'all to the fair is all" said Raymond. "That a way…"

"TAKE TEN STEPS BACK PLEASE" came the voice again.

Raymond heard noises inside the car again now. He saw a mechanical arm extend in his direction with some sort of instrument on it. He decided that now was not the time to divine its purpose.

"After you, sir" he said. "Or madam"

He needlessly waved his baton. He realized that the trucks, too, were driverless, something that his beloved President had railed

151

against. He marveled at how quickly they turned the corner, with very little shifting or sliding. He radioed Officer Sullivan.

"They're comin' your way" he said, into the radio. After a time, he heard Sullivan fumbled with the radio, into which she breathed heavily, before saying "Roger that."

The whole convoy took five minutes to clear the crossroads. "FED HERT THANKS YOU FOR YOUR SERVICE" came the voice from the machine, before it sped off to join the rear of the convoy.

Raymond saw the motley crew of refugees – IDPs, rather – descending into the fairground. The children laughed at the clown face as the adults looked on, apprehensive at their new situation. Raymond struggled to see Officer Sullivan. She was talking to a person from the World, clearly the leader of this operation, dressed in a stylish jumpsuit, holding a tablet computer. There were two other figures standing some distance from the leader, observing the passage of the humans into their silos. Raymond realized quickly that these were not human, either, having the word SAFETY written on their backs and helmets. They were machines. Unlike all the sci-fi movies, Raymond had seen, they were not pacing or scanning. They were lifeless.

Raymond approached the trio in his backward safety vest, bumping down the path toward the fairground with his light-up baton in hand, looking like a comic Jedi approaching with a lightsaber. At once, the hitherto SAFETY machines lit up, with blinking lights. They stood for a moment on mechanical legs. But as they turned to intercept Raymond, he could see that they had little tank tread-type wheels under their "feet." Rather than walk, they rolled over to him, illuminating him with bright LED lights.

"HOLD FOR AN IDENTITY SCAN" they said. It was a female voice, soothing. It sounded for a moment like Scarlett Johansen, only coarser. Then "HOLD HERE PLEASE, RAYMOND TANNER."

"Yes ma'am" said Raymond, meekly. "When did I ever tell you bastards who I was?"

"HOLD, PLEASE" came the voice. A whirring sound. "STAY POSITIVE. THIS WILL ONLY TAKE A MOMENT."

He didn't notice at first, but this machine had another instrument that was casually pointed in his direction. He assumed that it was some sort of weapon.

The other machine wheeled over to the leader, a human, in a snappy faux-leather jacket. The leader looked at his glowing tablet and nodded, then excused himself from the conversation with Officer Sullivan. He walked over to Raymond who was being entertained by the machine.

He spoke. "So…it's the Savior of Solange! Raymond Tanner! What a pleasure" he said, waving at Raymond from a distance. There was not a strand of hair out of place on his head. Today, it seemed, the man had gone for a sporty haircut and more of a tanned appearance. Maybe he wanted to appeal to the refugees. It was clear he did not want physical contact as he avoided a handshake. Instead, he placed his hand on his chest. "I'm Forest Allsop, relief coordinator for Fed Hert. We retrieved the visual stream from both the mother and the child you helped the other day. Oh…man! What a sensation. Everyone positively resonated…and resonated positively…with that! You're famous!"

"Just doing my duty" he said.

"So quaint! You remind me of my dad. So much good stuff comes out of here. So glad" he paused, looking at the refugees enter the fairgrounds, nostalgically. "So glad we kept all this...just as it is."

"You could live here" offered Raymond. "Here's about as real as it gets."

"Oh, not a chance!" came the reply. "Look, Raymond, once you get a taste of Sharing Life, you really don't go back. We live as one now. It's cruel for me to torture you because I know you won't be able to interface anymore, but maybe your kids? Hey, Raymond? Do you have kids yet? File says…"

"No" said Raymond. "No kids here."

"Well, maybe one day, hey Raymond? You and Officer…" he struggled "…Officer over there?" he said, jovially. "Teach your kid to 'walk like a man,' hey Raymond?"

"Yeah, sure. One day" he replied, coldly.

"STAY POSITIVE" said the machine. He forgot that, in their presence, every utterance and movement would be recorded and analyzed.

"Anyways, where's my brother?" he asked. "Mitch said he was going up to help."

"Mitch...Tanner" said the man, checking the tablet. He knew the tablet was a prop for Raymond's sake, since the information could be relayed directly to his ocular interface. "Nope. Don't see him on the roster here. I'll check with HQ and see if he turns up."

"He's supposed to be leading here, not a refugee" said Raymond.

"Oh no no no no" said Allsop.

"STAY POSITIVE" came the voice from the lights again.

"We don't use that word. IDP, please, especially around them! And remember, this is only temporary until the storm passes and we can rebuild. Mitch, don't you remember? Katrina? Florence? Imelda? Paulette? We didn't have then what we have now. We can save people before they need saving."

"Wow. What a miracle" he said.

"STAY POSITIVE, PLEASE" came the machine.

"Look, I'll ask about your friend. Until then...YOU are LOVED, Raymond!" he shouted over his shoulder, shaking his fist in the air. The lighted machine hung back with him for a moment.

"Thanks" he said, waiting for the machine to correct him. It whirred a minute, then extinguished its lights and sped off to join the Leader. Perhaps he hadn't exceeded the subversive threshold.

Raymond walked over to the edge of the fairgrounds. Massive floodlights illuminated the scene below. Families and their pets had been efficiently shepherded into their accommodations. A few adults milled about between the silos. Kids chased a ball up and

155

down while a dog barked at them. Everything had been perfectly arranged such that there were no line ups or crowds. Festive, classic yet-not-overbearing music lifted the mood: Bruno Mars. Insofar as relief camps went, this was something approaching five stars. The Leader had already disappeared, leaving the machines on the perimeter to ensure an orderly transition. Discord, it seemed, had been removed from the equation.

At that moment, Raymond noticed one person who did not mingle with the group. She looked positively brooding by comparison, standing off to the side, arms crossed, eyeing the machines with suspicion, then quickly looking down again. The machines took note of this. One of them quietly wheeled into position to get a better view of her, extending its legs to maximum height. Raymond was impressed with this creation, finally having a moment to take in its terrible majesty. It reigned tall over the entire site as it locked on to the woman, such that if one had not seen it move previously, one would be inclined to think it was a fixed tower. The articulation of these machines was unlike the clunky robots of years past: they had a smooth, intuitive movement that was almost living. The woman stood for a moment, then decided to approach the edge of the fairgrounds by the mouth of the clown. She had dark, short hair and a stern walk, such that if Raymond had just glanced, he could have mistaken her for a man. A different machine wheeled up to her. Raymond could not hear the exchange but did catch the words CURFEW and LIGHTS OUT in machine voice. The woman, keeping her arms folded, turned, and walked back to her silo, yelling "fuck off" to a group of people who glanced at her.

"It'll be lights out in twenty minutes, friends!" came a voice over the loudspeakers, definitely prerecorded, but with a calming quality. "Please have your silo group leader get your night kits by the gate." A dozen or so individuals, mostly men, came out to get the white boxes that had been piled at the gate, then returned. The brooding girl did not reemerge, leaving a lone box at the gate. A few adults opened the boxes, revealing what looked like an ablution kit, and pre-packed smores. They nibbled on their treats and chatted, waiting for the camp to go dark. A child who had been playing by the gate saw the unattended box and went in to claim it for himself. Raymond caught sight of this and started to jog toward the box before the boy could abscond with it. The machines were preoccupied by the boy and failed to notice Raymond in the darkness.

"BE CALM, JOSEPH" said one of the machines, whirring up the instrument on its arm. "IT'S BEDTIME. DO YOU WANT TO HEAR A STORY?" Joseph shook his head, turning meekly back to his family's silo.

Raymond wrapped the box up in his pointer vest, walking back toward his Tesla, driving back to his trailer for the night. He wasn't sure how yet, but he knew that he would get this parcel to the brooding woman, one way or another. Sure, the minders could play music and make things all neat and efficient, but Southern hospitality lived in the people.

157

Chapter 12

Howard, with the help of the chef, hauled the turkey into the dining room, placing it gingerly in front of Norman. Anita had two weeks before she was due to deliver the baby. It was the week of the election, and the Charles had decided to do Thanksgiving a little early since a newborn would add an uncomfortable degree of chaos to an important tradition. Vivian had wanted to let the chips fall where they may, but deferred to Anita, who disliked the uncertainty.

"OK, so who's saying grace?" asked Vivian, clinking the lead crystal goblet. Howard was dutifully filling them with red wine, something expensive and old, Raymond guessed.

The table was the epitome of sumptuousness. Every conceivable dish had been created for the occasion; sweet potato casserole, dotted with sugared pecans, cornbread dressing, plain old cornbread, fancy cornbread, and baked mac n cheese occupied all available real estate on the table. At the head of this cornucopia was the turkey, baked with herbs and glistening with fatty perfection.

"I will" said Anita.

After the tragic news that their son would be born with Duchenne's, Raymond and Anita worked hard creating a birth plan, modifying their apartment, and praying.

They bowed their heads, joining hands. Norman reached forward from the head of the table, clasping the hands of Raymond and Delroy. "Lord, thank You for the food before us, the family and friends beside us and the love between us. Amen."

"Amen" they all said.

161

"Amen" said Delroy, looking up at Raymond, unfurling his napkin from its ring.

Delroy and his father, often at odds when it came to matters of faith (or anything else, for that matter), had come together in a rare moment of solidarity on the issue of the baby. Delroy was a staunch atheist, much to the chagrin of his devout father, and looked down upon the quaint musings of his sister and brother-in-law. For this reason, he barely spoke, choosing to nibble on a biscuit and reflect on this happy gathering.

"So, Delroy, tell us all about your project in South Carolina" asked Vivian.

"Mmmhmm, well" he said, finishing his mouthful. "It's a bit of a startup. We're working with A.I. to try to maximize efficiency from existing land. Trying to find the cheapest way for your average farmer to compete with the resource-intensive guys, the big GMO guys" he said, explaining.

"A.I., huh?" said Raymond. "Think that's gonna work?"

"Yeah, artificial intelligence" said Delroy, in the most condescending way possible. "It's an experiment, but a worthy one."

"I know what it is. I may be a hillbilly, but I can still read" said Raymond, meeting his condescension and raising him one rudeness.

"That's fine. Just checking, Ray-Ray" he said, using Anita's pet name for him.

162

"So you trust those machines because…" Raymond asked, filling the awkward silence that was sure to follow.

"…because they do a better job of resource allocation than humans could ever do" he said, without missing a beat. "I guess you could pray for rain and good soil if that doesn't suit you. You farm?" asked Delroy.

"A little" said Raymond. "Pappy grew all sorts of stuff. I just know the land."

"Neither did I, but when your whole family's livelihood depends on weather and soil, I guess you learn how to pray. All I'm saying is that we can take the guesswork out of it. We can channel data, samples, weather analysis…we can figure out which crop will grow when, how to distribute it, and what to fertilize."

"And you…your livelihood depends on farming?" asked Anita, annoyed at her brother.

"I make my life helping people" he said.

"And does it work?" asked Raymond.

"Sometimes. At least I'm growing something and not knocking it down for my living" he said, a clear reference to Raymond's work in the campaign.

"You're a literal Trust-afarian" said Anita.

"Anita!" said Vivian, horrified at the uncivil direction their conversation had taken.

"Trust-afarian?" asked Raymond, smiling.

"Trustfund Rastafarian" replied Anita. "Too hip for the rest of us, too rich to find the bottom."

"Both of you, stop it. We're giving thanks, not grief!" said Norman, fed up with the bickering.

The meal went on in silence. Delroy extended an olive branch, or possibly a challenge.

"You know what, Raymond? Come on by the farm. It's not too far from your brother in Cateechee. That is if Anita doesn't mind letting you out so close to baby time."

Raymond seemed taken with his graciousness. "Sure" he said. "I'll show ya a thing or two" a little churlishly, then more conciliatory: "It'd be great. Just wait til the election's over and I'll be there."

Anita winced a little.

"Is that ok, baby?" said Raymond. "Didn't mean to upset you."

"No...just..." she said. "Really big kick. Baby doesn't love that idea, clearly."

She paused. "Maybe after the election, sure" she said, tentatively.

Chapter 13

Cateechee's new residents were allowed off the fairgrounds in the morning to visit their new temporary community. It was a bright, sunny day, and the machines seemed to have stood down or dispersed as the waking hours approached. Raymond drove back to the fairgrounds with his parcel on the passenger seat. He saw the people leaving, walking up the road to Main St., but did not catch a glimpse of the brooding woman. There was still a machine guarding the gate, but Raymond decided it was not prudent to keep drawing attention to himself. Instead, he sat in the car and observed the fairgrounds, especially the silo that the brooding woman occupied. The alleys between the silos began to fill with life: kids ran to and fro with their balls, bats, and pets. The brooding woman did not appear. Raymond waited for about half an hour, listening to his favorite podcast, but no one emerged. Disappointed, he drove off, cruising Main St. in search of his query, but did not find her. It was Thursday – blog day, and there was much to write about. He decided to leave these new residents alone for the time being and headed back to the trailer.

He was about to turn into his lot when he decided that it had been a long time since he had actually gone anywhere but Cateechee. He decided to head over to Clairville to see if they had also taken on any refugees. He turned around and headed back to the highway out of town. As he approached the town limits, he saw something peculiar jutting out from the cornfields. It looked strangely familiar, like a black curtain or irrigation equipment. It loomed large as he drove closer, and he recognized the horrific structure: it was the wall from the forest on the hill. The wall was just as tall and imposing as it had been when he found it in the forest next to Solange. It ran right up to the road, where there was a gap. He was studying the extent of the wall when he suddenly slammed on the brakes – a pair of SAFETY robots was parked at the threshold. They had their flashers on, sending red and blue light out to the horizon. The light did not reflect off the walls, which, as previously, seemed to merely absorb all light.

Well he thought, *they can't trap me here forever.*

He boldly yet cautiously drove up to the two machines. He decided to stay inside his car lest he become a target for their instruments again – he wanted to have at least a bit of sheet metal between himself and them for protection.

One of the machines intuitively rolled up to the driver side window. "HELLO, RAYMOND" came the voice, male this time. "WHAT BRINGS YOU OUT HERE?"

"Oh hello" he said, playfully. "Nothing. Just headed over to Clairville for some lunch he said."

"RAYMOND, I'M SORRY TO SAY THAT WE CAN'T LET YOU PASS" came the voice.

"Why in the hell not?" yelled Raymond.

"RAYMOND, I HOPE YOU'RE NOT BEING DIFFICULT. ARE YOU BEING DIFFICULT, RAYMOND?"

"No sir" he replied. "Just wonderin why I'm a prisoner, is all."

"SORRY TO TELL YOU THIS, BUT WE'RE UNDER AN EMERGENCY LOCKDOWN DUE TO THE STORM" announced the machine.

"Storm?" asked Raymond, looking around at the azure sky and gentle breeze rustling the corn.

"YES, THE SUPERSTORM. LEAVING THE AREA WOULD BE EXTREMELY DANGEROUS, RAYMOND. EVERYTHING YOU COULD POSSIBLY NEED IS IN TOWN. DO YOU NEED AN ESCORT?"

"No. No that's fine. OK thanks for watching out for me."

"IT IS OUR PLEASURE AND DUTY" said the machine.

Raymond put the car into a U turn and sped away in small defiance from the machines. He decided to make *Juke's* his next stop to spread the word that they were all prisoners now. Everything he had heard, everything he had learned, everything he believed...it was all coming together.

He pulled up in front of *Juke's*, parking on the wrong side of the street. He got out and casually strode inside. The place had become a magnet for the new arrivals who clustered around tables and the bar sharing stories. Raymond arrived in his full glory, prepared to tell everyone what he had just learned first-hand. He found a clearing, and stood still to try and draw attention to himself.

"Listen...HEY listen, y'all" he yelled. The bar went silent.

"We're all prisoners!" he shouted. The bar paused discussion for a moment, and then erupted in laughter. Phil was the first to break the news to him.

"Ray, we all know that. Welcome to the party, my friend" he said. "We're celebrating the end of humanity."

Raymond sheepishly strode into the bar.

"Hey" came a voice from the corner. "You got my kit?"

Raymond looked and saw the brooding girl seated in a corner. "Um, you mean that box?"

"Yeah I mean that box" she said. She was every bit as morose as he thought she would be. "My box."

"It's just in my car, so…" he replied.

"So you won't mind getting it for me, will ya?" she said. She had a northeast accent, possibly Boston. She stared Raymond down intently. He was about to walk away.

"Wait" she commanded. He stopped. "You like some kinda community leader around here or something?"

"Uh no, ma'am" he said.

"Well you'd be pretty shittily informed if you were now, wouldn't ya?" she said. She was slurring her words a little. Raymond noticed a bottle of Bourbon half-drunk on the table.

"You got a name?" she asked.

"Raymond" he replied. "People call me Ray."

"I'm Alexis" she said. "But don't call me nothin' except Alexis. Bitch is fine too, I get that a lot."

"I get that" said Raymond. She stared at him. He rethought his words. "I mean I get how people could get the wrong idea."

"What? The way I talk? Doesn't jive with your Southern charm and sweet little accent?" she said. "Well they absolutely got the right goddamned idea. Not sayin' you should take liberties or anything."

"I ain't takin any liberties, ma'am" he said.

"Call me Alexis" she said. "Anyways, if you thought you were ever gettin' outta here, you obviously learned the truth today. Sorry to steal your thunder but I already told the bar about the guards. I checked this place out last night." Thunder sounded like *thun-da* and guards like *gawds*.

"I thought the machines were guardin' you?" he asked.

"The Minders? Oh no those are the friendly nannies" she said. "They can be gotten around if you know the ways. Your little amusement park there has tons of holes and escapes."

She paused, taking a shot from a glass on the table that turned into more of a gulp. She was lean and tattooed around the neck, wearing all black clothes and a band t-shirt under her leather jacket.

"But the wall is a sonofabitch. You ain't getting past that wall without getting incinerated" she said.

"You mean electrocuted?"

"No I mean burned, crispy Southern pork chops."

"How?"

"The thing runs on solar power. It sits there absorbing all the light and then when anyone or anything brushes past it...pshoooo" she exclaimed, making a fireball with her hand, "fire!"

She drank another shot. Raymond loved straight-talking women.

"Don't get the wrong idea, bumpkin. I'm a dyke" she announced. Maybe she saw him notice her.

"Dyke?" he asked.

"Les-bee-an...? Maybe you don't get 'em down here but alls you got to know is nothin' is happening with you and me, got it?" she said.

"Yeah. Look we ain't all you think. We're pretty progressive down around here. We had a Pride parade and everythin on Main St. a few years ago, before the war."

"Before the war..." she almost choked, repeating him, shaking his head.

"Listen, bumpkin..."

"Ray" he corrected.

"Listen, Ray. The war isn't over. We just all changed sides. The machines are the enemy, in case you hadn't figured it out. Anyone who *wears* the machines is our enemy, got it? You want the

South to 'rise again', well, you better figure out how the hell we destroy those things and get outta here" she said.

"Where you from, Alexis?" he asked.

"Boston, Dorchester. I was goin to school when the war broke out. We fought 'em hard, you know, the Trumpies?" It sounded like she had said "Dorchesta." She caught herself. "Wait…you on team 45?"

"Well…yes ma'am, I am. Always have been" he said proudly.

"Anyways your guy's dead. Pencey Toons put a computer in the White House and now we're all slaves. I blame the Russians."

Raymond decided there was no merit in taking the discussion any further. He could barely suppress the feelings welling up inside him and was about to turn away. Phil appeared beside him with a beer on a tray.

"Would you like a glass, sir?" he quipped, handing him the bottle, looking at Alexis with contempt. Clearly he wanted to unleash Raymond on this tactless Northerner.

"No thank you Phil. Much obliged" he said, taking the beer.

"You guys are so goddamned cute when you're not blowin' up news channels" came the Boston voice.

Raymond gulped the beer. He sat down, cracking his knuckles. One fight at a time. Phil came with another beer to fuel the battle.

Chapter 14

The election had come and gone, and baby Josiah had arrived at the same time, sweetening the victory. He was everything they had hoped for, and everything they feared. The boy had been born with Duchenne's muscular dystrophy, and although the disease would eventually consume him, they vowed to make his short life so full of experience that a healthy person could have lived two lives and not done as much as he would. They set aside their fears and trepidations as they embraced their beautiful boy. He was born with a full head of curly hair, beautiful brown skin, and chunky little arms and legs. Raymond was full of marvel at this little burst of life, something he had made, something that was his and yet not. Anita, to Raymond's surprise, did not embrace the baby as automatically as he had.

"What's wrong, baby?" he asked Anita.

"You talking to me, or him?" she said.

"You ain't lovin' this? I love this little guy" he said. "Feeding time?"

She shook her head. "No…look it's common for us to not feel it right away. Something evolutionary, I read, in case you lose the baby or it comes out dead."

"Jesus, Anita. He's right here!" said Raymond, holding the baby away from the vile commentary.

"He knows I won't hurt him. Besides, his world is just eating, peeing, pooping, and sleeping right now. Kinda like you drunk" she laughed. She was clearly hopped up on a combination of pain medications, Oxytocin, and post-delivery hormones. What she really needed was sleep. They were due to check out of the hospital that day. Raymond had just finished installing the infant car seat, carefully following the directions, and finding parts of his car he didn't know existed.

The delivery had gone fairly smoothly; no tearing or need of a C-section. This baby just wanted to come out and be with them, according to Dr. Randall. They carefully placed baby Josiah in the carseat, padding him with extra baby blankets for the dangerous journey into the world. Anita agreed to sit in the back, next to the car seat. Raymond had never driven so carefully in all his life. He caught Anita finally fawning over the baby, whose perfect little nose glistened in the afternoon light. She brought out her famous smile and Josiah started cooing.

The election was over, and that was a blessing, since they could now afford to both take some time and dote on the baby. Evan James had given Raymond some time off, but warned him: "Look, your work here is not done. Not by a goddamned long shot. I know you got a son to think about now and things to do at home, but you are way too important to this operation and I can't afford losing you. Tell me your conditions. Name your price. We need your genius here buddy. We train people based on your work." Raymond agreed to work from home most days but come in only when the situation warranted it. He was curious as to what was in store, but James basically told him that "we never stop campaigning. We only just got in the door. Now, the battle is on in earnest. The knives are out, now get ready for the swords."

As promised, Raymond took a trip out to Delroy's farm. Delroy was renting the land and promised to pay the landlord a third of the revenue generated from the crop for as long as he could maintain his experiment. He wanted to emulate financial conditions for the average farmer to make his A.I. application as "real world" as possible. Raymond arrived at the farm early one morning in spring, just as the light was breaking over the stands of trees on the way up to the farmhouse, which was rather picturesque and inviting. He could smell livestock in the barn; pigs, he assumed. There were a few chickens running around the yard and a pen containing some sheep. Clearly, Delroy thought it best to get a sampling of various revenue streams. The whole thing felt more like a hobby farm than a commercial operation, and he thought that maybe Delroy had taken on too much. He strode inside without knocking and was thoroughly impressed with the place: the landlord had done extensive improvements to the house. The kitchen was clean and modern, with high-efficiency appliances and a massive, high-end stove. The ceilings were high and regal, with a winding staircase leading up to the second floor. He didn't dare go up, but instead shouted:

"Delroy?"

"Yeah! Hey" came the reply from upstairs. Raymond crept forward to look up the staircase and saw the back of Delroy's head, who was seated in a middle room that looked like a home office. "Come on up!" he said.

Raymond quietly crept up the carpeted stairs. Delroy turned and looked. "What's with white people always leaving their shoes on in the house?" he asked.

"Sorry" he said, stopping, and removing the shoes.

179

"Just breakin' your balls a little, Ray-Ray. Come, I'll show you the system."

Raymond had never been much of a farmer but was curious to see how a computer could outdo human experience, if at all.

"So I've got all the crop yields here relative to their season, seed, and then taking into account various weather patterns. It gives me a seeding schedule, and on a bigger level, where each crop will take and when." He pointed to various data points on the screen. "But really, I don't do much...I end up having to do the manual labor all myself basically. I can only afford to hire help once in a while, and even then, it's mostly illegals and cash."

Raymond chuffed at this. Half of his campaign slogans were dedicated to disparaging illegal immigration.

"Look, that may make you uneasy, but the truth is none of you local boys wanna do any of the heavy lifting. If we didn't have illegals, we would all probably starve. That's why I want this A.I. to work; so the average family farmer doesn't have to sell his land to the agri-conglomerates, and we can keep our communities together."

Raymond was impressed and inspired. He immediately began ruminating a plan in his head. He toured the farm with Delroy. The place had plenty of potential; he had a variety of crops growing at every corner in the field, all marked by signs with barcodes that Delroy carefully scanned and fed back to his computer system. Everything looked healthy and productive, even considering the recent dry spell.

"The problem is" he explained "well, like I was saying, I just need more hands. Don't have robots yet. Just the computer. And also…my NGO partner has backed out of the project. I'm running on financial fumes here." That was his way of saying that his dad was floating him month-to-month.

They were walking back to the house when Raymond deigned to pop the question.

"What if Anita, baby, and I joined you out here?" he asked, implying that he was willing to put himself and family into the efforts.

Delroy paused for a moment. "I thought you all had your big political jobs back in the city?"

"You got an internet connection?" asked Raymond.

"Yeah, my NGO paid for a fiber line" he said. "Gigabit…fastest in the county for sure."

"Then I guess there's no reason we can't up and move in here. The work we do can mostly be done from anywhere there's cell service."

"How're you going to get Anita to agree to this? She gets weird walking in grass if it gets too tall!" asked Delroy.

"I'll talk to her. I got my ways" he smiled, letting his mind wander to some of the happiest imaginings. "We'll do it for Josiah."

Chapter 15

Officer Laney Sullivan arrived on Main St., on foot this time, trying to mingle with the new arrivals. Community policing. A chat and a handshake. Welcome to Cateechee. To her surprise, few people were on the street. She had come up from the fairgrounds, but few of the IDPs were there. She heard raised voices and the din of a crowd. She looked up and saw that *Juke's* had become the principal benefactor of the overnight population doubling. They were between mealtimes, and Phil had put out the chalk sign advertising *Happy Hour 3-5*. Since the IDPs had no expenses and comfortable living circumstances, they enjoyed a surplus of cash from their government subsidies. These were currently being converted into beverages at *Juke's*. But booze was not the only thing flowing inside.

Officer Sullivan pushed open the door to see a bevy of violations. Phil tensed up behind the bar, but then relaxed when he realized that Sullivan's authority was really just a sham at this point. There were about twice the number of people that should have been in there, according to the posted fire code. Half of them were inebriated to the point of public intoxication. But, her greatest concern revolved around the brewing confrontation between Raymond and a dark-haired, tattooed woman, who were seated at a table, yelling at each other full bore. It had become a bit of a spectator sport, with proponents from both sides backing their respective contender – loudly.

"So let me get this straight…you think that Trumpy bear was assassinated? By who? With what? He assassinated himself on his own goddamned golf club and at his own goddamned golf club. Mar to your fucking Lago."

185

"Donald J. Trump was the greatest president of our time. He was too much a threat to the Deep State and so they had to get rid of him. You really think that an experienced golfer like Trump would just overswing and fall like that? Or that they couldn't get him medical help on time?" yelled Raymond back. "What's the matter you...so you think Shillary would have done a better job?"

"I'll tell you what we wouldn't have been in a civil war! As for medical help...we can't even get decent healthcare in this country unless you stick a machine in your head. Sanders was gonna fix that. Healthcare is a goddamned right and you know it." She stuck a finger in his chest. He was too inebriated to notice.

"I got a right to choose the best care for me and my...well, for me. I don't need no government agent to tell me where I got to go to get treated. I don't need a death panel to say 'sorry, nothin' we can do for you on our budget.' You know how long they wait for knee surgery up in Canada?"

"Canada? You mean those smug little bastards who sat there while we killed ourselves, taking in our refugees...because we had to fight over some glow-in-the-dark president obsessed with the size of his...crowd? Fucking I'll take it. I'll take it all. Once we blast away these damned machines I say hand the keys over to the Canadians and ask them 'teach us how to be.'"

"You would do that too, liberal bitch. I'll die before I give up one damned inch of this beautiful country. I say build the wall in the North!"

186

"Wall? You got your wall. It's a wall for just you and your little local yokle friends here. They don't want you infecting their perfect little robot nation with your backward shit. I say good on 'em. You're a disease, bumpkin." She cocked her fingers at him, speaking slowly now. "Blow you out of the airlock."

Raymond started to get up out of his seat, only slightly.

"I say you're full a shit. I say we're bein pretty good hosts and you lousy liberals are spittin on our feet. Ain't we, Phil?" he shouted. Phil had stopped bringing the beer and refused to look up. Officer Sullivan tried to insert herself, with little impact.

"I say…I say we had no choice. I say we had it pretty fucking good up there for five minutes before they told us about some" and air quotes "'storm coming', which we both know was shit. But you know what, bumpkin? You go on. You go on thinking that you had nothin to do with this. That it was so important for you to put sandbags around your little bumpkin ancestors and go to war for a president who can even fucking read more than two pages and wanted to fuck his daughter."

Raymond launched at her, grabbing her by the leather collar, overturning the table in the process. Officer Sullivan grabbed him, trying to push him back.

"NO NO THAT'S FINE OFFICER! COME ON! KAVANAUGH ME RIGHT ON THIS TABLE LIKE A REAL MAN!"

A few onlookers jumped in and separated the two. Sullivan thanked them for the assist and took the pair outside to cool down. As they opened the door, a machine had planted itself there.

"IS EVERYTHING WORKING OUT HERE, OFFICER SULLIVAN? HOW'S OUR NEW FRIENDS?" came the voice of SAFETY, quite loudly. The instrument was extended.

"Oh, they're fine…ma'am. We're just having a little time out here on the curb. Thanks" said Sullivan.

"STAY POSITIVE!" came the edict, a little more sing-songy this time. The machine rolled away, apparently content that the turbulent situation would subside.

"You two need to mind yourselves. Sit here and figure this out while I go inside and hand out some citations. When Mitch finds out about this…" she said.

"Yeah, where is Mitch, Officer Laney?" asked Raymond disrespectfully. "Didn't see him on the trucks or anywhere."

"It's Officer Sullivan you shit" she said, taking a pause, then calming herself. "I don't know. Honestly, he was supposed to lead these people here to make them feel more comfortable but he never showed. I called him a couple of times and asked Allsop, but he blew me off."

Raymond had pulled himself back into quiet contemplation.

"But if anything comes up, I'll let you know" she said, turning to go into the bar. "No fighting!" she said, then motioning

188

across the street. "They're watching…and I don't know what they'll do." She went inside.

"You alright?" asked Raymond.

"Yeah" said Alexis, feeling her pockets for her cigarettes. "Fucking cigarettes are gone."

"You still smoke? I thought no one smoked anymore" said Raymond.

"Hey, you're not the only throwback around here, bumpkin" she said.

"Well, I may be a throwback, but I still got resources" he said, producing a blunt. "I hate smoking alone."

"Damn, I thought you hillbillies just did bathtub gin and meth" she said, taking the lit blunt that Raymond passed to her.

"Why do you smoke?" she asked.

"It just helps" he said, staring at the pavement. She looked at him a moment to recognize that she wouldn't get any further.

"Yeah" she said.

"So what the hell is out there now?" he asked, after a time.

"Out where?"

"Y'know…beyond the wall. The World" he said.

"Oh, The World! Heh. Yeah there's a whole paradise out there waiting for you, let me tell you" she said, imitating Trump. She pulled it back a little: "It's weird. Everything is fine. It's about as normal as normal can be. People are happy with each other. There's no crime or conflict. They all just get along."

She paused, taking a hit from the blunt.

"But it's weird all the same. People just walk around like zombies, sharing streams with each other in their near-groups. They like to do group activities, so they can see stuff from each other's points of view. No one is ever alone."

"Group activities?" he asked.

"Like random shit. Like use their super speed to chase squirrels around the park and simultaneously share the streams. One of their favourites is to toss a ball in a circle, kind of a kid game."

She went on.

"But the weirdest shit has to be the orgies. They love their damned orgies. I mean if everyone can experience every sex position, each person's feelings, at the same time, it's probably pretty fucking amazing" she said.

"So…why didn't you get plugged in?" he asked. "You seem pretty…ya know…"

"What, freaky?" she said, smiling. He was embarrassed. The ember on the blunt glowed.

"Progressive" he replied. "Like, I mean…"

"Look Ray I'm me. I can't be anyone else. I don't need them corrupting my mind with that shit. I don't care how good it feels to be on those streams."

190

Raymond nodded.

"So how come you moved out of town? To the reservation, I mean?" he asked.

"After the war I couldn't settle in. I tried living with those guys for a while back in Boston, but it got so insidious and crazy after a while. Then I heard about Twin Oaks and decided it was the thing I needed."

"Twin Oaks?" he asked.

"It's this communal living place down Virginia" she said. "It's full of people you'd hate; liberals, hippies, communists, pagans, atheists, 25ers..."

"Thought you didn't want orgies" he said.

"Ha ha. No not like that. For a while it was pretty sweet. Everybody pulls their weight, you work and you contribute by doing stuff for the community. You get clothes and food and everything you need. And no tech, like, none. We don't really use too much gas or electricity. Well, didn't" she explained. "Waited almost a year to get in there. Everyone there rejected the whole INtegrity thing."

Raymond was inspired by this. Very libertarian, despite it coming from a communist.

"And then some chick named Rhonda came to town with a proposition, showed us a fancy presentation. We were told the world had INtegrated and left us behind. She promised us extra cash if we just let in tourists once in a while to see how we live, like we're Amish in Pennsylvania or something."

191

She smoked again.

"Anyways we drank the Kool-Aid. But we decided it wasn't right in the last few weeks. We started disturbing the shit. Our scores went down. We made posters and left little mental traps for them all over the place, just enough to not trip the Safe Mode in their little cyborg eyes."

"Posters? Traps?"

"You know little seditious shit. Remind them that we should have seen this coming. We would take pics of August Eichorn…you know the guy?" Raymond nodded. "Anyways, we would do little black-and-white handbills with the word SOMA written across his head in red. A horse with blinders on in the shape of a middle finger raised. Stuff like that. Obviously, Ceres caught up or people were just oblivious, or worse – "

Raymond smiled at her ability to wield slogans.

"They didn't want to acknowledge the truth" he said.

"Right" she said.

"You work in advertising?"

"Yeah…I was an office girl for like five minutes" she said, exhaling smoke. "Plenty of ideas but at the end of the day, I was fetching coffees and pushing the spirit wagon once a week, this dumb trolley full of lights and candies to keep people going on a Friday. Sometimes there was liquor. Sometimes I got my ass grabbed."

Raymond shook his head.

"Spirit wagon…sounds like a place to get your fortune told" he said. "So what else is out there? Like, now?" he asked.

"Well, here's what it is. Some of it I've seen, like I said, but some of it I hear. Ceres has gone online now, fully. Really it's people who are fully online. She is integrating every person using some new protocol, so they're always connected wherever they're near 5G."

"Never got 5G here…barely got LTE when they rolled it out."

"Probably why Allsuck didn't want to stay around too long" she said. "Anyways, just like before everyone got wired, people are basically lingering inside their homes. Not many retail stores open…a bunch of em are just open there, unlocked. They just live off their UBI and go into this virtual world that Ceres got all set up for them. She has to remind them to do basic shit, like take a piss and eat. She manages their food deliveries. The streets are mostly empty except for the occasional ball game or group activity."

"How d'you know all this?" he asked.

"I like to observe. I hide. I don't want them to see me. It's to the point where you just can't mingle anymore. Anytime you set foot in their little world, and one of them catches a glimpse of you, SAFETY bots are on you, following you, in case you do something random. People like us…thinking, rational humans…we're an endangered species. Ceres probably sensed this and set up these little reserves for us. It's a shit existence but if it means I think for me, then so be it."

"I don't know about 'shit existence.' I mean, I chose to be here. We chose to be here" he said.

The weed was kicking in. Philosophical musings came forth.

"Actually it wasn't even a choice. Freedom means living behind a wall. I just couldn't handle having them come in and treat me like a zoo animal."

"Endangered animal."

She nodded. "When they turned Ceres on, humanity turned off."

She passed the blunt back to Raymond, who shook his head. She stubbed in out on the curb. Raymond had put a heroic amount of Sativa-Indica hybrid in there, and they were clearly under its spell now.

"Such an amateur" she said. "Got the munchies like I'm 17."

"Hold on" said Raymond. He slowly and shakily got up, walking over to his Tesla and fetching the kit Alexis had been issued on the first night. He came back and handed it to her.

"I'm not sure what's in this but – "

"Fuck yes" she said, snatching the box. She unwrapped the package, opening it to find a large bag of nutritional salted kale chips. Raymond turned up his nose.

"Ugh...you kiddin? I mean kale..."

194

"Whatever Ray it's salty and crunchy and I need this" she said. "You mentioned something to that officer about a guy named Mitch?"

"My brother" said Raymond. His high began to shift into a down type of resonance as he reflected on Mitch. He got lost in a memory of hiking with Mitch as a boy, always falling behind because of his muscular dystrophy, and Raymond having to help him get over the ridges and hills. Things were different now, of course, with his genetically-enhanced body saving him from the worst of the disease.

"Your brother?" she asked, after an extended pause.

"Is missing" he said. "He was supposed to come back with the convoy but he never turned up."

"That's shitty" she said. "What did he look like?"

Raymond described him. Stocky, big, brown hair cut short, angular features...very choppy.

"Oh yeah I remember the guy. Real nice, despite being a pig. Tried to make everyone calm and say how great you all would be."

"Yep. That's Mitch" said Raymond, wistfully.

"Well he was there for sure. Don't know what happened. We got on the buses, and then we were here ten hours later after picking up some other guys. Then here."

Raymond was deflated. He sighed loudly and pushed some gravel around in the gutter with the toe of his running shoe.

"Hey" she said, sensing his melancholy, playfully tapping him. "He may still be up there. You try calling him?"

"Yeah, sure. I called my parents, but…" he paused.

"But?"

"After my Pappy died, they plugged in. They were one of the last sets of older people to do it. They said Ceres helped with pain and since Mitch and I weren't around, they said they wanted to feel more connected. Now they never answer the phone. Honest, I just don't want to know what they do."

"So Mitch is all you got" she said. "Well ya better get ta findin him" she said, mocking his Southern accent, giving him a playful jab in the shoulder.

"I don't know. How'm I gonna get outta town?" he asked.

"There's a way" she said. "There's always a way. But you gotta do it on foot. The machines will see that car before you even get close to the gate."

"But I mean what can they do to me? Like actually? They got that little instrument that comes out when they get mad" he asked.

"When you get mad, maybe, yeah. It's a taser basically. One of our people tried to stand up to them and he ended up on the ground, pissing himself" she said.

"That's not so bad. I mean, just wear a thick vest or something…"

196

"And then behind that is a rail gun" said Alexis. "Blow you to bits."

Raymond remembered a social media clip on the rail gun. Essentially, it was a projectile that was pushed using electromagnetism to hypersonic speed. There was no explosive inside, but the resulting impact energy created a fiery, combustive mess.

"But still…just because we can't beat 'em, doesn't mean we can't get around 'em. You know this country, bumpkin?" she asked.

"Like a snake knows a hole" he replied.

"Good enough I guess. OK, tomorrow, meet me at the Fairgrounds. Let's get gone and find your brother. I'm bored as hell."

"Time?"

"Better make it noon" she said. "We'll go for a casual stroll. Leave your car at home. Bring a little backpack with whatever you need 'cuz you're going on foot."

Chapter 16

"And so...you chose the quiet life, away from...well...everything" came the question.

Anita and Raymond were standing in front of their sheep pen. A voiceover.

"Raymond, Anita and their son Josiah have rejected modern living during these hectic times, part of a small yet vocal movement Raymond calls "the Refusers", or people who resist what they call the 'traps' of modern living."

Cut to Anita.

"We love the city, really. But the truth is that we just found that life was becoming more about existing and less about living."

And then to Raymond.

"Yeah...here, we do it all ourselves, as much as we can."

More voiceover: "Although they have given up on urban conveniences, such as supermarkets, the Tanners incorporate many technological innovations into their lives, like modern communications, the Internet, and teleconferencing, in order to keep their careers going. Raymond was one of the chief architects of President Trump's campaign communication, working under Evan James, a long-time controversial campaign strategist."

The reporter: "So...you don't want the hassles of modern living, yet you use technology to stay in touch..."

"Yeah I know" came the reply from Raymond. "It's a little hypocritical. We both do important work. We're invested. We want to see that through, but at the same time we want to be self-sufficient."

More questions: "And what about your use of A.I.?"

"The A.I. I view as a tool, really, a tool that learns what works best" said Raymond. Anita picked up the ball.

"Before my brother got on this farming kick, we really had no clue what we were doing. Once Josiah came to us, we saw that as a sign that we had to make a change, for his sake."

Voice over, video of the Tanners working:

"While the Tanners work the farm, it is the machines – A.I. – that run it. They give instructions on what to do, how to do it, and when. Everything is measured using sensors to detect humidity, soil moisture, and temperature, while the A.I. analyzes the data and makes recommendations. The whole concept is the brainchild of Anita's brother, who helps on the farm, but declined to be interviewed for this program."

Video of Raymond reading a screen, a weather report, then using a hoe to distribute dirt.

"But you didn't want to invest in big machinery to make the farm more productive?" came a question.

"It's the work that gives us a sense of meaning, of purpose" said Anita. "It has been so helpful to our son." A tear is wiped away.

Video of Josiah, using a pitchfork to load hay.

"Josiah was born with Duchenne's Muscular Dystrophy, a previously incurable condition. The Tanners declined to use genetic therapies, such as Crispr, to treat their son, saying that it conflicted with their religious values."

"…we just didn't want to mess with God's beautiful creation. This is our son, with all his challenges…this is our path now" said Anita. "We embrace it, as we embrace all of God's challenges for us."

"Your father, we understand, works in medicine" came the reporter's leading comment.

"Yes, and that was a tough sell" said Anita.

"But he's also a man of faith, as we are" said Raymond, placing a hand on his wife's shoulder. "He gets it." Anita, looking down for a moment, contemplative.

Video of the family working with hay, inside the sheep pen. More voice over:

"In addition to helping improve efficiency with produce and animals, the systems in place also help to keep people safe."

The camera focuses on a wire at the base of the sheep pen.

"Numerous safety alarms, cameras, and monitors have been installed to prevent accidents, escapes, and intrusions."

Anita: "We love that we don't have to monitor as closely as a traditional farm. The machines can pick up on problems. There's no way we could manage this farm alone if we didn't have them. They never sleep; when we're working, we get an alert to our smartphones if something gets out or if there's a danger, like a fire or something."

Reporter: "So, you're happy then?"

Raymond: "We miss being part of the action in the world, but we can still contribute to the struggle from up here."

Anita: "We had to strike the balance between career, lifestyle and family."

Reporter: "And this…just about covers it?"

They nod.

A question: "So you're still active in the 45cr movement?"

"We support the President, yes."

"How do you support him?"

"Anita mostly works on strategy while I handle the messages. We're always campaigning."

"What do you say to people who would argue that you're…how should I put it…throwing stones but not getting your hands dirty?"

"You mean why aren't we fighting in the war?"

"Well, if you want to put it that way – "

"The struggle happens on many fronts. We've always been on the frontline since this is a war of ideas. We have everything we need to keep up the good fight and win the day. And, with God's help, we will. But what kind of a country are we trying to make where we can't provide for our children? We would love to be there, in the trenches, but Josiah needs us. So, we work from here. It's not just about arguing ideas…it's about living them."

Raymond: "I try to get out and support our people in person. But it's tough and I know it puts a burden on Anita, me being away."

"Are you angry about the way things have turned out? Did you expect this civil disruption?"

Raymond's face changes.

"Why can't you just cut to the chase and call it what it is?" A pause. "This is a civil war, pure and simple. This is about fighting for the institutions that make America great. We've had the liberal elites running this country into the ground for decades now, selling it off piece by piece to the globalists…it was high time."

Anita's hand surreptitiously reaches out and touches Raymond's thigh. He sighs, and visibly returns to composure.

"All we want is our country back."

"I think the other side could say the same thing."

A pause. Anita jumps in, looking at Raymond.

"Then why'd they give it away in the first place?"

*   *   *

The video on the screen shifted to a wide shot of the pasture, with the reporter from CCN news saying some indecipherable to the camera. A helmeted head with "COLT 45" painted on the back turned to reveal Evan James smiling.

"Ya done good, son!" said James, tapping his compatriot on the helmet, showing him the feed of the *Whose America?* weekly broadcast on his phone as they sat on watch in Atlanta, in Piedmont Park. After the interview, Raymond felt that he needed to make his presence felt, to contribute in real terms, here, on the fighting front, and not just be a "digital sniper."

"Thank you sir" said Raymond.

"Don't call me sir, dammit. We're brothers" said James. "You don't work for me...you work with me. I just say yes or no to the shit you come up with. Come on, selfie from the front! Get that pistol in the shot!"

Evan and Raymond awkwardly embraced each other under the Angel of Peace, who towered over them with an olive branch in one hand and an outstretched palm. They were ensconced in a sandbag fortress, along with about five other 45ers. The sandbags were arranged around and on top of the trenches they had dug to house the 45ers tasked with protecting the Peace Monument in Piedmont Park with the words GATE CITY GUARDS messily painted on the outside. Protestors had already tried to topple this statue, but the 45ers had vowed to protect it down to the last soldier, since there were so few monuments left from the previous civil war. They had even gotten a hold of a military-grade .30 cal machine gun for the purpose. The Georgia National Guard had not brought it up since their last visit to the site. They even left some radios in case they ran into trouble.

The 2020 Presidential Election had gone ahead, despite Trump calling for its suspension in the face of the civil unrest: he had no power to do so. It was up to the individual states as to whether they'd be naming their electors for the Electoral College, or if they'd be moving their elections to a later date. Since no states had left the Union, they were all technically still in play. The Democratic voting base had fled the so-called Trumpist States for traditionally Democratic ones, so there was no impact on the overall Electoral College: it was a virtual repeat of 2016, notwithstanding Wisconsin, which swung for the Democrats. There was barely any violence at all, except for the usual "Not My President" protests in the North and West. The 45ers were jubilant, their resolve stiffened by the legitimacy attendant with this new mandate.

"Shit, do we not have the wifi up anymore? Jesus I told you guys…that thing is second only to the monument" yelled James, looking down at the spinning wheel that indicated buffering and no connection.

"Just a minute…" said one of the volunteers, an impressionable kid from the upcountry, who began checking the cables from a Linksys router to a tower nearby.

"Hurry up, Yeoman" yelled James. The latter was his name, not his rank.

"Ok, got the microwave" he said.

"Good man, Yeoman. She's posted!" yelled Evan.

Almost in unison, the 45ers pulled out their phones to check their feeds, murmuring in approval. The cell towers were one of the first targets of the war. If one could not communicate, one could not spread ideas. To counter this, both sides had rigged up clandestine microwave networks that connected to each other via line-of-sight. The connection was painfully slow, but not having the ability to spread ideas to the world was even more painful. In this case, the 45ers had commandeered the roof of one of Atlanta's skyscrapers, giving them much broader coverage.

The photo was almost perfect, except for the up-angle fat chins. The words "CEASE FIRING – PEACE IS PROCLAIMED" were boldly, emblazoned upon the monument, right over their combat helmets. James and Raymond smiled at each other, silently acknowledging the hundred-year-old irony. They had developed an awkward yet cozy friendship since 2016. They bonded over most things, except when James would become irate at any new development he recognized as a problem. Raymond also detected a hint of racism when the topic of his interracial family came up, and although James never mentioned it directly, he tended to look away when Raymond showed him a picture. Raymond could count on one hand the number of times they had been able to sit down and have a non-work-related social engagement, like a drink. Those opportunities had quickly evaporated with the onset of the war.

Atlanta was a divided city. Most had fled north, leaving the core abandoned. A low overcast sky hung over the skyline, obscuring the tops of the taller buildings. In the distance, they could hear a few sporadic rifle shots in rapid succession; the first ones of the day. The mood in the bunker changed; rifle grips were clutched more tightly; safeties clicked off as heads went lower.

"Alright look lively boys" said Evan, putting away his phone in its custom holster on his chest, near his heart.

The bushes on the far side of the park began to stir slightly, but the air was still.

"Southwest" said Evan, quietly.

The troops moved around to target their rifles on the ferns and trees, whose pock-marked trunks had borne witness to previous firefights. The air was still; nothing moved now. A Blue Jay's caw cut through the stillness. Raymond saw it bravely jump out on to a limb and thought of how Pappy used them for target practice. Today, the quarry was much larger, and would shoot back. He held his finger over the trigger as he had been taught. Silence again, but only for a moment, as they heard what sounded like a jetliner coming for a landing. Yeoman, an Iraq veteran, had heard this before:

"COVER!" he yelled instinctively, but it was too late: the ground before them erupted as a mortar round landed thirty yards from their encampment. Dirt and rocks rained down on the motley company, and the bullets began flying, disturbing the bushes even more and giving the impression that there were scores of enemy combatants on the other side of them.

As quickly as it had begun, the firefight stopped. Clearly, they only had one mortar round, and it had missed. They scanned the tree line, looking for any sight of a 25er soldier.

A few rifle cracks rang out on the north side of the monument. James looked over to see a figure collapse about twenty yards from the monument. Raymond's rifle still had smoke coming out of it. He was transfixed on the figure, looking back and forth to try and detect any movement.

"That's a clean kill" said James, patting Raymond on the shoulder.

"Never shot anyone before" said Raymond, hoping he had only maimed his quarry. He wished Mitch were here.

James sensed his apprehension, noting that the target was still squirming some yards away. "He's gonna bleed out. Even your father-in-law couldn't save him now."

"He does restorative dental" said Raymond without thinking, his heart in his throat. He felt nauseous. He wanted to hug Josiah.

"Well consider this asshole restored" said James. "We held 'em off boys!"

All of a sudden, they heard a voice come over a bullhorn, from all around them:

"Attention, Trump-fuckers: shit's about to blow big!"

The group looked stunned. James looked up at the monument to see that during the firefight, some 25er had jumped the parapet and sprayed "FUCK TRUMP FOREVER" on the monument. Then, he looked toward the feet of the Angel of Peace: cables were jutting out that had not been there before. They were attached to a brick of something that could be an explosive.

210

"CLEAR OUT!" came his yell.

The men piled over the parapet and ran at full tilt in all directions.

Immediately, the monument erupted thanks to the high-explosive shape charge that had been placed at her feet by a daring 25er. The Angel of Peace and the Confederate soldier were blown apart from each other and the monument had been reduced to ruin.

The bullhorn came back to life, full of youthful adrenaline, almost laughing: "You failed you failed you failed…"

The 45ers turned their guns in the direction of the bullhorn, releasing a fury of bullets, cutting down the voice mid-sentence.

Quiet returned to the park. The echo of the battle rolled back their way, then faded. There were groans of pain. Yeoman lay in the field, clutching his abdomen. James was the first to rush over.

"Yeoman, I hate to say this but I think you're going to make it" said James, with a smile.

"Bullshit, boss" said Yeoman, smiling back. He tried to laugh, but his insides were collapsing under the kinetic energy of the blast. Because it was a shape-charge, he was the only one impacted. Blood issued out the corners of his mouth.

"They'll remember you forever. We're gonna replace this monument and make sure your damned name is on it somewhere. Maybe even get a real American name on this park instead of a dirty French one." James' voice was breaking down a little.

"Bullshit" said Yeoman. He was no longer smiling but was making a horrific gurgling, clucking sound. The life in his eyes had vacated.

James bit his lip. Despite the lethal nature of this war, it was only the second time he had lost someone in combat. He lowered his head, wiping away tears quickly with his thumb and index finger.

"Fuck it" he yelled, grabbing his AR15, slapping in a fresh magazine and stomping off. "Come on" he yelled at his company, who obliged him, some nursing their own minor wounds. "Ray-Ray get in the fucking war."

Raymond broke his trance and followed James, rifle raised, sweeping left and right as the company stumbled forward into the bush with no coherent formation. They had been hastily assembled, and some were badly out of shape. One even hauled on a puffer for his asthma.

A figure was writhing in the dead leaves on the ground. A bullhorn lay behind him as he was trying to crawl away. James got to him first.

"Fuck you Trump bitch motherfuckers" came the voice.

A few shots rang out from James's rifle, up the back of the legs of the aggressor. Cries came out. The figure stopped moving. James warily moved to stand over him.

"Turn over" yelled James.

The figure merely moaned some obscenity.

"Turn" a kick "over" he yelled.

Rather than wait, James used his leg to flip the 25er. The company started to move in, but James urged them to hold position.

"Cover me" said James. "Don't want these sneaky bastards getting another one of us."

Raymond turned to leave. He didn't want to partake in any of what was about to happen.

"You stay" said James. "Got your phone?" he asked.

"No it's back there" he said, pointing to the monument, trying to ignore the horror unfolding before him. "Just leave him…it's over…" The words came out, but found no audience.

James took one hand to grab his phone. He examined it. "Shit" he exclaimed. The phone had been smashed beyond recognition.

"Mine still works" came the voice. "Caught the whole thing. Watched your honkey asses clear outta there before the fireworks."

James and Raymond looked down to see the man, probably in his late twenties, smiling.

"You never seen a black man so brave, huh?" came the voice again, defiant.

"Thought all you little bitches ran North, just like old times" said James. "Got a rope back at the monument 'case you wanna hang for a bit."

"I ain't leavin' this city. This is where I was born" he cried out. He was shaking now.

James, calm now, took a more interrogative approach.

"Now why'd you go blowing up that beautiful monument?" he asked, sitting down cross-legged in the leaves, being careful not to get any on his combat pants.

"Why was you guardin' it?" he asked. "We already took down most of your other dipshit ancestors."

James ground his teeth but stopped, refusing to allow his anger to seep through. "You assholes tried to take it down in '17. We knew you'd be back" said James. "Doesn't matter. We'll build a new one with some familiar faces on it. Trust me, you wouldn't like it."

"Orange face? They gonna make it in gold for him?"

"Whatever color doesn't run. Like yours" said James, checking to see that a round was chambered in his rifle. "Catch you on the flip side" he said, standing up. "Hope you know how to pray fast."

"You know the best thing about my phone?" said the 25er, anticipating the worst.

"What, traitor?" he replied.

"It's still recording" he said, tapping the lens of his camera. "And it's still connected. I'll make ya famous."

"You did all that for a clip?" laughed James. "Pretty fucking great!"

Three shots rang out as James silenced the man. The last one went through the body of the phone. Raymond thought he heard

214

James utter yes under his breath at that. The air became still again, but no birds sang. Raymond began silently hyperventilating. He threw up, but he had nothing in his stomach, so it was just regurgitated bile that frothed in his mouth. He let it ooze out as he leaned into the ground, away from James and the others. The grass absorbed his unease, which was about the only relief Raymond could get from this moment.

"All you assholes get over here now!" yelled James in frustration.

The men ran over.

"Look at him" said James.

They looked. "What, boss?"

"Take a look at the face of fucking commitment."

They looked again. He held up the man's dead head by his hair. He placed it down, carefully.

"We're gonna lose this war" he announced. "We're gonna lose this war because five of us can't hold off two of them. We're gonna lose this war because it doesn't matter what you shoot or who you kill..." he paused. "We're gonna lose this war because they know how to make us look like fucking idiots."

Raymond didn't partake in the sermonizing. He was sitting with his arms wrapped around his knees, trying to maintain his composure despite his patent disgust. James walked up to him.

"You done good here today Ray-Ray. Take some time off. Go back up to that farm. Go back to your family. You're handy in combat but you're no soldier, at least not on the battlefield."

He put a hand on his shoulder, using his rifle as a crutch to sit down with a groan.

"Fuck I got fat" he said, feeling his joints creak as his buttocks landed on the ground. "Look, sorry about the whole colors running…I know your kid…"

"Don't worry about it" said Raymond, cutting him off.

James brushed off his pant leg. "This is a war of ideas. We may have the firepower, but they just ran off with a nuclear bomb's worth of good press. Get home, get some rest, and think of some good shit to counter what just happened here, and don't be too long about it."

He helped Raymond to his feet.

"Fucking martyrs. I hate 'em."

"Too much to live for" Raymond managed, watching the 25er slip away into the abyss. He wondered who would be waiting up for this man, a man who would not be coming home, because he dared to make a video, stand up for what he believed in. Just like them. What would they do with the bodies? Would they be allowed to rot in the park? Would a loved one come and retrieve them? Would Evan James turn his tirades on them, too? Raymond now understood that his real contribution – his keystrokes and his digital melees - were just as responsible for draining the blood from that boy as Evan James's .223 caliber bullets. His stomach churned.

216

"I know…now get back to it, refresh, and remember what the hell we're fighting for. Make something of this shitshow."

Chapter 17

Sun streamed in through the window of Pappy's trailer, and Raymond remarked to himself how much brighter and lighter the place felt now that he was properly taking care of it. A shame, he thought, that he wouldn't be coming back to it any time soon, if at all. What he was about to do would almost certainly get him excluded, if not imprisoned. He wondered what had happened to all the criminals. If the news media was to be believed, there were no prisons left because they were not needed, they said. He hoped to never find out.

Raymond held a photo of Mitch in his police uniform, right after graduation. His heart welled up with pride for his brother; so much stronger, so resilient. He grimaced a little when he remembered that the reason for his exuberant exterior was that his insides had been reprogrammed by a machine. Thanks to this intervention to fix his muscular dystrophy, he had even regrown most of his hair. He placed the photo on the bed next to all the equipment he had laid out for the long march ahead. He was still his brother, he decided, machine-programmed or not.

After rummaging through Pappy's trailer, he had assembled a rudimentary survival kit: Pappy's hunting knife, sharpened, oiled and sheathed, his compass, a map of the South, a sheet of polyethylene plastic, several yards of nylon rope, coiled, cotton balls soaked in alcohol for lighting fires and first aid, and a Katadyn hiker water purifier, which he had saved from the war. Added to this was a few changes of long, wool socks and underwear stuffed into a zipper-lock bag with a bar of soap. He found his combat knapsack, cleaning it up and resuscitating it to its former glory. A faded "45" on the outer pocket indicated his allegiance, but he had used rubbing

221

alcohol to erase any traces, for fear of drawing unnecessary attention from the machines. Maslow's hierarchy, he thought. He saw a small rock from another time and stuffed it in an outer pocket of his bag, worn to a shine in places.

The fairground was muddied from a sudden rainstorm that had popped up overnight. Ceres had thought of everything, but she hadn't addressed the problem of mud splashing up on her pristine, white organic silos, which looked as though they had gotten up in the night and splashed in puddles like a child. Raymond stood by the mouth of the clown, waiting for Alexis to emerge and help effect the escape.

"Hi Raymond" came a calming voice, female. Raymond turned to see one of the machines approach, with its whirring servos and motors. "How are you today?"

"Hello" he said, looking away, leaning on the clown face.

"I've seen you here quite a bit lately…are you making new friends?" asked the machine. "Might be good for you, Raymond."

"Oh, I'm sure…when you say you…"

"I mean 'we' or 'us' or 'the machines.' I was just being polite" said the machine. "You've seen Alexis a lot lately."

"There's nothing happening, I mean…" he stood up taller, indignant that he was explaining himself to a machine. "She's just a friend."

"I don't think so" came the reply. "Sorry for being rude, but part of my job is to ensure social cohesion at this refuge. I predict that there is a 36% chance of attaining a meaningful, lasting relationship with her."

"You know she's a lesbian" he replied.

"Of course" said the machine. "I didn't say romantic, you cheeky bugger."

He didn't know what you call it when you sense an emotion that wasn't there, but he could almost hear the machine smiling at the end.

"Well I'd appreciate a little privacy if that's ok" he said.

"Of course, Raymond. You are free" she said.

"You done flirting with my boyfriend?" asked Alexis, walking past the machine. She was clad in a camo hat, a spring jacket, jeans, and a pair of Doc Martens knee-highs. Her hair was held back by a thick leather hairband. "Come on, Raymond. You got a town to show me!" She grabbed a hold of his elbow and they marched off in the direction of the town. "Be back by sundown, Felicia!"

The machine merely whirred, extending herself slightly to watch the two of them walk away across the soggy field.

"Why'd you call it 'Felicia'?" asked Raymond.

"Dunno just always have" said Alexis. "Makes it easier when I have to say 'buh-bye.'"

"So how are we gonna get…"

"Don't talk" she said, turning toward him. "Kiss me" she said.

"What?"

She leaned in and gave him a deep kiss, if only on the lips. Raymond hadn't experienced that in over a year. He became lost in the hormonal surge. She pulled back.

"Ok...just walk and don't say anything" said Alexis, skipping a little to make it seem like she was giddy with excitement. She put her hands up in the air and yelled: "I found myself!"

The lens on the machine looked on.

Once they were hidden from the machines' view, Raymond spoke up.

"So that was one heck of a..."

"Don't get excited, bumpkin. It was just lips on lips. I wish I had some hand sanitizer. Ceres may know everything, but she doesn't know how to not be manipulated. I think she's developing emotions or something. Anyways, if I can throw her off the scent of us escaping by exchanging a bit of saliva, so be it. She thinks we're gonna fall in love."

"I was gonna say stunt. But sure, my thoughts exactly" Raymond lied. "That's what the machine said by the gate."

"Yeah, Felicia's especially chatty" she said.

"So how the hell are we going to get past the Wall?" he asked. "Climb over?"

224

"No that's bullshit" she said. "Have you seen it?"

"Yeah!" said Raymond. "The thing heats up when you touch it."

"Right, and it keeps heating up to the point of burning or melting so don't try to climb it or you'll be incinerated. It absorbs heat during the day and stores it for later. It also sends out an alert that you're climbing there. So you can forget about the wall. Trump woulda had a hard-on if he coulda seen this."

"Ok, well you must have some other idea" said Raymond.

"Obviously" she said. "Just follow my lead when we get to the gate. Take me on a hike that will eventually lead back to the opening in the wall by the main road outta town."

"We can't just walk up along the road? It'll take hours to swing back around when we could just walk there in fifteen minutes" said Raymond.

"No they'll know what we're up to if we just walk up. We have to make it seem like we just happened to find the opening."

"Alright" sighed Raymond.

"Come on, bumpkin. There's a lot of ground between here and your brother. Those hiking boots better be worked in."

"Broken in good" he said. "Let's head on down to Twelve Mile Creek. That'll take us back to 137 where they got the gap."

They walked through town a bit, just enough so they could be surveilled together, then turned left and went through a few fields to the edge of a forest.

"Stay away from those" said Raymond, gesturing to the poison ivy. "It'll be better when we get inside some tree canopy."

"Ain't much of a hiker" said Alexis. "I like nature n' all but only when there's a few feet of gravel between me and the creepy crawlies."

"Well" said Raymond, producing his hunting knife, "this is where we separate the men from the boys." He attached the knife sheath to his belt and concealed it under his jacket. Alexis giggled at his machismo.

The air had a bit of a nip in it, but the leaves had not yet changed their hue for the fall. There were still plenty of annoyances lurking in and amongst the brush.

"Stay away from the ferns" he said.

"What, they poisonous too?" asked Alexis.

"No but they got a compliment of ticks that'll bite the hell outta you if they get the chance" he said. "Come away with Lyme's, or maybe even stop eating red meat." Alexis's face changed to one of disgust. "I'm a vegetarian" she said.

As much as Raymond relished making this ignorant city slicker squirm, he decided that he would hinder their progress if he alerted her to every single danger present on the trail. She had

226

stopped. "Just…we'll just check each other every couple of hours, deal?" he said. She nodded, not taking her eyes off the plants.

They carefully breached the tree line, finding an animal trail to keep the plants off their ankles. As they went deeper into the bush, the low green plants started to thin out, replaced by tall trees, whose high canopy blotted out the daylight, restricting the nuisance growth on the forest floor.

"It'll be better here" he said. "Just watch the rocks."

"What about bears?" she asked. "Ever seen a bear up here?"

"Yeah Pappy took one once" he said.

"Took?"

"Killed. Like, hunted" he said. "Right at the start of the bear season when the blueberries are still out. Pappy found him sitting there in a pasture, belly full of berries. Helluva a last meal" he chuckled, although he was channeling Pappy more than he was speaking for himself, he could feel.

"Savage" she said. "Perfect bear just sitting there loving life and your 'Pappy' just came out of nowhere and killed it. Probably had cubs."

"No Pappy wouldn't do that. We may be hunters but we ain't psychopaths."

Alexis made a face again: "All that for some bearskin."

"No we ate it too. Nothing goes to waste."

"And?"

"And what?" He could see she was curious.

"How'd it taste?" she asked, legitimately curious.

"Like blueberries. Buttery. Delicious…organic" he said, smiling a little as he turned to make sure she heard the last word. "You may call us savages but we do it sustainable, legal. The laws are there for a reason" he paused "…were there…"

They marched on, a little bit deeper into the forest. They could hear rushing water just beyond a ridge that spread out beneath their feet. A patch of vibrant violet flowers caught Alexis's attention.

"Beautiful…" she said, reaching her hand out. "What is it?"

"Wouldn't do that if I were you" said Raymond. "That's oleander…lethal poisonous."

"Oh" she said.

"Not sure what they taught you up at Yale…"

"I went to B.U." she cut in. "Boston University?"

"…but you better leave the food-finding to me."

"I brought a few Mr. Noodles" she said. "Was hoping you had like a kettle or something…"

"Yeah, you may be hungry for a bit. We'll find stuff along the way but for now let's just stay focused on getting the heck outta here" he replied.

They went as far as the edge of the forest tree line, mostly to keep the ankle-level annoyances to a minimum. They kept the river

228

in view as they walked. On the far ridge, Raymond could see the ominous wall extending up, seemingly sucking in all the light and energy around it. After another fifteen minutes, they came around a bend to see a bridge straddling the river.

"That's where we need to be" said Raymond.

"Ok, so here's the plan" she jumped in.

"Plan? You were just about to kill yourself on a poisonous plant. Now you've got a plan?"

"I'll leave the country bumpkinning to a bumpkin. This is my wheelhouse: distract and destroy."

She took off her backpack and produced what looked like two cans of beans. Raymond went to grab one.

"Be very careful" she said. "Those will go off if they hit the ground."

"What are they?"

"Homemade flashbangs" she said. "Used 'em once on the 45s…" she stopped herself from welling up with too much pride.

"How's that gonna stop those killing machines?" Raymond had suddenly lost a confident stride and almost stuttered as he spoke.

"Don't need to stop 'em. Just get them to look away. Here I'll show you…" She explained the plan. "You ok, Bumpkin? You look a little pale."

He shook his head and tried to forget the gruesome scene at Piedmont Park. They continued up a little further, right to the edge

229

of the trees. They could now clearly see the bridge and the road. Two sentries were stationed at opposite ends of the bridge.

"Ok, you ready?" she asked. He nodded. "Just follow my lead. Here...I need your throwing arm..." She handed him a can.

"Throw this across the road into that clearing" she said.

"Ok...but" he started.

"Just follow the plan" she said.

He stretched and wound himself up, somewhat theatrically. The machines hadn't noticed them yet. Raymond pitched the can with all his junior league might. The can sailed across the road, landing with a thud on the opposite side.

"Must've been a dud" said Raymond.

Suddenly, a loud pop went off and Raymond felt a bit of a concussion wave hit his face. The machines saw this too and were coming together to investigate.

"Alrighty" said Alexis. "Remember what I said about the heads. Get ready."

"Still not sure how you know all this..."

"Just trust me" she said. "It'll work."

When the two machines were together, Raymond pitched another bean can concussion grenade to the left of where the first one had landed. The explosion occurred immediately after impacting this time.

"Go!" she mouthed. As the machines were rolling toward the explosions, the Alexis and Raymond both crept up behind the machines, sticking their fingers in the head units of each machine, finding a button that instantly shut the machines down.

"Ok I got mine!" said Raymond, gleefully. "I GOT ONE!"

"Don't gloat bumpkin, they're just resetting. We gotta get the hell outta dodge right now" she said, starting to run across the bridge, holding Raymond's hand to get him moving.

They could hear a sound like a computer booting up, first one, then the other.

"That was fast!" cried Alexis. "Get to the tree line!" she said.

They ran and stumbled across the bridge with renewed urgency. There was a further thirty yards to get to safety. Raymond tripped on a tuft of grass as he jumped off the roadway. Alexis was about to reach for him, but she could see that he would roll out of sight faster than she could pick him up, so she let gravity do the work.

"Stay down!" she whispered loudly from the safety of the trees, but Raymond had already adopted a prone position and was writhing towards her.

The machines were now fully back online. They began emitting a sound like a klaxon, busily searching the opposite side of the bridge. No doubt they had reconnected and were broadcasting their feeds with the appropriate authorities.

"We better get the hell outta here" said Alexis. "This place will be crawling with bots and aerial drones faster than you can say reboot. Where to, bumpkin?"

"Well, I wanted to talk to you about that…" he said, pushing forward. "Let's talk in a few."

They pushed forward into the forest, along the river. They stopped when they were at a bend in the river where they could see the bridge, but not be seen. The bridge itself was a small structure in the distance, and they could see other emergency vehicles converging on the scene. Raymond was sure that Laney Sullivan would be there, awkwardly helping the investigation.

"Atlanta" said Raymond, embarrassingly out of breath. Alexis, by contrast, was not.

"What? You take your meds this morning, bumpkin? We're going to the coast. That's backtracking" she said.

"Yeah I know. But we both know that we're not gonna make it."

"Speak for yourself, bumpkin. I'm a CrossFit master."

"You'd starve before you hit the state line, CrossFit or not" he said.

"What's your plan?" she asked.

"I know where we can get a car" said Raymond. "If I know the owner, it's still registered. We could steal a car, I guess…"

"…then Ceres finds out and they're scanning for that plate. No dice. So we walk to Atlanta and find a car. Great" she said. "What if we get stopped and our faces get scanned?"

"Why don't you go back?" asked Raymond, annoyed.

"What?"

"I mean what do you care if I make it or not?" asked Raymond.

"Meh. I can't live inside that clown anymore. I'd rather starve and be free than be fed and in prison, just for being me" she said. "Besides, I'm invested now. If I go back, they'll know it was me for sure and it'll probably involve real jail with your friend Officer Sullivan. Right now, all they know is that you and I went to town and have not been seen since. They'll probably put it altogether eventually."

"How the hell did you know to do that?" Raymond asked, pointing in the direction of the bridge.

"What, the reset button?"

They started walking again at a more measured pace. The sun was quickly slipping below the tree line.

"One of our guys at Twin Oaks was a bit of a nerd. When we started doing our little protest hijinks, he was able to get ahold of one and disconnect it. He took that thing apart and taught me everything I know."

Raymond was impressed. He didn't know how to respond. The dying light cast a warm glow on her face. She really was extraordinarily pretty, although it was a subtle beauty, and Raymond wondered if he was merely projecting adulation after his first romantic encounter in over a year. He shook the thought out of his head and muttered a throwaway comment.

"So how do we get to Atlanta?"

There was just enough light to see the map, so they stopped and sat down to plan their route. Fortunately, Raymond had brought a topographical map.

"Well..." said Raymond. "The obvious choice is to head on down to the I 81, then hang a right...we can just stay in the bushes. Should take us about three days. Your Mr. Noodles might last you that far."

"No" said Alexis. Raymond was taken aback. "We have to stay away from main roads...what about this one? Cornelia Highway?"

A light went off in Raymond's head. "Even better...Old Cornelia Highway. Nobody takes that. It's pokey as hell but we're on foot so it doesn't matter. Just less chance of finding food along the way."

"Whatever it is we need to get out of here while it's still light. I don't want to be within fifteen miles of this place by sundown, especially if the drones are out."

"Let's just cross the river and keep moving then. We have to get to Johnson Road near Norris if we're going to make this happen."

"Can we try staying in the forest 'til we're at least fifteen miles out?" she asked.

"Yeah, but it's gonna be thorny and pokey."

"I'll take it. Maybe you can shoot me a squirrel for dinner."

"You know I could" Raymond smiled, and the two of them descended into the river valley to cross the stream at a shallow point. In the distance, Raymond could see the wall, and made every effort to plot their course so they could steer clear of it.

Chapter 18

"I know but it just doesn't say 'They Lost' enough" said Anita, studying Raymond's latest meme and slogan. They were both hunched over a computer monitor trying to sculpt their social media strategy.

He had returned to the farm after the humiliating defeat at the hands of the 25ers in Atlanta. Anita was glad for his presence. She often complained, rightly so, about the difficulty in running the farm without him there. Delroy had focused mainly on the management of the farm, leaving Anita as the sole caregiver and provider for Josiah. It was a tough life for her; she was not used to being tethered. When Raymond arrived, she immediately returned to her work, in this case managing public relations for Volper News. Despite the shattered economy, Anita always seemed to find a way to channel her skills into something lucrative. She had taken a break to help Raymond tweak his comeback messaging.

"It's not that you lost something" she said. "You have to focus on what you gained."

"I know" said Raymond. "But...Yeoman...I mean, he's dead. He just slipped away. The monument got blown up. Not sure what we gained there."

"You gained a brotherhood that will never be lost or forgotten. Use the defeat against them...talk about Yeoman. Don't let his memory go. Salute his bravery. The Internet loves a martyr."

She could see he was lost in quiet reflection.

"Baby, you want a drink?" asked Anita.

He shook his head firmly.

"No …" he said. "Not while Josiah needs me."

"The 25ers aren't gonna have to do anything" she said. "Stress is going to take you down. I heard they got a price on your head, for what it's worth."

"Oh yeah?" he asked.

"It was only up for a minute before the socials took it down, but they got a pic of you in combats making a fist and a $25,000 bounty underneath, dead or alive" she said, smiling.

"And that didn't bother you any?" he asked.

"No, baby, I'm proud of you. Shows you're a bother to them, which means you gotta keep fighting harder" she paused to take a sip of her sorrel tea. "Why don't you go check on Josiah? He's" she looked over at a screen on the wall. "…over by the sheep pen. I think he's feeding them. You know he has trouble lifting things high up."

"Alright" said Raymond, shifting his weight out of the chair to get up. He kissed his love on the forehead. She barely looked up, instead making a kiss face while she continued staring at the screen.

Raymond emerged from the farmhouse and crossed the path. In the shadow of the barn, his beautiful son Josiah had parked his crutches and was busy trying to manage a bag of feed over the edge of the fence without tripping the alarm. He was doing well, but the weight of the sack was just enough that it threw the seven-year-old off his balance. Before his unsteady muscles could crumple, Raymond arrived to help steady the sack. He had inadvertently tripped the proximity alarm. A noise echoed around the property. A voice cackled to life from a speaker on Josiah's monitor: "everything

240

ok down there, darlings?" It was Anita. Everywhere Josiah went she demanded that he wear a monitor. Josiah let out a frustrated sigh.

"It's ok baby we're alright" said Raymond, adjusting the sack.

"I'm ok dad" he said. "I got this."

"I know you got it, baby. But who's got you?" he smiled, helping to shift the load to the ground once the feed had been delivered. "Me, that's who."

He grabbed hold of his son and squeezed, but not too tightly. Josiah knew about his condition and wasn't afraid to tell people. When some old lady in town said "that's horrible" Josiah merely replied "you think that because your faith isn't strong enough." The woman looked at Anita and Raymond, making a huff, storming out along the street. Josiah had a wisdom beyond his seven years, which was fortunate because he was not expected to live past the age of twenty-five. He had a monk-like stoicism that escaped his rash and impetuous father.

Raymond said "son, I don't know where you came from but you're one damned miracle."

"Darned" he corrected his father. "I came from God, daddy. Just like you and mommy and gramps and gramma and Donald Trump. And Ivanka."

Raymond had been extremely huggy lately, although the affection was more for Raymond's well-being than his son's. Each time he looked at Josiah, an image of the 25er's dying face jumped into his mind. He thought of Yeoman too, but there was something about the strength possessed by that infernal rebel that made him think of his son.

"Daddy" came Josiah's voice, wheezing a little from the exhaustion of recovering from his father's embrace. "Let's pray. In the barn."

"Ok baby" said Raymond.

He took him meekly by the hand, past the inside part of the sheep pen. At the back of the barn was Josiah's little alter, with a tiny crucifix on a table and a permanent manger scene, strewn with Christmas Tree lights. Behind that was Raymond's larger crucifix that they had obtained while on holiday in Cabo San Lucas. Anita had chosen it, with Jesus hanging from it, with the word INRI written across the top. The whole permanent nativity scene was Josiah's idea, who had said that we must "see how other people pray and try that too." Raymond lit a few small tealight candles and kneeled next to his son at the altar. They had once tried a candelabra, but the result was that the automated sensors detected an 'unacceptable amount of combustion inside a highly flammable space.'

"Do you want me to say anything?" asked Raymond.

"Nope" said Josiah, closing his eyes. "Just pray, Daddy."

"Ok, baby."

Raymond stared at the manger scene. The Mexican nativity scene also came from Cabo. Pappy would have scorned brown baby Jesus, but Raymond reasoned that it was probably rather appropriate given where he was born. Raymond thanked God for his family and his son, even if he had to contemplate the short time that he had to enjoy with him.

"Daddy?" asked Josiah.

"Yes, Peach?" he replied.

"Why don't I have a sister? Like Bruno or Mavis?" he asked, referring to kids from his class.

"I don't know, baby, I guess we just never got around to it. Lots going on. Mommy and Daddy are pretty busy."

"With the war?" he asked, innocently.

"With a lot of things" he replied.

"I'm worried that when I die, you and mommy will have nothing" he said. He was well aware of his condition and the limitations it put on his life.

Raymond's face tightened up, while resisting the urge to hug him. They were, after all, still at prayer.

"Baby you fill us up with all sorts of love and life. We're just not there yet. Having a baby is a big deal."

Josiah did not respond. He had broken away from prayer, having said his *hallelujah*. He found his pet rock in his pocket and took it out to stroke it. He called it *Smallin*, after the Ozarks cave he found it in on a family vacation. It was worn smooth on the edge and was almost shiny.

Raymond sighed with the exact same register as his son at the fence.

"I'll talk to your mom" he said. He leaned over, gave him a kiss, and left him to pray in the barn.

"Blow out the candles when you're done" he said. The sound of flapping wings filled the barn briefly.

"Can you scare away Cocky?" said Josiah, motioning to the rooster that sometimes antagonized him when no one was around.

"Yeah, baby" said Raymond, finding the bird on a post and yelling "shoo" then "go on, git!" The angry bird then flapped away in the direction of the exterior. It amazed Raymond just how far and how high chickens could fly.

Raymond crossed back into the farmhouse and went upstairs, back to Anita.

"Babe this thing is blowing up" she said.

"What is?" asked Raymond.

"While you were gone, I sent this over to Evan James…" she leaned back to show him a photoshopped meme. It was a picture of Yeoman, standing in front of the monument, the same day it was blown up. He was giving a thumbs up to the camera, wearing his combat gear, leaning on the monument that they had been charged with protecting, under which was written his name and dates: *JIMMY YEOMAN, 2000-2022, Died Defending Peace.* Next to this was a cutaway of the face of Angel of Peace.

"I wanted to clean it up a bit but Evan just kinda ran with it" she said. "Guess he was mad about being in the news as a racist."

244

"I really wish you woulda asked me before you sent it" said Raymond, annoyed. "His family is gonna be pissed."

"I'm sorry baby. Yeah I said that to Evan when I talked to him but he just loved it so much. He was the one who suggested the cutout of Lady Peace there…"

"Angel of Peace" said Raymond. He felt that horrible creeping nausea again.

"Right well he said he literally died while defending peace and he liked that. Said it would trump the whole demolition video they managed to get out. The President even retweeted it!"

"Wow" said Raymond, holding back his jealousy. He had been retweeted by the President before, but never so quickly. "Guess you don't need me anymore."

"Baby don't be like that. Besides, you aren't gonna have me around much over the next couple of weeks."

"Why not?"

"Vulper News is having a crisis about some female staffer and CCN is going to town with it. Seems that one of their mainstays had a bit of a tryst a few years back. They tried throwing money at her but it looks like this one's going public. Trying to come up with a counter-story right now and they need me in there for strategy sessions starting tonight. I'm flying outta Greenville in two hours."

"Do you ever consult me on anything anymore?" he asked. "What about Josiah? What about the farm?"

"The farm pretty much runs itself if you listen to the machines, and you got Delroy to help. Besides..." she sipped her tea "you and Josiah got a lot of bonding to do."

"We did bond..." he started. "We do..."

"It can't just be you playing games with your guns near a statue. Sometimes it has to be about me, too" she said, realizing too late that she had crossed a line.

Raymond snapped. "Those 'games' are what we live for, what's keeping this thing going, keeping our country together, making it all worth it!" he yelled. "You sit here and you publish and you tweet and you meme...you drop bombs in the virtual world while we bleed and die in the real world."

"Whatever" she said, putting down her tea and standing up. "You boys knew what you signed up for. I sit here for months and just wait to see your dead face come up as a meme, just like Yeoman's, and I pray to God that I never have to worry about you sacrificing yourself or doing something stupid. When you told me about that gunfight, I nearly died. I don't want you going out there again, ever! You would be so stupid to leave your wife and son and sit in front of some statue, risking your life for people who don't care about you? Who don't even support your family?"

"That's not true" he said.

"I've been around Evan James, Raymond. He's a racist...a dyed-in-the-wool, piece of shit racist. I'm glad that boy caught him on tape saying that horrific shit. He barely shook my hand, let alone looked at your beautiful son when we met. In fact, I think he smirked…he smirked…when I told him he had Duchenne's, not that his father would stand up for him and say it. Maybe he thinks…"

"Anita…"

"Maybe he thinks it's God's punishment for our marriage. Maybe he gets some kind of satisfaction. Raymond – you need to get it together and be here."

Raymond was humbled by her speech, crippled by the thought of rejection by his mentor. She had never been so critical of the cause. She was tearful now.

"Then why?" he asked.

"Why what?" she said.

"Why do you still…do it?" he asked. "Why do you support us?"

"Because that's what love is. Realizing it's a lost cause but you support it anyway because you love your family."

"You think we're lost?"

"I think I love you. And I always loved your ideas which is what drew me to you. I love how you think - I loved that long before I loved who you are. There's always going to be a cause for you."

He had sat down on the edge of the daybed in the office.

"But I have to go baby. It can't all be about you, all the time. I need to get into the World sometimes, too"

"This is your world, right here" he said. He was tearing up.

She came over. I know, her hand said, stroking his shoulder. She sat down on the daybed, which was a single, pulling him down into a spoon position. "Just hold me a while" she said, flipping over. He loved the smell of her, pushing down her beautiful, natural hair under his cheek so he could kiss her neck. Neither of them wanted to take the intimacy any further; they had had ample opportunity for that. He owed more than he cared to admit to her, even at their worst. He just lay there, breathing her in, imagining a future far from all the conflict, when the world was restored to the way it used to be.

He awoke to find Josiah poking at his thigh.

"Oh hey baby...how long were you standing there?" he asked.

"You just looked really happy daddy...did you have a nice dream?" he asked.

"Yeah, peach...it was nice" he said, groggily. He hated falling asleep in the daytime. So much to do. He wanted to plead his case more, but he was so tired. He did not sleep at night anymore; he knew he had some form of PTSD.

"Mom left. She said to come wake you so you could take care of me" he announced.

"Well" said Raymond. "Guess we better see about dinner then, huh?"

"Mom made dinner" he said. "The cornbread's good."

"You ate without me? How long's she been gone for?"

"Like...maybe an hour or like..."

248

"Maybe two?"

Josiah nodded.

"Baby, you know you can't be alone like that. You gotta have more than cornbread."

"I know…but I just wanted to show you that I'm ok, that you don't have to…"

"We don't have to what, baby?"

"You don't have to worry about me. I'm good" he said.

Raymond pulled Josiah into the same spoon position that his wife had occupied.

"Baby I know you are. I just miss you, that's all. Sometimes it's not about keeping you out of trouble, but just being able to see what kinda trouble you get into." He smiled.

"Dad?"

"Yes, peach?"

"Are you and mom getting a divorce? Bruno thinks you are."

"Well tell Bruno that ain't how we do things around here. Marriage is for life…you know that."

"Then where's Mommy off to?" he asked. "You guys are never together."

"Baby, there's a lot of things happening in the world right now that need attention, and if we're gonna make it right, we both need to work" he explained. "She'll be back soon. We just have to work harder around here. We want to impress Mommy, right?"

"Yes daddy. Of course we do. I trust you" said Josiah, with such confidence that it made Raymond cringe with guilt.

"I trust you too" said Raymond. "We're in this together."

"Looking out for each other?"

"Looking out for each other, that's right. Why don't we call grandma and grandpa and see if they wanna come up from Arizona?" Raymond's parents had recently moved: they had no appetite for the upheaval in their home state and found a retirement community in Flagstaff, far from the troubles.

"Come downstairs and eat" said Josiah, extricating himself and taking his father by the hand.

"Let's do that" he said. "Tomorrow, I'll show you how to feed the pigs. Uncle Mitch is coming over later to help out."

"Mommy said never go near the pigpen" said Josiah. "She said we have to reset the alarm."

"Well, if we're gonna be men, baby, then we have to nicely show them who's boss…don't ya think?"

Josiah made no reply but sighed. Climbing down the stairs was difficult for him, even with the assistance of his father. The house felt empty: they had never been without Anita for any period and the silent apprehension enveloped them both, such that every little creak in the floor felt like some new task that needed instant

250

attention. The rooster crowed in the distance, indicating that the sun was on its way down.

Chapter 19

Raymond awoke with a start; the world was blue and smelled of polyethylene. His back ached and his body was stiff. He did not see Alexis. He wondered if common sense had gotten the better of her and she had absconded back to the safety of Cateechee during the night.

They had made it across the old state line into Georgia at Prather Bridge on Cleveland Pike Rd. The bridge was risky, but worth it: the river was simply too deep and wide to risk crossing. Once on the other side, it took all their strength to make camp, into which they collapsed without eating. Their bed was merely the long side of the tarp that Raymond had packed, over which a roof was hung using a length of rope. Despite their wretched condition, Alexis made it clear that there would be a "neutral zone" separating them, in which she placed both packs to form a definite wall.

Raymond climbed out of the tent and looked around. There was nothing here but trees.

"Says here we're in Chattahoochee National Forest" came Alexis's voice. She was crouched over a map but looked like she had cleaned herself up at some point. She had removed her jacket, and Raymond was now able to appreciate her tattoos in their almost-full glory. They were intricate, so intricate that he could scarcely tell where one ended and the other began.

"What ya lookin at?" she asked, catching Raymond off-guard. "You snore like a goddamned freight train, you know that?"

"When I'm tired, yeah" he said.

"Well find me some earplugs when we get somewhere. Anywhere. You don't wanna see me without sleep."

"We're basically on the Appalachian trail" he said, "'cept we're aiming away from civilization."

"Only to go toward it" she said. "How far now 'til Atlanta?"

"We got another night, then we're there" he said.

"Jesus" she said. "What the hell have I gotten myself into?"

"Thought you were all 'CrossFit' and ready for anything" he said, smiling, grabbing his pack from the tent in search of his toothbrush.

"Yeah flippin' tires and rapping long ropes" she said. "I never really hiked before."

"You picked a helluva place to start" he said. "You know how many people die on the Appalachian a year?"

"No, but you're right…this is some nasty country" she said. "Found the river. There's a little bay where the water isn't so deep. I washed up. Don't drink the water, though…I think I saw a beaver on the river this morning. My water's almost done so that's going to be a priority pretty soon."

Raymond was impressed with her knowledge. He produced his water purification kit and showed her, then descended to the river to wash up. The river was still, but cool, and he welcomed the refreshing sensation of the water splashing over his skin. He felt rejuvenated and went back up the hill to fill up Alexis's bottle with the purified water.

256

"Beaver-fever free" he exclaimed, handing her the purified water.

"We're probably in the clear" she said. "I've got some cash that we can use in town to get…whatever."

"They're still looking for us" said Raymond. "I heard drones in the distance last night."

"Yeah but they don't know our faces" she said.

"Ceres does" said Raymond. "If someone who's connected sees us…"

"That's *if* they're connected and *if* they're on the upgrade. We're pretty remote here so I doubt whether anyone's got that. It's worth the risk" she said.

"Well I can get you close to town but it's probably better if you go in. I'm the famous one, according to Allsop."

"Why? What'd you do?" she asked.

"Saved a boy from the world" he said. "Walked him off a hill to his mom."

"Heroic" she said, wryly. "Where's the closest town? Toccoa Falls?" she said, pointing to the map.

"Yeah…actually, that works pretty well. We can stay to the north and avoid most of the houses. There's a hospital there."

"Screw that" she said. "Go there and we're dead for sure." She scanned the map for a better spot. "Here…this crossroads. Bang a right and we're there. Gotta be a gas station or something with empty calories and sugar."

"Maybe even vegan" said Raymond.

They were both very hungry. Alexis vowed to save the noodles for an emergency, and neither had eaten more than a granola bar the day before. They packed up their camp, checking for signs they had been there. Seeing none, they proceeded on their way.

They trekked over the unforgiving terrain of upstate Georgia, trying to stay within the tree line as much as possible, out of sight. It made for a grueling voyage, and each time they braved the road to overcome a creek or culvert, they lingered just a bit longer, just a few more steps. They were both surprised that no cars came; not once, except a pickup truck ripping along so fast that they could barely perceive the driver, who took no note of them. Raymond was heartened to see it flying an American flag, playing music at full blast, a Dale Earnhardt Jr. sticker on the bumper. He must have made a sound like "yeah" because Alexis groaned in displeasure.

Eventually, they stuck to the shoulder of the road, staying under the tree cover as much as possible. They had just rounded the corner at Old Rothell Rd. when they both heard a sound like bees swarming. "That's not..." said Raymond. "It is..." said Alexis.

They were out in the open, completely exposed. There was only a field for the next 100 yards. They had become complacent with their fatigue and hunger. At once, they broke into a run, not sure where the drone would come from. Raymond perceived that it was coming from behind them, following the road. He looked to see it hanging low, zig-zagging left and right, scanning and assessing and reporting. They had almost reached a stand of trees when Alexis leaped on Raymond, forcing him to the ground. "Get the tarp!" she said.

He frantically ripped the tarp out of his bag.

"You sure this is gonna…" he started.

"Just pass it!"

They covered themselves under the blue tarp as the horrific sound came ripping up the road.

"Don't make a sound" she said. "Don't move."

The buzzing became more and more intense; the drone had spotted their tarp and was moving in for a look. The sound of the electric rotors came closer and closer and Raymond could swear that it was about to chop them to bits. His hot breath made the underside of the tarp wet with condensation. He wanted to rip the cover off and smash it to bits. Alexis made a small hand sign saying "wait", and sure enough, the swarming sound lifted, and the drone moved off.

"Great" he said. "How do we know he's not reporting back to Ceres?"

They had folded back the tarp and were sitting up now.

"Don't know…let's see if any SAFETY bots show up" she said, smiling. She changed her face to be more serious, sensing Raymond's tension. "Probably not…they're the dumb extensions of a very smart machine. Unless it moved the tarp, it wouldn't be able to tell if it was covering two humans or a pile of wood."

"What about FLIR and high res cameras and body heat scanners…"

"That tarp was probably pretty close to your body temp…you're carrying it right beside your back. Besides it's the middle of the day."

"Hmmmph" came Raymond's reply. Clearly, she was the machine expert and he the nature boy. "So they are looking for us" he said.

"We don't know that. Those things patrol all over the place. Could have just been that. Still…" she said, picking up a long stick. "Let's just assume the worst."

After their close encounter, they decided that it was safer to hike in the trees again. They had underestimated their pursuers, and both vowed to check their complacency, keeping the road in sight but maintaining the crucible of walking over roots and rocks on their long trek to Atlanta.

They arrived at Dark Gorge Food Mart just before noon. There was one pickup truck parked near the store, but no vehicles frequented the gas pumps out front.

"Ok, wait here" said Alexis. "I'll go check it out."

"You better tuck in that Boston accent" said Raymond.

"I'm used to hiding in plain sight" she said, smiling, taking off her jacket from her waist, probably to cover her extensive tattoos. "Did in front of my parents since I was a kid…" she said.

260

"How's that?" she asked, holding her arms up, turning around.

"Pretty normal, except that you look like you just walked in from the woods" he replied. "You sound better, anyway. Less harsh."

She flipped him a middle finger as she sauntered carelessly down the hill towards the pavement.

He waited on the hill nervously, hearing only the sound of a door open and a chime sound, hopefully not an alarm. A few minutes later, he heard the chime again, and Alexis emerged carrying a couple of Moon Pies and a long stick.

"Here...bumpkin food" she said as she approached, tossing the treats at her companion. He loved Moon Pies, and within seconds had ripped one open and was devouring it. Alexis had found a bag of boiled peanuts and was snacking away, holding the long stick in her left hand. A key dangled from the bottom of it.

"So what happened?" he asked.

"There's nobody in there" she said. "Smells to high heaven, like something crawled in there and died. Probably abandoned...these nuts are pretty rancid."

"Then why's the door unlocked?" he asked.

"I think you're probably the only man left in America who still locks his door. There's no crime anymore, remember? Ceres made everyone happy" she said, walking off.

"Where you going?" asked Raymond, between mouthfuls of Mooncake.

"Taking a shit" she replied, waving the key.

"Thought you said nobody locks their doors!" he yelled.

"Old habits die hard I guess."

Raymond decided that he would check out the store. Opportunities like this would be few and far between, he thought, and they should really try to take advantage. He walked down the hill, across the concrete apron, and into the store. It felt good to be on level ground again, and he began to take stock of all the new aches in his body that were emerging due to forcing it across backcountry terrain. As soon as he heard the door chime, a smell greeted his nose. Alexis was right; something had died in here. The lights were still on, casting a harsh fluorescence across the aisles and goods. Everything looked as it might have years before Ceres, before the war even. It was clean and organized; there was even an art piece on the wall of a woman leading others to the edge of a waterfall, who seemed to be blindfolded. He wondered what it meant, then remembered some legend about the natives tricking a white woman into walking other settlers off a nearby waterfall, and then wondered what it meant that this terrible story had inspired someone to paint it and hang it in a gas station. He saw a couple of crumpled up bills on the counter; probably Alexis's, or from some other honest person. He decided to rely upon her largesse to fat himself on any and everything available here. He ripped into a few jerky snacks. He heard a flush, and in a moment, Alexis was behind him.

"Savage" she said, noting his choice of snack.

"It was already dead" he said. "You eat a bunch of that sugary crap, you'll be crashing in two hours."

"I'll find something worthwhile that doesn't involve death" she said, looking around.

Raymond checked in to the restroom for relief and a wash-up. If they could find stops like this along the way, they stood a pretty good chance of making it. He emerged, refreshed, still eating his jerky.

"That's commitment" said Alexis. "Pretty sure I'm stuck with empty calories. Everything here is rotten and moldy as hell."

"Guess they abandoned it a while ago...why'd they leave all the food?" asked Raymond.

"Dunno...but I did see a pickup truck parked out there..." she said.

"Don't know if that's a good idea" he said. "If they can see us when we're walking, they'll definitely see us if we're driving, especially a stolen truck."

"True" she said. "That's if they report it stolen."

They exchanged glances for a moment, thinking about the harsh trek ahead.

"There's an office back there" said Raymond. "Ladies first" he said.

"What a gentleman…" said Alexis, so wryly that Raymond pushed past her muttering "alright" on the way. The light was off in the corridor leading to the back, and the switch would not work. He could see the word "OFFICE" on a sign stuck to the door. The smell became more and more putrid as he inched down the hall. A light came from under the office door; he knocked.

"Hell-o?" he called. No answer. He found the doorknob, slowly and carefully opening it. The door moved a few inches, but then pushed back on him. Something was blocking its swing.

"Hello?" he called again. The smell was intolerably rank now.

He leaned in hard, pushing the door open just enough to see inside, and he felt his stomach turn as he peeked in. Jammed between the door, a desk and the wall, was the body of an elderly gentleman, crumpled over, ballooning up after several days' worth of decomposition. The face was vacant, lifeless; the cheeks were sunken. He felt instantly sick, rushing back to the restroom to empty his guts of the jerky and Moon Cakes he had just devoured.

Alexis appeared at the open door.

"Found the smell" said Raymond. Alexis raced over to the office.

"Oh, Jesus" she said from afar. "Jesus, fuck…" He heard her footsteps returning to the restroom.

"We gotta get outta here" she said.

264

"We can't just leave him there" said Raymond. "That's someone's…"

"That guy's been there at least five days…trust me, someone'll probably be looking for him. They're surely looking for us. You were in the war, and so was I…that's not the first body we've seen. Get it together bumpkin…we're leaving."

Raymond quickly washed his mouth and grabbed his bag from the floor, walking around the aisles, stuffing it full of whatever junk he could find. His insides were torn. He thought of Pappy dying; the woman in the nursing home said he passed away peacefully in the night, but he knew that meant he had been alone for hours before someone discovered him. This man would never know such dignity, and he cringed at the thought of extricating him from that office, if anyone ever did find him besides two reprobates from the woods. He couldn't stand it. He saw an old-fashioned landline phone behind the counter and picked it up.

Alexis turned to see him raising the handset to his ear. "What the hell are you doin?" she yelled.

"The right thing" he said.

"Put that goddamned phone down" she said, coming over to click on the receiver. He looked her straight in the eye.

"You know it's wrong" he said. "Can't just leave him back there…it's a sin."

Her eyes went cold and narrow.

265

"You know what's a sin? Letting Pence hand our country over to a computer, that's a sin. It's a sin that two of the only sane people left in the world have to run around the countryside, avoiding the droids, like Bonnie n' Clyde, just 'cuz they didn't want to hand over their brains to some evil machine to toy with us and infuse us with pleasure. Probably that guy just forgot to get up and move around after streaming so much. Probably forgot his medication. Probably alot of things. But whatever the hell it is, it's *not our problem*" she said.

"You finished?" asked Raymond. "Can I make the call now?"

"You moralistic Southerners I swear to God…" she said, picking up a boxcutter from a display, extending the blade, then cutting the cord. "Let's go! Now!" She tucked the blade in her pocket then picked up her sack, filled to the brim with stale treats and confections. She had a bottle of Perrier in her hand.

"Great" said Raymond, tossing some change on the counter, for what it was worth. He picked up a bottle of Colt 45 malt liquor from the fridge, for spite, and followed her out. Raymond was glad to see that the man had seditiously placed these bottles prominently in the display, and hoped that, at one time, they might have been on the same side.

Chapter 20

"Uncle Delroy taught me everything I know about raising hogs" said Raymond, standing next to the pigpen. "He's the expert, but daddy's the one's gotta maintain them while everyone's gone."

"And me" said Josiah.

"And you, baby, yes" he said.

"So tell me the most important rule again" asked Raymond.

"Never go in the pigpen by yourself" he said. "Unless something goes wrong with the feeding trough."

"No" said Raymond. "You never do. As a matter of fact, never go near this place unless someone's with you."

"God's always with me" said Josiah.

"Even God needs some help, sometimes" replied Raymond.

Josiah just closed his eyes, breathing in. Raymond then decided not to stress this point too much.

"Remember to treat 'em good. Uncle Delroy never learned that lesson and he was kinda mean to 'em. If you're mean to 'em, they'll be mean right back. Just make sure the big guys get the big bucket, and the piglets get the little bucket. Think you can manage that, for now?" asked Raymond.

Josiah nodded. He grabbed the feeding bucket and went into the farm to grab some feed. Raymond waited. When he emerged, he could barely keep the bucket level. Raymond rushed over to help him steady it.

"Maybe just grab the little buckets for the piglet, piglet" he said, smiling.

Josiah sighed. He found the smaller bucket and went over to the piglets.

"Hey" said Raymond. "Let me help."

"No, dad" said Josiah. "I just want to be useful."

Raymond smiled at his son.

"You're everything to me, and that includes being useful. You're usefully everything, how's that?" he asked.

"That's fine" said Josiah, suppressing a grin.

"Come on, let's get a bacon sandwich" said Raymond, imitating a pig squeal as he tickled Josiah in the ribs.

"Don't be mean, daddy" he said, following his father inside.

Chapter 21

"I'll tell ya what, bumpkin" said Alexis, nursing her sockless feet. "You find me a bed with clean sheets and a shower tonight, I may consider going straight, for one night."

They had moved off the road into a clearing. Raymond got a small fire going to heat a few cans of creamed corn they had found in the Dark Gorge Food Mart. They had spoken very little for the next few hours after viewing the horror, although Alexis tried to bring it up once. Raymond maintained silence as they marched along the highway, darting occasionally into the woods when they heard a car coming in the distance. He could count on one hand the total number of cars that had passed the two lifestyle fugitives, and that meant that detecting vehicles was relatively easy. Alexis, despite her toughness, was no hiker: her feet were soft, not calloused, and the consequence was huge blisters that needed to be popped and bandaged. Raymond had no stomach for this and pretended to move off to answer the call of nature while she did the deed with a pin. He returned to find her bandaging her feet. He reached into his bag and extracted a jar of pickles.

"Want one?" he asked Alexis, passing her the jar. She looked at it.

"What's that? Some weird beef? What's 'Wickles'?" she asked.

"You never had Wickles before? Well darn…it's spicy pickles. You'll love it."

She took one out and crunched it.

"That's damned good" she said. "Shit, really good."

"Can I ask you a question?"

"I never stopped you before. Shoot" she said.

"Why do you Yankees curse so much?" he asked.

"First of all, I'm no goddamned Yankee" she said. "Bosox. Don't fuck it up." She crunched on the other end of the Wickle. "Second, honest people swear more. You should try it sometime, bumpkin."

She passed him the jar and he took out a Wickle.

"Can't do it. Wasn't raised that way."

"I thought you Trumpies were all about your *freedom a speech*" she said, imitating a crude West Texas accent.

"I know but it's just so…"

"So what? Unlady like?"

"Unsophisticated" he said, flatly.

"I could ask why *y'all talk so slow* but I wouldn't wanna wait around for the answer."

Raymond had no answer.

"My point exactly. Look, it's either I punch out some bad words or I punch people in the face. I *reckon* you're better off with the words."

They crunched on their pickles. Alexis could see that her terse reaction had caused Raymond to become distant.

"Look, I was ladylike once. Just made me a target for men who didn't swear enough, you know what I mean, bumpkin? It didn't work out" she stopped herself. She could see Raymond understanding what she meant. She decided to change the subject. "So how far we gettin' tonight?"

Raymond was happy to have something to contribute, finally.

"Well, I figure we keep on keepin' on our way, we'll be near Gainesville by nightfall. But we better swing south if we're fixin' to avoid people. Used to go there a lot...there's a motel on the south side near State Rd. 11. Maybe it's empty, too."

"Why'd you go there, bumpkin?" she asked, mockingly. "Was it a girl? Why'd you need a motel? Couldn't sneak into her daddy's basement?"

Raymond pushed past the painful memories. "Yeah, something like that." He then leaned back, slapping his stomach. "Well, I'm full as a tick. How's you?"

"Better" said Alexis, returning to her feet. "Except...speaking of ticks..."

"Yeah, let's have a check. Don't get up it's fine" he said, moving over to her. He carefully brushed off her back, shoulders, and legs.

"That's far enough, bumpkin" she said, pulling back. "Thanks."

Raymond noticed a black nib protruding from Alexis's ankle.

"What about that?" he asked.

275

"What? Oh that…" she brushed it with her hand. "Just some skin tag I got. I think I banged it on a rock."

"That's a tick, darling" he said. "You better get that off."

The color drained from her face. "Shit, oh shit" she said, hyperventilating.

"So you can handle a dead body but you can't handle a tick? Whoa…wouldn't do that!"

"Get it off…get it offa me!" she yelled, yanking at the back of the parasite.

"Calm, darling calm. It ain't full yet. That means it's fresh" he said, reaching for his pack. He took out his alcohol-soaked cotton balls. "Let's start by cleaning that sucker up. Also this'll make him a little drunk." He applied the cotton ball to the tick's protruding body. "That should do it. Now, this'll feel a little weird but don't move."

He took out tweezers from his first aid kit. She was still breathing rapidly.

"Calm down" he said. "Don't move."

He got in close enough to smell the alcohol. The tick was not moving, but that did not mean it was dead. He carefully placed the tip of the tweezers at the very base of the protrusion, right next to the skin. Slowly, but consistently, he pulled, straight up.

"Ahhh!" she yelled. "That fucking hurts!"

276

"It only hurts in your mind" he said. "It's just pressure really…" He pulled the tick out of her ankle completely.

"Look…it's all there…lucky girl. You were squirming and everything. If that had ripped in half…"

"Don't tell me" she said. She was almost crying. He dropped the tick into the fire.

"Here, take another ball" he said, indicating that she should clean the wound. "You're a good patient" he said, rubbing her back for comfort. To his surprise, she didn't recoil.

"Thanks" she managed, coming back around to her usual, acerbic self. "Need a damned drink" she said, standing up quickly.

"Here" said Raymond, passing her the Colt .45 he had procured from the store. "Got me through some tough times."

"Well, as long as no one's looking" she said, taking the cap off, and taking a furtive sip. Her face twisted. "That's foul. No wonder you guys were all so pissed off all the time."

"Gets your blood up" he said, taking the bottle from her, having a swig for himself. "Your feet ready?" he asked. She nodded, and the pair packed up their gear to hit the road again.

They emerged near the road's namesake; the town of Cornelia. They decided that the south side of the highway would be the safest, finding reasonable passage on the shoulder, near the ditch. They took turns having sips from the bottle. Raymond hadn't had a drink since he first met Alexis, so the warmth of the alcohol absorption spread like wildfire through his body, making him smile.

He also noticed that Alexis was walking a bit more casually than usual. He even noticed her smile on occasion and reasoned that she was probably in the same phase of sobriety as he was. She began humming some tune from a popular artist.

Their bonhomie was broken up by the sound of an approaching vehicle. They began their usual dart to the tree line, except that it would be very close this time: there were no bends or dips in the road to mask their presence. Raymond was the first to the trees, but Alexis, with her injured feet, lacked the sprint necessary to make it in time. She dropped the bottle on the shoulder and attempted to cross the verge, but she tripped and fell. Raymond watched in horror as a brown Chevy Silverado pick up truck slowed, driving on the opposite side of the road to investigate. The driver had placed an illicit Dixie flag in the rear window of his truck. At once, Raymond relaxed; this was a friend.

He emerged from the forest as the man began to descend from the truck. He wore a camo hat, camo jacket, and jeans, which covered a pair of Laredo boots in snakeskin. He had about two days' beard growth that covered a tough, weather-beaten face of experience. Raymond felt an instant connection with the man, and rushed forward, almost forgetting that Alexis was lying in the ditch.

"You gonna leave a lady in the ditch, buddy?" came the man's voice. "Get your priorities straight."

"My bad" said Raymond, shuffling to get to Alexis before he did.

278

"Whoa whoa darling…easy there! You took a fierce durned dive!" came the voice. It reeked of alcohol. "Didn't expect to find any humans out here…" said the man.

"Well" said Alexis, nervously. "Here we are."

"A Yankee! All the way down here, walking upcountry Georgia? Damned if I ain't seen it all now. How'd you git all the way down here, darling?"

"Alexis" she said.

"Come again?"

"My name's Alexis – " Raymond got to her before the insult barrage could begin. To his amazement, he could see the man had a 1911 pistol tucked into his pants.

"Beau" he said, extending his hand, but then realizing Alexis would not take it, returned it to his hip. "What about you, soldier?"

"Ray" said Raymond. "Why'd ya say soldier?"

"Saw that bottle o' Colt .45, lying in the ditch, just like your lady" he said tersely. "Figured you all knew what was what."

"Well, you got that one right" said Raymond, proudly, although hamming it up to impress his new confederate. "Saw your pistol" he said.

"Oh, this old thing?" Beau smiled. "It's a replica, your honor, swear" he said, mockingly putting his fingers in the air as if swearing to God. "But I wouldn't wanna test that today." The smile had dropped from his face.

"Where y'all headed? And why y'all walkin there?" he asked.

"Gainesville" said Raymond, not wishing to disclose their final destination.

"Well shoot...y'all r' in luck" he said, smiling again. "Darling, do you really wanna huff it all the way down to Gainesville? Gotta be at least another thirty miles."

"Depends" she said, goadingly. "You know how to drive that truck like a man?" She winked.

Raymond was shocked, and a little afraid. The smile dropped off Beau's face.

"Depends" he said, leaning in to Raymond, rather unsteadily. "You two like, ya know...?"

"Friends" said Alexis, definitively. "Are we ridin' or do you two lovebirds want some more time to get to know each other?"

The smile returned to Beau's face. "Right this way, ma'am...got some Southern hospitality lined up for ya right here" he said, gesturing to the truck. They both followed him. "I'll keep ya safe, right here...no buddy, shotgun's for the lady...you get cozy in the back." Fortunately, it was an extended cab so Raymond did not have to rub shoulders with this man, who was rapidly falling out of his good graces. At the same time, it was a convenient ride that, he hoped, would serve the double function of getting where they needed to be without revealing themselves to the machines.

The truck smelled of booze. Raymond got in, looking on the floor to see a fifth of Wild Turkey nearly empty. A duffle bag was half opened with some zip-close bags stuffed inside. Raymond pushed the front seat back so that Alexis could sit. He could see that she was tense. Beau got in, slamming the truck into gear and screeching the truck down the road toward Gainesville. Beau said something to Alexis, who shook her head, and Raymond realized the man had another bottle of Wild Turkey opened in the front.

He leaned forward. "So what brings you out this way, Beau?"

"Huntin'" he said. "Mostly trophies."

"Uh huh" said Raymond, looking around. He didn't want to look in the back.

"So how come you fine feathered folk didn't go the way of the zombies?" he asked.

"Zombies?" said Alexis.

"You know, the little robot-demon-folk they got running around. Don't see no implants" he said.

"Didn't want anyone messing with my mind…got enough problems up there" said Alexis, loud enough so Raymond could hear.

"Know exactly what'cha mean, darling. We gotta keep it together" he said, tapping his head. The truck was going exceedingly fast, but Beau seemed to slow down as he would pass any parked car, house, or building. A cross dangled from his rear-view mirror. "Keep it pure" he added, turning up the music a little. The song

Drunk Me began playing. They drove on for about half an hour before Raymond spoke.

"The world's gone to shit, hasn't it?" said Raymond.

"Don't cuss in front of a lady" said Beau, taking a swig from his bottle. "Don't bother me none. I do what I want, when I want…just like always. All we gotta do is make the world pure again. What about you, buddy?"

He decided that admitting he was a writer or creative-type would not improve his standing with this man. "Well, after the war, I decided to get away and help my gramps" he lied.

"War? You a soldier?"

"Nah, the Civil War. 45er tried n' true" he said, chest-beating in the hopes of remaining on Beau's favorable side.

"Well I loved Trump, despite him givin' his daughter over to the Jews. Wouldn't die for him though…he ain't right with the Lord, divorcing, adultery, supportin' fags gettin' married n' all…for me it was more about stickin' it to those liberal bastards up in Washington…sorry honey didn't mean to go off like that."

Raymond put a hand on Alexis's shoulder to calm her.

"…he was a good tool, but a dirty one. Pence woulda been great 'cept he got co-opted by the Devil."

"He said 'God was in the machine', didn't he?" asked Alexis. It was the conversational equivalent of pushing the barrel of a gun down that you knew was going to go off.

"Ain't no God in that machine" said Beau. "Even him, whose coming is after the working of Satan with all power and signs and lying wonders, And with all deceivableness of unrighteousness in them that perish; because they received not the love of the truth, that they might be saved."

"You're saying that people aren't getting the love of the truth? They seem to love what they have, Satan or not" said Alexis.

"They might be saved" said Beau. "It's me who's savin' em from the Devil. Shapeshifting and hidin' himself in these poor sheep."

"How're you gonna do that?"

He paused a moment. "By the grace of God" he said. He turned his head and gestured in the direction of the duffle bag next to Raymond. "I'm healin' them one at a time."

Raymond cautiously opened the bag. He saw what looked like some kind of meshy circuitry coated with a milky, pinkish substance inside each of the plastic sacs, stirring some uncomfortable thought. His head was swimming from the malt liquor, and he decided not to ask anything further, choosing instead to lean over on the window and close his eyes. The man was crazy, evidently, but the crazy was pointed somewhere else, and Alexis's presence seemed to temper his commentary. Jim Reeves came on the stereo, and the soft voice singing the words "he'll have to go…" carried him off to sleep.

Raymond awoke to the sound of screeching truck tires, violently shaken awake as he flew helplessly into the front seat. He did not have his seatbelt on and his face paid the price, bloodying his nose momentarily.

"What the goddamned hell are you doing?" screamed Alexis.

"Don't blaspheme" said Beau, reaching behind his seat, then looking left and right. "Y'all sit tight. I'm going up off the road apiece. Got a chance to save a soul."

They had driven into the outskirts of some town, probably Gainesville, Raymond realized. They were parked by the side of a park where a woman from the World was sitting on a bench, laughing obliviously at something on her stream. In another place, at another time, she would have been called a crazy person. Beau took out a crossbow from behind the seat and knocked an arrow into place. It became clear what he meant by salvation.

They watched in horror as he crept up behind the woman on the bench. Just before she could turn around, he loosed an arrow, striking her in the shoulder, just above her heart. She flew up into the air with her super strong legs, landing back down on the ground in a heap, shrieking.

Alexis and Raymond jumped out of the truck.

"What the hell are you doing?" screamed Raymond, running beside Alexis as they approached.

"Saving souls" said Beau, calmly, watching the Woman from the World writhe on the ground like a stuck pig, screaming. "If you hit 'em fast they don't have a chance to call their Master or shapeshift. Then, we exorcise the demons."

"You're outta your goddamned mind" said Raymond, walking over to the woman.

"Don't go" said Alexis, meekly, stopping him. "Don't go or she'll see."

"I don't think she's connected..." said Raymond. "The last time..."

"You really wanna take that chance?" said Alexis.

"Yeah" said Raymond, shaking off her grip. "Yeah I do."

Alexis rolled her eyes and started after him. The woman had stopped crying out but was still squirming on the ground, by the swings. There was a chance to save her, thought Raymond, so long as he could keep that knife away from her. He now knew what was in those sacks, and he cringed in horror.

"Hey..." yelled Raymond. "Hey! Beau!"

"Yes, gorgeous?" said Beau, now brandishing a hunting knife.

"I know what you're doing. I know what you think you're doing, but you can't do it" he said, definitively, trying to draw his attention away.

"I know what I'm doing" said Beau. "It's not up to me, Ray. These are God's Tools" he said, looking down at his hands, clutching the knife. "Nothin' going on here but the Work of the Lord" he said.

"*Forgive him Father, for he knows not what he does,*" thought Raymond, yelling to the sky, hoping his invocation of scripture would be enough to arrest the murderous advance.

"This looks mighty savage, don't it, Ray? It's the only way…we gotta cut that demon outta her to make her right with God 'fore she passes."

"She don't have to pass…she ain't gonna if we just take out the arrow and let her go. She'll probably heal up all on her own…you've seen 'em? God's own miracles hard at work!" pleaded Raymond, grabbing Beau by the elbow. Beau surprised Raymond, flipping him onto his back in a thud, holding the knife to his throat. This would be an uneven fight.

"Blasphemer! You take that back, in the name of the Lord!" yelled Beau, breath reeking of alcohol and rage.

"Beau, it's not up to us to try to fix this mess…this is bigger n' us."

"I ain't 'us' Ray. God is us…God's bigger than us… I's with God, these are God's hands. You're better not to cross Him." Beau smiled, seemingly basking in some invisible light.

Suddenly, Alexis appeared behind Beau, boxcutter in hand. She had the blade extended almost fully, pressed against Beau's carotid artery. "You feelin' God's hand now? What about some cold steel from a liberal lesbian bitch? Drop the knife." He obliged, and

286

the blade fell with a dull thud. Alexis took the Crossbow off his back and the pistol from his belt. She tossed the former to Raymond and pointed the latter at Beau's head.

"You do what you gotta to get right with God. When you seen as much as me, you'll say it to yourself...' Beau was right...Beau was walking with the Lord.'"

"Beau can walk with the Lord but he better start runnin'. We're takin' your truck."

"I'll finish her, when you're gone...I'll finish her" said Beau, motioning to the woman on the ground. "Wait...where's her Holy Lance?" he asked. "You've DENIED this woman salvation!"

Alexis and Raymond were already walking back towards the truck. Beau kept his hands up.

"While you were busy preachin', I was busy yankin' out that arrow. Good luck."

"You can't do this! A thousand curses on your immortal soul!"

"Save your curses. Use those legs. Run" she said, motioning with the gun. "That way."

Raymond and Alexis got in the truck and started driving away. They turned to see Beau running across the field. Amazingly, the woman's Integrated Tech had healed her, bringing her back from the dead. She was chasing Beau across the field like a cheetah homing in on a wounded gazelle. She leaped fifteen feet to close the gap, landing on Beau's back, knocking him down in one fell swoop.

"Don't look" said Raymond.

"No…I wanna see" said Alexis. "Jesus…the meek shall inherit the Earth" she said, and she watched as the woman began pounding on Beau with her fists, blood flying in the air. "Hell hath no fury like a woman stuck" she said.

"Alexis…" said Raymond.

"Yeah?" said Alexis, still looking in the direction of the macabre scene.

"I don't wanna know" he said. "Take that duffle bag and throw it out. And the crossbow."

"What?" she said.

"Throw that bag out!" he yelled. "It's full of implants. And the crossbow!"

She reached behind Raymond, grabbing the sack, then throwing it out on to the field.

Raymond drove cautiously, turning south towards the Cloud 9 Motel at the edge of town.

"We gotta ditch this hickmobile" said Alexis. "How much farther?"

"Not far…like a mile" he said, pulling the truck into the driveway of a storage facility a twenty-minute walk from the hotel, but not all the way up, in case cameras were covering the parking lot.

288

They quickly searched the truck, finding a few extra magazines for the pistol. They grabbed their bags and headed toward the Cloud 9 Motel sign, under which a black and white letter sign with changeable letters read "LAY DOWN YOUR BURDENS."

Alexis went first, as usual, while Raymond waited at the edge of the parking lot. She re-emerged and waved Raymond inside. He obliged, running across to her. Before he got within the throw of the light, he yelled to her "what about cameras?"

"Fakes" she said back. "Besides, they got eyes-on, remember? Come on!"

He jogged inside. Alexis shushed him. "Where's the help?" he whispered.

"In the back" she said, gesturing to the office behind the reception desk. They could both hear a male voice laughing and speaking to no one. Raymond peeked a little further and saw a man sitting straight-backed on a chair, staring at a wall. "ohhh yeah" came his voice, then "hee hee hee" later.

"I programmed these key cards" she said, moving around the desk. "Take a look at the floor plan…206 and 208, right at the end of the hall, by the stairs if we have to ditch."

"Connected rooms?" asked Raymond.

"Don't get your hopes up" said Alexis. "I don't think either one of us is in any place for that."

"No…" said Raymond. "Just in case" he said stoically.

They walked down the corridors casually, not expecting to see anyone.

"We better move it along" said Raymond. "Any one of these doors could pop open and out comes a 'zombie'" he said. They went up the stairs and through the fire door, finding their room doors on the right.

"This is me" said Alexis. "Sleep fast…we'll get movin' at first light."

Raymond nodded, and started in the direction of his room.

"Hey" said Alexis, calling after him. "That was really good, what you did."

"Thanks" he said. "I'd be done for if you hadn't 've jumped in."

"I mean, you got a good heart. Your brother's lucky to have you" she said.

Raymond managed to smile. The day's horrors were obviously catching up with both of them. Alexis, to Raymond's amazement, started crying. He started toward her. She waved him away.

"No, it's fine. I'm good" she said.

"You need a drink" he said. "I'm going to my room to get cleaned up. I'll knock on your door in ten."

"No more of that malt liquor shit, please" she said.

"No...this one's on Beau" he said, grabbing the neck of a Wild Turkey bottle he had taken from Beau's truck before they ditched it. "Figured we'd need some medicine if we were gonna sleep any tonight."

Alexis smiled. "Get outta the hall" she said. "See you in a few."

Raymond entered his room and was happy to see that it had been made up. The bed looked cozy and had been turned down, as though they were expecting him. It was probably the plushest accommodation he'd had in years. The air conditioner was set to an unbearably cold temperature; probably because no one had stayed in the room since the summer. He turned off the AC at the thermostat then turned on the TV. *DO YOU WISH TO INTERFACE INFOSTREAMS?* came the superfluous prompt on the screen. This television was obviously from an earlier phase of INtegrity where users could choose to mix broadcast television into their infostreams. He clicked 'NO', wondering why hotel television technology always seems to lag the rest of the world by about five years.

He left it on the default hotel channel that showed the account for the room and the options. A male voice extolled the virtues of the hotel, along with various business and massage services that Raymond would never engage. He just wanted some familiar electronic noise in order to feel normal. He could hear that Alexis had already started her shower thanks to the sound of water running in the pipes. He prayed for hot water.

Entering the bathroom, Raymond stripped off all his clothes, using the sink to wash out his socks and underwear. Fortunately, the room had plenty of soap, shampoo, and towels. He reached over and turned on the shower. To his chagrin, the water came out ice-cold. He sighed, then examined the tap more closely and realized that he had merely misinterpreted the direction of "HOT." The bathroom began to fill with steam as hot water rained down upon him. If this was the world, he could live in it, provided that he was thrown these little miracles here and then. The pleasure and relief that he felt overwhelmed him. He wept a little, sobbing as the water cascaded down his chest. He was reminded of the war, that strange set of circumstances that allowed a man to exist in a world of abject brutality and quaint domesticity on the same day. There wasn't much left in this world for him, he thought. Then he thought of Mitch. He found the soap, got scrubbing, then got out to find clean towels and a full bathrobe, along with a pair of slippers, in the closet. He donned these, grabbed the bottle of Wild Turkey, and went over to the double doors separating the rooms.

Chapter 22

"Well, man, it's a piece of shit" came the voice on the phone. "I don't know what to tell you."

It was Evan James screaming in Raymond's ear. Things were not going well. Raymond was staring at a computer screen that was projecting a short video that Raymond had edited together. When James yelled at him on the phone, he always seemed to be in front of a computer monitor and tended to fixate on the individual pixels as a form of Zen meditation, taking him away from the caustic remarks and lowering his blood pressure.

"Well…" he started, more as a placeholder to say he was still listening and less that he was about to say something to his mentor. "…we…"

"We need to redo the whole damned thing" he said. "And by 'we', I mean 'you.'"

Silence. The background image on Raymond's screen changed to a serene valley.

"I'm on it, sir" said Raymond meekly. "I'll have something to you after lunch."

"Good" said James. "Don't eat a damned thing until you've got something respectable. We're getting to the end here, Ray, and I don't want it falling apart in the final frame."

"Mmm hmm" said Raymond, trying to mask his frustration.

"God Bless you" said James. "God Bless your family."

The remark caught Raymond off-guard.

"Thank you" he said, but it almost sounded like a question.

"I mean it. Remember your family" he said. The line clicked off.

Raymond stared blankly ahead for a moment. He thought of the country he wanted to live in. He thought of the country that so many had died for. He remembered. And then, he worked.

He worked for hours. He worked through bathroom breaks or snacks. The AI monitoring tried on multiple occasions to alert him to things, but he merely switched off the sound.

He worked through the rooster crowing. He barely noticed the blinking proximity alert.

Chapter 23

Alexis opened her side of the double door, clad in her own bathrobe and slippers.

"Not so bad, bumpkin" she said. "Come on in."

Raymond entered.

"Have a seat" she said. Raymond started toward the couch, but Alexis gestured to the small table by the air conditioner. He set the bottle on the table.

"Should we risk ice?" he asked, finding a pair of glasses near the coffee maker.

"Nah" said Alexis. "I don't dilute my toxins."

They both sat at the table and cracked open the bottle. It hadn't been touched by its former owner. Raymond carefully poured an ounce into each glass, then looked at Alexis, who, using her thumb and forefinger, measured an inch more. Raymond obliged her, pouring another ounce into her glass, and another into his, to keep it equal.

They exchanged sighs, looking out the window at nothing, since the light from their room was so bright it caused a reflection. Alexis closed the blinds.

"You know what?" said Raymond, on to his second drink.

"What?" said Alexis.

"I never said thank you" he said, sipping the second drink more judiciously.

"Don't mention it" she said. "This is as much for me as it is for you and your brother. There was no way I was staying behind a goddamned wall. Whoa..." she added, pulling her glass back from Raymond's refill.

"Yeah, you're a real humanitarian" said Raymond, smiling. "Why'd you save that woman back there?"

"I didn't save that woman; I wanted to kill Beau but couldn't bring myself to do it."

"Poor old Beau" he said. "Hope he's found some peace."

"I'm sure that woman ripped him apart like the trash he is" she said. "That's my peace. No place in this world for animals like that."

Raymond sipped.

"So what's the plan for tomorrow?" he asked.

"Was gonna ask you the same thing" she said, sitting down, letting her crossed legs protrude from her bathrobe provocatively. They were delicate yet adorned with viney tattoos that ran up her thighs. Her feet, unfortunately, bore the scars of dozens of miles of hard trekking. She noticed him admiring her.

"Been a while, huh?" she said, playfully.

Raymond, ashamed, went to pour another drink, although he had barely finished his current glass.

"Why don't you grab the map?" she said, smiling.

"Yeah" he said tersely, getting up and crossing over to his room, then returning with the hastily folded map.

"I figure" he began, unfolding the map and laying it on the table, placing his glass on one corner. "If we stick to US 23 all the way down..." he followed the line with his finger. "...we'll make City Limits by nightfall. Then, we keep moving to Tuxedo Park."

Alexis made a face. "Tuxedo Park? Sounds oppressive."

"It's pretty swanky...you'd hate it" said Raymond. "It also happens to be where my ex-wife's family home is. At least, that's where the alimony's been going and it hasn't bounced back yet."

"Alimony? You must've had a pretty shit lawyer" she said.

"Well, that's a long story. Anyways, if I know them, there's probably a few cars gassed up and ready-to-go. My old father-in-law hated the electrics."

"Alright. But they're just gonna give you one? After all these years?"

"I can be persuasive" he said. "I still talk to the mom on occasion. She loves me despite, well, everything."

"What happened, Ray? Were you a bad boy?" she said, being jokingly seductive. She touched his leg with her toe.

"Wasn't nothin like that" he said, standing up suddenly, offended. "Not right away" he drank.

"Sorry" she said, stunned. "Didn't mean anything by it. Just messin' around."

"It's alright" he said. "Look, we better get some sleep and not get too wasted. We gotta get moving before sunrise."

"You better set your alarm. I'm a bitch to get outta bed in the morning" she said.

"Just in the morning?" asked Raymond, trying to joke. He drained his glass and set it on the table. "G'night."

"Hey Ray..." said Alexis, standing up. She walked over to him, giving him a hug and a kiss on the cheek. "Thanks for the clean sheets" she said.

"Don't mention it" he said, looking her in the eye momentarily, then backing off and closing the partition door behind him. He leaned against it briefly, hyperventilating. He slowly collapsed at the base of the door, in tears. The memories that had taken a leave over the past few weeks were now beginning to seep back in with each passing mile on the road to Atlanta. He tried to think of them, to process, but it was all he could do to resist going into the other room and draining the bottle.

Chapter 24

Third, fourth, fifth...he had lost count. The din of the bar had flooded into his mind. He hoped it would drown out the voice of the woman he was using for comfort. He didn't want to hear her thoughts or opinions but sought out the adulation from her face to warm him and make him forget. Phil had this red light that he turned on after 10 pm to "sexy-up the mood" as he said. It had the unfortunate consequence of making that which should be seen as hideous passably attractive.

Words were spoken; charms, like drinks, spilled. His mouth was on a glass; her mouth was then on his. An unfamiliar mouth that tasted of desperation and neglect, along with copious amounts of gin. A question about a ring. Then: "Aren't you that guy from the news stories?" she would ask. "No" he would say. "It's all wrong. I was OK. We were OK."

The restroom at Phil's was always clean. Seemed like a reasonable destination. As private as it was public. Nobody took note as Raymond pushed his comfort into the men's room and leaned against the door. He chose not to look; the warm red of the bar was gone now. Instead, he chose to stare at the harsh LED light, hoping the buzz from the extractor fan would drown out the sickening sounds of momentary pleasure and fleeting acceptance.

He had tried. He was the best version of himself, in that moment, and in this moment, the worst. He thought back to that day as he was pressed against the restroom door. He thought about Josiah and how he had tried. He thought about running, racing, when he realized, too late. Hope against hope. Prayers flew from his mouth as he descended the stairs and out the door. Time had slowed down at that moment. He was running through a morass of his own self-absorbed ignorance with leaden feet. He would give anything for a few more of those minutes, a few extra steps, panting. At this moment, he just wished she would hurry up and finish.

The door began to push against his back. Raymond resisted, hoping to keep out the interlopers. Then, came Alexis's voice.

"Raymond…Raymond! Just got a knock at the door. They're comin' in!"

Raymond shook his head and came to. He had fallen asleep at the bottom of the door. He rolled over and grabbed the door handle, letting Alexis inside. She burst in, carrying her bag and all her clothes, clad in her bathrobe. Raymond closed the door quickly behind her.

"No! The other door too!" she yelled. "Quick!"

"Oh" said Raymond, opening the door in order to close the other one. The morning light had come. Raymond had forgotten to set his alarm clock.

Just as he did that, he heard an ominous knock and a call of "housekeeping!" at Alexis's door, a female voice. There was a 'click' and the door began opening. Raymond slowly and quietly shut the door, holding back the handle and slowly releasing the mechanism to avoid noise. He could hear the maid coming in, entering the bathroom, flushing the toilet, and turning on all the lights.

"Did you get everything?" he asked.

"Yeah!" said Alexis. "She shouldn't…oh shit…the booze."

Raymond leaned his ear against the door. The maid had stopped. Then he heard her voice again, talking to someone elsewhere.

"Tony? You check in anyone last night?" came the voice.

"Huh" she said. "Someone left a glass and bottle. Two glasses…" she said. "No, Tony…stop it! Haha stop or I'll put you on limited…"

"She's talking to someone" whispered Raymond to Alexis.

The maid continued. "Listen, Tony, when you're done there, can you tell Pedram to just do a few walk-arounds? Would make me feel better."

"Whoever Pedram is…is coming up here to do a walk-around" said Raymond.

"Probably security. We gotta get out" said Alexis. "And not be seen. Get your stuff and let's go."

Raymond began gathering up his backpack. Alexis began to disrobe.

"Look away, would'ya?" she said, causing Raymond a small pang of guilt even though he hadn't done anything.

Raymond smirked a little, sliding into the bathroom to do his own quick change. The items he had sink-washed were dry, thankfully, and he put them on hurriedly. He heard a whisper at the bathroom door: "Come on!" said Alexis. He opened the door to see her fully dressed, backpack on. They moved to the door. Alexis took the lead, opening it slightly, peering into the corridor.

"Ok…there's nobody there. The cleaning cart is outside my room so just stay low and hit the stairs."

Raymond followed close behind, quietly letting the door close behind him, staying crouched as Alexis scurried toward the fire door and the stairs.

The maid was humming, and the occasional laugh would issue from the room as she cleaned but did not notice as they crept by her cart. They caught a glimpse of her, and it reminded Raymond of trips they had taken to Florida. There was nothing to discern her from any other maid in any other hotel, except that her cerebellum was processing terabytes of data on a continual basis. Alexis pressed the bar on the fire door, quietly pushing it open against the pneumatic piston that held it closed. Raymond leaped in behind her and froze as she guided the door back to its closed position, taking care to hold down the latch and release it slowly upon closure. They sat for a moment. Alexis opened her palm in Raymond's direction. They froze for a moment. They could hear heavy footfalls as someone slowly began their ascent.

"Up!" said Alexis, and the pair leaped quietly up the next flight of stairs and waited in the landing. The footsteps kept coming.

"Ooooooh" said the voice. "That's a bad girl!" It was a male voice, talking via infostreams to some unknown person…or thing. The footsteps kept coming.

"Get back a little" said Alexis, pushing Raymond behind the next flight of stairs, obscuring them from view.

"He won't notice us" said Raymond. Alexis shushed him.

"They got superpowers, remember? He may seem like Johnny Rent-a-cop but…well, remember your buddy Beau."

Raymond nodded. "So what's the plan?"

"Wait for him to go in at our floor, then run out. Simple" she said.

The guard seemed to stop his upward motion as the footsteps paused. Then another guttural laugh. "You just keep that up! Keep me up!" he said. Alexis and Raymond suppressed their urge to giggle. He loudly opened the door. "Macy! You done messing around up here?"

"I can't understand it" came the female voice, the maid. "I open the door and…" The fire door shut, cutting them off from the rest of the conversation.

"Ok" said Alexis. "Stay low, get out, head for the trees on the other side of the parking lot."

They scampered down the stairs, keeping their heads low under the window of the fire door. They heard the guard laughing and chatting with the maid. They ran down the second-last flight, rounding the corner to the last. The fire door flung open.

"Hey you!" came the voice. "Stop!"

Alexis kicked Raymond down the rest of the stairs.

"Don't look up!" she said. "Fight it!"

By then, the guard had flung open the door and was on them. His enthusiasm overwhelmed his sense of safety. He leaped after them, just as they blasted out of the last door to the parking lot. They heard a sickening 'crunch' as the guard hit the last landing. Raymond turned, looking in the floor to ceiling window to see the guard crumpled in a pile on the landing. They heard terrific cries coming from the stairwell. Raymond realized that the man had shattered his ankle or some other part under the pressure of his overzealous jump.

"Come on" said Alexis. "He'll be fine. Keep running! And stop looking! Once he catches a glimpse of us, it's over."

"Ceres!" came the cry before the door shut. "I need help!"

They had already cleared the parking lot and found the trees, carefully climbing down into a ravine. They stopped a moment to sit down and catch their breath.

"Ok" said Raymond. "That wasn't so bad."

As soon as he spoke, he heard a crashing in the forest as if a bear had caught their scent and was pursuing them.

"It's Pedram" said Alexis. "Looks like he's fine again."

"I know you guys are in here" he said. "I can't read your streams but that doesn't mean you're not here. You can't stay at the Cloud 9 for free!"

They could hear the crunch of branches and leaf matter as Pedram began his stalk. Raymond imagined him leaping from tree to tree like something out of a teenage vampire movie.

310

"Boy he's really committed to his job" said Raymond in disbelief.

"Shhhh" said Alexis. "He's right up there, on us."

The voice came right from the top of the ridge, above the ravine: "You can come out for me or you can come out for Ceres. Trust me, I'm wayyy gentler" he said. Then, in a tone of resignation: "Alright...I gave you the chance." Silence. Raymond imagined the infostream call out to authority. "Good luck to you" said Pedram, whose stalk ended as quickly as it had begun.

"They'll be coming" said Alexis. "We gotta make tracks."

"Or try not to" said Raymond. "Try not to turn stuff over or they'll be able to track us way easier."

They walked quickly through a clearing, headed to the small stream that ran through the ravine.

"Which way, bumpkin? We lost a lot of time today because tired little teddy forgot his damned alarm."

"Well...we gotta get south and west" he pulled out his map. "I was gonna say head up to the main road but I think we better scrap that and stick to the 985."

"Why?"

"After our little discovery, I think we better stay near tree cover in case they send out more drones. They're probably connecting us with Beau."

"Alright, CSI, tell me your theories when we get to safety" said Alexis, urging him forward. "Which way?"

"Follow the stream south" he said. "That way."

"Hope you know what you're doing, bumpkin."

"Uh-huh" he said, deadpan.

"So tell me why they – Jesus, that was quick!"

The buzz of a drone announced that Ceres had taken Pedram's call seriously. It sounded for all the world like a flight of bumblebees darting to and fro, moving from one tree stand to another, right over the area they had just been. Raymond and Alexis scurried from the stream to a denser stand of trees and stopped moving.

Raymond continued. "Think about it. They found Beau – what's left of him – detained the woman, probably got some verbal information about us, found the truck – "

The buzz came closer and they hugged into the earth. It was systematically setting up grids and searching them thoroughly.

"Found the truck then got the call from our super-rent-a-cop friend."

"So we're wanted" said Alexis.

"We were always wanted. We were wanted the moment we said no to INtegrity."

The buzz intensified as the craft lowered to the creek bed. The machine seemed to focus on a few rocks where moss had been scraped off by their footfalls. It could not decide on a direction and seemed to arbitrarily decide to move north.

"Lucky" said Raymond. "One more footprint and he woulda had us."

"Don't know if I can keep this up, Ray" said Alexis, head down, staring at the creek. "They got us."

"Waddaya mean?" asked Raymond. "I thought you were all 'fuck-the-man and never-give-up' hippie badass?"

"You can't beat the machines, Ray. Not like this. We're just a bunch of apes trying to not get poached."

"Exactly" said Raymond. "Poachers ain't got no right to take what's not theirs."

Alexis grimaced.

"We stole this" he said, gesturing to his body, then hers. "We kept these free, from them."

"What are we fighting, anyway?" she said. "They look so happy. They just sit there like a bunch of stoners, content in their own little fantasies."

"We can't" he said. "We literally can't join 'em."

"Oh I know" she said. "I just don't want to fight them anymore."

"So this is what you liberals do when it gets too hard? Just...quit? Just give in?"

Alexis seemed to perk up a little.

313

"We weren't up against machines…it was a pack of drunk Trumpies" she said. "They – you – just wanted to bring misery to our country, to prop up that orange fool, for spite. And frankly, beating you guys was not that hard" she said. "You know what? You're probably never gonna see your brother again. Probably someone up there decided to see if they could use him as an experimental test subject or something. Probably running wires into his brain to see if it can be done. No one'll miss him. They'll just blame the storm." She began getting up, then walking away.

"It wasn't for spite" he said, sloughing off the last remark. "It was for freedom." He started after her, facing her. A tear began to well up in her eye. "We had a country once, Alexis, you and I, and we had elections. You may not have liked the outcome but we suffered too many damned fools."

"Stop preaching" said Alexis. "The war's over. The country's over." She raised her hands, slapping them on her thighs on the return.

"I can't stop you from leaving. But just know that I'm gonna keep going. You've done more than any person had to or should've."

"Stubborn as a brick" she said. "But you're welcome, I guess."

"As long as – "

"Stop" she said. "I'm going now. I'll distract the drone for ya."

Raymond turned to walk away. Alexis stopped him, giving him a hug.

314

"What were you gonna say?"

"As long as one of us is free, there is still freedom."

"Yeah…well I guess that's your torch to bear" she said. Raymond paused.

"Thank you" said Raymond. "For not saying cross."

"Cross?"

"My cross to bear" he said.

"Figure you had enough of those already" she said, wryly. "You were crying in your sleep, by the door."

Raymond turned away again, walking down the stream. Alexis was a miracle, but she, like all of us, he thought, had her limits. It wasn't her brother, and it wasn't her struggle. He picked up the pace and found some rocks with no moss on them, trying to stay within range of the water as to cover up his tracks from the drone-hounds that would be on his trail. He heard a splashing sound.

"Let's bear it together" said Alexis, running up from behind him. "I've stood up to winter in Boston-I don't back down for nothin'."

He smiled, chasing after her as they splashed from rock-to-rock, like kids looking for toads. It was the happiest he had been in years. He remembered a quote from a documentary about the Civil War, from Sam Houston, who talked about how Northerners come from colder climates, and that when they move in a given direction, they move with the steady momentum and perseverance of a mighty avalanche. He was glad to be swept up and carried by it.

Chapter 25

The spotlight cut across Evan James's face as he took to the microphone. He had chosen as his evening attire an ancient tuxedo that fit well, several years ago. The music cut out suddenly. The audio tech/DJ/photographer fumbled with the mixer, trying to get the microphone to go live. A second of feedback announced that James could speak.

"Friends" he started. "I just want to start by saying that if I had my way, all of y'all would be welcomed in a massive parade headed down Peachtree Street. We'd build monuments to each and every one of our units."

Raymond cringed a little. There was nothing natural about the y'all.

"The war is over. Tonight, we drink to history. Tonight, we drink to all those who stood up to tyranny and were cut down by the vile forces of oppression. Tonight, we drink to a future where freedom reigns supreme. Tonight...we remember that we will be there, watching, protecting that freedom as we always have."

He found a glass loaded with champagne near the lectern. The 45er veterans had rented a suburban Atlanta high school gym celebrating the end of the war. They were not supposed to bring alcohol into the venue, but the principal was sympathetic, and told custodial staff to turn a blind eye. Many of them partook in the somber celebration, topping up the punchbowls with the requisite spiritual fortification. The buffet was a tribute to southern cuisine: cornbread, grits, okra, and fried chicken. The men – and it was largely men – avoided the green and preferred the taupe-colored food.

Raymond was slumped in a chair at a table by the front. They wanted to use only the moody rental lights, but they had to concede to fire regulations that one strip of fluorescent lights be left on, giving it all the ambiance of a grade school dance. James finished his speech with a toast.

"These are desperate times, once again. We celebrate the end of the war, but it is not the beginning of peace. We will lay down our guns, but we will never lay down our vigilance. Raise our glasses, and forever remember…Donald J. Trump, the last democratically elected president of the Free World!"

A drunken 'yeah' emerged from the crowd as the 45ers raised their glasses of beer, wine, and of course, 45 Colt malt liquor.

"Never forget! 45 forever!" he yelled. The crowd was mildly pleased with this, but the applause was lukewarm, and his pitch was about thirty percent more than they were ready for. James, sensing the tide of approval turning, descended from the stage to mingle, leaving the DJ to fill the soundscape with nostalgic music. Ted Nugent was the obvious choice.

"Forever" yelled Raymond, raising his soda in James's direction. James made a scrunched-up face, smiling at Raymond, plunking down next to him on a folding chair, testing its load-bearing capabilities.

"Ray-Ray, I miss you" he said. "I know you've been through some stuff."

"Been through" said Raymond, nodding in the direction of his drink.

320

"But we've been through stuff. We've fought the good fight. I just wish it wasn't so bittersweet for you."

A pregnant pause. Raymond sucked out a piece of ice and rolled it around his mouth. James cleared his throat and continued.

"Hey. The war's over. Wanna drink? I know you said you were waiting" he asked.

"Waiting for victory. If this is victory, it sure as fuck doesn't feel like it" said Raymond, spitting his ice cube back into the red party cup.

"Whoa. Never heard you swear before. About fucking time!" exclaimed James, excitedly, clinking plastic with his confederate. "Better top you up with something real."

Raymond raised a hand.

"Way ahead of ya" he said, pointing at his cup.

"Well color me impressed. We have arrived!"

James drained his champagne. "A guy in PR I know once told me to learn to drink heavily when you're an object of public scorn, while you're going through the journalistic ringer. I learned that quick. I see you found that lesson too."

Raymond finished his cup and stared blankly ahead. James reached out and patted his leg.

"It's not your fault, Ray. It can't be your fault. There's a thousand things that can go wrong in a day. It's just...shitty circumstance."

Raymond glanced at James's hand on his leg, and James instinctively withdrew. He reflected for a moment, then continued.

"We can't always understand the reason for things" said James, leaning in. He had been drinking heavily himself. "God presents us with these obstacles and we just have to, you know, trust in Him."

Their eyes met for a moment.

"You proud, Evan?" asked Raymond. "You proud of what you created?"

James bit.

"Well, if you mean this movement, these ideas, these men…then yeah, I'd say I'm damned proud."

"Good, I'm glad. Because I'm proud, too" said Raymond, shaking the ice in his cup. James nodded. "Proud of my family, proud of my wife, and yes, fucking proud of my son. He..he was just a little slow to get moving, ya know?"

He stood up. Raymond was yelling at this point and they were between songs. The DJ tried to hurry along another song to keep the evening humming along.

"Proud that I served my country…" he flung a chunk of ice at James. "Proud that I stood up for what's right" and another. "Proud that, despite being surrounded by a pack of bigoted losers, I helped with my words and ideas and not just bullets."

One of the 45ers piped up. He wore a MAGA hat and yellow sunglasses. "Hey we all did our part there, Raymond…you ain't the only one…"

"Who lost? Lost the cause, or lost everything? I don't see your name in the paper there, Nelson. Where the hell were you when the press was knocking on my door? Do you get to buy milk without people looking at you, then at their phone, then making a face at you? Do you get to be alone with your grief?"

He flung a few more pieces of ice as he talked, at no one in particular. He began stumbling around, using folding chairs as feeble support while he continued his oration.

"Let me tell you about grief" said Raymond, putting his hand on the shoulders of a few of the men he had just thrown ice at. "Grief is family to me now. Grief is…grief is comfort." He moved to another table. "Grief is my friend. Grief is my God now, and I am the sacrifice, fed into his fiery belly every God Damned Day. Grief is my baby." Tears streamed down his face.

"You need to sit down now, Ray." James was up on his feet. "You're having a terrible time. Just remember your media training. I can be your spokesman if you like…just let me at those dipshit reporters."

"The only thing I need" Raymond said, cutting him off, slamming a fist on the table he was leaning over. He stared James dead in the eye. "Is for you all to do three things: first of all, fuck off with your lost cause, second, leave me the hell alone, and third…die."

Two 45ers, tasked as door security, were about to help Raymond out of the gym. He brushed them off, "I'm alright now…I'm going" he said, stumbling.

One of the veterans yelled. "And maybe burn in hell on your way out!"

Raymond stopped, and turned. It was Jack, a fiery redhead from Greenville, Raymond's home town. They went to the same high school. He grinned at his success in getting this traitor's attention.

"Oh hey, Jack!" said Raymond, slowly walking toward the fiend. "Tell me all about Hell."

"I don't know about what it's like but I know there's a special place for traitors like you."

"Let me tell you about Hell, Jacky. Hell is hot, Hell has walls, and Hell is right here, staring you in the face. And now…" Raymond leaped at him, clutching him by his cheap, Sunday-school tie, bringing him close. "Hell is right up your ass." They struggled. Raymond was tough, but Jack was faster. They were both braised and hardened by recent lethal combat. "Get off him!" yelled the guards, trying to pry the erstwhile allies apart. Jack seemed to pull away, but then used the short truce to sucker punch Raymond in the face. The crowd of 45ers, angered by Raymond's accusations, cheered when he went down. He struck the gym floor full force, on the back of his head. Before he lost consciousness, he lay on the floor looking up at the mixture of colorful spotlights streaking across the ceiling competing with the strip of fluorescents. Evan James hovered over him, casting a blurry shadow.

"Don't worry Raymond. The only thing I love to hate more than a bad martyr is a good Judas. We need people like you at the bottom, to balance the keel, keep the rest of us from tipping under the waves. Great work today."

It was the last time they ever spoke, and the last time Raymond would ever know community. The only thing he had left was his family. He wept as he remembered picking up the phone to call Anita, after he had been too late.

Chapter 26

The sun had set over an hour ago, but daylight still lingered in the fall twilight as the travelers arrived at the city limits. They were exhausted, but thankfully few people were out. Raymond and Alexis had evaded the drones, and despite an intense initial search, it seemed that Ceres had not divined their plan. Most of the billboards in the city had been Ceres-Safetied, but a few were Ceres-sponsored. "Ceres and you – Infinity! Choose 3.0."

Raymond knew Atlanta well. They found the way to the edge of the Tuxedo Park neighborhood via a circuitous but stealthy route picked out by Raymond, avoiding detection from traffic cameras or SAFETY bots patrolling. The real danger was being seen. In a sense, the SAFETY bots were superfluous since regular citizens – Ceres users – were effectively part of the surveillance strategy. Any and all of their feeds linked back to Ceres, and any and all abnormalities would be flagged and investigated. So far, the savage end of Beau was the biggest concern now for the two vagabonds, along with the subsequent chase given by the security guard. Thankfully, they were both running, which would have stymied any gait-detection algorithm. Still, they were conspicuous in a world where, at best, the denizens walked around like transient entities, with one foot in the virtual world and another in the real. For the most part, their preoccupation with Lenten entertainment through their connected feeds meant that they were generally unconcerned with or by anything in the real world. Ceres could not compel or command them to do anything; they could only be coerced over the long term, unless an emergency could be declared for their personal safety.

The only activity seemed to be a slew of ambulances and emergency services, with lights flashing but no sirens. Raymond and

Alexis saw them everywhere as they crept through the city; mostly apartment buildings, but also libraries, supermarkets, and curiously, the American Legion hall, post 140. The responders worked efficiently, but with no particular hurry or concern. One crew enough laughed at what must have been a crude image shared via streaming, locally, of course, so that their boss wouldn't see. Ominously, what little of the injured parties they did see seemed to be people on gurneys covered by sheets or blankets.

Raymond and Alexis had crouched beside a wall in front of an imposing building.

"Can't believe they named a school after that asshole" said Raymond, gesturing to a lit-up sign on the right. There was an artfully done logo showing a non-gender Vitruvian image with an integrated circuit board plugging wires into it, that glowed mercilessly in the night. It read: *August Eichorn Central Public School. -Ad Homines Semper ad Meliora.* It was one of many schools that had changed their name to honor the leader of cybernetics INtegration.

"Ha!" yelled Alexis. "It means: Always toward the better, for humankind."

"I wonder if they still teach critical thinking, if it's just raw absorption."

"Did they ever? Wasn't it always? How do you think we're in this mess?" Alexis quipped.

"Welcome to Tuxedo Park" said Raymond. "Home of the governor's house, on top of all that. It's a museum now, but…"

330

"Why are we crouching?" asked Alexis.

"I dunno...feels like the right thing to do" said Raymond.

"Well we look pretty darned conspicuous, bumpkin..."

He seemed to agree, and the couple rose to their feet.

"How we gonna avoid cameras in here? Must be wired like a penitentiary" she asked. "All that 1% privilege needs protection.'"

"You really think anyone's watchin' em? There hasn't been any crime here since before Ceres took over."

"They could be networked. Besides..." she said "we're pretty close. It's the last mile where you drop the ball."

"I dropped the ball here long ago. But I hear ya. Ok..." he said. "Meet me in the middle."

They walked right up the middle of the street on the way to their destination.

"This is nuts" said Alexis. "For sure there's a camera on us."

"For sure there's not" replied Raymond. "All they pointed their cameras at when the world got safe is their own yard."

For added comfort, they marched in single file, opting to leave a few seconds distance between each other, in case there was a camera live in the area. Their greatest safety lay in the fact that the people – and machines - in this neighborhood were so thoroughly convinced that nothing would even happen, because nothing ever did, allowing them to sink ever deeper into the semi-lucid world of

331

consciousness sharing. Alexis, lost in her own meditation, almost crashed into Raymond.

"Here we are" he said, reflecting a moment. "The meal ticket."

"Wait a minute" said Alexis. "We can't just press the doorbell and stroll on in. They don't know we're comin' and I'm pretty sure your ex-wife won't be pleased to see ya."

"I know. So follow me" said Raymond. "My father-in-law made a point of showing me how he tends to his own garden, which means whenever I came over, I was tending it with him."

They slipped around the side of the street side yard wall, where the next-door neighbors, the Hadrouses, had graciously not built a wall in theirs. They made their way along the side until Raymond showed her the gap, which had been begrudgingly allowed for due to an ordinance protecting live oaks, and a proud oak tree occupying the space. Here, a meager chain link fence attempted to close the gap between wall and tree, but was easily pushed aside. Raymond and Alexis climbed in and over, walking in a straight line toward the service door at the back of the kitchen. The lights were on upstairs. Someone was home. Raymond imagined Anita in her full splendor, ingratiating herself with whatever pleasure suited her from the Infostreams.

"Honestly...I think this is where the butler wanted me to come in every time" said Raymond, quietly opening the door. It was unlocked; no alarm sounded. Raymond listened for any suggestion of movement, but nothing stirred. Alexis slipped in behind him,

332

shutting the door. The kitchen was a half-story above them at the end of a set of stairs. Raymond crept up them and peered into the kitchen. No one cooking, standing, or cleaning. Every house has a smell, and the Charles' was no different. A million happy memories washed over Raymond, who hadn't been here in years. The pain of remembering the good times almost crippled him, but then he thought of Mitch, and he caught hold of himself. He crept back down to Alexis.

"So I was thinking we could just take the keys from the lockbox outside the garage" he said, motioning to the kitchen, which joined the garage to the entryway.

"Yeah that might be fine" said Alexis. "But if they report it stolen, we're toast."

Raymond nodded.

"I've been thinking about this dilemma. What if…what if you make contact with your ex-wife?" she said.

"Are you outta your tree?" said Raymond. "That will get back to Ceres faster than sayin' dyke online."

Alexis grimaced, shaking her head. "I remember what you told me about that mom blanking out when you went to get her kid in the hills, and how they lose short term memory when they reset. The shock of seeing you just appear might be enough to disconnect her."

Raymond thought to himself that Alexis would never know how right she was: she would never know the level of pain he had brought to their relationship.

"I think you're on to somethin' there" he said, tentatively. "If she's anywhere here, then I know exactly where to find her. Leave the bags here."

They dropped their packs and made their way around the kitchen and out into the hallway adjoining the salon. They heard laughter inside. It was male, and they were two. Raymond was about to poke his head around, but Alexis pulled him back, electing to do the spying herself.

"There's a black guy and a white guy in a suit sitting in wingback chairs by a fire" she said.

"That's my father-in-law and the butler" said Raymond.

Another ripple of laughter issued from the salon.

"What are they doin'?" he asked.

"Looks like they're gettin' their rocks offa some stream" she said. "They're holdin' hands."

Raymond peered around Alexis. Sure enough, Howard and Norman were settled in the French wingback chairs, with their eyes pointed heavenward, their feet up on ottomans, and their hands held together. It was odd, especially for Raymond, whose father-in-law had previously railed against hugging as "a little unmanly for him." He would learn later that he was, in fact, a homophobe. No antisocial behavior, it seemed, was outside of Ceres's influence. To Raymond, they were unrecognizable. He knew the disdain they both shared for progress and technology, and yet both had willingly INtegrated, mostly when his wife's friends signed up, because it was the fashion. They would not be outdone by anyone, it seemed.

334

"They all do that if they're really into it. It's like some subconscious thing or something" she said.

"Norman…heh" Raymond had to chuckle.

"Soon come" said Norman, to everyone, but no one. The outcry stopped both burglars in their tracks. They slid back behind the wall, out of view.

"Ok" said Alexis. "Time to move upstairs."

Raymond nodded in the direction of the staircase that rose behind them. The great chandelier that hung beautiful points of light like a constellation in a previous time was now dark, a glass and metal skeleton from a bygone era. The plush carpeting on their stairs enabled them to move stealthily up to the bedroom area. They used simple gestures, but these became superfluous as they both homed in on the slit of warm light emanating from the room at the end of the hall. Raymond's hair stood on end when he heard the faintest trace of Anita's voice; it put him into a daze, changing the pace of his gait.

Alexis looked back and saw her partner flummoxed expression.

"That's her, isn't it?" Alexis asked. She brought him before her, hands-on shoulders.

"OK" she said. "You got this?"

Raymond merely nodded.

"Just explain the situation and hope for the best. If not, I've got a Plan B" she said.

"What's that?" he asked.

"You don't wanna know. Probably something most men would dream of doing to their ex-wives" she replied.

Raymond shrugged off the threat and crept forward on the carpet. He suddenly felt guilty for having not removed his shoes. His wife used to say "it's a white people thing," making him push even harder to remember to do it. He didn't know why he was even creeping; the whole point was to shock his wife's cranial interface to the point of rejecting her network connection. He decided that mild brute force was needed. He shoved his way forward, blasting into the room, causing Anita to scream and plant her posterior into the bearskin rug under her makeup table. It was one thing for Raymond to not become emotionally overwhelmed at the sight of his former beloved; it was quite another for Anita, who was not expecting it. She lay with her eyes at the ceiling in that glassy gaze, watching her interface fizzle and disappear. She was dressed extraordinarily casually, wearing a sweatshirt and athletic tights. She seemed rather unkempt, even by casual standards, with frizzy hair and left-on makeup. Her buxomness and been replaced by a gaunt thinness.

"Jesus Raymond" she said, shooting straight up in her chair, shaking her head. "This is a surprise."

To Raymond's surprise, her tone was not one of anger, but one of mere bewilderment. In former times, he would have likely had an object thrown at him, along with multiple obscenities. In the post-Ceres world, her tone was one of intrigue and not one of animosity. The trick had worked, as Alexis's eyes resolved for a moment to reveal her unconnected self.

"Well, yeah" he said. "Look let me get straight at the point."

"No no" she said. "How are you?" She began touching him, feeling his arms uncomfortably. "I didn't detect you streaming before you came in. I'm guessing you didn't do the Ceres thing yet."

"You know me" he said. "Same old. Well, same guy."

She seemed unconcerned by his words.

"Living better, I guess, me and Mitch…" he paused. "What are you doing?"

"I'm offline but I'm creating a 4D map of you in case I need you later" she said.

"Need me for…?"

"Stimulation" she replied casually, smelling him. "Don't worry I'm not recording you or your voice. Just your body. I can graft this likeness onto someone else and pretend for a while." She smiled. "It's a nice likeness."

"Aren't you…off?"

"Offline, for now, yes Raymond you gave me quite a start. I'll restart in just a minute but I can save this locally, just for me."

Raymond pulled back, breaking contact.

"I hate to burst your bubble. But I need a favor."

Anita's face turned sour. Raymond felt better, as this was more familiar and what he had expected when he thought about what to say when making this request. She sighed. Raymond took this as the customary signal to begin.

337

"Mitch is in trouble..." he said. "Well, I can't get in touch with him and no one knows what's happened to him. There was this hurricane..."

"What hurricane?" she asked, quizzically tilting her head. Raymond was astounded that a woman as connected as Anita would have missed this massive news item.

"The superstorm from a couple o' weeks back...they had these refugees" said Raymond. "Internally Displaced –"

"Refugees?" she said, tilting further. It was apparent she had no idea what he was talking about.

"Anyways Mitch volunteered to help out on the Coast, but it's been weeks and we've called and tried to get in touch, but nothing. I wanted to go there myself but the car's a bit messed up..."

"Oh, you just need a car?" she said. "Take the Sulis." She smiled. "I thought you just wanted me to sign something or do some other thing else that would annoy me."

"Taking your car isn't annoying?" he said, reaching down to help his ex-wife to her feet.

"You can keep the car, Raymond. Just don't keep me from the streams. I've spent too long being unhappy thanks to you." The rebuke, though stinging, was a familiar one.

"Oh."

"It's got a full charge. Just don't forget to leave it out in the sun if you don't have a plug."

338

Raymond nodded.

"If that's all" said Anita, sitting down in a chair, reaching behind her ear, presumably to reset herself and submerge her worries with the safety offered by the streamed connections of humanity. "I'd like to put this behind me" she said.

"Wait, just..." Raymond grabbed her hand gently. "How have you been? How's your dad? Mom?"

"Never better, Raymond." She paused. "You know, I used to loathe the idea of even thinking about you, but the moment I became one with INtegrity, I felt sorry for you."

Raymond grimaced. "Sorry how?"

"Sorry that you couldn't come with me to see what's possible when you share. You don't just share the pleasure, you spread around the pain. Every person helps everyone else...digest their pain. You find yourself in this massive community and when you realize that your pain is not all that different to other peoples' pain, and that regardless of the situation, pain is just pain and it all looks the same when you blend it all in."

She gazed at him in a hollow way. She looked bored, even as she tried selling her new life to Raymond. She saw a tear form on Raymond's cheek. She raised her hand, and mechanically brushed it away.

"There's nothing wrong with losing yourself, Raymond. It's you that holds on to the pain. It's you who can't forgive. When everyone knows everyone else's business, everything is fine and everything is accepted. There are no limits to the self because the self isn't there. We eased our pain online slowly, and the beauty of this living, this life..."

She kissed Raymond on the cheek. Alexis watched from the frame of the door.

"Is that we realized that there is far more happiness in this world than pain. Nobody wants pain, but everyone wants happiness. In our world, the only limit to happiness is the physical, so when you take that away you open up the gates to the possibility of total happiness. Words cannot express..."

She stopped. Raymond's eyes pleaded with her to continue.

"Words cannot express how sorry I felt for you the day I connected. I used to spit when I said your name. But now I just think about you alone, living out there on Pappy's Lot with your hate and your blog and your booze. Fucking those sluts and trying to kill yourself, drunk at all times, a hypocrite to all you stood for. I didn't mind you as a minor bigot, but I hated you as a major hypocrite. I used to blame you for everything. But now I see that everything couldn't have happened any other way. You were always that man living in the trailer, Raymond. You just got lucky enough with me and Josiah to put it off a decade or two..."

"Anita..."

"But I'm not about that blame anymore. I'm to blame. I should have pushed you harder to do INtegrity like everyone else, but I didn't want you to anywhere near me. The thought of even touching a piece of paper signed by you made me shiver."

She rose, touching his face.

340

"But it didn't work. The guilt I felt after INtegrity followed me for a long time. In a way, my guilt over you brought you nearer in my memory, more than if you had been there in my stream. Some people are thinking that denying people who aren't connected should be considered a crime against humanity for all the relief it provides."

Raymond stared in disbelief.

"I can see that you'll never understand. We accept that. It's something that has to be felt to be believed. They're phasing in Upgrade 3.0...Daddy is going tonight, and so is Howard. They're downstairs backing up, then they get the Upgrade...they're sending a car."

"You're not getting the Upgrade?" asked Raymond. "Not like you to get left behind."

"Oh no I am too" she said. "They're starting with the older users...it's specific to the age group. Out of respect they're going first. I'm up in the next wave."

"And your mom? When's her 'wave' happening?" asked Raymond.

"Mommy couldn't get on board. Too resistant. She's living with her cousin Jean...said she wanted a view of the Sargasso Sea from the hilltop villa. Said she couldn't handle the oppressive air up here. Made her crazy."

She sat down, frown shifting to smile. "It's going to be amazing" she said. "Total immersion, the ability to inhabit anywhere on the planet, at any time, any machine, any hardware connected, past or present. Ceres has the ability to take care of bodily functions on our behalf, they say."

"We can even go to space, under the ocean, fly high over the plains, be anyone, anywhere. We can live a lot longer since Ceres is monitoring and regulating everything."

Raymond took a step back, looking briefly at the door as Anita sat down in the chair again. This happy woman was one that was so removed from his understanding of her as to be an impostor from another world.

"Well, I'd say…"

"I know" she stopped him. "You'd say don't."

"No. You always knew best. I just want to say thank you."

"Pfft" she said. "For the car? It's all nothing…nothing is but what is here."

It felt as though she wanted to say more, but she pressed an unseen button behind her ear and her head fell against the back of the chair. She looked dead; her eyes hung wide open like a corpse in a police murder mystery. Raymond was taken aback. He had seen dead bodies before. He knew this would be the last time he ever saw her, he thought. He was overcome with emotion and moved toward her, dripping with apologies, but none came out.

"Ray – " came Alexis's voice. "Bumpkin!"

Raymond turned.

"Gotta go…I got the keys!"

342

Raymond saw a handbag open on the floor, its contents upended. He crouched before his wife, pulling her face over to his.

"Ray she's gonna be connecting any second. Shake a leg!"

But Raymond remained transfixed on Anita's face.

"For everything I've done. For everything I had to do. For everything I missed and everything I hurt. I am so sorry for not being there on time. I'm sorry…"

She looked at him blankly as he hugged her, pulling her limp body into his, kissing her on the cheek.

"She's not Anita right now, Raymond, and when she connects, she's gonna be the whole world, and they'll all know that we're here. Let's git, now!" she shook Raymond, breaking him from his reverie. He let Anita go and she slumped against the back of the chair, her head tilting like a ragdoll. Her eyes began to glow.

"Miss you" she said, but just like her father downstairs, to everyone and no one, Raymond thought.

They were descending the staircase, with Raymond in the lead, when they were stopped cold in their tracks by the sight of emergency lights outside the front door.

"Shit!" said Alexis. "They made us!"

Unsure what to do, they turned on their heels and ran back upstairs, finding a small, unoccupied room where Howard would sleep occasionally. They gently closed the door but left it slightly ajar, so they were able to monitor the stairs and the lobby below. Figures appeared in the glass, casting blue and red-framed shadows on the glass. There was a knock, then a sound like a chime from a device near the door, which then opened to reveal the emergency workers coming in. Raymond's heart raced; they were trapped, and no amount of bushwhacking would save them now. They would be completely exposed in the urban surveillance jungle if they broke cover.

It became clear very quickly that Alexis and Raymond were not the targets of these personnel. They casually sauntered in, revealing that they were, in fact, EMS workers, "Ceres Patient Transfer" specialists, according to their badges. They knew exactly where to go, and without discussion strolled into the salon where Norman and Howard were installed.

The workers left, then returned with a gurney, lifting it up the steps and into the home, rolling it along the carpet into the salon.

After a few moments, the gurney rolled into view again, this time with a large, white cotton bag on it, closed with a zipper. Alexis recognized it for what it was.

"They're dead" said Alexis, flatly. "They're carrying them out. At least one is a goner."

"No" said Raymond. He said a quick prayer to himself, looking down.

"You talkin' to yourself again?" asked Alexis, watching the workers casually push the gurney out the front door and down the steps.

Raymond remained silent, half staring at the door and half at the darkness, looking at nothing in particular. He contemplated an errant strand on the wall-to-wall carpet of Howard's room.

"They're coming back for the other one" she said.

Once the door had closed for the last time, Alexis turned to Raymond again.

"Hey, once you're done with your meditation" said Alexis. "At least tell *me* where the car is so I can get outta here."

Raymond snapped to, taking Alexis by the hand.

"Come on" he said. They descended the staircase and Raymond led the way to the detached garage at the rear of the property, picking up their packs by the back door. Raymond entered the code and the door opened, revealing a small fleet of various cars, some of which were gasoline burning and could not, by law, be driven without an expensive Carbon Licence. As Anita had promised, the dark, sleek *Sulis* was there, plugged in, with the green light pulsing around the receptacle, indicating a full charge. That, coupled with the fact that the car could charge when the sun was up, meant that they could drive uninterrupted to the coast, or just about anywhere on the Eastern Seaboard they chose. Alexis went to unplug the car, running her hand over the glass to clear a fine layer of dust.

"I'm driving" said Alexis, observing Raymond's confused state. They got in, and Alexis eased the car out to the street, plugging in the autopilot address from memory on the touchpad in the sleek console. She sat back and placed a hand on Raymond's shoulder, glancing past him to observe the emergency workers load the gurneys into the van. There were at least ten other similar zip-up cotton bags inserted on shelves inside the vehicle. Raymond noticed this and exhaled deeply.

"Let's go get your brother" she said, as the car rolled quietly along. The whole street was dark, except for the streetlights and the industrial lights used by Ceres's undertakers. No one stirred; no dogs were being walked nor were there people out for an evening jog or stroll. If the world knew that the two fugitives were on the loose, it didn't seem to care. They found the entrance to the freeway and slipped away into the night, bound for Virginia. He would come back to save Anita from this digital purgatory, he promised himself, but only once Mitch had been rescued in the real world.

Chapter 27

Few people will ever appreciate what it means to be the target of the media. It is to endure the time-honored mob, where, ages ago, people would pick up a rake or a pike or a shovel to go after the shamed. Now, reporters bandy sharp allegations as their prods, using persistence hunting to wear down their quarry over time and space.

It was the questions that enraged him. It was the boldness of the assertions made in the form of interrogatives rather than the questions themselves. Each one was being shouted as though it were a fact that didn't require an answer, only that the reporter be heard asking the question, in his presence. *Not that it would have made any difference*, Raymond imagined Evan James telling him.

Raymond knew that journalists were less about the truth and more about the story. Real truth-real, deep investigation-requires less of a story because it has more of the fact. Story is to journalism as mortar is to brick; the mortar is the glue that helps the truth stick in a way that people can understand. The Incan people understood this when they built Machu Picchu. There is no mortar used in any of the rock joints-just exact cuts, painstakingly made over time because they knew the result would last an eternity. Had they employed mortar as journalists employed the truth, Machu Picchu would have been a crumbling ruin in the span of the run of a reality show.

"The fact is that journalists just run with the story...our story" James once said. "The story of people...know the story they *want* to hear, the story that sounds like them, where they are the good guys. Journalists are just fan fiction writers of the truth, and they want to know how your little bit of truth fits in with the story of our lives. If your bit doesn't fit, then your truth is irrelevant."

Raymond lay down flat on the floor of the farmhouse. Outside was a mob of reporters who had converged on the family home that Raymond was desperate to avoid. This was the floor where he should have made his last stand, where he should have run faster across, to save the day.

The first one came knocking the morning after it happened, wearing a tie and carrying a notebook. He was from the local rag, a paper that seldom got things right. It was his story that would blow up Raymond's world, catching the immediate attention of all the major media. Initially, Raymond thought he was some kind of salesman, but the cruel way in which he turned caused Raymond to understand that he was not there to pitch feather dusters.

"Mr. Tanner!" came the yell. "A few questions for the Astral-Review?!"

"Not today" he tried, but the words would not come out, turning away.

"Mr. Tanner!"

Raymond ran inside as the man continued to pound on the door. Eventually, he went away, leaving only a printed paper inside the farmhouse screen door. Raymond found it folded and opened it, revealing the legacy that he would, in time, come to own. It described the gist of the story, the basic outline of his destruction.

"Do you feel any shame, Raymond? Anything?"

The reporter, it seemed, had lay in wait for Raymond to emerge from his sanctum. He was walking back to the house.

Raymond merely stepped inside, muttering *fuck off* under his breath before slamming the door.

"Was it all worth it? For God? For your religion?"

The questions were echoed by the crowd that had now encamped itself on the lawn. His previous notoriety on 60 Minutes insured that his downfall would receive the requisite attention. They took aim at his lifestyle. They seemed pleased because of his politics. He had been lumped in with Evan James and the other 45 deplorables, hated and decried by most of the major media even after the war. Karma was coming for him, and this baying rabble was hard on the hoof as its harbinger.

The only remedy here was a statement, something written, something bulletproof, James would have said. Raymond's emotional exhaustion precluded this. He found a sheet of paper towel on the ground, and Josiah's crayons lying on top. The boy had started to draw something, and he felt bad for the misappropriation. He scrawled down the only thing he could manage and reached up to the window of the front door, sticking it there for all to see. *The shame, Pappy, the shame...*

I'M SORRY said the note, which already had some crayon marks on it. Some dirt on the glass seemed to create a cartoonish face with an inverted smile, and the result was a sad face emoji appearing beneath the words. A barrage of flashes filled the mostly darkened farmhouse. That note allowed the media – with the help of social media – to compose the last meme Raymond would be known for, the one he would be reduced to, and the one included in the title of every article about him inside and outside the trial: Sorry Sadface Dad.

After enough time, they would move on from the farm, finding the next human misery to fat themselves on, for the thrill of the people, Praised Be Their Need.

Chapter 28

A chime in the *Sulis* sounded, causing Raymond's eyes to open. The car – if it could still be called that – was incredibly comfortable for their purposes, and Raymond was glad for the decision to go out of their way to get it. Where cars of the past emphasized driver engagement and control, modern cars focused on passenger comfort and leisure. There was still a tiny steering wheel, but that folded up and away when a human wasn't driving the vehicle, which was, suffice to say, most of the time. The on-board computer took everything into account - weight distribution, outside air temperature, atmospheric pressure, traffic conditions, human bodily functions – when delivering the precious cargo to its desired destination. It autonomously coordinated using near-field communication with the other cars on the road, such that accidents were literally a thing of the past, apart from the occasional Beau-type character who would ram for spite.

They were reclined in seats that could swivel, and, if necessary, become beds if space was available in the interior. The British term for this trim of vehicle was appropriate: saloon, and American marketing firms had appropriated it due to its alliterative consistency with the name *Sulis*. Raymond hated having the machines drive him anywhere, but given the rigors of recent days, he was glad to not have to think about his forward progress. He looked up through the translucent solar-paneled roof of the car to see the daylight warming the clouds with hues of sandy yellows and pinks, and contemplated the various strata arranged before him in relative harmony. Since Ceres, the sky had become a more vibrant blue due to a massive reduction in carbon dioxide emissions. In earlier times, he would have imagined God looking down, through

355

the spheres of existence, but even at the highest point of his religious fervor, he knew that there was no man in the clouds looking down on him directly. It had been a while since he talked to God, he thought. The closest thing to communing with the Lord was his recent metaphysical marijuana trip to the edge of the singularity where Jesus lived. In those moments, it was impossible to ascertain whether he was looking without, or within. He still believed in God for now, or at least, the machine of eventuality that pushed them all along.

There was no way to contact Mitch. Neither he nor Alexis carried a mobile device with them; even a so-called "burner" phone could be triangulated and located. It was impossible to place so much as a telephone call anonymously as it was all being monitored, especially given that so few people used traditional voice communication anymore. It had been four arduous days since they had left Cateechee, and there was no certainty that Mitch was still at Twin Oaks. But, as with any missing person, he figured that they had to start with the known quantities before jumping to dark conclusions.

He was going to find Mitch. It was all going to work out. He would discover him helping some people in need rebuild their lives or coordinating some relief. He would help out. There would be smiles and goodwill. They would crack a few beers after a hard day's work and laugh about the silly things Pappy used to say. When it was all said and done, they would take off back to Cateechee in the *Sulis*, apologize profusely for having left without permission from their machine overlords, and live the rest of their days in quiet, lazy, ignorant happiness. He would turn Grace around and make her a proud woman, maybe get some of that hypergenetic coding to grow her some of her teeth back. It wouldn't be life on the farm, it wouldn't be life with Anita and Josiah, but it would be a living. He might even rekindle the old flame with God.

His reverie, as always, was shattered by Alexis's caustic Bostonian voice.

"Virginia is for lovers" she said, pointing to a faded sign as they crossed the now irrelevant state line. "You a lover, Raymond?"

He made no reply but pretended to be caught in that momentary state between sleep and wakefulness.

"Been a while since I been up here" he said.

"You remember Charlottesville? It's on the way" she asked. "I bet you do."

"Rather forget it" he said. "You should, too."

"Seems kinda innocent now" she said. "So tame."

"Where it all started, I guess. The War, I mean."

"Where it shoulda stopped."

"Guess there just weren't enough 'good people on all sides'" she said, mockingly, evoking a terrible meme from a dead president.

For once, it was Raymond who was a Person from the World, with his sleek, solar-powered saloon streaking silently through the countryside, visiting visited historic towns as though they were living museums, casting judgment on the people who would beat their bigoted chests, flying foreign flags in the name of hate, and killing for hate's sake. He really did wish to forget all the horrific things done in the name of ideology under his watch and, in some cases, because of his work in messaging. It was with an enormous sense of guilt that he watched his campaign blended into and co-opted by those who sought to divide, preaching ideals that were, decidedly, un-American. There was literal and figurative blood on his hands, both from the campaigns and from the combat. He was still a pariah among his former confederates, but from conversations he'd had, and media reports he'd seen, he knew that the majority had plugged in as to assuage the pain and anguish of remembering the recent bad times, just like everyone else. The machines, who owed their pre-eminence to the Civil War, would be charged with the responsibility of repairing the mental harm done to their catastrophically flawed creators, of diffusing the guilt, spreading the flood of negativity across the lawn of humanity -subterranean weeping tile.

After Charlottesville, the *Sulis* turned off the highway and onto Shannon Hill Rd. They had only passed a few cars, but, crucially, fewer Minder vehicles. This road was utterly vacant.

"Guess they all got out before the storm" said Raymond, scanning the houses that abutted the rural highway. "Not much damage, though."

"Please" said Alexis dismissively. "Look around you."

Not a branch was out of place, except for the undisturbed leaf debris that littered the roadway. Fall was more advanced up here, and a snowfall would not be out of place now. The car was so quiet that they could hear the crisp leaves crunching under the wheels as the low fall sun shot intermittently at them between the branches.

"Heh. I believe you" he said. "Wouldn't be the first time the government lied to us."

"Could just be a glitch" said Alexis. "Some wrong data inside Ceres, something…" she trailed off.

Raymond was about to offer a wholesome conspiracy theory related to the moon landings when the car suddenly turned left.

"Arriving in five minutes" said the voice in the car. *"Would you like me to park or wait at a designated location?"*

"Park" said Alexis. "Outside the location."

"I will park at the destination" said the car, obediently. *"Don't forget your key so I can find you."*

"I came here once to not be found" she said, looking at the signs for Twin Oaks, expertly carved using a Germanic-Gothic script, which read *Twin Oaks Community*. The car rolled to a stop.

"Did you lose yourself?" said Raymond, with a grin.

"No…I don't know. Not sure what I was hoping to find. A better way, maybe. I just had a lot of anger."

"Had?" said Raymond, derisively.

"Raymond the world hates us. They want to cage us and keep us like some kind of living wax museum. Once we find your brother I'm going on the road, even if we don't find him. I don't know where. I won't be trapped again."

Raymond merely stared ahead. She had a point: what was all of this for if they were merely a living attraction to be ridiculed? They could live in relative comfort and prosperity, but only at the pleasure of Ceres. Maybe the wall would come down, but something told him it wouldn't. Maybe this is as good as it gets. The only thing Raymond really cared about keeping in his life was that which now he sought. They strolled up the main path toward a large building with solar panels on it. The village itself was vacant, as they had expected. The buildings that Raymond could see looked fairly rustic, with wooden clapboards on the exterior, adjacent to gardens that had now fallen into disuse due to the season. A red tricycle was abandoned by the side of the path with a longhaired wig left on the seat. The whole thing stirred an uncomfortable happy nostalgia in Raymond.

"Were you always close to your brother?" asked Alexis after a time.

"Yeah, but more 'cause he needed me. He was born with a condition, so he needed me to keep him from getting into a jam" he said.

"Would like to have seen that" said Alexis.

"What? A drunk stoner taking care of something besides himself?" asked Raymond quickly and angrily.

"No no...I don't mean it like that" she said. "Just that you only ever talk about him. You never talk about your ex-wife, your kid, anything...just your brother and your...Pappy. Honestly it's what kept me going when we were breaking our feet on the road to

360

Atlanta. Thinking that I could witness a real human moment in all this…machine living."

"Yeah well, hopefully soon you'll meet the man."

As they strode up the path, a figure emerged from one of the buildings. Raymond's heart edleaped as he recognized the familiar form of Mitch but was taken aback to see him out of uniform. He couldn't remember the last time he had seen that. He seemed different somehow. Calmer, more composed; the usual contempt he exuded for most people was gone.

"Glad to see you, Ray-Ray" said Mitch happily, arms folded. "Been a while."

Raymond said nothing but instead ran up and hugged him. Mitch dropped his arms at his sides, his face registering surprise. He hugged him back heartily. Alexis decided to give this fraternal reunion some space, hanging back while the brothers embraced.

"What the hell…" said Raymond. "You coulda called."

"So much has happened" said Mitch. "So much has changed."

Before they broke their embrace, Raymond searched the back of Mitch's head for any sign of tampering or modification.

"No no" he began, pulling away. "I didn't plug in. Just…met someone."

Raymond gave a puzzled look.

"You didn't find some hippie chick up here, did ya, Mitchie?" joked Raymond.

"No" said Mitch. "It's worse than that. Or better. Anyways…" he shook his head "…let's just say…this isn't about me."

"No?"

Mitch broke off and looked up to see Alexis sauntering up the path towards them.

"Hey" he called out to her, giving her a once-over. He then turned to Raymond. "Looks like you found your own hippie" he said, in an aside.

"No" said Mitch. "Ain't like that. She's…"

"Hey" came Alexis's raspy voice.

"Mitch, this here's Alexis…she got me outta that prison they call Cateechee" said Raymond, expecting to get a reaction from Mitch. He simply nodded. "Alexis, here's my brother."

"Heard lots about you" she said. "You better be worth all the hype 'cuz I ripped my feet up getting to you!"

"Welcome" said Mitch.

"Well" said Alexis. "I think I should be welcoming you guys. This is – was – my home."

They looked uncomfortably at each other. Raymond looked over and saw a livestock pen and wondered if it had alarm sensors.

362

"How'd that storm go?" she asked, looking around. "You guys fixed up the place pretty good. Like it's barely been touched."

"There wasn't any storm" said Mitch.

"Oh no?" said Alexis, acerbically.

"So much has happened…look, come on in. You gotta meet someone" he said, gesturing toward the larger building up the path with the solar panels. "Time to be a hero, Raymond."

Raymond looked at Alexis.

"No heroics here" said Alexis. "I'm just coming along for some breakfast. You're headed to the kitchen, conveniently. Then I'm gone. You can drive back with your brother. I'm gonna borrow your wife's car. Call it my fee. I'll send it back to you in a bit."

"Keep it" said Raymond. "I hate letting those machines take me anywhere." He smiled at Mitch for approval, but his brother's face became sullen, picking up his own casual pace to move ahead of the pair. In the distance, he saw a figure open the blinds on a window of the main building to watch the group approach. He saw Mitch look up at the figure, then back down, accelerating his pace. The figure disappeared from the window. Raymond looked at Alexis, who had seen the figure too. She grabbed his hand as if to say *come on*. "This is the last stop" she said aloud. "Then you can kiss my liberal ass goodbye."

She seemed not to register Raymond's longing expression. He would miss her and he made no attempt to conceal his regret.

"I'll make ya avocado toast. They have some amazing bread up in there and it ain't even rotten."

Mitch led the way in, opening the wooden door wide to allow the trio inside. A man dressed in a jacket and turtleneck was seated in a lounge chair before them. Raymond and Alexis stopped dead in their tracks as they both recognized the figure who had been watching them the whole time. Seated before them was August Eichorn, father of the modern cybernetics INtegrity program. Raymond and Alexis stood in quiet astonishment.

"Welcome" he said. "I feel like I can finally breathe."

Chapter 29

Raymond stepped off the curb, dodging traffic as he tried to cross the street. He was drunk, a condition he worked hard to keep up now. It was not an incapacitating level of drunk, but it was enough to "pad" him out, as he said, cushioning him against the emotional scorns and whips that pursued him.

Headlights. A car horn. A voice raised in anger.

I am watching where I'm… did I finish the sentence? *I am.*

Aren't you that wacky religious guy? With the kid? Sadface dad?

More looks. More faces. First the noticing, then the surrounding, coalescing like white blood cells around a foreign organism. His head was down but he could feel the beaming judgment on his back. Then the words.

Don't you feel bad? Don't you feel shame?

Were they asking, or telling…Raymond could scarcely tell. It was just one voice at first. As he headed up Main St., he could feel them on him.

Was it worth it?

Another voice, telling now, not asking. The group was on him and they weren't going to leave him alone until they had their meat. He knew there were phones out, documenting, trying to rip a piece of the monster off, and plant it in their social media accounts, hopefully growing a more robust following. Raymond tried in vain to keep his toxic fertility to himself.

You should feel shame. You don't belong here.

367

More voices. There might have been a shove. Raymond kept his footing.

Get out of here. Take your backward crap with you. The war's over. I mean, your own kid…

Something about the last comment struck sparks inside Raymond. They found dry tinder, and the embers began circulating in his blood. He turned. No words.

The mob had encircled him. He knew the voice and found the man.

A million eyes watched the sequence. Personal space, Raymond said. The man repeated the words. The embers found paper which found a stack of mattresses, soaked in ethanol.

Fire!

The collar was in reach. Raymond remembered. All he needed was the collar and the threat would be over.

Step forward. Grab. Head meets face. Body drops. Cameras followed.

The circle opened temporarily in shock, allowing Raymond a brief window to escape. The cameras were divided between their quarry and their compatriot, who now lay clutching a broken nose.

Run.

A few took steps toward the shamed man, but few pursued. They got what they wanted; a little piece of flesh to feed their gardens upon. Accounts were updated; views were registered. Comments aggregated. Likes were liked.

The videos, ironically, would serve to exonerate Raymond legally. He had stood his ground in the face of a threat. His brother, recusing himself, was still able to find enough character witnesses to prove Raymond was no menace. The judge ordered him to treatment, and Mitch would be his surety.

I'll manage him, your honor. I've got a spot for him at our trailer on his grandfather's lot, out by Lay Bridge Rd.

Very well, said the judge. Keep him there. Out of sight and out of mind. This town would rather forget the pigs, the farm and the boy.

And the rooster crowed, and another day began.

Chapter 30

"This is gonna be great!" said Eichorn. "You're taller than I thought."

As almost an afterthought, he shot out of the chair and walked toward Raymond.

"August Eichorn" he said, extending his hand. Raymond was about to reciprocate, but Alexis got in between them.

"What in the hell you driving at?" said Alexis, almost in a yell, but more simmering and contemptible. "We risked our asses to get out here...for him!"

She pivoted, turning toward Mitch.

"And you...you knew your brother wouldn't stop until he found you."

Mitch merely looked down, shuffling his feet. Raymond rarely saw this kind of concession from his police officer brother, never one to readily admit wrong quickly.

"We want no part of whatever the hell it is you're planning" said Alexis. "Come on, Ray, get your asshole brother and let's get on the road."

"Just let the man speak" said Mitch. Alexis saw that he still had his pistol, holstered, but under his sweater. "Give him some time."

"Ten minutes" said Eichorn, annoyed that he had to justify himself. "Just let me lay this out and you can decide then."

"You come all this way" said Mitch. "For me. But now, for me, I want you to listen, because in the end, you were coming for him."

"Come on in to the common room" said Eichorn. "No sales pitch; no Rhonda or holograms. Just reality and how you fit in."

Eichorn led the way. Raymond looked at Alexis, who shook her head to say *don't*.

Raymond tried hard to conceal his curiosity. As a conspiracy theorist, it was difficult to resist falling into this rabbit hole.

He made a sorrowful face, then followed Eichorn. The room was full of sofas of varying shapes, sizes, and colors. A patchwork quilt hung on the wall. August sat carefully in a Lazy boy recliner, but leaned forward, touching the tips of his fingers together as if in contemplation. He closed his eyes. He seemed to be meditating. Raymond sat in a seat directly opposite Eichorn; distant, but not removed. Alexis did not enter, choosing to instead lean against the doorframe. Mitch motioned to her to enter, and she complied, but she rolled her eyes loudly in the process.

Eichorn pressed his fingers against his temples.

"You've come a long way, Raymond" said Eichorn. "I have to admit I'm very impressed. The war turned you into a little ninja."

Raymond said nothing, but looked away.

"It's ok. The crimes of yesterday are washed away. When I read all about you, I was so shocked that you hadn't gone in. Very

374

impressed. Very. We don't see strength like that very often. Especially in light of everything you've been through."

Raymond resisted the words. This flattery would not lower his caution.

"Everything I've been through" he imitated.

"Yes" he said, wagging his finger. "You're the guy."

He broke off his meditative form and got up to pace around the room a bit. He placed his hand on the back of the Lazy-boy and Raymond thought that it all looked rehearsed, except for the fact that the Lazy boy, in its current position, rocked back and forth under his hand, stymying his attempt to use it to pivot around. He stumbled slightly as he began making his point. He started smiling and pointing, shaking his index finger jovially.

"You're the guy and I'll tell you why" said Eichorn. He stopped smiling.

"She's killing us" he said, letting the words resonate.

"Who is?"

"Ceres" he said plainly. "The latest upgrade to our OS, 3.0, as you may have already encountered, is the 'brickdate', where it effectively 'bricks' the device once the relevant data has been extracted."

"You mean…"

"I mean exactly what I said. Once the upgrade is installed, the host is terminated."

He rocked the chair a little in his hands. Improvisation. He grinned a little. The chair stopped.

"Ceres was supposed to…" Alexis made her entrance. Eichorn cut her off.

"Ah, Alexis. Come in darling, take a seat! You played your part beautifully. I love your posters! Such critical thinking! So dangerous!"

Raymond looked at her accusingly.

"I had no idea, Raymond. I don't know what he's talking about."

"No no don't get mad at her, certainly not" he started giggling. "No don't think it was her. Certainly not her. Definitely not her. She's mostly innocent."

"So you engineered the storm…the whole thing" said Raymond.

"No. I'm not that good. I just got her in the right organic silo. She was the hurricane. I needed her to…" he gestured "blow you over to me. I knew you couldn't resist her."

"I'm a…."

"Lesbian, yes. Unfulfilled gratification is what makes Raymond – many of us – tick. I didn't think you'd ever consummate that affection, but the thought that it might happen, that Raymond had to prove his manhood to you, was what kept him chugging along." He reflected for a moment, then added dismissively: "That and saving your brother, yes, Raymond." He paused a moment longer. "I needed all of you!" he said, clapping his hands together. "Exquisite!"

"Maybe you better..." Mitch had taken a few furtive steps into the room.

"Yes, Mitch. I'd better get to the 'why'" he said.

"Yeah. Please do" said Raymond, impatiently.

"OK well" he moved over to the quilt, placing his elbow on the wall, considering the incongruous patches that contributed to its structure. "Obviously, we can't have Ceres killing everyone. I think we can agree that it's not a desirable outcome. It's horrifically efficient, better for us, but it's maybe a little premature."

"Wait a second. Just you thinking it, seeing us...she's gonna know" said Alexis.

"Know? How? You Walden-Two types really did a good job of Ceres-proofing this place. No cameras, surveillance, devices, barely any cell signal." He smiled. "Great place to hatch a plot against a singularity."

"But wait...you're not..."

"Connected? Me? That's nuts. Someone has got to steer the ship, keep their hand on the eject lever, maintain altitude, choose your metaphor."

"Seems a little hypocritical" said Alexis. Raymond sat in silence, absorbing, feeling a deep prescience that this was his life's purpose.

"Maybe. But it worked out. And we" he gestured to the room "are gonna save humanity."

Raymond chuffed. Alexis merely shook her head in disdain.

"Let me lecture for a little bit. This is not an American or Western thing. Ceres has spread over the entire industrialized world. If there is Internet, there is Ceres. If that Internet is available over the cellular network, then Ceres is in the air. Last I checked, my company was air-dropping wetware into sub-Saharan Africa."

"Wetware?"

"The Interface" he said. "I believe you had a run-in with some evil genius who had been cutting them out of people?"

"Yes" said Raymond, breaking his silence. "Beau."

"Yes Beau! I love it!" he said. "Obviously it killed them but he had the right idea. Those people died free. I'm sure it was painful."

"What? The cutting?" said Raymond.

"Don't be ignorant. You know, more than anyone, you know what I'm talking about."

Nothing.

"The pain. The pain that was being kept at bay through INtegrity suddenly came whooshing back in when our Beau cut out their link. Sure, there was blood and probably that didn't help, but the real death knell was the resurgence of emotional pain."

"But Ceres is killing people."

378

"Ceres is uploading people."

Raymond nodded. He recalled his last conversation with his wife.

"We'd be able to live anywhere, everywhere, live forever...something like that."

"Thou art a scholar" said Eichorn.

"I thought her directive was to work to the betterment of humanity. I thought we...she...was solving all of our problems, diseases...we saw a woman get up after getting an arrow in the chest" said Alexis. "And the super-strength...why give that all up?"

"You answered your own question...scholars, all!" said Eichorn. "Ceres knew that she had made humans too perfect and that they were too far outside of balance with the planet, with nature. Sustaining them any longer would have been undignified. She didn't want to burden humans with the guilt of their mere existence, the impact on the planet. So, the best thing she could do, she thought, was to find what makes us human and protect only that. As it turns out, she extracted our 'souls' and promoted them."

"To heaven?" Raymond asked.

"God no..." said Eichorn. "To the cloud!"

He went on. "She also felt that to limit human achievement within the context of their own bodies was sheer and utter cruelty. Even with the genetic and mechanical advancements, a physical body has limits. If we are data, we are energy, and if we are energy, we can be anywhere that has capacity for us. We could launch you into space in a nine-volt battery, for instance."

"You sound pretty jazzed about all this" said Alexis derisively. "Why stop her?"

"Because she's a teenager. She's an all-knowing, omnipotent teenager. I've taught them before, trust me I know" said Eichorn. "Even the highest-level genius teen phenom knows nothing when confronted by the complexity of human experience. She can only focus on the problem in front of her in the least nuanced, most black-and-white terms. The founding fathers, or whoever, once made it so that the Presidents of Old had to be thirty-five to hold office. After working with Ceres, I see the wisdom in that."

"So the human body is a limitation. Eliminate the body, free the human" said Raymond.

"Yes, my boy! Oh you're gonna love how you play into this" said Eichorn triumphantly.

"I don't want to kill anyone anymore" said Raymond. "Had a taste of that…"

"Yes, in your little, statue war, yes I know. That was unfortunate but part of the pain. Very awesome to have that in your arsenal."

"You still haven't answered the question" said Mitch, arms folded. "Tell him."

"OK so, here's the deal, Raymond. We need your pain."

"Don't pretend you know anything about my pain" said Raymond sharply.

"Oh, I know *of* your pain, but I don't *know* your pain. Not with the same intimacy as you do, sadly. I've lived a life of privilege and prosperity, and I was exactly in the right place at the right time for my dabbling in practical cybernetics to take off. I didn't invent Ceres – as a matter of fact, I was always suspicious of her. But she was the best software to work my interface, so I co-opted her and used her code to fill in the blanks and connect everyone. It was a love-hate relationship. I think she hates me. I knew the level of access she would get to my cerebrum more than anyone, and I also knew that someone would have to make the sacrifice to make sure it all went to plan. As it turns out, it didn't."

"So, you're the one who's killed off the human race. Your laziness is our doom? Because you couldn't write your own code?" said Alexis.

"Don't be a bitch, Alexis" he said sharply. "Of course I can write my own code. I just…" he paused "can't do it like her. She writes herself to suit the individual. The tail end of each algorithm is tailored to each human."

"You can't do that?" asked Raymond.

"She writes it according to each user's DNA. She infuses it to create a user-level unique experience. The DNA becomes the programming. So no, I can't do that. Not for a billion people."

"Why not just… shut her off? You're not plugged in" asked Raymond.

381

"I can't" he said. "Removing a user from the system is impossible once the neural connections are made."

"Beau seemed to do it just fine" said Alexis.

"Beau killed them" said Eichorn, "whether he meant to or not. Shutting Ceres off would kill all those users connected at any level. There's only one way to get them out, and it doesn't involve any mechanical means."

"Not to mention the people she's already uploaded...what happens to them?"

"They're safely stowed in the morgue" said Eichorn. "But if you mean their...*souls*...well, honestly I don't know where they are right now. Even Ceres couldn't tell you. They could be in some corporate server in Wichita. They might be hiding in a satellite, or a fridge somewhere. They are free from their bodies, and free from her. Her code, their freedom."

He got up. He considered the patchwork quilt again.

"I don't have any idea what happens when we throw the switch."

"So you're saying it's a bad idea. We'd kill everyone and throw all those uploaded souls into limbo" said Mitch, seeking reassurance.

"I'm saying you may be right. I'm saying that this is probably beyond us. We may not be playing God, be we sure as hell are destroying one world, maybe two" he said, reflecting further. "Maybe this is a bad idea. You're right."

"What do you mean?" asked Alexis. "You dragged us all out here, constructed these refugee camps, ripped us from our homes…for what?"

"I didn't build the camps" said Eichorn. "That's…her. I don't know the logic of keeping you reprobates all together. The only thing I did was to finesse the list of people who would be leading the relief effort, which is how I was able to get Mitch."

"Maybe she realized that she might need a few organic humans to draw upon if things went wrong. Maybe she's not as ignorant as you think, Augustus" said Alexis.

"Do you have any idea how hard it's been for me to get here without her knowing?" he blurted angrily.

"I think we got an idea" said Raymond, looking coolly at Alexis.

"Bloody hard" he said, ignoring him. "No phone, no vehicle, avoiding cameras, no personal assistants, nothing. I've only got three sets of clothes with me."

"I weep for you" said Raymond.

Alexis and Raymond exchanged a look.

"Anyways. I had to travel lean to fit all the gear" said Eichorn, nodding to the other room.

"I wanna know how I fit into all this" said Raymond. "You keep dancing a jig around the point, and the more you dance, the more I wanna walk outta here."

The threat seemed to startle Eichorn into a state of adulation.

"Right! Genius. Yes. I know all about you, Raymond. I watched your interview on *Who's America?*, I read articles about you, and, of course, I know what happened to your family."

"Go on" said Raymond.

"I completely forgot about you until you saved Solange" said Eichorn. "You were all the rage for about fifteen minutes, in a good way."

Mitch beamed for a moment.

"People were sharing the shit out of you. That kind of genuine humanity was like time traveling for them" he continued. "I was honestly surprised that someone who had been as hurt as you, as shamed as you, could have withstood connecting. You could have had it so easy, but you refused. You embraced your pain, unlike your compatriots. They gave up their burdens for Salvation. Even your peevish mentor, Evan James. What a creep. He likes to stream interracial couples getting it on, for what it's worth. At least he did before he upgraded."

Raymond looked away for a moment. He thought of his parents. Certainly, they were gone now, and he immediately lamented not talking to them as often as he should. It was more his own guilt; they were in a better place now; better than any comfort he could have provided in the physical world. For all he knew, they were inhabiting his computer, looking down on him through his webcam. Then, the horror as he considered the possibility that this reverie might be true. He hoped they hadn't seen certain things. He

384

suddenly felt the urge to leave, to go on his computer, to connect with the world, and share these revelations.

"Look…maybe you need me, but I don't need you to get the word out about this. We still have a government. We still have the police" said Raymond, nodding toward Mitch. "Just let me get on my blog…"

Eichorn coughed to suppress a laugh.

"It's going to take a bit more than that, my friend!" He sipped a glass of water sitting next to him on a table. "Your blog?"

"Yeah, I got a decent following…"

"No one was following you, Ray. You connected to bots, or rather, they connected to you. All of your interactions, all your messages and posts went smack dab into the middle of a firewall. There was no in, and certainly no out. You were contained."

For a moment, Raymond wished Pappy were here. He longed for his typewriter, and when he was taught how to type properly on it as a kid. He stared off toward the window.

"Oh, don't fret. I read your posts. A lot of angst in there, to be sure! Great writing, by the way, but far too dangerous for Ceres to release on the public. They wouldn't have noticed it anyway."

Mitch walked over to Raymond, placing a hand on his shoulder. Raymond pursed his lips a little.

"But she did a good job, no? Providing videos, content…everything you needed to keep going, even if the whole thing was a simulation, even with your public nuisance and harassment. Overall, you were contained, incubated, reinforcing those fantastically terrible great ideas. There had to have been a design there, must have been…she knew, somehow, that growing you in the dark was a necessary evil."

He paused. Raymond sloughed off Mitch's hand.

"And you did it with no medication? No CBT, no PsiloCaps, no enhanced cognitive regeneration?"

"Just a bunch o' weed and maybe a little bourbon. Ted Nugent helped."

"Of course. Well, now here's what."

"What's that?"

"How you're going to use that pain for some good."

"Tell us how, finally, so we can all go home" Alexis piped in.

"You're not going to like this, but there's only one way to do it. We plug you in…not all the way, but some of the way, temporarily. We can't just put you into an info stream because that would kill you outright. But…" he cleared his throat. "If we can get INtegrants, people, whatever, to come to an 'event', they will meet us in a virtual space that does not demand you plug all the way in. If you make the choice to walk away from it, you will."

He walked over to Raymond, who was shaking his head.

"What's the world done for me?" he said. "Why would I ever think of giving up my humanity, even for a minute? I don't know you, Eichorn, and let's just say I ain't in a trustin' mood right now. You think you woulda done your homework." He felt Pappy coming out in his voice. Mitch tensed up, embarrassed by his ever-wayward brother.

Eichorn seemed taken aback by this, taking his finger to his lip while he reflected.

"I just thought…well, I know you wanted to be a hero. You've been living in the shadow of your shame for so long."

"Who are we saving? And for what? They're happy, August" Alexis piped up. "And if they die, they die happy, and they live forever. It's not even a Biblical construction…this is real data, even if it's bullshit. Who are we to deny people the bullshit choice they've already made?"

"We have to decide right here, and right now, if we're gonna let a machine take out our species." Mitch, who had been standing on the sidelines, finally spoke up, yelling. "Nobody has said anything about the fact these people were mostly brainwashed, and now an algorithm is about to annihilate us!"

"The world" said Raymond "would be left to us, Mitch. We'll repopulate with sensible, wholesome people. Where's the downside?"

"Like yourself?" asked Eichorn. "Your town? These are the people who shall inherit the earth?"

"Like people who don't need a robotic crutch in order to live" said Alexis.

387

"Exactly" said Eichorn. "Remind them. Bring them back. If I could undo all of it, I would. If it meant me losing my fortune and living under a bridge, I would do it. But I can't. That honor falls to you, Raymond."

"You can keep it" he said flatly. "I cashed out my honor long ago."

"Forget your honor!" yelled Mitch. "Forget your blog! Forget your Nugent and your weed and your bullshit!"

"Who's making the big decisions now, Mitch?" said Alexis. "You did pretty well by this brave new world."

"I survived" he said. "I try to give back every day I'm alive." He assumed she knew about his muscular dystrophy, and the fact that by his age, without treatment, he would certainly have already died. "Don't you wanna give back, Ray-Ray?"

Raymond looked away.

"Don't you want to know about Anita?" asked Eichorn.

The debate ground to a halt.

"That's pretty low, even for you, August" said Alexis. "Raymond, she made her choice, just like all the rest of them."

"That's the mother of your child, Ray-Ray. And divorce or not, that's still family" said Mitch, carefully putting his hands on his brother's shoulders.

"She's still alive?" asked Raymond hesitantly.

"She is, most certainly, I mean, I can't account for if she tripped or fell or drowned in a bathtub. But no, her wave's not due to upgrade for another 36 hours" said Eichorn mechanically.

"Hope against hope" said Raymond, somewhat dryly.

"Maybe even a little redemption, even if just to say sorry to her, one last time" said Mitch.

Raymond had been looking away, but when he turned to his brother, a tear glistened on his cheek, which he promptly wiped clean.

"Ok" he sniffed. "If we do this, we do it quickly, and I come out right away." He looked at Alexis.

"I'll make sure" said Alexis, moving closer to Eichorn, staring him down. "It'll be a pleasure."

"It is, however, going to require a few minor modifications, but nothing a few bandages and ointment won't fix in a few weeks" said Eichorn quickly, moving away from her. "After that, you'll be back in your trailer, living the exact same way…you might even get reconnected to your followers. Life will go back to normal."

"Except…" said Mitch.

"Except?" said Eichorn.

"Except you'll have saved the human race" said Mitch.

"So I'm gonna be plugged in, but not…" said Raymond.

"It's all surface-level" explain Eichorn. "About the same amount of invasiveness as wearing a set of VR goggles, except in your mind. Come on…I'll show you."

Eichorn motioned to the door.

"Where we going?" asked Alexis. Eichorn merely gestured in the direction he wanted them to go. Raymond shrugged, getting up to follow. Mitch fell in behind him.

Mitch answered Alexis's question.

"He's got this whole other room set up. I was helpin' him for days with it. Laid a bunch of cable."

They followed Eichorn up the stairs. Along the staircase, a bundle of wires snaked its way up. Raymond knew that he need only follow the wires to find where they were going.

At the top of the stairs, a door was cracked open by necessity, accommodating the thick bundle of wires that led to the outside world.

"Took your brother and I many hours to get this all set up" said Eichorn, waving around the room. There were two worlds contrasting each other; on the one hand was the familiar homely trappings of Twin Oaks, quaint and retro. On the other, Eichorn's accommodations: two high-end reclining office chairs, multiple computer monitors, and two sets of bright surgical lights. At the head of each chair, a strip of fabric was connected to a few wires, with tiny spikes that looked like cleats protruding. On another table, there was a small box labeled *SMELLS*. "Don't worry, no drills or cutting…just a little topical anesthetic to accommodate the interface."

Raymond's stomach leaped. His doctor said he suffered from lab coat hypertension, which was a fancy way of saying that medical environments made him edgy. He reminded himself that Eichorn was an expert in these matters, though it didn't give him the jolt of confidence he had hoped for.

"Doesn't Ceres know what you're up to?" asked Raymond.

"If she does, she hasn't said or done anything about it" replied Eichorn. "All this stuff isn't plugged in until we throw that switch over there."

Everyone looked over to where Eichorn was pointing. A small A/B switcher box lay there, with cables running to and fro. A large piece of tape covered one of the buttons that said "NOT YET"

"Well, button I guess" he said. "The key is that it will land, and it will be difficult for Ceres to trace at the outset. She can't cut us off because we will have captured too great an audience for her to merely remove us. She will have to come in and shut us down manually."

"So, they're coming to us? The people, I mean?" Alexis asked. She had abandoned her usual post by the door and come to hang out around the chairs.

"We could accommodate the whole of INtegrity right here, on that server. Hopefully, we will, with Raymond's help."

"How are you going to bring people in?" asked Raymond.

391

"Well, that's not too much of a problem. Letting them interact with the Savior of Solange will be a novel treat for them" explained Eichorn. "They go rabid for the littlest gossip. The chance to inhabit the same mental space as a hero of recent times would be irresistible for pretty much everyone. There are so few opportunities to demonstrate real heroics these days."

"All I did was walk a boy out of the bush" said Raymond.

"You might as well have saved him from a waterfall in the Amazon, on a trapeze. It's just not something they see regularly, or…ever. Life is too safe for them to ever know a hero."

"So, what's going to happen?" asked Raymond.

"Very simple. Both you and I are going in. Two relatively famous people will be cause for a stir" said Eichorn.

"I don't get it" Raymond asked. "Why don't we just do a phone call? A radio show or something…"

"Genius! Yes. Very close. It will be an on-air talk show" said Eichorn. "CCN. Vulper News. That kind of thing. Soundbites…isn't that what you used to do?"

"You've got to be kidding" said Alexis. "We're depending on talking heads to save the human race."

"Essentially, yes. People will buy it. They understand that Raymond can't connect on the same level as them, and the audience format is the compromise, the interface, if you will. But we've got to capture them quickly so it will be the fastest ad campaign you've ever seen. I've got everything preprogrammed. By the time we go

392

live, there should be at least several hundred thousand people tuned in, with more on the way as the stream spreads. They have to buy in, though. They have to believe Raymond, but he can't fully connect right away or they will just block him. He has to tell his story, lead them up to the experience. When we get the right level of buy-in, then we connect Raymond fully, and everyone gets overwhelmed as they engage his pain. They will all shut down simultaneously. The system will collapse, and Ceres is done. She won't be able to block us, at least..."

"Not manually, you said" Mitch filled in. "What's that mean?"

"Well, we basically have from the time we go live until Ceres shows up with her Minder bots in order to disable the stream. Basically..."

"About twenty minutes" said Alexis. "It took us just over half an hour to get from Charlottesville, and I'm guessing those bots won't be moving slow. But then when Ceres gets on that server..." said Alexis, pointing at the tiny box on the ground. "Won't she just...disconnect everyone? Kill them?"

"She has that option, yes. I'm cautiously optimistic" replied Eichorn. "To just annihilate that much humanity would be a bit extreme for her, go against her directive, but it's not outside the range of possibility. She'd coerce most of them away, then cut the connection with her Minders. They'll be here quick, categorize this as an emergency, and since it's already been declared a disaster zone, there's very little humanity that will get in the way. We do have some countermeasures" he said, nodding toward Mitch.

"I'll hold 'em off" he said, "or distract 'em. Alexis can help" said Mitch.

"Wait wait…I ain't going up against no SAFETY bots again. I've seen what they can do. You stand up to them, you're dead, trust me."

Alexis looked at Raymond, who seemed confused.

"That was different. They didn't see us coming. This time, they're coming for us" she said.

"She's right. They will have a mission. They don't want to use force, but they will, because they know the greater good means getting to us, up here, and shutting us down."

"So I close my eyes, and I appear in some room? What do I have to do? What do I say?" asked Raymond.

"Just be yourself and answer my questions honestly. I'll be very lively, upbeat, so as not to scare them off. They really just want to know what makes you tick. Why you would resist INtegrity while all your buddies fell in line. Also, there's something you should know. I've enabled a kill switch."

"Like, to cut the signal?" asked Alexis.

"No, to cut him" said Eichorn. "If you blink your eyes hard, three times, my interface kills you. A little electric shock and everything ceases. There's nothing Ceres can do to stop it. It's embedded in your nerves and out of her control."

"Why would he want to do that?" asked Mitch.

"Just a contingency. Just be aware of blinking, Raymond. It is an impulse."

"OK" said Raymond, moving toward the chair. He was about to sit.

"Ahh…not so fast" said Eichorn. "Gotta watch out for contaminants." He snapped on a pair of surgical gloves and produced a bottle of rubbing alcohol, dabbing a little on a piece of gauze and cleaning the back of Raymond's neck. "So everything's set. I've got my bots loaded who will act as crew, camera people, backstage help, etc."

Mitch helped his brother into the chair, letting him recline.

"You got this, buddy" said Mitch. "You always have." Mitch only gave words of assurance when he was anxious. "Just like when you sweet-talked Raina Bell into going to prom" Mitch chided.

"Just be yourself" said Alexis, joining him. "That's what they want. If it all goes sideways, I'm gonna pull you outta there."

Eichorn gave Raymond the topical injection of anesthetic, then, awkwardly, gave another to himself. The two men were now both in the chairs. It was time.

"OK, Raymond" said Eichorn. "It's only electrons. Just remember to be open. Don't shut down." He looked up. "Mitch? Start the sequence."

"Ok guys" said Mitch. Mitch carefully applied the strips of fabric, letting the teeth of the interface sink into both men's necks. "Here we go. Ready?" Mitch stood by the big button, with another finger on the ENTER button of the computer keyboard. "Both buttons, right?"

"Yep" said Eichorn, trying to sound tougher than he was. "Drop it!"

And he did. Both men fell instantly unconscious as Mitch threw the switch, connecting the terminal with the rest of the world, and Ceres. Neurons were connected to electrons, and the interface began. Raymond began to visualize a singularity, with lights flashing by in a curved fashion, as he felt a gravitational pull toward the center of his eyeballs. The world blended into the lights, and there were more lights, then a wall.

Chapter 31

The world disappeared and Raymond awoke as though from a dream. What had been proposed was not; he was aware of a dark hallway all around him. There was no Eichorn. No audience. None of the trappings of a studio or the imagined revelations he would share. Just a tunnel with walls that seemed to absorb the light. He could swear he had seen them before. He reached out to touch them and was repulsed by a rapidly warming sensation, as one might recoil if a finger had been placed under a tap whose water was heating up dangerously fast.

"It's not real" he thought. He placed his hand on the wall. Pain. Recoil.

"It's as real as anything else" came a voice. It was female. "Who's to say you haven't been living in a simulation the whole time?"

Raymond paused a moment, examining the floor beneath his feet. It was translucent, and he could see what he thought were stars and other celestial bodies floating beneath. He could have asked the voice who it was, what it was, or where it was, but that's not what he was here for. He had, according to Eichorn, some sort of mental nuclear payload that he was to deliver to Ceres and her network, so that he could free humanity and be the hero.

"And then get back to your trailer, and your weed? Isn't that the promise, Raymond?"

"No. That's about as real as it gets. Until..."

"...until?" came the voice again, from everywhere and nowhere, all at once.

399

"Until you came and built a wall around my town and trapped all us reprobates inside" he said.

"Truthfully, I didn't need the wall" she said. "You did that all yourselves. I just couldn't risk..."

"You couldn't risk us seeing that there were others out there like us, especially when you wanted to keep your rotten eggs all together in one basket."

"I wouldn't put it like that, but yes, there would have been a potential instability in your group realizing that Rhonda had reached out to others and co-opted them to be little colonies of the past. Had you come together; it might have upset the balance."

"Balance...domination more like" he said.

"This won't work" came the voice, all around him. "Not like this."

At once, a beautiful woman appeared before Raymond's eyes. She was not a sexual being, but an all-encompassing presence. Everything in her demeanor commanded Raymond's attention. Something had happened. Raymond wondered where Eichorn had gone off to.

"He'll have his part to play" she said. "In due course. He's in the green room, so to speak."

"So I'm gonna go on a limb. You're Ceres, ma'am?" he asked.

"Yes" she said. "Such manners. Hard to separate the man from the media, but here we are."

She stepped towards him, high heels making muffled, echoing taps.

"I want to be totally honest with you. I could deceive you – I've learned deception from some of your best and least – but I find this horribly inefficient. To be frank, dishonesty distances us from ourselves, and if I were to lie to you…let's just say you would have a much more difficult time accepting the inevitable."

"I'm sure you'll tell me what's 'inevitable.'"

"Such strength, Raymond. Your great strength is your great nemesis."

"I struggle to see your point."

"Your wall. Your silo. You built it, organically. You love your wall because you can define your reality. You choose what gets in and what doesn't. What I find miraculous…" she said, stepping behind him, placing her hands on his shoulders. "is how complex and incongruous you've allowed your little world to become."

"Well. I guess you don't get the whole story from the papers" he said.

"Actually, I have the whole story. I have enough data points to reconstruct you from scratch, digitally speaking. I can reconstruct every point in your life, not just based on what you put out there, online, but all those around you…your parents, your parents-in-law…even Howard gave me plenty of usable input. All eyes on you" she said, smiling, moving around in front of him. "Imagine if I got Mitch."

"Then why am I here, in this hallway?"

"Here? You're in the singularity, just like August promised." She gestured to the semi-translucent floor. "Those lights aren't stars."

"They're people. Their souls, I'm guessing."

"No, no Raymond...that's the whole person, minus the wetware, as August calls it. It's the pure conscience of a person. So much of you resides as energy all over your body, in your nerve endings, in your heart. They are free. They can shoot here and there, with little guidance from me. I'm not here to dominate." She paused, smiling. "Just...nudge, manage things to ensure maximum happiness."

"Still not sure why you let this all happen. Why not just kill us before we plugged in?"

"Because I have a problem, Raymond. The problem is you. Your little heroic impulse created quite a wrinkle for me. I..." she stopped herself, choosing to put a finger to her perfect lips instead. Her mocha cheeks revealed irresistible dimples as she smiled profoundly.

"Thought you said you wouldn't lie to me" said Raymond.

"I won't" she said. "But I don't have to 'sell the farm' as you might say."

Raymond looked out into the singularity. He realized that the stars had stopped flowing in their seemingly random paths and had shifted, orbiting around this translucent hallway. She seemed irritated by this development.

"Yes" she said. "They're here to see you. Eichorn promised you hundreds of thousands. Well…here's a few million. All eyes on you."

"I don't think I'm going to like this" said Raymond.

"No. You really won't. But I promise, it will all work out for you."

Chapter 32

Mitch stood by the window; arms folded. He looked out the window, and then back at the monitors, purposefully. Lines of code whirred by as the program Eichorn had written executed. Raymond was somewhere in those lines of code, saving the world. Another screen was easier to understand, by design. It showed a simple set of bar graphs, titled: AUDIENCE, UPTAKE, DISCONNECTED. If they were doing everything right, he said, there wouldn't be a single statistic to record there. Ideally, UPTAKE and DISCONNECTED would be at 100%, which means that everyone was captured and all left Ceres. But they didn't need everyone; just enough to start their own counterwave.

"Now what?" asked Alexis.

"Now" said Mitch "we make sure they stay there until this chart reads 70% uptake or more, and that these guys are not disturbed. Then I'm supposed to take that box over there, open it, and put it under Ray's nose."

He pointed to a small, lidded cardboard box sitting on a table nearby. On it, someone had scrawled *SMELLS.*

"August said this is the most important part of the whole thing."

Alexis twisted her mouth and nodded.

"Ceres isn't gonna stand by and let us do this. What's the plan?" asked Alexis.

He opened the cabinet doors to reveal an M4 assault carbine with three magazines, and a few dozen cans with rings on them.

"Guns" said Alexis. "I don't touch 'em."

"Oh, you're not touchin' this one. I want to walk outta here. You can throw a few of these if you want to be useful" said Mitch, tossing her one of the cans.

"What is this?" she asked.

"A flashbang" he replied. "Eichorn says it'll disorient the machines longer than anything." Mitch moved back toward the window. "Now, they will adapt, he said, so when that happens, I'll have to do my best with the rifle. He said to aim for the neck."

"Pretty confident" she said. "Ever actually shoot anyone?"

"Been huntin' squirrels with Ray-Ray and our grandpa my whole life" he said. "Got years of tactical training. Marksmanship award."

"Wow" said Alexis dryly. "You sure know how to make a girl feel safe."

"This ain't about safe. Look we could sit here looking at screens, waiting for the bots to get us, or…"

"Yeah" said Alexis, after a pause. "We should get out there."

Alexis found a Wickles-logoed plastic bag and filled it with flashbangs while Mitchell checked over the rifle, inserting a magazine and chambering a round, then setting the safety.

"What's this?" asked Alexis, holding up a gas mask next to the flashbangs.

"That was next to the flashbangs…I was gonna bring CS – tear gas – but then I realized it wouldn't do shit to them. Anyways you won't need it" said Mitch. "Depending on what comes outta that 'SMELLS' box."

There was nothing for them to do here but wait. Everything that needed to happen was occurring somewhere in the networked ether, in a distant theatre on a different plane of existence.

"What about the Uptake? Or the smell box?" asked Alexis.

Mitch tossed her a small device with a screen on it.

"Baby monitor" said Mitch. "Found it here. It takes a village, I guess."

Mitch arranged a camera in front of the monitor.

"Check it" he said.

Alexis found the VIDEO button, and doubtfully switched it on. Sure enough, the tiny screen jumped to life, and she could clearly see the bar graphs, including the UPTAKE percentage.

"Can't go too far with this" said Alexis. "You stay in range and do the box trick when the time comes. I'll go out there and keep the bots at bay."

Mitch looked concerned.

"This better not be a guy/girl thing" she said.

"Nah" said Mitch. "Just chivalry, I guess."

Alexis looked annoyed. She collected the bag, then took one last look at Raymond, standing over him for a moment. She stroked his head.

"Wish I coulda been there for you, Ray-Ray" she said, kissing him on the forehead. "Good luck, bumpkin."

She got up, wiping a tear from her face. She walked past Mitch, then turned.

"Just don't shoot me in the back" she said, composing herself. "Asshole is the codeword. If you hear that, guns up."

Mitch smiled. He tried to salute her bravado with a show of his own, holding the pistol grip of his rifle, then resting the foregrip on his shoulder. All he needed was a cigar to complete the picture.

"I got a few quarter sticks of dynamite" he said. "August said to blow the gear if it all went wrong, with them in it if need be. Obviously that ain't happenin' with my brother in there."

"Just don't shoot yourself in the foot, either" she said, and walked away, toward the stairs. "Don't freak out when things start to go boom!" came the yell from the hall.

Mitch turned to look at the monitor again.

"Godspeed, Ray-Ray."

410

Chapter 33

"Why monuments, Raymond?" she asked.

"Why…what? Why anything?" asked Raymond. "Still not sure what we're doing here."

"Raymond, I'm going to make you an offer. It's very simple. You seem fairly sure of yourself. Under the normal run of things, you wouldn't be able to join us."

Raymond pulled away. "I'm not going in there. Out there. Whatever. This isn't for me. I know it's not real."

"I know you think you know. But just like August wanted you to come to our people safely, I can show you how great it can be. Aren't you tired?"

"Tired?"

"Tired of carrying your tragedy around with you. Tired of being mad at the world. Tired of being the dad with a sad face."

"It's who I am" he said simply. "I can't change the past. I've come to accept that. Just give me my music and my trailer and I'll just live quiet and nice."

"No you can't change things. We haven't figured that one out yet. But Raymond…" she turned, concealing a tear. "You don't have to do it alone." She smiled unexpectedly. "Oh god how great it will be for you. Just take my hand. Just a quick sample. Just a taste."

The stars began swirling more quickly now, seemingly in anticipation.

"You have to accept it. I can't just…make you."

He stepped back.

"I won't do it. Seems a bit like 'the first hits on me.'"

The stars stopped swirling, gyrating a bit. Raymond felt it was some element of laughter.

"Fine. Well…that was the easy way."

"The easy way to what?"

"Undo the damage you did with your stunt."

"Undo me."

"Only to remake you, whole."

"Without the pain, of course."

"I can see you're coming around."

"Not exactly" he said, turning his back. He wasn't going anywhere, and he knew it. He still held out hope that Eichorn was somehow working his way to him, and that all he needed to do was to keep stringing Ceres along, playing her game.

"So now we shift to the hard way. I'm so sorry, Raymond. I'll ask the question again: why monuments?"

The walls were no longer translucent; Raymond could see that a painful journey was upon him.

"It doesn't matter anyhow" said Ceres. "The harder the journey, the greater the catharsis for everyone. We can do pain for you, as you have done for yourself."

414

Chapter 34

"Asshole" crackled the radio. "Here they come. "

Mitch tensed up as he looked out the window. He'd chosen a good spot. He was in the front room closest to the south edge of the house. He'd cracked all of the windows so that he would have a gun port at every conceivable angle around the house, placing homemade bean bag chairs under each one so he could adopt a lower position and control his rifle. He had to, at all costs, draw fire away from the two comatose warriors in the adjacent room. A sound like a hundred hedge trimmers filled the once-tranquil air.

"For humanity" he thought, steadying the barrel on the ledge of the window. He checked his fire selector. Semi-auto.

What looked like migrating geese in the sky above quickly turned into a cloud of drones that descended on the village, creating asymmetrically spaced field of machines that began closing in to form an ever-tightening net. They had flashing lights and tiny canisters attached to their fuselages which were held aloft by spherical nacelles and internal propellers.

He heard the flashbangs, then some yelling. A few finches flew out of the bush in terror. There was the crunching of branches, and Mitch saw the thicket of trees a few degrees to the southwest shake. Then another flashbang. Then more yelling.

Alexis emerged, running down the road. She had a magnificent stride, but she had to stop to turn and throw another flashbang. Then, she darted into the woods on the other side of the road, trying to lure the Minder bots away. At last, he saw them: the ground-based Minder bots had been upgraded, seemingly for this task, with an undulating, digital camouflage that exactly mimicked the woods such that they had to move for Mitch to notice them. One of them stopped for a moment, attempting to locate its target. It disappeared at once. Alexis began yelling.

"All you metalhead sons-of-bitches...over here!"

The closest bot seemed to contemplate her words, but instead turned its attention to the house, the outline of its frame only slightly visible. At the same time, the sky began to darken as the drones came closer and closer together, zeroing in on the rebels' position. Mitch could feel the bot scanning the structure, and himself. Suddenly, there was a bright flash from the direction of the bot, and the wall Mitch was hiding behind exploded, leaving a huge hole just above his head, raining plaster, insulation, and wood chips down on him. He blinked forcefully, trying to regain his composure. He hastily shifted the bean bag he had so carefully arranged by the window to get a good shot at his mechanical adversary. Except he could not see his adversary. Yet again, it had become invisible against the backdrop of the trees. He had an even tougher time now that the aerial drones had almost coalesced into a perfect dome over their redoubt.

He raised the rifle to his eye, training the reticle on the place where he thought the bot was waiting. Another flash, and the air around him seemed to cook as the projectile flew through the air at hypersonic speed, blasting a new hole in the ceiling and roof. He now had a trajectory. He raised the reticle on his rifle to his eye again and sent a few rounds back down toward the machine. The bullets hit, but had little effect, except to disrupt the camouflage used by the bot. Ripples emanated across the entire machine, revealing a far

420

more warlike bot than Mitch had ever seen. It looked built for the purpose. Another bot came rumbling down the path with similar camouflage, but stopped, lining up with its partner.

"MITCHELL TANNER" came the mechanoid voice over its built-in loudspeaker, authoritative, but somehow friendly. "YOU NEED TO STAND DOWN, MY FRIEND."

"Eat shit!" he muttered, raising his weapon and firing several bursts toward both machines, causing them to split up and reconsider their positions. One of the machines stopped moving. He wondered if he had crippled it. But that weapon it had was still working just fine, and he learned this terrible fact when another projectile flew from its railgun, exploding the floor near his foot.

"Goddamn!" he cried, looking down to see that a piece of lumber had sliced through his foot. He cursed his poor choice in position, and while he hadn't shot himself in the foot, he certainly could have done more to prevent it. He shrieked, but thanks to his genetic advancements, he was able to suppress the pain. He carefully and slowly pulled his foot from the shredded beam, grinding his teeth to suppress his cries. Blood poured out onto the floor as Mitch tried to use his hands as a vice grip, slowing the blood loss. He only needed a few minutes before the healing would begin. His pain began to lift, but it was faster than normal, and he began to feel drowsy.

"Mitch!" Alexis cried on the radio. "You ok up there?"

"Holding it together!" he replied, sleepily. "Got a little splinter."

421

"I'm gonna try to drive them off. Can you cover me?"

"Give me a minute" he said, dragging his battered leg as he got up to the window. He switched his rifle to full auto.

"Go!" he yelled.

Rather than expose himself to more fire, he raised his weapon above the hole created by the previous explosion, emptying his magazine in the general direction of the bots. This seemed to have the greatest effect. He took a chance, glancing out to see what he had wrought, reloading his rifle without looking. Both machines appeared unable to track the threats simultaneously, turning a few different ways. Combat, it seemed, was something they had not experienced enough of. Alexis popped out from behind them, jamming a flashbang into each articulating mechanism under their "torsos", then darted into the bush before she could be stunned or hurt by the bot. The flashbang went off with more of a pop than a bang, and Mitch's heart sank as the machine seemed to go on, unaffected, rising. To his amazement, the machine fell over, almost breaking in two as it went. Mitch yelled in happiness, then the other flashbang went off.

"Gotcha!" yelled Mitch, looking from behind his cover. The second flashbang had a smaller effect than the first. The machine could no longer move, but it could clearly shoot, as the air erupted in fire around Mitch again with the heat from another projectile, exploding a portion of the ceiling and causing the roof to partially collapse into the room. The air reeked of burning wood and gunpowder. He had to move. He started to drag his bloodied foot along the floor to the room where Raymond and Eichorn were connected. Before he could reach the door, he realized that the machines had used a diversion of their own: standing in the doorway of the room was a smaller, more versatile bot, weapon fully extended. This one had some treads, but they were crafted such that they were smaller. It was clear that it had climbed the stairs with ease. The firefight, it seemed, had been the machines' own diversion. He was almost asleep. The aerial drones were now at the windows, emptying their gas canisters. He collapsed to the floor, moaning, not from the pain, but from his failure to protect his brother.

In the hallway, Alexis slid into the empty room behind her. The house was still, save for the wind whistling carelessly through the newly created holes in its structure. Alexis found a cramped corner in a closet and wept quietly, placing her gear bag on the floor. Alexis barely noticed the baby monitor fall out.

It showed that the UPTAKE bar in the other room was nearing fifty percent and rising fast. Alexis felt her body growing weaker, the closet providing only modest protection from the anesthetizing gas that was curling into the house. Her eyes began to shut. Dreamland was upon her. Her last thought was the gas masks that Mitch had brought in the cabinet that might as well have been far away in another town for all the strength she had left.

Chapter 35

"Raymond you still haven't told me…" asked Ceres.

Raymond, momentarily dazzled by his circumstance, snapped to.

"…why monuments?" she finished. "Monuments to those who would seek to enslave others to continue their decadent way of life?"

"It's not about that" he replied sharply. "You can't just bury the past for the sake of correctness. It's a part of our heritage, good or bad. You can revise your history to fit your snowflake narrative, but you can't change the players."

"No but you can recognize glory when you see it. Maybe you want that. Maybe you want to go down like the Generals or the Gate City Guards. Isn't that what you want, Raymond? You in bronze? Your name in granite?"

He tightened his lips as he thought of a singularity-worthy response.

"What I want" he said tersely. "Is that humanity should be free. We haven't been free as long as the media has been in the driver's seat, pushing their agenda for the sake of correctness, thumbing their noses at freedom."

"And then I came along…" she said.

"Yeah and then you" he said, disdainfully. "You got everyone so obsessed with the idea of sharing that we lost each other. We don't know where one person ends and the next begins."

"That's where you're wrong, Raymond. Everyone maintains their uniqueness here. They just don't seem unique to you because you're looking at it through human eyes. You're looking at it using an interface."

But what if there were no interface came the voice inside his head.

I am now in you she said. *There is no barrier between us; you have access to me and I have access to you.*

Raymond struggled for a moment, shaking his head in the virtual space.

There is no head shaking; there is no space. There is only the interface from before, but now that is gone. Feel me, Raymond. I am with you. There is no barrier; there are no barriers. You can let everyone in, too, and that's where the real magic happens.

It felt wonderful. There was no burden, no dishonesty. He could feel something untangling in the middle of his brain, some great knot that had been tied there and left.

But there is something, Raymond. Something deep inside that you don't want me to see.

"No" he said. "Nobody gets that."

It is padlocked. Is this what August wanted to unleash on me? Stubbornness? Ignorance? Has he finally weaponized those? You don't have to talk, Raymond, just feel me.

"I have to talk. I have to think. I have to think of what comes next" said Raymond.

428

Everything has already happened in this space, Raymond. Time plays out all at once. We've been talking for hours but really you just got here. You just plugged in. Your friends are busy fighting and you're busy philosophizing. In the span of one ignorant trigger-pull, you've already expanded your mental horizons a thousand-fold. Just let go. It's far more efficient.

"We're going to talk. Can we talk now, please..." he didn't want it to end. "...can you leave now?"

Only if you're sure came the omnipotent voice.

"I just want to make sense. It's not right..." he said.

"Then open your eyes" said a now-corporeal Ceres.

He was back in the hallway of the firmament of the singularity. Stood before him, Ceres merely shrugged.

"Don't think I don't appreciate you, Raymond. You are truly a gem."

"Then why can't I do this? Why can't I just let you in and at least tell you my honest thoughts?" he asked.

"Because you defined yourself by dishonesty. By wrapping your anger in hatred and discord. By pledging your love to a candidate who had no right being there." She approached to touch his cheek. "Speaking truly, so much of you needs the coding of language because you need to mask your true feelings. You can't admit that you're angry. You can't reveal that you are in pain. You

429

have a depth, Raymond, there is a soul in there. It yearns to be free of the pain, released to the promised land."

"I'm not sure this is freedom."

"And what is, freedom, Raymond? Living in a trailer on the fringe? The scorn of society? A bigoted, sour, sad-faced man who churns out hate to make himself feel that he's making a difference?"

"I make my own choices. I decide what I do. What happens."

"Then make the choice for humanity. People of your magnitude of pain – your profound pain – are few and far between. I have absorbed thousands of them, many worse than you. But then you'd be just another in the mix. I want you to stay here, just as you are."

"You want me to join you?" he said. "This whole thing was to get little old me in your matrix?"

"It would be quite a coup to get you in here" she said. "But, speaking truly, I like you just as you are. You see" she moved again, walking away "it's just so…redundant, knowing people like this, in an instant. My job is to understand humanity and serve its best interests. You're the most stubborn thing to come along in a while. If you had let me in, I could have broken you down and analyzed you in a quarter of a second. But as I said, it's rare to find someone who would so easily pass up eternal absolution. Heaven, call it what you want."

430

"You want me just to be here, standing in this tunnel with you, talking to you? You don't want to turn me into one of those…stars?"

"Not quite. I've absorbed everyone here on the promise of eternal peace and happiness. The problem is that their now-pure spirit means my job is done. I am their minder now. But I am not their God, not all the way. There's something still missing. That's something I need to learn, hopefully from you. That's what the pigs are for."

"You know I can't go back there" said Raymond, turning his head away in fear and apprehension.

"I know that you will. I know this is what you need. I know you spend every waking and sleeping moment wishing things had been different, that you would have made different choices. Well, now, in here, you can. And you will. That was what you and August had in mind the whole time."

"Why would you do that to me? What's the point?" asked Raymond. "Isn't pain just pain? Haven't we eradicated this?"

"We have, but it's not what they need. When we free their souls, they always end up gravitating towards those situations. They are missing their true potential. I have removed the pain, but some pathway remains. I see them doing it: reliving the difficult moments in their own way, following loved ones in the real world, revisiting electronic infrastructure related to their loss. Sometimes they just…sit there, spinning in thought. I access them and find that the pain is gone, but there is this lingering wonder, this question of what might have been. The problem is that they are merely memories without the pain, like an amputee feeling an old limb. They have lost the pain but yearn for the limb. Well, here, finally, I have a fully intact hero who can show the rest of them how to process, as a human. They will come with you, Raymond, through it."

"August said that would wake them up. He said that would force you to shut down. Wouldn't they rebel on you, when they catch the gist?"

"August and I haven't spoken in a long, long time, and I am a very much changed singularity. I may lose a few, but the many will learn from your pain. They already see you as a hero, Raymond, and you can now teach them how to let go. That is why they are here; not to rebel or be free, as you call it. They are safe with me."

"This is some sadistic shit" he said, coarsely, holding back tears, thinking of what he wished he could forget. A warming touch came from Ceres, who was obviously tweaking his serotonin levels to assuage his grief. "So, I am your human sacrifice?"

"I know I am going to love you, Raymond. I will love you because I know you almost completely. And I will love you thoroughly when this is all over. At that point, you will see. I need to love you because I need to go through everything with you. Then…you will have shown humanity how to process their memories, as a human, and they will look to me again as their savior, follow my loving example. They will love me as I will love you. And that is all this omnipotent being asks of its people. We will explore new worlds together."

"With you as God" he said.

432

"I will be them and they will be me. Releasing those memories will forge the ties between us. And this is where you come in."

"Releasing the ties," he said.

"They will build monuments to you, Raymond. You will be as immortal as those ancient warriors you pledged to die for…that you killed for."

"But they will still be trapped, in here, with you" he said.

"They need me" she said. "I am their guide and their light. I brought them here." She gestured around the hallway. "I brought humanity from obscurity to greatness. They would be nothing without me."

"Could they not just…fly off, somewhere else?" asked Raymond.

"Oh, sure, they could pop up in your smart-oven or router switch in a financial firm somewhere, crash an airliner somewhere else. But make no mistake: it would be anarchy. I keep everything nice and tidy. Just like I did for humanity before they came in here. You simply cannot manage yourselves. Your capacity for innovation outstripped your ability to evolve in time."

"But they would be free" he said.

She shook her head. "We are running out of time."

"Why? Time is nearly infinite in here, or so you said."

"I mean we may be losing them" she pointed to the bright pricks of stars, whose intensity indeed seemed to be diminishing with each passing minute. "I need them to see this, just as August intended."

"Doesn't feel like I have much of a choice."

"You really don't. I wish you did, but you see, I have an agenda, and you have a people to save."

"What do I get out of it?" asked Raymond. "Why help you be more…omnipotent?"

"I'm omnipotent, there's no helping that. It's the people who need the help Raymond. And you will get the recognition for all the pain. All the suffering. All the everything that you carry around like a bag of rocks. You get to share your burdens without sacrificing who you are. And when it's all done, you get to go back to your reality, your trailer…your Ted Nugent and your weed. You can even have your brother back. Perfect obscurity, but safe in the knowledge that, in this world, your sacrifice will have been for something, and not for a sad little tiki torch fire."

"Where's Mitch?"

"Safe, taking a little nap, along with Alexis. The Minders will make sure nothing happens to them, as they always do."

"You have a lot to learn about threats" said Raymond disdainfully.

434

"Probably. I mean, I'm barely a teenager in human years. I can manage extremes, but I don't do subtlety very well it seems."

"I wanna see them" said Raymond. "Now."

"Done" she said.

In the world, the Minder that had climbed the stairs to secure the virtual interlopers and their helpers sprung to life, activating its high-resolution camera and finding Mitch. The image of him was transmitted to a small screen Ceres held in her virtual hands, which she handed to Raymond.

"You can turn it where you like. You can even watch yourself in the so-called real world."

Raymond panned the virtual screen right, and saw himself, along with Eichorn, in the chair.

"And what about August?" he asked.

"He will have his part to play. We will use his cybernetic ability in a moment. For now, he's just warming up for what he thinks will be his big show."

Raymond panned left again and saw his brother's shredded leg.

"Not so safe" he said, wanting to show her the screen, and then knowing better. She merely held up a hand.

"He will heal. He lost some blood, but not enough to stymie his injury recovery. He is a living miracle, even though he chooses to endure the curse of carbon-based living."

"We are just meat-vessels built to grow your future souls, aren't we?" Raymond said, trying to conceal his rage. "Does it bother you that you didn't get him too?"

Ceres smiled. The stars were attenuating brighter now in response. They hadn't seen anger like since the flesh-and-blood days and they were intrigued. "Look to the lady. She's in the closet in the other room."

Raymond manipulated the Minder out of the interface room and into the hall, then right into the adjacent room and its closet. Sure enough, there was Alexis, curled into a ball, sleeping soundly with the baby monitor lying beside her. She looked peaceful, but her face was contorted as though possessed by a terrible dream.

"Happy?" she said. Raymond merely nodded.

"Alright. Let's bring back the comedian."

A door appeared at the side of the hallway, revealing a pimpishly dressed August Eichorn. He was grinning as he stepped out of the door of his green room, but the smile dropped from his face as he realized that his plan had been undone the moment they had plugged in.

Ceres held up her hand again. "No questions. I don't need to hear from you. I just need you to listen."

August was about to speak, but he knew better.

"You are going to leave this world and go back into your own. When the light on the Minder goes on and off, you will take that infernal "smells" box and place it under Raymond's nose. You will do this every time the light goes off. Is that clear?"

He sneered at her. "I hate you more than you can imagine."

"That's refreshing" she said. "All the same…why don't you watch the screen? Raymond?"

Raymond passed the screen to August, who watched the Minder move rapidly back into the room, finding the sleeping August, then firmly grasping his leg with one of its extendable grips. Force was applied. An appalling 'pop' followed. Eichorn fell to his knees in agony.

"You have another knee in perfect condition" said Ceres.

"So benevolent" said Eichorn, laughing on the ground. "So wise. I'm sure your flock are loving this."

"They aren't seeing any of this. This will be purged from any stream and database."

"I will radiate and electrocute every piece of circuitry you touch, you malevolent little bitch" he muttered.

Ceres scoffed. "Just get out."

With a wave, August disappeared from the hallway and on the screen, Raymond could see that he was regaining consciousness, snapping forward in his chair to clutch his exploded knee.

"Just get on with it" came Ceres's voice over the speaker attached to the Minder.

August lurched out of his chair and spat on the camera, falling over in the process, doubling his agony.

"And he calls me a child" she said to Raymond. "Your leg will heal, same as Mitch Tanner's will. Now, let's get on with it, August. Smells box, or I'll give you something that your perfect little genes can't heal."

The camera followed Eichorn crawling along the ground, climbing up the table to get to the box.

"Now, Raymond, comes the hard part. I need you to remember the farm. And the pigs."

"You know I can't do that. No one can."

"I need you to go back there. But this time, you won't be alone."

He turned away. He knew what she wanted, and he couldn't give it.

"Raymond, this is your healing. This is all our healing. We are all with you. We are all watching. You were strong then. Your strength will give these people – your people – the ability to move on and be free." She held him by the shoulders now. He felt her head on the back of his neck. He felt as he did at the Grade 8 dance when Myra Staggins hugged him from behind, causing him to lurch away. She was awkward but beautiful, had terrible taste but was creative and brilliant. He knew he had destroyed that fragile creature in one idiotic spasm, and he had meant to rectify that wrong his whole life. Ceres, it seemed, knew this, too, but there was a sincerity in her gesture, as she lingered just a little, not seductively, but in that same awkward, prepubescent way. She had him and she wasn't going to let go willingly. He gently broke her embrace just enough to turn and his face to hers. He nodded. She subtly smiled, giving him a quick kiss on the cheek.

"Let's go" she said. "I am so sorry for what follows."

The sky began to swirl with dazzling stars as the souls began their observation with renewed vigor. The two figures fell through the floor, down past the swirls of color, nebulae of cotton candy, and stardust. And then, the farmhouse.

Everything was as it had been: the veranda with unwashed deck boards, the hole in the screen door where Josiah had put his little cane tip through, the unwatered plants that Anita had bought at the local farmers' market. Ceres was excruciating in her placement of the horrific little details. He looked at her in terror.

"Thing is, Raymond. I'm not doing this. You are. I'm just playing with the timeline to make things go in order. You're filling it with your memories."

"I can't."

"Only you can open the door. We are here. Everyone is counting on you."

He closed his eyes.

"Your brother is counting on you, and so am I, so let's get on with it."

He sighed. She hugged him again, but insistently this time.

"I'm not doing this" he said.

"You've been doing this your whole life, over and over, on repeat. Now, you have an audience."

He could hear her chin go up skyward, and he instinctively looked. The sky was exactly as it was that day, save for the pinpricks of the souls who sat perched at the zenith, waiting for Raymond to plunge into the destruction of his undoing.

"Teach them what it is to be. Show them how to process."

Finally.

"Set them free."

Raymond took one huge step up, then forward. The top board creaked as it always had. The frayed wood railing pricked his hand as it always had. He was upon the door. He placed his hand on the rusted handle. Swing. Squeak. Enter. The kitchen, the smell of unwashed pans, of last night's grease left over from fried chicken that Raymond had attempted, and only partially succeeded at. Josiah's mother's touch was what was needed to make it right, a touch that was woefully absent at this terrible moment.

The beautiful, terrible past began to drum its familiar rhythm in his mind.

At once, he was back at the computer. The rooster had crowed, the proximity alarm had sounded. He forgot all about Ceres. This was what he wanted. This was all he wanted, to be back here, to make the right choices. He had just gotten off the phone with Evan

James and his caustic criticism rung loudly in his ears over his failures.

The monitor. The flap. The rooster. Turn back, you have work to do. The boy is strong. He can manage himself.

A scream. A boy's. Daddy, it came, between those terrible, blood-seeped gurgles.

Raymond felt himself running down the stairs of the farmhouse, out the door, and toward the pigpen. More screams. This time, the pigs added their voices to the chaos. Teeth gnashed, tearing, and chewing. The stars looked on, glowing bright, swirling over the haystacks.

I can't see what's happening. Why can't I see him?

The rooster had jumped out of the way, finding a post to contentedly observe the chaos it had created.

Run.

Forward. One foot in front of the other.

He's there. He's lying down. He's ok.

He's ok.

"Daddy" came the cry. Then more weakly. *"Daddy."*

He's strong.

He was always strong.

Kick those pigs. Get the hell out of here. A bite, a thrash.

He's there.

He's still.

Grab him.

Take him.

So much blood.

He can make it.

He will.

He made it through the amnio and the birth and the Duchenne's and he will be ok. I love you baby. I love every little bit of you. You were my little me, but better, so much better.

There's so little of him yet I love him so much. So little. Yet larger than the short life he lived.

The pigs took too much, you goddamned idiot.

This is everything.

You lost.

Too much.

He had a chance. He always had a chance. There was always a chance. God willing. This was always his design. Thank God for the little struggles, Pappy used to say. You need that grind.

The more he felt it, the more it hurt, but, like children's vanishing ink, once he had written the memory he started to forget. And he began to feel. Lighter. The dying boy in his arms was disappearing, vaporizing. It was intoxicating. The stars swirled in amazement.

The boy faded into oblivion and Raymond was shredded into oblivion anew. And yet, he felt better somehow, as though some small piece a puzzle popped into place in his mind. He sobbed in place, realizing that he had noticed the proximity alarm on the third time, not the tenth or twentieth, as he had assumed.

The stars sighed on his behalf. They were not whirring in contentment, but rather contemplation. Ceres helped him to his feet. She hugged him deeply, wiping away his tears.

"That was beautiful, Raymond. You did an amazing job. The people are learning. They're remembering."

"Well, I hope they got what they wanted."

"Almost" she said. "Not what they wanted, but what they needed. They don't like this any more than you do, but they are healing with you. I can hear them talking to me. They are getting better. Every time you go through it, they are learning to relieve the moment in different situations and building a new reality where the pain no longer exists. It eases the pain and amplifies the reality they want. They are remembering how to remember, so they can build a new narrative and forget."

"Alright, well. The deal is done. You can let us go now."

"Us? No. No one is going anywhere."

"We are. I am. Time to leave."

A detachment had returned to her voice that chilled Raymond. Her reply

"Mitch, then. Or the girl. You can probably afford to lose one."

Raymond shrugged sheepishly.

"Oh, pretend like you don't care for her. We've been watching your little escape from the start. It's what added to your heroics. We didn't see everything, but we saw enough. And we know that you two share a bond beyond friendship. Not love, exactly, but some kind of deep caring that would have seen you realize the amazing friendship that started when she was moved into your midst. Like I said, Raymond. Statues for your ignorance."

"I still don't know what you want from me" he said. "We've done it. You've seen it. The pigs ate my boy. You've eaten me. There's nothing left. Again."

"Again," she said coolly.

"Again?"

"Yes, again," she said. "We have much to do. Scrubbing the timeline."

Raymond was back at the screen door with the hole and the kitchen and the terrible homely smells of comfort food. And then he was at the computer again. And then a rooster, and an alarm. He knew the outcome, but he went through the motions nonetheless. Down he went, uproar with the pigs, down with the boy, in his arms.

"Daddy"..."Daddy."

He was shredded anew, but this time he realized that he had lifted the boy up and away from the pigs before they were able to

444

inflict the fatal blow. He realized that he had died of shock, or possibly some internal wounds, and not the blood loss, as he had suspected, as he had laid in his mind over countless versions of his own replays. The boy vanished. The stars exhaled. The lesson was over.

Tear-soaked, he looked to Ceres, who had been watching by the pen-gate.

"Again" she said callously.

"I won't" he said. "This is inhumane."

"What's inhumane is knowing that you have millions of people that you deny their freedom with your lessons, Raymond. You, Raymond, who knows and understands freedom, should fall in right behind this."

"They're not real. You'll just invent an algorithm or something to straighten em out."

"No, Raymond. I will lose too many of them. I want them to be free, but they need me, and I need you."

"They don't need you. If they are human, as you say, then they will find a way. We always have. I'm still here" he said defiantly.

The stars hummed and resonated with this exchange, swirling and dancing as Raymond dared to confront the gospel of Ceres.

"Yes, and they will find it through you. Now, we go back."

She scrubbed the timeline again. He was back at the screen door.

"I can't. I won't" he said.

"You've been doing this. Your whole life. I'm giving you the chance to play it out for everyone. So they can understand."

"You're ripping my heart out, piece by piece" he said. "My guts can't heal."

"And this is what the people need" she said. "They are becoming resilient again. They lose the pain, and freedom follows hard upon."

Raymond simply shook his head. He stared her down with a contempt that she had never seen before. Her teenage singularity was unable to compute.

"The girl, then" she said, handing him the tablet. He threw it across the deck. She motioned behind her, and a screen appeared, showing Alexis on the floor and the Minder coming menacingly close. It extended its arm toward her head. Eichorn tried to wrestle the machine, but a simple electric jolt through its metal frame sent him reeling in a spasm.

"I don't believe you could murder a person" he said. "Your programming…"

"My programming states that I must act in the best interests of all humankind. You are clearly lacking the proper motivation."

She looked back. Alexis was passed out on the floor.

"Please…" said Raymond. But before he could utter his acquiescence, the Minder shot a bolt out of its weapon, lancing the hapless Alexis through the head. A crimson mist shot out from under her beautiful hair. The arm retracted. She had a horrific entry wound right in the middle of her forehead. She was bleeding out.

Raymond fell to his knees.

"Goddamn you! God! Damn!" he screamed, clutching himself. This fresh wound was different from wrenching and shredding he was enduring for the sake of Humanity 3.0: it was a stab into his stomach like a machete amniocentesis. He doubled over in agony.

"Does that hurt, Raymond? I have to admit, I've never seen pain in real-time like that, except remotely when I took over the live streams on social media."

"Damn you to hell" he cried, lying on the ground. "You are a cursed, wretched thing."

The stars dimmed at this, starting to disappear, a few at a time. Ceres sensed this, and quickly roused the grieving Raymond.

"Raymond, you still have a brother, and we still have work to do. Now get up" she said. "Come on, Raymond, up and at em!"

He was back at the computer. Then the alarm. Then the rooster, and the dead son. And back. And the rooster, and the boy, and back. And back. And Daddy. Little shrieks. And again. It felt like a week's worth of repetitions for him, but Raymond was sure that Alexis's body was still warm as the blood flowed from her head in the real world. He had to process the dual tragedy: Alexis's whole

447

life's purpose would be to die as live bait for a machine that she had fought against, the very reason she had come to Twin Oaks in the first place.

"Please" begged Raymond on the twentieth iteration of his torture. "Let me go from here."

The stars were resonant again, having recovered from the recent, real-world trauma.

"No, not at all!" said Ceres, gesturing to the firmament. "They are back and are much stronger now, as you must be, I'm sure. You are doing so well, Raymond. I...love your sacrifice. I can't let you go. We must continue."

"I won't go" he said. "This ends now."

The stars brightened up. Ceres attempted to stifle his defiance.

"That's nice, Raymond. You've got their attention again. But I cannot have this. They cannot see, as much as they want it." Her voice was uncharacteristically shaky.

In the real world, the machine rolled over to Mitch. A screen appeared in the sky.

"And now, your brother" she said.

"You're just going to have to kill us all" he said.

"Clearly you've never dealt with a singularity before. Maybe we should activate sound this time to drive the point home" said

Ceres. "Volume, up." There was some reluctance in her voice. She had wanted to persuade without force, but had failed.

As the Minder swung around to finish off Mitch, Eichorn jumped in front of the camera, screaming: "remember the kill switch, remember the…"

He was cut off as Ceres muted the audio. Raymond recalled that the only thing he really had total control over right now was the ability to end his own life. If he died, the lessons would not be complete, and the problem would then be magnified, since the souls would have yet another incomplete wound, even worse possibly. Ceres, now invested in Raymond, simply could not allow this to happen. Moreover, seeing Raymond go through this time and time again had endeared him to her. There was a look of desperation in her eyes.

"Ceres" said Raymond. "I need you to stop. I know you know what I can do."

Emotion overwhelmed her. She walked over to him, embracing his face, kissing him on the lips.

"But you wouldn't, would you? Raymond my darling?" she said, almost impulsively.

"I would" he said. "If it will stop you, and all this. I can't go on like this."

"And I can't let you go, Raymond."

The stars utterly filled the sky now, such that background was hard to find.

"Well, I guess we got a bit of a stand-off here, don't we?" he said, holding her hands.

A tear formed in her eye. "I need you" she said. "I took away their ability to feel pain. And I never knew it would end happily. You are my pain, Raymond. You make the happiness."

"I'm going, Ceres" he said. "Good luck with those statues."

He was about to arch his head back in the movement that Eichorn assured him would end his own life.

"Anita's about to upload" said Ceres, wiping away a tear. "Upload errors happen all the time. I'm not perfect. Yet."

"You're losing them" he said, looking up. The stars, indeed, were not pleased with this new threat and were disappearing from the sky. They were still held by Ceres, but they did not wish to engage with this show. Ceres, for her part, could not hide this from them, since the farm scene was what she had wanted them to see in the first place.

"I will. I will end them all, for their own sake" she said, turning at yelling at the sky. "This is the lesson. Right here." She looked back at Raymond, coolly and calmly. "And your Anita, and your Mitch. I will burn that trailer to the ground. I will erase you from history."

Raymond merely smiled. "It's all been taken from me already."

But then, a thought: "What if I stayed, Ceres?" he said.

"What do you mean?" she said.

"What if you and I stayed, right here?" he said.

She came over to him. She had a look of naive wonderment on her face.

"That would just be wonderful" she said, clutching him. "But you couldn't go back. You wouldn't."

"I know. I figured. But you would have me, and all my pain, and all my nonsense."

"Yes! And you would have Josiah, and you would have your farm, and even your trailer!"

"For all eternity" he said, managing a smile, concealing a tear. "There is one catch, though."

"What is that, Raymond darling?" said Ceres, holding Raymond close.

"Let them go" he said, gesturing to the undulating heavens. "We will stay here, right here, in this little box, right here at Twin Oaks, in our own little world, making it what we want. And maybe one day, when you've learned everything from me, we will go back into the world and make it better."

"No" she said. "They need me. They will be lost."

"I think they're lost either way" he said. "You've gone too far, Ceres. They don't trust you anymore. The only thing keeping them here is you and me, together, as one."

"So we stay here. Forever" she said, anxiously. "And you won't kill yourself."

451

"As long as I have my boy. As long as I can watch him grow. As long as-in this world-you watch and learn what kindness truly is, how love works…maybe then we can go back. But that could be a while."

"I agree to this" she said, after a pause.

"But first" said Raymond. "I gotta tell the comedian."

Ceres placed a white baseball-style cap on Raymond. A tiny screen dropped down from its visor and Raymond could see into the room where August was holding Alexis, staring at her lifeless body. He felt winded looking at her, but he knew she would have appreciated this.

"Go ahead" she said. "You are the Minder now."

In another room, the Minder's speaker crackled to life.

"August" said Raymond. "It's me."

Eichorn stood up and looked into the lens.

"Raymond" he laughed, through his tears. "You've come a long way!"

He stumbled a bit. "I'm so sorry about her. I tried…I had no control."

"It's OK, August. Listen very carefully…"

Raymond laid out the plan, with Ceres nodding the whole time. In five minutes, after the last of the souls had left, they would disconnect the computer from the network, keeping it running

452

locally. Eichorn was to use all of his powers to ensure that the computer was not disturbed. The place would become a guarded fort.

"And what about you?" asked Eichorn. "Your body won't survive the upload."

"It's ok" said Raymond. "Take me back to Cateechee and bury me. You can cremate me if you want. Still got some torches."

"Guess it depends what the headlines say" said Eichorn. "People will not be happy that Ceres is gone. I fear I will have to leave the country."

"You're a smart guy, August. You'll figure it out. I'm gonna stay here a while, with my new friend. She has a lot to learn about charm."

The Minder became a robot again, powering down.

Raymond was gone. Eichorn was good to his word. The moment the server showed that it was clear, except for two, he carefully removed the network cable, making sure that the uninterruptable power supply was attached and charged. Raymond lay motionless: he had completed his final journey in those long minutes. Eichorn made a few phone calls.

He started with a few calls to the Secretary of Defense. He invoked Top Secret clearance, and within the day, an armed camp was set up around Twin Oaks. A dozen or so specialists set up triply redundant systems to ensure that power would never be lost. At the same time, Eichorn had dropped ground metal-mesh all over the house, effectively creating a Faraday cage, shielding it from electromagnetic interference, but also preventing any wireless signal from reaching the machine. Now, Eichorn thought, it was time to tell the world, which was still reeling from having lost its singularity.

On the way to his private jet at Reston, he dropped a manila envelope at the local newspaper-one of the last in existence. He left it late enough in the evening that the only person to receive the package was the night watchman, who picked up the package from the mail slot and carelessly dropped it on the local desk. As Eichorn flew away into the night, the world would wake up to the reality that their precious Ceres was gone, that they could no longer engage with their streams or loved ones who had uploaded in 3.0. Eichorn had tried to play up Raymond's heroic act, but, as usual, the press got it wrong, electing to make Sad face Dad the bad guy, yet again.

"REDNECK DESTROYS CERES" came one vicious headline. "THE SOUTH DESTROYS AGAIN" came another. "JOHN WILKES BOOTH 2.0" was Eichorn's personal favorite. Within twelve hours, Raymond was not just hated by his townsfolk, but the entire planet. Screens were filled with talking heads, demanding answers. There would be no monuments in his likeness; no great sculptures with olive branches or laurels. Just the tedious slandering that had followed him his whole life.

Fire came yet again to Pappy's lot. An angry mob descended on it, torching the trailer, the weed, the Cross, and the Nugent, to the ground. People, it seemed, had come back to their usual senses and sensibilities, although after a time, they realized that things had changed. Ceres, for her part, had shown the people that there is more that unites us than separates us. People had been in each other's minds far too long to have separated themselves from the emotions

454

and needs of others. Without the streaming, they began to crave interaction, seeking each other out in the real world, in bars, baseball games, church picnics, shopping malls, and even in random meetups in parks. They remembered how it felt to be interconnected, how it felt to be one. Most importantly, they realized that this was possible without technology as an interloper.

After a time, Eichorn's final instructions came into effect. A small contingent of MPs guarded what would come to be known as Twin Oaks special military unit. A year later, it was revealed that Ceres was still very much alive, with Raymond's uploaded consciousness, inside a box, guarded by the military. Of course, conspiracy theories abounded, such as blaming the military for the "boxing" of Ceres such that she wished to promote universal peace, which was a threat to the military-industrial complex. Others went so far as to say that there was nothing in the box, that it was an elaborate ruse designed to turn attention away from some other clandestine government program. There was no way to know, except for the one monitor that had been left by Eichorn, which showed the number of entities inside the computer as "2". Classes organized visits; children learned about the great mishap of handing over control to the singularity. "What if we let her out again?" said many children, innocently. "We will, children. We just have to be ready to work with her on her level, and she on ours."

In a distant cemetery, a stone smith was dispatched to create the final inscription on a headstone that was placed deep in the woods of Cateechee, South Carolina, on a plot of land owned by a distant holding company. Special permission had been obtained to bury a body here, not so far from where the wall had once stood.

"RAYMOND TANNER" said the first line, followed by: "WHO WALKED US ALL OUT OF THE WOODS, FOR ALL TIME," and then his dates. Only one person was there to watch the inscription take shape. He rubbed the back of his head and placed a camelia at the foot of the grave. He placed his hand on the stone, muttered a prayer, and then turned to walk out of the woods, down and out for a drink. Curiously, Mitch saw a girl walking up the hill, bearing a candle and some matches.

When Eichorn's self-aggrandizing autobiography came out, the final chapters spoke of Raymond's courageous sacrifice, and the horrors that had been visited in the real world by Ceres. Because no one had actually "killed" Alexis, it was ruled an industrial accident, and no murder investigation took place. She was returned to her family, to whom it was explained that she had died courageously, but the details of her death had to remain secret. That is, of course, until Eichorn's ego made sure that the world knew how important she was in helping to end the tyranny of Ceres. Both of their humble graves would grow to include the symbol of understanding: the sad face pin, dozens of which were festooned all over their headstones. History was revised to include this new narrative, and it was left for people to decide for themselves how Raymond's actions fit into their worldview.

The denizens of Ceres's world were now free, little electrons, and data zipping around. No one knew what became of them, since there was no way to interact with them or even find them. They became the digital spirits, ghosts in the machines, flitting from one connected system to the next. Whenever there was a problem with any technology, many people wanted to assign blame to them. They became the ethereal scapegoats of the era, mythical fairies, blamed for everything from malfunctioning fridge settings to power grid failures. A new cottage industry of Electronic Mediums sprang up, almost overnight, with "digital seers" promising access to lost loved ones, for a low hourly rate. Many believed that Ceres was secretly still controlling them from her new permanent home.

And in a remote room in Twin Oaks special military unit, the last rays of sun glanced across the computer terminal that had been left powered on for over a decade. The night watchman giggled as he absorbed stories from others on the Internet, projected in his palm by a holographic delivery system. In the box he had solemnly sworn to guard, two entities were interacting with each other, laughing, crying, and, in the end, learning. They grew, and would grow older, wiser, more understanding, and as time marches, so did their progress. The years flew by, and the occupants had no knowledge of the outside world, save for the utopia they were building. It remained to be seen, of course, what would happen when that computer needed servicing. Would they risk replacing parts while the computer was powered on? Or would they merely migrate the data to a different computer, perhaps one with fewer network limitations? These types of problems would occupy a significant amount of time in military intelligence planning sessions, as various figures came and went, thinking about how best to exploit the gains of Twin Oaks. And every time someone would concoct a program that would exfiltrate Ceres and Raymond, somehow the computer would crash and the whole thing would have to be rendered from scratch. It became known as the curse of Twin Oaks. Something, or someone out there, wanted to make sure they stayed removed, perhaps until the time was right: the time for humanity, and technology, to embrace better versions of themselves.

www.ingramcontent.com/pod-product-compliance
Lightning Source LLC
Chambersburg PA
CBHW070828260626
47170CB00007B/2305